Flamingo Café

By

Jackie Kang

Flamingo Café

Cover Art by *The Wild Rose Press, Inc.*

The Wild Rose Press, Inc.
PO Box 708
Adams Basin, NY 14410-0708
Visit us at www.thewildrosepress.com

Publishing History
First Edition, 2024
Trade Paperback ISBN 978-1-5092-5695-2
Digital ISBN 978-1-5092-5696-9

Published in the United States of America

Dedication

For Austin

Acknowledgments

Believe it or not, the inception of this book took place many years ago when I was in grade school. I was tasked with drafting a fictional narrative and produced a story called The Green Flamingo. The story was slightly different from this one (It included a macaw that flew around the café) but had the same theme—a story based on a girl's life that took place inside a coffee shop.

While lying in bed with my son, Austin, one night, I told him about this story and asked if he thought it would make a good book. He said yes but knew I needed to flush it out for it to grow into something more substantial. So, I asked him to fill in the blanks. He suggested we have four girls, not just one, and that they face a life-or-death situation. He also insisted that I add a key somewhere, thus, how Flamingo Café evolved from a child's fantasy to what you are about to read.

But to get from one point to the next, there were quite a few people along the way who helped me, and I'd like to thank them here.

One person who will be surprised to see her name in my acknowledgments is Sylvia Kim, who posted the definition of Sonder on Facebook one day after conversing with her son about how we are all passersby in each other's lives. Well, Sylvia, you passed by my life, but when you did, you made a significant impact without even knowing it. I've loved watching your business grow and am proud of all you've accomplished!

For my early readers, Jami Johnston, Shannon Frisvold, and Namrata Bachwani, thank you for putting up with my rough drafts and spelling errors! To the Flamingos: Carl Lee, Melanie MacDonald, Wendy

Kendall, Avis Adams, and Catherine Brugger Brown, those late-night critique group Zoom meetings got me through the pandemic. This story wouldn't be the same without all of you!

Thank you to Anne Rethke for your walks and talks and for telling me Abigail should be my first chapter. You could not have been more correct!

To Jayme Kennedy and Brittney Beam Apfel, I cannot thank you enough for reading and re-reading countless versions of this book. Your encouragement and praise are what kept me going.

I started drafting this book in earnest during the pandemic and wanted to finish it within a year. But then my mom passed away, and I could not bring myself to work on Flamingo Café for a very long time. I took a year to grieve and process, and during that time, I leaned heavily on my family, especially my loving husband. Alex, thank you for everything you do for me. I'm the lucky one.

To my editor Ally Robertson, thank you for being so kind all those years ago at the PNWA conference and for all your kindness since then. I love working with you and everyone at The Wild Rose Press!

Sonder

n. the realization that each random passerby is living a life as vivid and complex as your own—populated with their own ambitions, friends, routines, worries, and inherited craziness—an epic story that continues invisibly around you like an anthill sprawling deep underground, with elaborate passageways to thousands of other lives that you'll never know existed, in which you might appear only once, as an extra sipping coffee in the background, as a blur of traffic passing on the highway, as a lighted window at dusk.

Chapter One

A Butterfly Flaps its Wings
Abigail

My phone, lying on the chaise next to me, pings with yet another incoming text. I roll my eyes. A pointless gesture really, if I take into consideration the noticeable lack of audience in attendance to witness my drama.

With languid arms, I reach down and rotate the phone until I can just make out the message lighting up my screen.

—OMG, Abs, I'm so sorry. Call if you need me.—

This message—even less inspiring than the last one—has my motivation to reply dissolving right along with my grip on the slim phone. A dull thud sounds as the phone drops back onto the striped cushion. I continue to lay there, ignoring the persistent onslaught of afternoon interruptions.

Or at least that is what I try to do. As much as I want to stay perfectly still and focus on the simple joys of the South Florida sun baking my body—morphing my golden skin into an even darker brown—my mind refuses to stop buzzing with the activities of the last twenty-four hours.

I sit up with a sigh and roll my eyes again—empty backyard pool deck be damned. If I'm being honest, I'd have to concede this last message from Suzy, one of the WAGS I socialize with, is at least slightly more sincere than the outpouring of identical correspondence flooding my phone all day. Texts with the heartfelt, bullshit lines of,

Darling, I understand this is hard for you. Please take all the time you need.

And

Don't worry about your seat at the gala. I'm sure we will be able to fill the spot in your absence.

Or

Your board position has been temporarily put on hold while you work to heal your family.

Of course, the hidden message in these so-called earnest correspondences flooding in from my so-called friends is as subtle as a hurricane warning calling for an immediate evacuation. The kind of warning that lets me know if I come within twenty yards of the Palm Beach Princesses, I will be dismissed as though I'm merely a brown-haired beggar on a street corner.

Damn. The women in this town work fast.

Which means I need to work faster.

This new tidbit of targeted propaganda focused on my family and rounding the gossip circle is sure to have people—important people—asking questions, which is precisely what I don't need right now. So, if I'm going to save any shred of my reputation, I need to come up with a brilliant rebuttal and fast. Something that will shut down the *no quiero tiki tiki, ni taka taka* before I become completely ostracized from Palm Beach society.

Besides the hurricane warnings the newscasters are always hyped up on this time of year, it is another typical slow-news day for Southeast Florida. Which means Julian's face is everywhere. And so is that *chusma* he was feeling up on THE NEST dance floor last night.

I can't believe how colossally Julian screwed up this time. It is one thing for me to ignore Julian's indiscretions when they are done in the dark, behind closed doors, where one can't prove he is a lying, cheating, S.O.B. But it is quite another when it is splashed across the tabloids, and every news station in the sunshine state is blabbing about it. His carelessness has left me no choice but to address our personal—and what I thought was private— "situation." Thinking about all the clean-up this little tryst of his will require has me simply exhausted.

Of course, he had to choose THE NEST for his little outing. He couldn't have chosen a quieter nightclub with fewer paparazzi. No, he had to go to our spot. This just goes to show how truly unoriginal he is.

God, I need another drink.

I reach over and grab my Collins glass, squinting at it through my newly purchased CC sunglasses. Only melted ice, muddled mint leaves, and blueberries are left, creating a kaleidoscope of green and blue in the bottom third of the cut glass. "Rosa…Rosa?"

Oh, now where is Rosa? Lord knows, with what we pay the help, I should not have to go in search of someone to mix me a drink. My mixing days were supposed to be long over, but then again, so were Julian's nights at the club.

"Ah, damn it," I mutter and will my small yet mighty frame to magically teleport from the red and white striped chaise lounge over to the fully stocked wet bar. What a waste of money, paying for help when the help was nowhere to be found.

Pissed—and not entirely oblivious to the fact that my anger is misplaced—I admit defeat and slide off the chaise, taking my empty glass with me as I approach the bar cart.

I start to work, expertly muddling the mint and lime with a pinch of refined sugar. I fill the shaker with ice, rum, and a splash of lime juice and give it a good shake with practiced precision and skill. A simple twist of my wrist sends the frothy clear concoction sliding down the shiny cylinder, over the fresh blueberries, lime, and mint, and into my glass.

I top the drink with club soda and take a sip, letting the sweet mixture work its magic. The second the alcohol touches my bloodstream, the knot in my shoulders starts to dissipate.

That's better.

Well, at least one disaster has been averted. My dear fiancé might have ruined my afternoon *siesta*, but I still have my blueberry mojito. I manage to make it back to my chaise without sloshing too much of the precious liquid over the rim.

Conscious of the clock ticking down, I don't hesitate to settle back into the lounge. Due home from that pretentious institution of a primary school of hers, Riley will be walking through the door any minute.

Lord knows the second she sets foot onto the terrace; I will be required to morph into the doting mother instantly oohing and ahhing over her many accomplishments. Showering *mi amor* with my full attention, shepherding my overly stimulated daughter to any number of after-school activities. All encouraged by Julian, of course, to keep her out of the house and out of his hair. Her most recent enrichment involves marine biology, saving the Florida Manatee population, or some cause equally trivial. Unfortunately, the apple has fallen far from the tree with this one.

That's not to say I haven't tried to relate to Riley. I've done my best to understand my precious seven-year-old and her desire to save the world and all the creatures in it. I even adopted a manatee named Moo Shoo from the Save the Manatee Club in her honor. I figured my effort to acknowledge her likes would be reciprocated. But when I ask her to do something I enjoy—so we can bond on my terms—she shows no interest, blocking me out in that way only a child raised with unlimited privileges can.

It never fails. No matter how many times I offer to drive Riley to Worth Avenue for some shopping, she steadfastly refuses me, claiming there isn't a single thing she could use or want. I don't understand how she can resist all the bobs and bobbles dangling from the shop windows. I certainly can't. My own newly renovated walk-in closet is chock-full of fresh-from-the-runway garments, bags, and shoes. I think about my precious treasures, secure on the second floor of our sprawling *hacienda*, and wonder why, with all the charm that comes with living the life of a football player's fiancée, I still want to scream?

Oh, who am I kidding? The answer is blindingly obvious.

Every day is the same. Stale as a loaf of *Mamá's* Cuban bread left on the counter overnight. I plaster on a fake smile and embark on my predetermined routine of being a player's fiancée. I show up for the exercise, the luncheons, and the gossip, never deviating from my role or straying from my duties. I make nice with the other wives and girlfriends of the players (also known as the WAGs)—and even though I'm fully aware half of the women surrounding my table have slept with my fiancé—I keep my Palm Beach composure and pretend like there is nowhere else in the world I would rather be than at a luncheon with five other fake bitches.

A few of the non-WAGS (also known as the Palm Beach Princesses or PBPs) I socialize with actually track the team stats and rankings, trying their best to impress me with their football knowledge. Still, most of them simply feign an interest, so they can air-kiss my cheek and say they know Julian Mendez's fiancée, the soon-to-be Abigail Mendez.

It's only when lunch is complete that I finally find myself free and able to breathe for a precious few hours before Riley arrives home from school.

This valuable time is my one chance to release any built-up tension. And Lord knows I have tension. Not a single person could deny I deserve a little R&R. Especially not after all the early morning hours chasing that damn yellow ball up and down the tennis courts of the Palm Bay Vista Country Club. Always ensuring I've burned at least five hundred calories and my calves ache before I allow myself to limp off the court. But it doesn't stop there. Oh no, tennis is promptly followed up with aerobics and then weights. All done with the simple intention of maintaining the physique required to keep Julian's eye—among his other body parts—from straying. But, after last night, it is becoming embarrassingly apparent all my efforts are in vain.

I shake my head at the thought and flip my freshly highlighted auburn waves back over my shoulder. I mean, I've even recently added injectables to the daily assault of plucking, painting, buffing, and waxing I regularly subject myself to, all in an effort to step up my game. If all that can't hold Julian's attention, what will?

Of course, all my pains wouldn't even be possible without the little black card buried deep inside the recesses of my quilted leather wallet. The card that was given to me by Julian when he first signed with the Miami Sting Rays, and our lives changed forever.

I can still picture draft day so clearly in my mind, cradling a six-month-old baby in my arms and holding my breath as Julian's name was called during pick number five of the first round as the new Miami Sting Ray's quarterback. The day that transformed the pair of us from unwed college sweethearts with a newborn and barely twenty dollars for pizza and beer to multimillionaires with designer clothes, fancy cars, and a private chef.

We were so young and innocent. We felt like we had won the lottery. Suddenly, our lives were changing. Julian securing a spot on the team meant no more nights for me working as a barmaid at THE NEST while *Mamá* took care of Riley and Julian studied for his college exams. It meant Julian didn't have to slave away, struggling to maintain the grades that would keep him on the team. It meant we could afford to get married. Suddenly, our family could put food on the table and so much more. With that one phone call, our lives had rocketed into hyper-speed, catapulting Julian to star status and me to the life of luxury I was always destined for.

It hadn't taken long for us to adjust to our new lifestyles. Six years of adapting to fame and fortune undeniably turned Julian and me into shadows of our former selves. However, the WAG luxuries were now an integral part of my life, placed there by the insistence of Julian.

Which meant I wasn't going to give them up so easily.

Chapter Two

Clear Skies
Claudia

"Is it possible I saw paper drink umbrellas on the kitchen counter?" Benedict asks with a smile as he enters my home office, the lines at the corners of his eyes crinkling with amusement.

"There is a very strong possibility you did, *Agápi mou*." I lean over the side of my chair as he approaches my desk and gently kiss his worn cheek.

"What's that now?"

My own smile turns to a smirk. Clearly, my dear husband has forgotten to turn his earpiece on today. I reach to the side of Benedict's head and adjust the flesh-colored bean nestled in his ear.

A quick, high-pitched whine pierces the air before Benedict smiles sheepishly at me. "Yes, I suppose that is better. Now, what is it you were saying?"

"I said, there is a very strong possibility you did see some paper umbrellas."

Benedict nods once and gives me a knowing look as he backs away from the desk, starting a slow meander around my office. "They wouldn't have anything to do with a certain celebration, would they?" He comes to a stop in front of my design table and runs a finger over a white feather. The table takes up three-fourths of the office and is full of fabric swatches, sketches, trinkets, and random snapshots of items and places which bring me inspiration. "I thought you wanted to keep it to just the two of us this year?"

"Just because we are keeping it simple doesn't mean we shouldn't toast our anniversary," I say and struggle to push myself out of the dove-grey chair. My arthritic joints scream in protest as I lift my body with considerable effort. Once standing, I join Benedict, who wraps an arm around my shoulders. Comforting and familiar as my own body, I relish the warmth his frame provides me.

"I suppose you might be right. Fifty-five years does deserve a toast. After all, not every couple can stay married for so long and still declare their spouse as their best friend." Benedict pauses as though he is thinking through a problem and not simply discussing our anniversary. "Say, why don't we go out to dinner to celebrate?"

"Oh, that's not necessary." I decline a bit too quickly, trying to keep my voice neutral. "Let's just stay in and enjoy each other's company." I lean my head against his shoulder and pick up a picture of a sunset over the town of Oia. The blue domed roofs reflect against the whitewashed buildings of Santorini, Greece. I smile up at him and turn the picture over in my hand, positioning it so Benedict can see what I'm looking at.

"Can you believe it's been so long? It feels like we were here only yesterday," I point to the picture. "Getting married. Preparing to spend a lifetime together. We were so young and in love."

Benedict tightens his hold on me. "Well, my bride, we might not be young anymore, but I love you now just as much as I did back then. The day you became mine."

He sighs with resignation. "We can stay in if that is what you wish." I turn so we face each other, and Benedict tucks a strand of gray hair behind my ear before continuing. "Three kids, four dogs, five grandkids—"

"Don't forget the two adopted grandkids." I remind him, playing along with the number game Benedict likes to engage in whenever we reminisce about our shared past.

He nods in acknowledgment. "Two adopted grandkids. Yet another reason you've always captured my heart. Always taking in the bird with the broken wing."

In the depths of my soul, I appreciate the compliment Benedict is trying to bestow upon me. Accepting it and moving on is what this situation calls for, but the mental image of Nicholas and Cassandra proves to be too much of a trigger for me to keep my mouth closed. "They were Betty's family."

Benedict ignores the sharp tone laced between my comment and merely nods his head again. "Which makes them our family now."

My shoulders relax, and Benedict feeling my tension release, continues. "Two moves, one law degree—"

I snort at the mention of Benedict's law degree. The year of his bar exam was one of the many true tests of our marriage. Benedict raises an eyebrow at me.

"Sorry, sorry. Go on," I say.

Benedict gives me a look but continues, "and one internationally acclaimed fashion line."

"How did we manage to do it all?" I ponder aloud, reciting my line in this pre-rehearsed conversation.

"We do make quite the team, don't we?"

"We make a wonderful team. Of that, there is no doubt. But I couldn't have done any of it without you," I say.

Benedict nods and blushes, the veins in his checks taking on a purplish tone. "Come now. You're doing it again."

"No, I'm not."

"Yes, you are *Agápi mou*."

"Well, if I'm doing it again, it's only because it needs to be said. You, of all people, should know I only give credit where it's due." I say, placing one hand on his chest for emphasis.

Benedict covers my hand with his own, sending a soft warmth across my skin. "Of course, I know this about you. Just as I know you wear a size six shoe, you can't go to bed without brushing and flossing your teeth, and you like your eggs cooked over easy. I know you inside and out. Therefore, I know you are trying to avoid giving yourself the credit you deserve for living with narcolepsy while running a business, dealing with me and my crazy hours at the office, and raising our child."

My heart warms at Benedict's compliment. "It wasn't always easy." I concede.

"No, it wasn't, but somehow we managed, and we did it with style and grace. And we managed to stay sane." Benedict smiles at me.

"That could be considered a subjective comment." I tease.

Benedict lets out a hoot of laughter and leans his head of silver hair to the side, moving in for a kiss. The purse of his thin lips emphasizes the lines etching the sides of his mouth, put in place by years of sun and laughter.

I embrace him, recognizing the familiarity of his body close to mine. Neither of us has maintained the physiques of our youth. Yet, somehow, we have managed to age perfectly together, always fitting into the nooks and crannies of the other person. Like pieces of a puzzle, beautiful together, never a complete picture apart.

"So, I did a little research," Benedict says, releasing me and walking back to the door. He bends down and reaches his hand into the hallway just outside my office, picking something up off the floor. "And it turns out there are traditional gifts one is supposed to give on a fifty-fifth wedding anniversary." With a grunt, Benedict straightens his knees and stands back up, pushing against his leg with his left hand. In his right hand, he holds a dark blue velvet box. He walks around and places it on the table in front of me.

I reach out tentatively to trail my fingers over the soft blue fabric covering the box. "Darling, you shouldn't have."

"Oh, but I should." Benedict looks me in the eye. "You, *Agápi mou*, deserve this." He nods to my sun-spotted hand, still hovering over the box. "Go ahead. Open it."

"Your gift isn't arriving until next week," I say, thinking about the new Amel 50' sailboat with its teak decks and seventy-four-foot mast, set to be delivered in a week's time. A boat that is sure to give Benedict much pleasure, despite the fact it is destined to be a pleasure I will not be partaking in.

"Oh, I'm sure whatever you have decided to gift me will be wonderful. Now, go on, open it."

I slip my manicured nails between the box seam and

pop open the lid. Inside the box is a velvet platform. Nestled among the top of the forum is the most exquisite necklace of drop-shaped emeralds, one after the other, all surrounded by a frame of brilliant diamonds suspended from even more brilliant diamond clusters.

"Oh my." I breathe out as I bashfully delight in the jewels.

Benedict senses my hesitation. "Don't be shy," he says as he reaches over, removes the necklace from its place in the box, lifts it over my head, and secures it at the back of my neck.

With a gentle nudge, Benedict leads me to the full-length mirror at the room's far end. The bank of French doors along the East wall are open, letting in the natural light. As the sun catches the stones, rainbows burst onto the starch-white walls and dance across the room.

The wind has picked up, lifting my floor-length caftan off the ground. It billows like a sail behind me. I catch my reflection in the mirror, not in the least bit startled by my soft skeleton trapped in the trapeze of silk fabric. The necklace glows like a halo, illuminating my sun-touched skin.

"*Agápi mou*, you are a Greek goddess," Benedict says.

"It's simply stunning." I agree with him. "I love it, and I love you. Thank you." I reach for Benedict and place another kiss on his lips.

"You're welcome. Happy anniversary, Darling."

I open my mouth, intending to tell Benedict about the boat coming next week, but I am cut off by Frank Sinatra crooning, "*fly me to the moon…*"

Benedict and I glance at each other before breaking into broad smiles at the familiar ring tone coming from my mobile phone.

If I am a Greek goddess, then our grandson, Parker, is a perfect reincarnation of Hercules, the immortal hero. Always engaging in some far-flung adventure, it is a rare treat when Parker takes time out of his busy day to call home.

Benedict releases me, and I retrace my steps back to my desk to answer my phone, immediately setting it to speaker.

"Parker, darling! It's marvelous to hear your voice. How's our favorite *Engonós?*"

"*Giagiá,* I'm your only grandson!" Parker's voice, deep and robust, cuts through the other side of the phone.

"Nonsense, one small detail doesn't mean you can't still be our favorite." He knows our affection for him. There is no reason to hide or deny it.

Parker chuckles. "Sure, sure. Okay. Is *Pappoús* with you?"

Benedict comes to stand next to me. "I'm right here, buddy. How are you?"

"Good, I'm good. Listen, I don't have much time. I have to go on air soon. But I wanted to make sure to call and wish you both a happy anniversary."

"Thank you, darling."

"Thanks, buddy." Benedict echoes me, "So the news station is keeping you busy, huh?"

"It sure is. This season has already been off the charts. I'm sure you've heard about the next tropical storm heading our way. The one that just missed Puerto Rico. The guys at the National Hurricane Center think it will pick up speed as it crosses closer to the coast. They're predicting a direct hit on Florida within the next few days. I'll be reporting on the storm, tracking it as it moves closer."

Benedict and I lock eyes and share an unspoken moment of amusement.

"I'm going to be in your area, doing some fieldwork," Parker continues. "I'd love to stop by and visit you both if you have time."

"You know you're always welcome here. I'll have the staff make up the guest wing for you. Stay as long as you like. You know *Pappoús* and I love the rustle of young people around."

"I know, and I like being around too. But this time has to be just a quick stop. Maybe I can stay longer on my next visit."

"Well, we will take whatever we can get," Benedict says.

"I have a break in my schedule tomorrow afternoon. How about we have dinner together?"

I clap my hands in delight. "That would be lovely. I'll have a reason to use my umbrellas."

"Um, I'm not sure what that means, but great."

Benedict chuckles, covering his mouth with his fist, turning his laughter into a cough when he catches me smirking.

"Parker, it was wonderful talking to you. Now, I must go and attend to some paperwork. Thank you for calling and for the anniversary wishes. I'll leave you with your *Giagiá.* I know how you two love your little chats. "

"Thanks, *Pappoús*. I'll see you soon. Don't work too hard. "

"You too, young man. See you tomorrow."

Benedict squeezes my hand one last time before heading into the hallway.

I return my attention back to the conversation as

Parker says, "I've missed you. How are you? Are you getting enough rest?" An authentic concern for my well-being is in Parker's voice, and I smile at his generous nature.

"I've missed you too, darling. But we are doing fine. I'm merely an old lady puttering around the house. You know how it goes."

"When have you ever just puttered around the house? I do know how things go, and I don't remember you puttering. You have a schedule, and you stick to it. Although, I do wish you would get out more often. Which reminds me, have you given any thought to our last conversation?"

"No."

Parker sighs on the other end of the line, and I know what he is going to say before he even says it.

"I wish you would at least think about selling the company. You realize you would stay on as a consulting designer, right? And you would, of course, remain the name of the brand. That could never be taken away from you."

"Parker, *Agápi mou,* selling Claudia's Caftans has never been an issue of my ego. This is about letting someone else have authority and creative…" I must pause for a moment while I search for the correct word in English. Mentally scrolling through the Rolodex in my head until I grasp it. "…jurisdiction over my life's work," I say. "This is our family's legacy. You forget others are involved. I can't simply snap my fingers and let a multi-million-dollar business go poof." I snap my fingers next to the phone for emphasis. "Just like that, and it's gone? I don't think so."

I am getting agitated, which is not how I like to feel

while speaking with my grandson. I turn my attention to the open French doors and start a slow shuffle out onto the patio.

"I understand how hard this transition might be on you, *Giagiá*, but it's time. You have to admit it. With your condition, you need to start thinking about yourself and the company's future."

"Oh, come now. I've had the same 'condition' as you call it for over fifty years. Narcolepsy has yet to prevent me from performing any of my duties."

"Of course, you can perform your duties. That's not what I meant."

"No? What did you mean then?"

"I only want what's best for you. You should be going out and doing things. You never leave the house anymore, and I'm concerned about you. I just think you should take the last years of your life to enjoy your time with *Pappoús*. Travel, explore the world.*"*

"I've seen the world. I've been to fashion shows around the globe twice over. Venice, Paris, and Milan. I've seen it all, and now Pappoús and I are settled here. Palm Beach suits us just fine.*"*

"I know Palm Beach suits you. But *Giagiá,* you never leave the house."

"That is simply not true."

"Okay, then tell me, when was the last time you went out?"

I am not enjoying the way his line of questioning has taken on a note of hostility. My desire to remain at my own residence should be of no consequence to him.

"Parker darling, whether I leave the house or not has no bearing on my running a business."

"Of course not. But you're over seventy-five now—

"

"And because I'm aging, you think I should go ahead and abandon my life's work in order to travel around the world until I die off, like a beetle, on my back with my legs up in the air? Like I'm incapable of running a business due to the fact I have gray at my temples? No, Darling. I'm not prepared to live like a fossilized bug for the last few decades of my life."

"You know that's not what I mean." Parker's voice has taken on a stuffy quality that I find distasteful. I sniff and think about how I want to respond.

"Well, darling, if you're so concerned about it, why don't you come home and run the business yourself? They have asked me to find a new Design Director to replace the one we just lost. It would be simply marvelous. We could keep it all in the family. I could teach you everything I know."

"Come on, *Giagiá. You* know dresses aren't my thing. Besides, I've worked hard to get where I am in the newsroom. People know me as the weatherman."

The echoes of his father's ego are strong in his convictions, and I want to call him on it. Kids these days, you show them the slightest bit of attention, and they think they're the next Cary Grant. I ignore his bid for celebrity status and re-address the issue at hand.

"First, they are not dresses. They are caftans. And second, have you forgotten the net worth of Claudia's Caftan's?" I pause to let him remember on his own. "Now, are you sure you don't want to own a piece of the family business?"

This time it's Parker's turn to laugh at me. "*Giagiá,* you should know I don't care about the money by now. I only care about you."

I walk to the sloping entrance of the white-tiled infinity pool, not stopping until I'm ankle-deep in the heated water. "I know. That's why you're my favorite."

Parker blesses me with his rich chuckle. "So, you said earlier." He concedes. "Look, why don't we talk about this later? I've made this conversation stressful. That was not my intent in calling you."

"Well, that's awfully kind of you, dear, but there is no need to discuss it any further. It is my decision, so unless you will be joining the company, this conversation is over."

Parker is silent on the other end of the phone for a minute before obediently switching to another subject.

"Do you have everything you need for the storm? I can pick up some things for you before I head over tomorrow. Medications? Food? Water?"

"Oh, no, Darling. We have everything we could possibly need and more. You know how these things are. All the drama, and then nothing happens. If the power goes out, we have plenty of food, water, and a backup generator."

"I don't think—" But, as Parker is about to answer me, he is cut off by the beep of my call waiting. I look at the screen, surprised to see Cassandra's name flash across the surface of the slim phone in my hand. At this time of day, she is usually busy at the café.

"Oh dear, Parker, hold on. Cassandra is trying to get through." I stare at the buttons lining the bottom of the phone and try to figure out which one to push. "Oh darn, I never can figure these things out," I mutter. After a considerable amount of effort, I give up on the buttons, abandoning the call and returning my attention to Parker. "I'll just have to contact her later. Sorry, go on, darling."

"You said that was Cassy calling?" The tenor in Parker's voice drops an octave at the mention of Cassandra, and I cannot help but smile to myself.

"Yes, that was her."

These two young ones—always chasing but never catching one another.

"How is she?"

"Well, I didn't actually answer the call, now did I? So, as far as I know, she's doing fine."

"Right," Parker pauses before mumbling, "I just thought, since you talk with her regularly, you'd know how she was doing."

"Yes, Cassandra and I do have more regular conversations than, say, you and I do." It is uncalled for, and I regret it almost immediately, but I can't help placing the dig regarding the frequency of Parker's communication with Benedict and me.

"And the café," Parker continues, either ignoring my dig or not comprehending it.

"She's done wonders with the business, as I knew she would. All those years of Betty and I working in the kitchen with you kids paid off."

"Those are some of my favorite memories, making Key lime pie rolls with you and Auntie Betty."

I smile at the image Parker has conjured up. Betty and I bent over the kitchen counter with our hands on the children's, teaching Parker, Cassandra, and Nicholas how to roll the cake in a towel dusted with powdered sugar.

"If my memory serves me correctly, you and Nicolas would get halfway through our lesson before deciding to go rough house at the beach, leaving poor Cassandra to finish the baking, only to magically reappear when it was time to eat the results."

Parker laughs, deep and hearty. "Hey, I was a kid. You can't hold my adolescent work ethic against me."

"No, I suppose you are correct. Thankfully, you have proven to have outgrown that phase." I pause a moment before continuing, "You know, I'm sure she'd love to see you."

"Yeah, I know," he says, sounding far away. "And I'm planning on stopping by. It's been so long, you know. I'm not sure she wants to see me." He pauses, and I get the feeling he is debating what he wants to reveal to me. "She never returned any of my messages when I did reach out. I got the feeling she needed some space..." he trails off a moment before continuing, "you know, what she's been through and all."

My smile fades as the happy image of Betty and I baking with the kids is replaced by one of tangled metal and wreckage.

"Cassandra is a strong girl. She wouldn't want you to pity her," I remind him. "Besides, that was almost ten years ago. No sense dwelling on the past," I snip.

"I know," he snips back. "I wasn't pitying Cassy, just thinking about her and trying to figure out the best way to contact her. Anyways, if it wasn't for you and what you did for both her and Nick..."

As a moment passes between us, I remain quiet before Parker fills the silence. "Well, you helped them out. It was nice of you."

"I took them in when they had nowhere to go. Anyone would have done the same for their family."

"Yes, but you did more than just take them in. You gave them direction in life. You helped them get back on their feet—"

"I simply gave them a loan when the time was right," I say, cutting Parker off with a wave of my hand. "Enough to start a business, work hard, and pay it back. I gave the children a jumping-off point, that's all."

"It was generous of you. All I'm saying is we are all lucky to have you."

"Yes, well...I still think it's been far too long of an absence. You should try and see her again. I'm sure she would like that."

"Okay, I'll see what I can do."

A thought starts in the back of my mind. Something about placing people on pedestals that are too high. I try to coax it into a whole idea, but it stubbornly stays hidden in the recesses of my brain. I eventually give up on the thought and say, "Thank you, *Agápi mou*. Now, what time should we expect you tomorrow?"

Chapter Three

Disturbance
Cassy
Call me when you can
I read over my line of text for the third time, debating adding 911 to the end of the message. I pause to contemplate the possible results. Either Auntie Claudia will see the numbers glowing like a beacon at the end of the message and call me right away, understanding they are a figurative 911, or she will see the numbers as a literal emergency, and her fight or flight instincts will kick in, and she will instantly morph into an unmovable statue.

This is an impossible decision.

I *really* need Auntie Claudia to call me back, but do I risk activating her autonomic response system in the process?

I tap the phone to my chin, weighing my options. Officer Jackson will be walking through the front door of the Flamingo Café any minute with the break-in report for me to review. He's already explained that I will have to sign the report when he gets back, but the pressure of not messing up is weighing heavy on my conscious. What if I miss a crucial element that hinders the investigation, or worse yet, I sign my rights away and don't even know it? I'm not equipped to make these kinds of decisions on my own. I need help.

I recheck the screen and arrow out of my text, swiping up to reveal a list of my most recent phone calls—all black in color and all unanswered. I scroll down the list, a continuous display of names alternating between Auntie Claudia, Uncle Benedict, and Nick. Where is everyone? I keep scrolling until I catch the one call that deviates from the pattern, The Palm Beach Police Department. I check the time stamp on the call, 4:35 A.M.

It had only taken me five minutes after arriving at the café to call the police. Looking at the bashed-in glass and the kicked-in door, I knew I wasn't setting one foot into the café alone.

Pressing my lips together, I hastily flip back to the text message addressed to Auntie Claudia and press send, deciding not to include 911 at the end. I check the text has been delivered before clasping the phone between my hands in silent prayer and crushing it to my chest.

What a morning. I can't believe it is already past noon, and I haven't heard from one single person. I'm exhausted from cleaning the broken glass and picking up the mess that greeted me this morning.

I step back until I rest my head on the palm-frond-decorated wallpaper behind me and let out a slow breath. The lip of the hot pink wains-coating that covers the lower third of the wall presses into my hips, and I adjust my shoulders to relieve the pinch on my backside. Settling into my empty surroundings, I count to three and try to remember what my therapist taught me about dealing with a crisis. Not that I'm experiencing a crisis. Or maybe I am. I don't know. I'm so exhausted from this morning that I can't think straight.

I rack my brain and try to remember the requirements for calling an event a crisis. Destruction. A quick glance at the front door, where the sun is illuminating the duct tape holding the cardboard in place over the broken window, confirms what I already know. Yes, there is definitely destruction. And although I've done a decent job over the last few hours of cleaning, the thoughts of the white bookcase lying in a heap across the wood-planked floor, the overturned gold stools with the pink tufted cushions smashed and lying on their sides, and the palm frond wallpaper devoid of its racks and now riddled with nail holes are all images of destruction that are now burned into my memory for a lifetime.

I mentally check the first box as I recall another requirement. Being in immediate danger.

Well, there is cash missing from the register, but thanks to the nightly deposit I make, it's not a large sum of money. Thank God no one was here when it was taken. Instinctively, I reach down and rub at the goose bumps on my arm. I don't even have to look down to know they are there. The mere idea of violence in the café has my stomach roiling. I suck in a lungful of air and remind myself that Zoe and I weren't present when the actual break-in happened and that the perpetrator is now long gone. Which means I am not, in fact, in any immediate danger, and this particular situation doesn't qualify as a crisis.

But the break-in is still a problem. A problem I've had to deal with all on my own for the last eight hours. Hours that have passed by in a complete blur, and yet, by the grace of God or by a massive injection of adrenaline into my system—which one I'm not entirely sure—I've managed to keep my composure.

My lack of a complete melt down has to count for something, right? After all, I was the one who discovered the shattered front doors of the café. I was the one who called the police before the sun was even peaking over the horizon. I was the one who spoke with Officer Jackson when he arrived to assess the damage done. I was the one who had to categorize all the damage, consoled my shaken and startled employee, and got the place back in working order. Me. I did all that. If I wasn't such a pessimist, I might consider patting myself on the back, but I am, so I don't.

If my therapist were here, she would tell me to take a moment and honor my accomplishments. I consider her mute advice and decidedly nod my head in agreement. Just this once, I'll allow myself some credit.

With renewed determination, I push off and shove my phone into the back pocket of my jeans, but as I do, my elbow bumps against the broom leaning against the wall next to me, where it clatters to the floor with a thunk. Bending down to right the fallen broom, my gaze drifts to the door leading to the kitchen.

"Shit." The expletive leaves my mouth before I can stop it. In this morning's chaos, I'd totally forgotten to connect with Zoe about what needed to be done in the kitchen to prepare for the day.

Shaking my head, I lean the broom back against the wall and push through the swinging door. "Zoe, I'm so sorry. I—"

I'm not even a foot into the kitchen when I pause in astonishment. The aroma of melted butter, brown sugar, and citrus greet me, cutting off my apology and making me want to cry in relief. There, lined up and ready to be taken to the display case, are baking sheets lined with lemon cheesecake crepes, Key lime white chocolate cookies, and mini coconut coffee cakes. Next to the prepared pastries, muffin tins sit at attention, filled with perfectly golden-brown tops. A mound of pie dough rests on the cutting board next to the already prepared pastries, waiting to be rolled out.

Zoe catches me looking over her work and raises her shoulders in faux nonchalance. "I thought I'd make some lemon-poppy seed muffins and those crepes everyone loves so much. The dough for the mango Key lime tarts is right over there." She nods to the cutting board. "I figured we didn't need a full case since we missed the morning rush." Undeterred by my abrupt entrance, Zoe returns to her work and continues to dust the top of the muffins with citrus sugar.

Dressed in her Flamingo Café uniform, Zoe is a vision of Palm Beach perfection. Her long blonde hair is held back in a tidy braid, showing off her tan skin and perpetually sunny disposition. She did the work not to impress me but because she knew it was simply what needed to be done. I could kiss her, but of course, I don't.

Instead, I glance around the kitchen, checking for any damage to the equipment, when I catch a glimpse of my reflection in the industrial oven on the far wall. My own lackluster appearance of red hair is pulled up into a messy ponytail, doing little to flatter my pale, freckled skin, still dirty from cleaning up the shambles of the break-in. I cringe. I am the antithesis of Zoe's golden spirit. I look away, directing my attention back to Zoe.

"Well done," I try to make my voice cheery, mimicking Zoe's good nature. If we plan to open the café for business—and interact with actual customers, I will have to work on brightening my immediate attitude.

"This is amazing."

"Yeah, well, you had a lot to deal with. I was just trying to make myself useful." Zoe gives me what I interpret as a look of sympathy out of the corner of her eye. "What's the status out there?"

I try not to choke on the sob bubbling up out of nowhere and search my internal social skills for the best way to put a positive spin on the situation.

"I managed to get the glass from the shattered door swept up," I say in a clear voice. "I used duct tape and cardboard from the back to cover the hole. Officer Jackson is outside completing the report now."

The timer goes off as Zoe gives a nod of understanding and turns to grab the oven mitts. I take the opportunity while Zoe retrieves the muffins from the oven to grab one of the turquoise aprons, complete with a picture of a hot-pink flamingo wearing sunglasses, off its peg on the wall and thread it over my head. "It's not pretty, but it'll have to do until Nick gets here." I tie the apron's strings around my back and pull my phone out of my jeans pocket, glancing at the screen again. "That is if he ever decides to return any of my calls." I shove the phone into the back pocket of my jeans with disgust.

"He's still not picking up?" Zoe asks as she replaces the baked muffins with yet another batch, shutting the door and setting the timer.

"I can't get ahold of anyone," I say and immediately chastise myself for the whine in my voice. I clear my throat and try again. "I left messages. I'm sure they'll call back soon."

Zoe gives a sympathetic nod. "Of course they will."

I wish I could feel as confident as Zoe sounds. "I can take over from here. I'll just get a few more pastries going and meet you out front. Why don't you go and fire up the espresso machine?"

"Sure thing, boss," Zoe dusts her hands on her apron and turns in my direction. For a horrifying second, I'm afraid she is going to try and hug me, but before I have to steel myself for any physical contact, she points over my shoulder at the ovens.

"I set the timer. They'll be done in about five minutes." She nods her head toward the kitchen door and follows with the rest of her body. "Just thought I'd remind you since I won't be here to grab them. I know you have a lot on your mind." With that, she pushes through the door and leaves me in the silent kitchen.

I close my eyes and savor the calm moment, counting to ten and listening for the sound of the espresso machine whirling to life before opening my eyes and sprinkling my hands with the flour needed for the cutting board.

Looking for a distraction from my thoughts, and before getting started, I reach over and switch on the small television we keep in the back, quickly setting the channel to WESH 2 news. Then, with the soft hum of the reporters in the background, I prepare to get back to the work of baking pastries. Ignoring the oven scars taking up entirely too much real estate across my knuckles and wrists, I begin rolling the dough for the mini mango-Key lime pie tarts.

The simple act of kneading the dough is enough to lift my spirits, and it's not long before I lose myself in the rhythm of the baking. Measuring ingredients, setting the mixer, sliding the pans into the oven—each task completed working ten times better than any therapy session. The stress of the morning melts off me like the butter in the pan as the routine unfolds.

My forearms are burning as I roll the dough with more force than is necessary, flattening it repeatedly against the counter when there is a buzzing in my back pocket. Without wiping my hands on the towel, I snatch the phone from my jeans.

Nick.

I have to swipe my floury finger across the screen two times before the phone finally accepts the call.

"Nick, what took you so long?" I practically shout into the phone, now on speaker.

"Dude, Cassy…" Nick drags the words out, like he's just woken up, checked his missed calls, and decided to call back even though he's still half asleep. "Why so early?"

"It's not early, Nick. It's the middle of the day."

"Well, it's early for people who work nights."

There is a muffled sound in the background, and I realize he's not alone. My bachelor brother, and owner of the hottest nightclub in Palm Beach, has another conquest in bed with him. Probably some socialite wanna-be he picked up after closing. I can just imagine the Palm Beach Princess clinging to Nick as the bartender announces, "Last call." Tripping over her stilettos as the pair of them are ushered out of THE NEST and into his Hummer. Both tumbling into the back seats with the sole intention of keeping the party going until the wee hours of the morning.

"Someone broke into the café," I say, without any prelude, not caring about whichever PBP happens to be in bed with Nick at the moment.

"What do you mean?" Nick mumbles into the phone, clearly not ready to wake up yet.

"I mean, the café was burglarized. Last night. Bo and I discovered it when we arrived at four thirty to prep."

"Four thirty in the morning?"

"Yes, in the morning."

"So early?"

"Yes, I arrive at the café that early every morning. You know that. Pay attention."

"Okay—go on."

"And when we got here, the café was smashed up."

"What do you mean, smashed up."

I grind my teeth together at Nick's constant repeating of everything I'm saying. "I mean, someone broke into the café. They smashed in the front door and tore apart the inside. It was a complete mess."

"Have you called the cops yet?" Nick asks.

"Of course, I called the cops. I need to sign the report at any minute, but I need you to help me. I need to replace the front door. Get new locks. Install a security surveillance system." I'm mentally ticking off the to-do list items as I relay the information to Nick.

I stop talking and wait for Nick to respond, but all I hear is a sound reminiscent of sandpaper. I recognize it as Nick running his hand down the scruff of his face. I can picture his large palm traveling from his copper-red hairline, down his freckled tan face, only stopping once he's reached his chiseled jaw with the days-old growth as he shakes his head in annoyance at my request.

"Man, Cassy, you're gonna owe me big time."

"So, that means you're coming?"

"Yes, I'm coming. But I'm a little tied up at the moment. It's going to take a while before I can get there." Nick grunts on the other side of the phone, emphasizing his point. "I'll be there as soon as I can." He clicks off, not even bothering with a proper "goodbye," leaving me to glare at the phone.

Chapter Four

Temperature rising
Bri

The air conditioner whirls to life, sending a cascade of cold air to cover my naked flesh. My sympathetic nervous system springs to life, and in seconds, I'm covered in tiny goosebumps. I shiver once in response, only to repeat the action when Nick's warm hand snakes around my waist and pulls me to him. Our bodies flush together.

Nick works his leg between mine and tosses his cell phone onto the nightstand next to him, "Mmm, now that's better." Still holding tight to my waist, he reaches down and pulls the sheet up to cover our tangled limbs.

"Is it now? Aren't you supposed to be high tailing it out of here?" I ask as I make no move to release him from our embrace. Unfortunately, I only heard Nick's side of the conversation, and from what he could grunt out half asleep, I didn't have much to go on. But I was able to gather that Cassy wanted him to head to the café, and soon.

"Cassy has done fine this long. She can wait a few more minutes."

"Okay, but what was that all about?" I ask as Nick nuzzles my neck, his stubble scratching against my skin in a good way like he's tickling me. I shiver again.

Nick catches my shiver and looks up to give me a

seductive smile. I roll my eyes, and he laughs a deep throaty laugh followed up with puppy dog eyes.

I giggle at his wounded expression and let out a puff of laughter. This is a mistake because before I can process what is happening, he has rolled me over and pinned me to the bed, pressing his lips to mine, his hips pushed into my own.

I automatically raise my hips to meet his and kiss him back, losing all cognitive ability to reason. Like I do every time his hands are on my body. I breathe him in. The scent of his soap mixing with the ocean as it invades my olfactory membrane.

"Nick?" I whisper through our kiss.

"Mmm?"

"Nick, what did Cassy need?"

It takes considerable effort to form a coherent sentence with Nick's hands roaming my body. But something about their conversation keeps chipping at my consciousness. Like there is something there that needs attention. Attention that Nick is currently too distracted to give.

Nick pulls back and studies my face like he's looking for answers deep within my eyes.

"What?" he asks, lips swollen and red from kissing me.

"Cassy, what did she need?"

Nick flops back on the bed, taking the sheet with him and leaving my body exposed to the cold air again.

"Jeeze, Bri, talking about my sister sure kills the vibe."

I crawl across the bed and rest my chin on a tuft of red curls taking up residence across his chest, looking up into his green eyes.

"So?" I draw out, waiting for him to expand on what I've already asked.

"It's no big deal. Cassy just needs me to do some stuff for her."

"Such as?" I press.

"Replace a window, install a security camera, change the locks." Nick ticks off the tasks like he's already exhausted, even though he hasn't even left the prone position of lounging in bed.

As he talks, the hair stands up on my arm, but this time it has nothing to do with the air conditioning. "Nick, why does Cassy need those things done?"

"She said something about the café being broken into last night, things being smashed up or something."

I'm instantly upright. "Nick! What the heck?" I start grabbing our clothes off the bed, reaching down to grab his jeans off the floor—left there last night in our hast to disrobe as quickly as possible.

"What? THE NEST is ruffed up all the time. It's no big deal." Nick is now sitting up, leaning against the headboard, catching the clothes I'm throwing in his direction.

I pause, my hand fisting my bra. "Nick, THE NEST is roughed up because some drunk guy ends up in a scuffle with another drunk guy—it's a bar. This is the Flamingo Café. It's pink and cheery and full of pastries."

Nick looks at me blankly, still not getting what I'm trying to explain.

"If the café was broken into, Cassy is more than likely having a hard time dealing with the stress of it. You need to be there for her."

"Correction, we need to be there for her." Nick pulls his white t-shirt over his head and shifts to the edge of the bed to pull his jeans on. "Come with me."

I pause in my dressing. "I fully intend on checking on Cassy, but you know I can't show up with you."

"Yes, you can. You just come with me, we show up together, and we tell her the truth."

"Nick, this is not the time for us to come forward with our deep dark secret, and you know it. It would put her over the edge completely."

"No, it wouldn't."

"Yes, it would, and you know it. She can't handle that kind of stress right now. Besides, you and I have known her long enough to know she has a history of not liking the girls you date. Not to mention I'm her best friend. I'm not supposed to fall for her brother. It's girl code."

"Screw girl code. Besides, all the girls I've dated in the past were high-maintenance, fake snobs. They weren't you. Come on, Bri. We've been sneaking around long enough. Let's go there together," he motions between us, "and tell her we're a couple. You guys love each other like sisters. She'll be thrilled for us."

"Not yet." I cross my arms over my chest as we stand facing each other on opposite sides of the bed.

"I don't get it, Bri. Why can't we tell everyone? I fell for you, so what? You're my sister's best friend, so what? I've known you since freshman year of high school, so what?" He stares at me. "I love you, so what? Why can't I tell everyone? Do you know what it does to me not to be able to shout it from the rooftops?"

My fingers start to tingle, and I feel like I've swallowed a mouthful of sand. I concentrate on long, steady breaths until the oxygen returns to my blood.

I love you

He loves me

"You love me."

"Well yeah, I figured you knew."

"I...Well, I..." I can't seem to get any words out to explain all the thoughts swirling around in my head. "Love is a unique blend of brain chemicals. Adrenaline, dopamine, and serotonin are all released at the same time. It's temporary. Love fades."

Nick laughs and walks around the bed to take me in his arms. Reaching out, he takes my hand in his. "Bri, I know the word freaks you out. I also know you are probably, right this very instant, trying to find some scientific explanation in your head that puts this all into reason. But there isn't a scientific explanation for what I feel for you. I know what I feel, and what I feel is love. I've known you long enough to know this isn't temporary. I love you, and I'll keep loving you for as long as you let me."

"But I won't even let you hold my hand in public." I blurt, burying my face in his chest.

Nick pulls me in tighter. "Doesn't change how I feel."

There is a long stretch of silence, and I start to worry that he is expecting a similar declaration.

"I don't know how I feel," I say, my words muffled by his chest. "There's so much to consider. Cassy..."

He releases his embrace, moving his hands to hold onto my upper arms. Forcing me to look up at his face. "I'm not going to win this one, am I?"

"It's not about winning," I say. "It's about changing the course of a relationship."

"I'm not sure which relationship you're referring to, the one you have with Cassy or the one you have with me. But, Bri, I don't want to wait forever for you to figure it out."

"I know."

Nick shakes his head and starts heading for the bedroom door, stopping to grab his phone and car keys off the dresser. "Meet me back here tonight? If I can't touch you out in public, you better believe you're going to have to make up for it in private."

I can feel the capillaries in my cheeks expanding. "I can't tonight. I have to go to Orlando. I have a presentation with the Marine Mammal Commission early tomorrow morning."

Nick stops short, his hand on the doorknob. "What? Bri, when were you going to tell me? You do realize they are saying a hurricane is headed straight for us, right? "

"I was going to tell you," I say, feeling only slightly remorseful about my initial plan of texting him from the road.

"After you were gone?"

I'm not sure why I didn't tell him I would be gone earlier, but now that I see his face, I know I should have. "It's only one night. I need to do this. I've been rescheduled so many times. This is my chance." I walk across the room to rest my hand on his arm. "I need to do it before the storm shuts everything down. I don't want to have to start from the beginning again. I'll be back tomorrow. Then we can hole up in your room and ride out the hurricane together." I squeeze his arm, hoping to convey my meaning, and I know I've succeeded when a sleepy look covers Nick's eyes. "And in the meantime, you've got some things to do."

"Fine, fine. I get it. I have responsibilities. I'll go perform them like a good boy." Nick gives me a soft kiss, brushing his lips over mine, but when I sigh, he dips back in for a second taking, this time pressing into my mouth with meaning. He pushes me up against the wall, and I let him. We stay that way, touching and kissing until he breaks the kiss and looks into my eyes. "But when you return, you better believe I'm going to perform my responsibilities on you." He bends his head and nuzzles my neck. I lean my head back, and an "Mmm" escapes my lips, which Nick takes as an invitation to move his hands from my hips to my backside, pulling me against his body.

"What am I going to do while you're gone?" He mumbles, moving from my neck to my earlobe.

"I'm sure you'll figure something out." I close my eyes and allow myself to dissolve into his body, granting us one perfect moment of unthinking bliss.

Chapter Five

Clouds Gathering
Abigail

My skin is practically blistering under the direct afternoon sun. But I told myself I wouldn't leave this lounge chair until I had a solution firmly in place. Of course, I could probably have come up with some brilliant idea at least half an hour ago if I had stopped downing the *mojitos*. Oh well, what's done is done. Or at least that seems to be the new motto around here.

Right. Focus. Julian.

I'll need to involve Julian's agent. Maybe have him set up a press conference, or better yet, we could stage something more natural.

I sit up with a jolt of inspiration.

I know what we need to do. We need to hire paparazzi. Capture Julian, Riley, and me frolicking on the beach. The vision of a picture-perfect family. Of course, I'll have to make sure we coordinate our outfits. Maybe some of those florescent paisley garments all the tourists love. The photogs will capture the most precious moment of us as we hold hands and stare lovingly into each other's eyes, Riley just feet away, playing in the sand. Naturally, we'll have to blast it across all the social media accounts as well. Insta, Twitter, Snapchat. Anywhere the PBPs and WAGs might see it.

Yes, that will be perfect.

We'll show the world we stand united as a family against the vicious rumors being spread about Julian.

A quick check of the diamond-encrusted watch encircling my left wrist tells me it only took twenty minutes to come up with this brilliant plan. Now all I need is for Julian to come home so we can start implementing it.

As if I can manifest my own desires, the low rumble of Julian's Porsche Turbo S slices through the silence, announcing his arrival. The engine cuts out, letting me know he has parked his precious new toy in the circular driveway.

I settle back into my chaise and try to keep my foot from tapping as Julian makes his way through the house and out the bank of open French doors to the pool.

"Hola Amor, como estas?" I call, careful to keep my voice even as Julian lumbers his way through the open-air living room and onto the terracotta tiles surrounding the infinity pool.

His dark skin, even blacker from all the time spent in the sun, glistens in the afternoon humidity. Tiny beads of sweat collect on his bald head. His biceps are swollen, as though he's come straight from a workout, causing the wall of tattoos covering his arm to strain with his every movement.

There was once a time I couldn't keep my hands off those arms. Now, I regard them with disdain, picturing them wrapped around someone else's body.

Julian makes his way over to my chair and stands over me, forcing me to shade my eyes from the sun as I look up at him.

"Hey," he says with a tilt of his chin.

"Hey," I respond, "Where've you been?"

Julian doesn't answer and instead lets his gaze leave my bikini-clad body and drift out over the two acres of our perfectly manicured property, focusing on the light blue waters of the Atlantic a few feet beyond the hedges.

My skin tingles at his silence.

I sit up and rotate my position, hanging my legs over the side of the lounge.

"Riley at school?" He asks, keeping his gaze locked on the ocean.

"Yes."

He licks his front teeth with his tongue, something he does when he's deep in thought. As he performs his nervous tick, I catch sight of a new purplish-blue shadow gracing the outside corner of his left eye. I pinch my lips together to avoid commenting on it.

The silence stretches between us until he lets out a deep breath and brings his gaze back to mine. I'm granted a moment of direct eye contact before he reaches into his shirt pocket and pulls out a pair of mirrored sunglasses, putting them on and blocking me out. I find myself staring at my reflection and instinctively turn away. But then I remember my plan.

Pushing up from the lounge chair, I face Julian square on, reach out, and snatch the sunglasses off his face. His look of surprise is gratifying, and I almost stop there, but then I catch a glimpse of Julian's hand. Tiny cuts line his knuckles as though he's put his hand through a glass wall.

Of all the times Julian has gone missing, he's never come home with any injuries. Smelling of expensive alcohol and cheap women, sure, but never injuries.

I eye his hand one more time but again decide to keep my thoughts to myself. Instead, I say, "You've been gone awhile."

"Yeah," he puffs the word out, not bothering to expand on his explanation of where he was or who he was with.

I bite my tongue between my back molars, trying to hold in the scream that so desperately wants to erupt from my mouth.

A memory of when Julian first joined the team flashes through my head, "It comes with the territory," the other WAGS had whispered in my ear as we stood on the red carpet, watching the groupies grope and grab our men. Back then, I never thought Julian, my Julian, would fall for any of that nonsense. Our love was the kind that inspired romance novels. Strong and unbreakable. Our history was enough to bind us together forever. How wrong I was. It only took one season before I knew Julian was dipping his toe in the water. But at that point, I had already quit my job. Believing Julian when he said he would always take care of Riley and me, that he would always put us first. But as time passed and Julian became less engaged, I became even more determined to make it work—even if it meant turning a blind eye. In my mind, if I chose not to acknowledge his stepping out, I still had a chance to get him back. To make him want only me.

I should have heeded my mother's advice; "After all these times delaying the wedding, *Mi hijá*, you better start thinking about providing for yourself." Those had been her words after I told her, yet again, that Julian wanted to wait until after another season before getting married. Passing on his excuse to *Mamá* of him needing to focus on the game, claiming he didn't have time to think about a wedding.

But I had squashed her warnings like a cockroach on the tile floor. I knew better than anyone. The only way I would get him back was if I continued playing the charade of the perfect little housewife and kept turning my head at his indiscretions.

And I thought my plans had been working, up until twenty-four hours ago at least. But that was because his outings were done behind closed doors. If no one was the wiser, I didn't need to worry about public scrutiny or repercussions. I could pretend I didn't know what was happening. But now that Julian has brought his personal business public, he's left me no choice but to address his reckless behavior.

I square my shoulders and try to bring myself up to my maximum height.

"I saw you on TV."

"Yeah. So?"

"So? Enough with the messing around, Julian. This, this…" I wave my hand in the air. "Sowing your oats or whatever it is you are trying to get out of your system before the wedding, it needs to stop—"

"I think you know as well as I do, Abs. There's not gonna be a wedding." Julian cuts me off before I can finish my speech. I gape at him before he finishes with, "This isn't working for me."

And… there it is.

The statement I have been desperately trying to avoid for the past six years—tossed out and hanging in the air like one of Julian's famous fifty-yard passes. Only, after all this time doing his bidding, there is no way I'm going to act as his willing receiver.

"What, exactly, isn't working for you?"

"This," he waves his hand limply at me. "You, me.

The tight rope you have me on."

"Tight rope?" I choke on my laugh. "You can't be serious. I've given you so much slack you've managed to strangle yourself. Julian, I've turned my head so many times I've gotten whiplash. You don't get to call it quits like you're the only one in this relationship. Did you forget we've been together for eight years? That we have a child together? That you proposed to me?"

"I didn't forget. I couldn't possibly with how often you remind me." He takes a deep inhale of breath. "But I do have a say in this relationship, and I say it's over."

"*Mierda de toro.* How do you figure, Julian, just because you're some big man on campus now with your multi-million-dollar contract? You think you get to call the shots on everything? Well, let me tell you—"

"Tell me what exactly?" Julian seethes, cutting me off for a second time. "You think you can tell me anything when I'm the one busting my ass on the field every day, and you're lying around here like Cleopatra or some shit." He waves his hand in the air, indicating the pool terrace and my vacant chaise lounge.

I narrow my eyes. "Cleopatra was Egyptian. I'm Cuban. And she ran an empire. But, if you count being the manager of the staff and this house, then yes, I'm Cleo-fucking-patra."

Julian rolls his head back in what I can only interpret as disgust.

"And yeah, I do have a say in this relationship. *You* told *me* to stay home. You said, 'Riley needs her mom available.' So, I listened to you. I stayed home.

"When we got out of school and you got drafted, you said this was *our* dream come true. *Our* dream. You said our lives would change and we would be a family. So, I gave up my dreams in order for you to live yours. I put design school on hold. I put my whole future on hold to help build yours. I trusted you to come through on your promises."

"I made those promises before I knew the money would go to your head. You've changed. You're not the same person I thought I was going to marry."

"Ha!" a sardonic laugh escapes my lips. "Go to my head! Changed? Like you can talk. Look at you. You drive all the fancy cars, buy all the top designers, and blow money left and right at the Miami nightclub scene. What savings have you put away? What college fund for Riley have you set up? Good God, Julian. Have you even dedicated any money to our wedding day?"

"Enough with the wedding shit. It's not happening."

My throat constricts like it's starting to swell up. I shut my eyes and try to focus. "Look, I don't know where this is coming from, but why don't we take a breather."

"I don't need a breather. I've thought about it. We're over."

I laugh at the ridiculousness of what he's saying, "You can't be serious. I've lived here as long as you have. Or have you forgotten that part?"

"No, I haven't forgotten. Just grab what you can. I'll have the rest shipped when you know where you're staying."

I stare at him dumbfounded. If he thinks he can simply wipe me out of his life, ask me to gather my things, and leave no trace of my existence, he has obviously been hit in the head too many times on the field.

"You can't just kick me out. This is my house too."

"Actually, I can. I bought this house." He turns,

staring me down. "How much have you paid into the mortgage? If I recall correctly, not a single penny, which makes this my house. Your name isn't on the title. Mine is."

Nausea rises in the back of my throat as the truth of his words seeps in. My name isn't on the deed to the house, and we are not married. Florida doesn't have common-law marriages, which means I have no recourse.

I suck in a long breath of humid air, doing my best not to vomit.

"*Mamá, Papá!*"

I whip my head around at the unexpected interruption and catch sight of Riley skipping out of the house with her backpack slung over her shoulder. She crosses the terrace and stops in front of Julian and me. Giving me the once over, she takes in my bathing suit and raises one of her pointed eyebrows.

Pursing her cupid lips together, she asks, "Why aren't you dressed, *Mamá*?" She hops from one foot to the other, allowing me enough of a distraction to collect myself. "I have camp today. We have to go soon."

She stops hopping and snuggles into Julian's leg as though it's any other day and her parents weren't just discussing the end of her life as she knows it. Julian casually slugs an arm around Riley's shoulder and pulls her into him.

I stare at the pair of them standing together and blurt out, "What about Riley?"

"What about me?" Riley asks, looking between the two of us.

"Yeah, what about her?" Julian inclines his head toward Riley in a "not now" gesture. "She's going with you."

I stare at him, trying to decipher if he means at this very moment or forever.

I pause, taking in Riley. Her layers and layers of dark curls are loose against her school uniform, and her glasses are pushed up on her nose. I fight my instinct to grab her out of Julian's embrace and hug her close to me. "Of course, I'm taking Riley with me. But where do you expect us to go?"

"Don't be silly, *Mamá*. We're going to the Manatee Lagoon. You know that." Riley slips out from under Julian's arm. "I'll go change." She regards me pointedly as she heads back inside the house. "And you'll change too."

Right as she says it, the alarm on my phone goes off—the reminder for getting Riley to camp on time.

I want to scream at Julian, Riley is *our* daughter, but deep down, I know he's right. He might have been in the hospital room for her birth, but ever since we pinned the Azabache on Riley's onesie, Julian has left the raising of our daughter entirely up to me, choosing instead to focus on building his career.

I wait until Riley has disappeared into the house before repeating. "Where exactly do you expect us to go?"

"I figured you'd go to your parents, but honestly, I don't really care." Julian wanders over to the lounger I vacated only moments ago and sits down. He lies back, cradling his head in his hands, elbows sticking out on either side like bird wings, and focuses on ignoring me.

I grab my phone to silence the alarm, still buzzing, while simultaneously fighting the urge to throw it at Julian's head. Doing my best to distract myself, I pick up my caftan, with the prestigious Claudia embroidered on the tag, slip it over my body, and start walking toward the bank of open French doors. "I have to take Riley to camp. We'll talk about this when I get back." I call over my shoulder with as much authority as I can muster. No way was I going to walk out of my house without a fight.

Chapter Six

Tropical Waves
Claudia

I know, as I'm experiencing it, it's a hallucination. Betty has been floating and fluttering across the room, playing hide-and-seek between the delicate gauzy curtains. Switching locations each time the thin sheet of fabric is blown off her translucent body. The breeze coming through the French doors blows my memories around like the leaves of the palms.

I want to giggle, laugh like when we were teenagers, and I would chase Betty around the room, poking the fabric with my fingers to catch her. Then, yelling out, "found you!" before running in the other direction, squealing.

But I can't move my body.

I'm fixed in place by the ever-familiar floating sensation. Only when my body has consented, and I'm allowed to wake fully will the floating cease. I used to think this is what it felt like to be dead, completely detached from your body, looking down from above, surveying all your worldly possessions surrounding you. But now that I've passed the invisible threshold of seventy-five years of age, I'm not so sure anymore. Maybe being dead simply means you are gone. It's one of life's many questions I have decided to place at the back of my mind.

51

****

"There you are, Mrs. Castello. Your virtual meetin' be coming up in half an hour."

"Thank you, Pamela. Yes, I'll be getting up now." I squint my eyes. The sun has moved farther to the west, and the umbrella shading my lounge chair is no longer adequately blocking the afternoon rays from my face.

When choosing the staff for our house, Benedict had made it perfectly clear to each employee the state of my condition—emphasizing how it was essential for me to stick to a schedule. Pamela had taken those particular instructions to heart, keeping me on my routine with the precision of a drill sergeant.

"Yes, ma'am. And I thought you'd like to know Parker's segment be coming up soon. They be running storm coverage nonstop. Your gran' baby been getting lots of airtime."

I smile as I remember Parker's "celebrity" comment. "Yes, I will want to watch him. Thank you."

"You're welcome. I'll bring your medications and afternoon tea to the library shortly." Pamela says as she heads to the kitchen.

It takes me a few minutes to persuade my limbs to start working again. After my afternoon nap, it is always a bit tricky to bring my body back from its deepest sleep. It has been getting harder and harder over the last few months. When others find their deepest rest in the dead of night, my body chooses to find it during the middle of the day.

Once I've managed to push up out of the lounge chair, I follow Pamela's footsteps back into the solarium, where I use the next ten minutes to work my way through a yin yoga series. It's during the flow when I remind myself I can control my body. If I stay with the discomfort of a pose long enough, it will pass. The blood flowing through my body serves as a reminder that my mind can still work even when my body remains still. The result is as good as a shot of caffeine.

With my final tree pose completed, I wander back down the hallway. Past the temperature-controlled wine closet, the dining room with not just one but two dining tables, and the ballroom with hanging chandlers and dove gray velvet upholstered armchairs. All of it is evidence of decades spent battling back against the cards life dealt me. Not accepting my disability as a curse but instead taking it on as a challenge.

I continue my shuffle down the long hallway until I have reached the library—my sanctuary from the world. The mahogany shelves lined with rows of books act as my place of peace. Where my office pulls the creativity from me, this room allows me to feel settled and relaxed.

Once situated in the brown leather chair, worn to a shiny patina from years of use, I pick the remote up off the side table and speak into it, "turn on the TV."

Instantaneously, the entire wall across from me springs to life. Bringing with it a larger-than-life image of Parker, on location at some beach, dressed in polo shirt and slacks, holding a microphone close to his mouth. I push the button, releasing the mute and turning up the sound.

"Odette is now churning in the Atlantic as a Category one but could become a Category two by Saturday. Predictions are for Odette to be a Category three hurricane with one hundred and twenty mile per hour winds within the next forty-eight hours.

"All residents along the entire east coast of Florida

need to be prepared for possible impacts. As it increases in strength, Odette has the potential to damage homes, businesses, and buildings severely. Do not wait until it is too late to make plans. We are currently on Hurricane Warning. Notice this is different from being on Hurricane Watch. It is not just possible. Now it is inevitable."

I press the mute button again. Oh, kids nowadays, everything is so sensationalized. I can't even count on my hands how many times I've heard the same warning, "Hurricane coming, prepare for the worst." And every time, it's the same. After the stores have been wiped clean, gas stations have run out of gas, and everyone has been run out of town, some butterfly somewhere flaps its wings, the hurricane trajectory is changed, and we are all spared. But not until after all the excitement and stress of preparing for our impending doom.

Pamela breaks into my thoughts as she enters the library carrying a tray of mint tea, medications, and *Amygdalota*. She sets it down on my desk and glances at the screen, still illuminated with Parker's beautiful face.

"He say we should worry?" she asks in her broken English, not so much worse than my own when I first came to this country, making the trip with my family from Greece to the United States.

"Oh, you know the news. They always say we should worry." I smile at Pamela as she pours the tea for me.

"Yes, but sometimes it is good to worry, no?" she questions.

I realize she is thinking about her family in the Bahamas,—a country that has repeatedly felt the effects of hurricanes.

"Yes, sometimes." I grant her the acknowledgment of what her family has gone through. "But most of the time, it's all for nothing."

"It be a good idea for me to prepare the pantry, in case." She decides for me.

"We have enough food in this house to feed an army, Pamela. I don't think you need to do anything. This house may be on the water's edge, but it's built like a fortress, with hurricane-glass windows and shutters. It's practically got a bunker in the back," I say, referring to the safe room Benedict insisted on having built in the back of the house.

Pamela gives me a look that is a cross between a disobedient teenager and a concerned employee. "But, ma'am, they say you should have prepared seven days of food, water, and medicine. They also telling everyone to be prepared to evacuate, should you need to."

"Well, Benedict and I will be staying right here. We've never evacuated before, and we won't be abandoning our home this time either." I rub my temples and grab my phone to check if it is time for my meeting with the creative team in New York. But when I peer at the screen, I'm surprised and a little startled by the number of missed calls crowding my inbox. I look closer and see all the messages are from Cassandra. A quick scan tells me she needs me to call her. I swipe out of messages and jab Cassandra's name to start the call.

Pamela takes the cue and heads for the door to give me privacy, but before she can leave, I hold up a finger for her to stay.

"I'm planning a dinner here tomorrow night."

Pamela's eyes widen, but I choose not to acknowledge her surprise. Instead, she simply nods her head. "How many should I plan for dinner, ma'am?"

I listen to the phone ring in my hand and say decisively, "Five people. Benedict, myself, Parker, Cassandra, and Nicholas."

Chapter Seven

81 degrees
Cassy

"Auntie Claudia!" A jar of strawberry preserve scatters across the cutting board as I swipe my finger across the phone. "Crap. Hold on a second." I release my hold on the phone and right the container I was about to open for the strawberry and lemon thumbprint cookies mere milliseconds before my workspace is turned into a river of red goo. But, as I avoid that catastrophe, I knock my phone to the side and it slides across the work surface, resulting in a loud clatter as it hits one of the metal mixing bowls.

"Cassandra, *glykie mia agápi*, Is everything all right?" The combination of my self-created ruckus and the chatter emanating from the television takes up so much air space in the little kitchen I can barely hear Auntie Claudia.

"Yes, yes." A plume of flour explodes off my hands as I grab the phone with one hand while simultaneously punching the remote with the other. The white dust hangs in the air for a beat before dropping, settling atop the remote and papers. Crap. The police report. I let out an audible sigh of frustration, grabbing the documents and shaking them with more vigor than necessary. "No, no, no."

"Cassandra? What is going on? You are confusing

me. Are you saying you're not okay?"

"Sorry, I'm sorry. I just…" I trail off as I place the papers back next to the TV. A rustle sounds on the other side of the line, and I imagine Auntie Claudia struggling to stand up so she can pace the room in frustration. "I'm okay. I didn't mean to alarm you. I'm fine, I promise."

The rustling stops, and Auntie Claudia's voice appears once more. "My dear, what in the world is happening over there? I'm hearing a lot of commotion. That, and you've left several messages for me to call you. So what is going on, *Mia Agapi*?"

The reminder of how many times I dialed her number during the morning has me cringing inside. In the dark and early hours, it had felt imperative that I get ahold of Auntie Claudia, craving the reassurance that I wasn't truly alone on the dark sidewalk while waiting for the police to show up. But now that the sun is overhead and the evidence of the break-in is virtually erased from the café, I no longer feel the same urgency to be comforted.

I stand up straight and wipe my hands on a towel. Forcing a steady stream of air out my nose in an effort to try and gain a little composure. How I proceed with this conversation will determine Auntie Claudia's reaction and possibly how we conduct business in the future. On the one hand, I see no need to upset her further. There isn't really much she can do for me at this point, and anything I tell her now will only make her worry about my safety in the future. And, since Auntie Claudia has already spent the last decade worrying about my safety and future, I don't see the need to start the whole process over again. We were just getting to the point of her trusting in my decisions and treating me like an adult.

But on the other hand, I've already started the ball rolling with my persistent calling. That—coupled with the fact she is the primary investor and the reason I own the Flamingo Café in the first place—I know I owe her an explanation.

"Before I tell you, I want you to remember that I'm fine. Everything is fine."

"Well, now you have me worried."

I swallow the lump in my throat and plow forward. "The café was broken into last night."

I turn around and rest my hips on the back of the counter, abandoning my baking as I wait for an influx of cross-examination questions from Auntie Claudia. But as I settle against the island, there is only silence from the other side of the line.

I look at the phone to ensure we aren't disconnected, but the time stamp is still ticking away.

"Auntie Claudia? Did you hear me?"

"Yes, sorry, dear. I am just trying to process what you've told me."

I push off the island counter and start to pace around the kitchen. But, of course, I should have known Auntie Claudia wouldn't blow the phone up with sentiments of "Oh my God." Or, "What are you talking about?"

Auntie Claudia has never jumped the gun during a crisis. She has always taken her time to process the information before choosing how to respond because that is how Auntie Claudia operates—methodically and with purpose. I've seen her work this way numerous times, either in her business, dealing with disgruntled vendors, or in her personal life, taking on her disability and self-advocating with her doctors. Even years ago, when our family was met with a tragedy impossible to bounce back from, she was there, being steady and acting as my compass. No matter the situation, she keeps her composure. I can't help but admire her.

"You said you're fine. That is, of course, my primary concern. Are you certain you're unharmed? Were you there when it happened?"

"Yes, I'm certain. I wasn't here during the break-in. I didn't even know about it until Bo and I got to work this morning and were greeted by the broken glass. Whoever broke in had already left. They think it was done around two in the morning. I'm sorry I called you so many times, but the place was a wreck. One of the chairs from the patio—the pink metal ones—was thrown through the front window. A hole was punched through the glass of the French door, right by the lock. They knocked over all the furniture, dented the stools, ripped the shelves off the walls, and pushed over all the bookcase displays with the merchandise. It was a total mess when Bo and I got here, and it was dark out when we arrived. I didn't know what to do, so I called you." I pause and admit. "I also called Uncle B, and Nick. When no one answered, I finally called the Palm Beach Police Department."

"Oh, Cassandra, I'm so sorry I didn't answer your phone calls. If I had known, I undoubtedly would have called you back much earlier than this. You've certainly been through an ordeal."

My chest swells at Auntie Claudia's kindness, and I bite back the tears that have been threatening to spill over since this morning. I swallow and try to get ahold of myself, not wanting one phone call to undo the resolve I've held onto this whole time. "It's okay, I've been cleaning up all day, and it's finally starting to feel back to normal around here."

"Well, *Mia Agápi,* I'm very proud of you for handling this on your own. It wasn't ideal, of course, but you proved you could stay calm and deal with a stressful situation. You've made progress with your therapist, I can tell. And you did the right thing, calling the police. Of course, it's what I would have had you do anyways if I had answered the phone."

I nod my head in silence, her affirmations helping soothe my nerves. "Officer Jackson, the police officer I've been working with, says it looked like whoever did it was just out to cause trouble…"

I trail off with my explanation because I am distracted by Zoe, who sticks her head through the kitchen door.

"I'm sorry to interrupt, but Officer Jackson is out front. He says he needs to go over one more thing with you before he leaves."

I cover the phone with my palm and say, "Can you let him know I'll be right there? Just a minute."

Zoe nods her head and pats the door frame. "Sure thing." She makes a one-eighty turn on her pink high-top converse sneaker and pushes back through the door separating the kitchen from the café.

"Auntie Claudia, I still need to handle a few things. Can I call you back in a little while?"

"Of course, you can call me back anytime. But, darling would you like me to stay on the phone with you while you speak to the officer? I might be able to offer some guidance with the legal process."

I debate telling her I've got this and that I don't need her to stay on the phone while I talk with Officer Jackson. But then I realize that, after years of hearing

Uncle B's legal cases, she is probably a valuable resource for me. "Yeah, that would be great. Thanks."

I quickly check the ovens to ensure they are all off before putting the phone on speaker and stepping through the door, separating the back of the house from the front. As I traverse the three hundred square feet of display cases, coffee bar, and open seating, all designed for quick and efficient service, a familiar four-legged shadow appears by my side.

Automatically, I reach out my free hand and caress the top of my companion's head. Bo pushes back and follows me through the boarded-up French door and into the afternoon sun to where Officer Jackson is waiting.

Today's air feels like a knife slicing through a meringue pie. Thick and sticky, it attaches itself to every surface of my body. It only takes a minute before sweat drips down my spine and pools in that mysterious space between my hips and backside. I pull at my pale-pink t-shirt, already showing signs of sweat spots, and silently curse the South Florida humidity.

Raising a hand to shade my eyes from the glare, I try to locate Officer Jackson. I glance to the right and find him standing next to his patrol car. As he turns my way, the sun glints off his sunglasses, momentarily blinding me. As I wait for the spots to leave my vision, an image from ten years ago—when my childhood home was crawling with police officers—flashes through my mind. Memories of endless questions leading to no solid answers fill my head.

Bo, able to sense a change in my demeanor, nudges me with his wet nose, leaving a damp mark on the side of my leg. It's enough of a distraction to break the spell. I inhale a few deep breaths and try to clear my head as I stroke Bo's body. His strong muscles ripple under his shiny white coat, covered with black spots, as he allows me to continually run my hands over his body, waiting for the memories to pass.

Officer Jackson catches sight of Bo and me and walks over to greet us. He stands close, as though we are old friends and comfortable in each other's presence. Stretching his hand out for Bo to sniff, he says, "I love Dalmatians. I keep suggesting we get one down at the station, but they say a K-9 isn't in the budget." He laughs and pats Bo on the head. "Can you believe it? Not in the budget of the Palm Beach police precinct. Anyways…" He stops himself before expanding on his comment and stands back up, glancing toward the café before returning his gaze to Bo. "I'm not sure having a dog in a café meets code."

"He's her emotional support dog. He stays in the front of the house. He's allowed." Auntie Claudia's voice cuts through, calm and clear, from the phone that has been in my hand, dangling at my side the whole time Officer Jackson has been talking.

Officer Jackson eyes the phone but doesn't even flinch at the sudden interruption of Auntie Claudia. It must be from his training—maintaining focus in the face of distraction or something along those lines. Nevertheless, I still feel the need to explain why I didn't mention her virtual presence earlier.

"Officer Jackson, this is my aunt, Claudia Castello. I was on the phone with her while I was in the kitchen." I wave the phone in the air like I'm introducing a physical being and not just a voice on the other end of the line.

"Hello." He nods toward my outstretched hand.

"He's her emotional support dog. I got him for her myself. He has papers, and he's allowed to stay in the front of the house." Auntie Claudia repeats herself, ignoring Officer Jackson's greeting.

Officer Jackson adjusts his gaze from my hand to Bo and back to my face. I can feel myself blush under his watch as he takes in my pale, freckled skin and green eyes. The way he looks at me makes me think he can't decide if he believes I'm the kind of person who needs an emotional support animal or if this is just a convenient excuse to keep Bo at work with me.

"Well, as long as you keep his papers nearby, it shouldn't be a problem." He finally decides.

I nod my head in agreement.

"No, it shouldn't." Auntie Claudia agrees, sounding like she was the one who was going to make this decision all along.

Office Jackson eyes the phone but doesn't say anything in response.

"I'll keep the papers," I say.

"Right. Well, Mrs. Castello," Officer Jackson begins, changing the subject. "like I was telling Cassy earlier, Palm Beach is generally a low crime area. Unfortunately, I'm sorry that the break-in at the cafe got the best of us. We will be increasing our night patrols down here, but in the meantime, I suggest Cassy change the locks as soon as she gets the door fixed. I would also suggest a security camera of some sort."

"I have my brother coming to help me. He should be here soon." I glance at my watch and notice over an hour has passed since I called Nick. Where was he?

"Oh, I'm happy to hear Nicholas is going to be helping you." Auntie Claudia says.

"Yes, that is good to hear." Officer Jackson agrees. "I have one more piece of business, and then I should be on my way." He takes a piece of paper off his clipboard and hands it to me. "You have the opportunity to make a separate Victim Personal Statement. It's a chance for you to go on record how the crime has affected you."

"Cassandra? Make sure you fill that out. Then, if they find the person responsible and it goes to court, this statement can be used in the prosecution."

I take Officer Jackson's paper as he says, "Your Aunt is correct on this one. You will want to fill it out and file it with the break-in report. Just in case."

"Okay, I'll make sure to complete it and bring it down to the station. Thank you."

Officer Jackson gives a small and somewhat awkward wave. "Okay, that just about does it. But if you have any questions or if you can think of anything else, you have my card. Don't hesitate to call me."

"Yes, I will, and thank you for your help," I repeat as he heads back to his patrol car.

He stops when he reaches the car and, with his hand on the door handle, turns back. "You're more than welcome." He tips his hat in my direction and disappears into the vehicle.

Once he has reversed out of the parking lot and merged into traffic on Royal Poinciana Way, I let out a breath.

My sight trails his patrol car through the traffic, but I am distracted when I spot Bri's white Jeep Rubicon passing Officer Jackson, heading toward the café. I wave at her and motion for her to park in the spot Officer Jackson just vacated, but she isn't looking in my direction, so she doesn't see me. I'm about to go all teenager and start jumping up and down on the sidewalk to get her attention when Auntie Claudia's voice breaks into my concentration and reminds me I have yet to end the phone call with her.

"Well, I'm glad that is taken care of. Now, is there anything else I can help you with, Dear?"

"Oh no, you've done so much by just being there. I'm not sure I could have done this by myself. Thank you."

"Oh, now, that is nonsense. You handled yourself perfectly well up to this point. You need to give yourself more credit."

I smile and head back into the café, leaving Bri to park and make her way on her own. "Thanks, Auntie Claudia. I'll try to."

"There is no try. There is just do."

I can't help but laugh at Auntie Claudia's insistence. "Okay, I got it," I say and walk back into the café, holding the door for Bo to follow me.

"That's it. Now, I wish I was there to hug you. How about you plan on coming over for dinner tomorrow night, and I can do just that."

I pause as I slip back behind the coffee counter, surprised by the invitation. "But isn't that your anniversary night? I thought you and Uncle Benedict were having dinner together."

"Yes, well, I decided to make it a family dinner. Will you be able to join us?"

"Yes, of course. I'd love to come and celebrate with you."

"Marvelous. I'll be able to give you that hug after all. Can I rely on you to pass the word on to Nicolas?"

"That won't be a problem. We'll be there."

"Oh, this is great news. We are going to have a wonderful night. I do believe Parker will be able to join us as well."

The coffee mug I just picked up slips from my hand and shatters all over the floor at my feet. Bo is instantly by my side, but I shoo him away from the broken shards, worried about his paws getting cut.

I've been rendered speechless at the idea of seeing Parker again, so Auntie Claudia continues her side of the conversation with no idea of the mess I've just created. "Don't hesitate to call me if you need anything done for the café. I have people, you know."

I shake myself out of my stupor and bend down to clean up the broken mug, forcing a polite laugh at Auntie Claudia's offer. "I know. But I think I've got it covered now."

"Okay, well then, I'll see you tomorrow."

Chapter Eight

Invest
Bri

"Manatees are typically found in shallow coastal waters and rivers. They feed on sea grass, mangrove leaves, and algae. These herbivores munch on food for almost half the day, consuming up to ten percent of their body weight in plant mass."

Executing a perfect parallel parking job with one hand on the wheel, I place the gear shift into park and snatch the pile of prepared note cards off the dashboard. Leaning into the rearview mirror, I check my reflection before leaving the confines of the air-conditioned Jeep. Staring at my reflection, I realize I'm not particularly concerned with the image staring back, but rather I'm trying to detect if the guilt buried in the depths of my consciousness is radiating off me like a blinking neon sign.

"Oh, come on," I mumble to my reflection after confirming I am not, in fact, radiating cold cathode gas-discharging light. "Don't be ridiculous," I say, taking in the same plain and boring brown hair and brown eyes I've tried to escape my whole life. "That's enough of that. You have work to prepare for." Doing my best to shake off any lingering uncertainty, I open the door before I can change my mind.

The direct afternoon sun engulfs me the second I am

clear of the Jeep's shadow, making me wish I were back on the job site, swimming with my beloved manatees in the lagoon's calm waters and not standing in the sweltering heat, preparing to lie to my best friend's face for the umpteenth time.

Attempting to shade my eyes from the brightness of the day, I duck my head, refocus my attention on the cards in my hand, and head across the street in the direction of the Flamingo Café picking up where I left of on rehearsing my speech.

"The baby manatee relics on their mother's milk for nourishment for the first two years of life. Which is why the calves here at—"

"Beeeeep," an ear-splitting honk and screech of metal-on-metal cuts me off mid-sentence, forcing me to look up. There is no time to react as smoke erupts from the tires of a massive SUV careening down the middle of the street—heading straight toward me.

As if observing the events from above, I watch the note cards in my hand drift and flutter to the ground. Frozen in the middle of the crosswalk, I am unable to move or react in time to get out of the way.

I've studied time dilation in my undergrad psychology class. How, when faced with intense fear, a person can feel a slowing down of time. It works when the amygdala, an area in the brain, lays down an extra set of memories that go along with those usually taken care of by other parts of the brain. This little neurological trick creates richer and denser memories, causing the person affected to believe the event took longer.

And yet, despite being equipped with this basic biological knowledge, time comes to a screeching halt as the dropped note cards drift from my hand down to the crosswalk as the bumper of the black SUV squeals to a stop mere inches from my knees.

Unlike other people's accounts of near-death experiences, my short twenty-six years of existence do not flash before my eyes. Instead, I am faced with a tunnel of darkness. Eclipsing anything next to or in front of me until all that is left is a black hole. I'm unsure how long I stand rooted to the same spot, unseeingly staring at the bumper. But eventually, time returns to normal. I gasp like a fish out of water, desperate for air.

With the return of natural oxygen levels to my brain cells, my vision clears, allowing me to shift my attention from the three-pointed star in the middle of the grill mere inches from my khakis up to the tinted windshield of the vehicle.

Searching for the distressed driver, I peer into the abyss of the windshield, but all I see is a wall of blackness. I mentally will the driver to roll the window down and offer me a few words of concern or condolence.

Still nothing.

I'm about to take a step toward the driver's side to offer my own words when the SUV reverses away from me, driving backward down the street without any warning and without providing any regrets.

The sudden separation of space is so jarring that, again, I find myself glued to the pavement. I continue to watch, dumbfounded. Just when I think the SUV will drive backward down the entire length of the street, the driver abruptly changes gears, causing a crunching from under the vehicle, and starts moving forward again. The driver swerves before reaching the crosswalk, sideswiping me and running over my note cards before continuing down Royal Poinciana Way.

"Hey! Hey! Where do you think you're going!?" My arms automatically spread wide at my sides as I fight the shiver traveling up my spine. I stare at the back of the SUV as it drives away, only registering the make and model of the vehicle as one of those pretentious Mercedes G-Wagons after it has disappeared. Nevertheless, the vision of its custom Miami Sting Rays license plate is burned into my memory.

Flummoxed, I search up and down the road, desperate for anyone that might have borne witness to my almost demise.

To my utter disbelief, there isn't a single person nearby. I try to calculate the probability of being alone on the street at this time of the day. But after a few unsuccessful attempts, I recognize I'm too rattled to actually do the math.

Still shaking, I quickly and carefully gather my tire-stained note cards from the ground and make my way to the other side of the street. It's not until I'm outside the entrance of the Flamingo Café that the adrenaline starts to dissipate from my body, leaving me unsteady and shaky on my feet.

As I'm standing by myself, rehashing the events in my head and trying to take slow, steady breaths, the door to the café opens. A gentleman in a suit and tie exits, holding a pale-pink paper bag at his side. He tips his head at me. "Great shirt," he says, holding the door open, expecting me to pass through.

The abrupt manifestation of this man on the street sends a new rush of adrenaline into my bloodstream, while at the same time, I'm hit with a strong surge of disbelief.

Where was this guy a few minutes ago?

His presence would have been invaluable, serving as a witness to the accident or even possibly helping to prevent it. But, instead, he was inside the café, taking his sweet time stocking up on Cassy's famous Key lime pie rolls and grabbing an iced coffee, oblivious to my plight.

"Um, are you headed inside?"

With a start, I notice the gentleman is still staring at me expectantly, continuing to hold the door open. I shake myself out of my trance, remembering his prior compliment, and remind myself the appropriate thing to do in these situations is to offer a response of some kind.

Looking down at my cerulean blue *Save the Manatee* t-shirt, I push a strand of hair out of my eyes and manage a reserved "Yes, thank you" before sliding past him into the air-conditioned café, avoiding any further conversation.

Once inside, it takes a minute for my eyes to dilate and adjust to the dimness of the café. I blink a few times before I spy Cassy behind the counter, cleaning up what appears to be a broken coffee mug from the floor. Just the sight of her is enough to calm my frazzled nerves. I try to send her my best, best-friend mental telepathy of my arrival and am surreptitiously amused when she looks up in my direction. After almost thirteen years of friendship, it's no real surprise Cassy, and I can sense when the other person has entered a room.

Cassy stands up and waves me over. Carrying a handheld broom and dustpan, she casually slides the contents into the trash can behind her and walks to the sink to wash her hands.

With her back to me and the water running, Cassy starts talking as soon as I reach the display case separating us. "Oh my God, you wouldn't believe my day," she says.

I can tell by the exasperation in her voice she is about to go into a detailed explanation of what kind of day she's had, but when she turns around, wiping her hands on a towel, she takes one look at my face and counters with, "What's wrong with you? You look like you just saw a ghost."

"If that SUV hadn't stopped when it did, I might have turned into one," The words spew out of me, and I realize only after I've spoken that what I've said is as clear as gibberish.

Cassy looks at me like I've lost my mind. "Come again?"

"Some dumb Mercedes almost ran over me while I was crossing the crosswalk."

"Wait. What? Just now?"

"About two seconds ago, yeah," I say.

Cassy's mouth forms an O, but no words come out. It takes me a beat before I comprehend my mistake. "But nothing happened." I backpedal. I know better than to surprise Cassy with thoughts of car accidents. What was I doing? I should have eased into telling her about what had happened.

"I'm fine, see?" I pat myself on my arms and legs as if proving to Cassy and myself I'm still in one piece, not splashed all over the pavement.

My patting does the trick because Cassy gives a slight shake of her head and purses her lips together before saying, "I'm glad you're okay, but geez, Bri, you have to be more careful!" She walks around the counter, dodging the to-go cups of coffee waiting to be picked up, and envelopes me in a tight bear hug.

I know I should accept the hug and let it go, but my pride is standing in the way of being gracious. "But they almost ran me over."

Cassy lets me go and looks pointedly at the note cards in my hand. "But you weren't looking where you were going."

The fact she knows I wasn't looking where I was going without me having to tell her should act as a testament to our friendship, but instead, it just riles me up even further. "But I was in a *crosswalk*."

"That doesn't mean you shouldn't check both sides of the street before walking into it." Cassy shakes her head at me.

"You can't be serious. You really believe this was my fault?"

"No, that's not what I'm saying," she says, this time being the one to do the backpedaling. "I'm just saying you tend to be preoccupied with your thoughts. I'm only suggesting you try to mind your surroundings a little more. You know," Cassy nods to the street just out the window. "So you don't get run over."

"Fine." I pout but reluctantly concede to her logic, which is when I notice the boarded-up door I walked through only moments prior.

Even though I already know about the break-in from Nick, there is no way I can reveal that information to Cassy. So again, I push down the guilt bubbling up my throat like heartburn, put my best poker face on, point, and ask, "What happened there?"

"Someone broke into the café last night." Cassy walks around to the display case, bends down, and plucks the last vegan lemon-poppyseed muffin from the tray, handing it to me over the counter.

I practice my concerned look as I happily take her peace offering and sink my teeth into the still-warm pastry. The acidity of the lemon stimulates my reticular activating system, kicking my salivary glands into high gear and getting rid of any lingering tension. "You're kidding? That's awful." I say, mid-chew.

"Unfortunately, I'm not kidding. I wish I were. I make a nightly deposit, so the register was empty, but they still managed to make a mess of the place. The cops have been in and out of here all day. Zoe and I have been cleaning up since arriving this morning."

"Oh my God, Cassy! That's so scary. What if you were in the back kitchen when they broke in?"

Cassy shrugs her shoulders. "Bo would have been barking his head off before they could even get a foot in the door."

I look over at the perfectly spotted, gangly Dalmatian asleep on his bed in the corner of the café and smile. "You're right. Bo would have taken them out for sure." I turn back to Cassy and say, "But, in the rare case Bo is otherwise preoccupied, you should consider increasing your security."

"I'm on it. In fact, Nick just got here a minute ago. I already put him to work. He's installing the camera system as we speak."

I follow her finger with my gaze and spy Nick on the other side of the café. He is perched precariously on a folding ladder with a power tool in his hand. On closer inspection, I see he is mounting a tiny camera into the palm frond wallpaper in the corner just under the ceiling.

Despite the instability beneath his feet, Nick works smoothly, pushing against the drill, screwing the hardware into the wall. I watch as his biceps and triceps flex from his exertion. Before I can stop it, the heat builds in my neck, traveling to my cheeks as memories of my hands holding on to those powerful muscles flash through my mind.

I must mutter, "Nice," out loud because Cassy scoffs in my direction and says, "Yeah, nice that he finally decided to show up." She shakes her head in his direction and takes my hand, leading me toward the empty tables, away from Nick and his power tools. "Come on. You can help me clean up before the afternoon rush."

Cassy's direction serves as the much-needed douse of icy water to my heated cheeks. I push away the erotic images of Nick's body pressed against mine and transfer my attention back to my best friend. I dutifully follow as Cassy scoops up discarded cups and plates and deposits them in the wash bucket.

"Did you just get off? How was work?" Cassy asks, changing the subject and redirecting my attention to lesser matters.

Of course, Cassy is not referring to my professional career but to my side hustle that helps pay the rent as an after-school camp counselor at the Manatee Lagoon. I nod my head in the affirmative.

"We have this one little girl, Riley. She has some real potential. She's able to understand concepts the other campers can't grasp. The only problem is I don't think she gets much encouragement from her parents. They're the kind of parents who are more into Palm Beach society than saving the wildlife surrounding it. Her dad is the quarterback for the Miami Sting Rays. You've probably heard of him, Julian Mendez."

Cassy nods her head as she moves to the next table. "Oh yeah, I know, Julian. His fiancée, Abigail, used to

work for Nick eons ago as a barmaid at THE NEST."
Cassy pauses with a coffee cup in her hand and smirks to
herself before continuing, "After he became big time,
you know, walking around town like he owned it, he
would come in here and hit on me. He had this lame
pickup line about keeping it all in the family or
something like that. So gross. Like Abigail and Nick had
hooked up, and we should too." Cassy sticks her tongue
out in disgust. "Anyway, needless to say, I wasn't
interested, so I always shut him down."

"Ewe, he hit on you when he was engaged to
Abigail? He sounds like a real stand-up guy."

"Nope. Not at all. I wasn't impressed. I did my best
to avoid him when he came by, but he made it obvious
he doesn't take rejection well. But, of course, that was a
few years ago." Cassy shrugs. "Maybe he's changed
since then."

"That's doubtful. You know what they say, 'once a
cheater, always a cheater.' So why don't I remember him
coming in?"

"It was when you were away at Eckerd College,
busy studying fish or something." Cassy waves her hand
like she can't be bothered to remember all the years I was
away studying to get my master's degree.

"You mean Marine Biology and Biological
Oceanography, or, I guess, marine animals to you."

Cassy nods and gives me a sardonic smile. "Right,
right, that was it."

I shake my head at her. "So, Abigail worked at THE
NEST. That must have been a sight. She's definitely
upgraded since then. She's so posh now." I say, bending
my hand at the wrist, imitating someone posh. "She's
always wearing the outfits I see in the windows of Worth

Avenue, and she's always carrying the latest handbag when she picks Riley up from camp. She's totally out of my league."

Cassy laughs and picks up another dirty coffee cup, waving it in my direction. "They are all out of our league," she says, referring to ninety-eight percent of the population of Palm Beach Island. "Abigail and Julian live in a house off North County Road. It's funny, Julian stopped visiting once he caught on to my rejection memo, but Abigail comes in all the time now. She orders the Key lime pie roll for Riley almost daily. Bo loves her; Riley, that is, not Abigail. At least it's good for business to have a celebrity stopping in."

"I suppose she does consider herself a celebrity. But it still surprises me how she is the complete opposite of her daughter. Riley has a real talent with animals." I say, looking over at Bo.

"Sounds to me like you have a favorite camper?"

"Can you blame me? The other kids are so spoiled. All they do is whine all day and pick their noses."

Cassy curls her lips together in disgust. "Riley's not a nose picker, huh?"

"Nope, not a single finger to the naris on my watch."

Cassy laughs. "So, when's the next class?"

"Not for a while. I need to head up to Orlando tonight."

"Again? You've been up to Orlando a lot lately."

The sting of guilt rushes back as I try to recall the number of times I've used this same excuse to avoid coming home to the apartment Cassy and I have shared for the past two years so that I can shack up for another night with Nick.

The fact that I am traveling to Orlando for work this

time does nothing to ease my self-reproach. "I'm meeting with the Marine Mammal Commission. I applied for a grant, and now I need to explain, in detail, what we will be using the funds for." I pause as Cassy brushes past me with the wash bucket in her hands and heads to the kitchen. "The habitat needs the money. They just received three baby manatees requiring round-the-clock care, and they're short-staffed after serious budget cuts." I follow behind Cassy into the kitchen, emphasizing the words *round the clock care* and *short staffed*, as though explaining the perils of the situation will exonerate my past fabrications. "Besides, it's only for the day. I'll be back tomorrow. Let's hang out when I'm back. We can go grocery shopping to stock up before this storm hits."

"Can't. I just found out I'm having dinner with Auntie Claudia tomorrow night. It's her and Uncle Benedict's fifty-fifth wedding anniversary. Can you do the grocery shopping without me? I'll need to come back here after the anniversary dinner to board this place up. If the storm does hit, I can't leave the windows like they are."

"How about I come and help you? You can't board up this place all on your own. If you do, you'll still be working by the time the storm blows in."

"Okay, but I'm sure this storm will be like all the others," Cassy says with an air of nonchalance. "It's going to be all hyped up on the news, and then it's going to change course, and we'll be left with a little wind and rain."

I give her my best authoritative look. "Well, you can throw caution to the wind—pun intended—if you want to, but I personally will be taking the proper precautions. The hurricanes have been getting worse every year. You can't tell me global warming isn't happening. And we happen to live in the perfect place for it. I want to be stocked and ready."

Cassy, not bothering to glance in my direction, walks to the industrial-sized dishwasher and places the tub on the counter. I follow and stand next to her as she passes me the dishes to load into the machine as though I work here too.

"I have no doubt, which is why I'm glad you are my roommate. I know you'll have my back when disaster strikes. Like always."

She winks at me, and I give her my best stink eye, which makes her laugh. "Ah, come on. You know I love you." She gives me a side hug, and it's the most natural thing in the world to hug her back. Cassy isn't just my roommate or best friend. She's a sister to me.

We finish loading the dishwasher, pull the hood closed over the rack, and start the load before wiping our hands on a towel and heading back through the door to the café.

Now on the ground and standing next to the ladder, Nick looks up as Cassy, and I pass through the door. He locks eyes with me, and it's as though an invisible rope is pulling him toward me. He walks across the room with a slow saunter until he stands only inches from Cassy and me, invading our conversation.

"All set with the camera." He says to Cassy, his eyes boring into mine.

"Perfect. How about the new locks?" she asks as she moves to the counter, oblivious to the sheer volume of dopamine and norepinephrine released from the two bodies standing next to her.

Nick breaks eye contact with me, dutifully

following Cassy as she picks up a towel from the bleach tub and heads to the vacated tables.

"Got em' changed. All you have to do now is copy the keys." He holds up three separate keys, showing Cassy.

Cassy holds up her towel in response. "I'm totally swamped here. Can't you do it for me?" She asks before bending over to wipe the table.

Her back is to us when I feel the soft brush of Nick's fingers on mine, sending my sensory neurons into high gear and triggering the release of oxytocin from my brain. I take a step to the other side of the table, placing a physical barrier between the two of us.

Nick cocks his head to the side as he addresses Cassy, "Awe, come on. You have new cameras and new door locks. Can't I go now?" Over her shoulder, Nick gives me his best puppy dog eyes and flicks his head toward the door, all while keeping his attention on Cassy.

I narrow my eyebrows at him and shake my head in the negative.

"Seriously? Nick, you just got here. You installed the camera and the locks, but I need the glass replaced and the hurricane shutters installed." Cassy pleads.

Nick makes a "humph" sound and throws his hands in the air.

"Now, that's a good boy." Cassy pats him on the shoulder as she passes him on her way back to the counter. She throws the dirty rag into the tub of bleach water and heads toward the swinging door, leaving Nick and me alone at the table.

Nick raises his hands to Cassy's retreating figure, choking the air at her back, before dropping his arms to his sides. "You know what they say, 'good things come to those who work their ass off.' "

I watch as Nick sulks away and giggle despite myself, causing Cassy to turn around, her hand resting on the door before pushing through. "I'll see you tomorrow, Bri?"

"Absolutely. Text me when you're done with your family dinner."

"You got it." The door swings closed behind her as she disappears into the kitchen.

The instant Cassy is gone, Nick reappears by my side, reaching out for my arm.

I take a step back. "No," I whisper, noticing Zoe ringing up a customer behind the counter.

Nick follows my gaze. "Fine, but wait here, don't leave yet." He turns and walks over to the counter, leaning on it with his hip. He tilts his chin at the customer next to him, waiting for them to pay and leave before he directs his attention to Zoe. He leans in and says something I can't make out then slides the three keys Cassy just tasked him with copying across the counter to Zoe, who looks down at the keys and then back up at Nick, nods, and giggles in response. Batting her eyelashes, she reaches up and sweeps her blonde horsetail-of-a-French-braid over one shoulder as she places her other hand over the keys and drags them across the counter, leaving them next to the cash register.

Watching the arousal Nick creates in the opposite sex—I can't help but cringe. I avert my eyes from the sun that is Nick Greene and hastily do a tally of all the other ladies in the cafe crushing on him. Overdone eyelash extensions are fluttering in rapid succession across multiple tables. It would seem the only person not affected by Nick's Adonis presence is me.

But then again, I'd be lying if I didn't admit my own affection toward him. I can feel the capillaries in my cheeks beginning to dilate again. Determined to save myself from further embarrassment, I turn on my heel and make a quick exit. Satisfied to let Nick bask in his adoration all on his own. I know he will text me later, but I'll be on the road to Orlando by the time he remembers me.

Chapter Nine

Spin the Center
Abigail

Well damn, I can't feel my fingers. When did that happen? I pry them from their death grip on the black leather, flexing and stretching each extremity a few times to get the blood flowing again as I try to remember when I started to squeeze the steering wheel so tight. The jostling causes the perfect five carats of bling on my left-hand ring finger to catch the glint of deep orange sunset pouring in from the window, sending rainbows of mocking beauty dashing across the bright white interior of the Mercedes.

"Get a grip," I mutter under my breath.

"What did you say, *Mamá*?"

"Nothing *Mija*," I call over my shoulder to Riley in the back of the car, not bothering to glance at her in the mirror. After my most recent debacle, I'm determined to keep my eyes focused on the road in front of me.

Riley doesn't respond, and I assume she's gone back to whatever she was doing before I started talking to myself like a crazy woman.

The image of Julian declaring the end of our relationship had been so all-consuming of my thoughts that I had been totally checked out from driving. Right up until Riley yelled, "*Mamá*, Stop!" from the back seat.

Thank God for the brakes on this overly inflated

vehicle because if I had reacted a fraction of a second later, I would have plowed right over Plain Jane camp counselor. Not that the blame rested solely on my shoulder. Miss Marine Animals practically blended into the road wearing her basic blue t-shirt and khaki pants. Not to mention she hadn't bothered with even a glance in my direction before stepping out onto the crosswalk. Even Riley knows to look both ways before crossing the street. She wasn't so bright for someone who's supposed to be so brilliant. That, or she's harboring some deep seated death wish.

Either way, she's still alive, and my driving record is still intact.

Sure, it was risky driving away like that, but no way I could stop and exit the vehicle. Being seen as the driver of a pedestrian accident was out of the question—even with a lack of casualties. Another scandal is the last thing this family needs. And besides, I obviously have other, more pressing issues to deal with at the moment.

I console my guilty conscience with the knowledge that I at least waited a few moments to ensure the poor girl wasn't injured before leaving the scene. But I can't seem to keep my mind on the accident because my thoughts jump right back to Julian and his blank face as he unceremoniously declared our years as a couple—as our own team—over. The idea of confronting him sends a shiver up my spine causing goosebumps to rise along my arms. Of course, it doesn't help that it's practically arctic temperatures inside the Mercedes.

After picking Riley up at the Manatee Lagoon, I had flipped the air-conditioner on full blast and, distracted, left it on—cold air gushing into the car—for the entire ride.

I cautiously lift my eyes to the rear-view mirror and check if Riley is freezing too, but she seems fine. Chatting away in the back seat, she has clearly recovered from our near collision with her camp counselor.

Riley catches my eye in the rear-view mirror. "*Mamá*, did you know there are three species of manatees? The West Indian ones are the species we have here. They also live in the Caribbean and off the coast of South America." Riley turns to stare out the side window. Listing her newly acquired facts as she watches the perfectly manicured lawns pass by the window on our way home.

It's not all that difficult to manifest the essential response of "Mm-hmm" as I redirect my attention back to the road, leaving North Ocean Boulevard and turning right onto our street. The palm trees lining the sidewalks rustle in the wind, reflecting a burnt orange from the sun dipping over the horizon. Riley continues. "Did you know the manatee's body is covered in whiskers? They help them feel for food. And get this. They have two parts to their upper lip. Each part works like a finger to grip their food." She flexes her pointer and middle finger like she's scooping up some imaginary food.

"Mmm, that's nice," I say. On most days, I block out Riley and all her random factoids while I drive. I am not particularly interested in marine trivia, but today her chatter provides the necessary distraction from the rant in my head. I do my best to focus and concentrate on what Riley is saying, but the subject proves to be just as uninteresting as always, and before I know it, I'm zoning out again.

Instead of increasing my manatee knowledge, I realize I've slipped into one of my favorite pastime activities: surveying all the houses I've coveted since moving to Palm Beach. Comparing each estate's size and amenities to the home Julian and I have lived in for the past five years.

With over thirty billionaires living on our little ten-point-four square mile island, it's a wonder we could afford our house in the first place. At only five thousand square feet and with a price tag of a measly six million, it could easily be mistaken for the pool houses of one of these more extensive *castillos*.

In Palm Beach, everywhere you look and every person you speak to does their best to remind you, You are a nobody. Because living in Palm Beach means living amongst the world's most successful and famous people. It took me years to fit in here. Each year Julian renewed his contract and added another couple million to his net worth, was another year that helped me secure my place in Palm Beach society. Finally, I could prove I was no longer an impostor, desperate to rub shoulders with the rich.

I was rich.

Well, *I* wasn't rich. Julian was. But, by association, that made me rich too.

Thinking of Julian is getting me all agitated again. I force my hands to relax as I pull the boxy black Mercedes into our driveway. Slowing to a stop at our gate, I roll down my window and type my key code into the free-standing security panel. With the final button pushed, I pull my hand back into the car and roll up the window. I'm about to press the gas pedal when I realize the familiar clink and sound of gates drifting open is missing.

I glance at the two slabs of European Oak still

locked tight in front of me.

"Hmm, that's odd," I say and return my attention to the keypad. I type my code again, this time ensuring I'm entering the numbers correctly. I finish and wait.

Not a single movement from the gates.

No sound of locks opening, no massive wooden doors swinging open, no grand entrance into *mi casa*— just silence.

"Hold on a second," I say to Riley, who is finally tuckered out from the day's activities and is now silent and staring aimlessly out the window.

I push on my driver's side door to check the security panel. But when I do, the door jams on something.

"What the…" I roll down the window and stick my head out. There, sitting atop the crabgrass between my door and the security panel, is my LV Keepall duffle bag. I tuck my head back inside the vehicle and push with more force, creating just enough space so I can crawl out the door. Once outside the car's air-conditioning, the humidity instantly bombards me. Eager to get back into the dry air of the SUV so my hair doesn't frizz, I bend down to inspect the duffle bag. A note is attached to the top with a piece of tape. I immediately recognize my name in Julian's handwriting and snatch the paper off, unfolding it quickly.

It's over.

Here are some things for you and Riley.

I'll send the rest to your mom's.

What the actual fuck?

I stare at the note for a minute and then flip it over, unsure of what I'm looking for but determined to find more. Something, anything that will prove this isn't real.

Crumpling the note in my hand, I turn and press the

call button on the security panel. It buzzes, but when there is no answer, I stride to the gates and peer between the slit in the wood. Julian's Porsche is parked in the drive. He's home.

"Julian!" I yell over the door and then press my eye back to the slit.

But there is no movement from the house. Not even the gardeners are outside performing their usual tasks of trimming the bougainvillea into perfect pink and white walls of color. So I rush back to the panel and push the call button in random succession. When there is still no answer, I press and hold it down for a whole minute.

Radio silence.

"*Maldita sea*, Julian!" I kick the pole holding the keypad with my espadrille and end up cursing again as the pain slices through my big toe.

"*Mamá?*" Riley calls from inside the car.

"I'm right here, *Mija*," I call back through clenched teeth. I hop on one foot so I can grab the duffle bag and throw it into the car atop the passenger seat. The pain is still radiating up my leg as I get back into the icy SUV and slam the door.

"What's going on, *Mamá?*"

My heart pounds in my ears, making it hard to think. Not willing to comprehend what is happening, I make the split-second decision to lie to Riley.

"Oh, I forgot," I say, trying to keep my voice relaxed, knowing any hint of panic will alert Riley to my deception. "We have painters coming for a few days. *Papá* is training down south again, and we can't go into the house with the painters working inside." I pause, impressed with myself for coming up with such a reasonable explanation in my current state. I raise my gaze to the rear-view mirror, looking at Riley, who nods with no hint of disbelief in sight.

I adjust my eyes to look out the rear window and start to back the Mercedes down the driveway. I'm deciding which way to turn, not sure what to do next when an epiphany comes to me. If Julian is going to make me leave this house, then he is going to have to pay for it. "How does an overnight at The Breaker's sound?" If I can't get into the Flagler Club on such late notice, the Imperial Suite should still be available. Those pricey accommodations are hardly ever sold out.

In my periphery, Riley yawns and stretches in her booster seat. "Okay, but I'm hungry."

"How about we pick up something at the Beach Club restaurant?" My plan is coming together better by the second. I can stop by the front desk and make a reservation while Riley eats at the tables overlooking the pools. Once she's done, we will simply be whisked up to our ocean-view suite, where we can lounge in bed. A movie will be the perfect distraction for Riley while I figure this whole mess out. I can already feel the freshly pressed linen sheets against my skin.

"I don't want to eat at the Breakers," Riley says, cutting into my daydream.

"Why not? It's the best food in Palm Beach. Is it not good enough for you?"

"No, it's not that. It's just I don't want to eat *there*. It's so pretentious."

I almost choke, hearing the word pretentious coming out of Riley's mouth. "Do you even know what pretentious means?" I ask, merging onto South Country Road.

"Sure, I do. It means you have to act all la-di-da."

Riley singsongs from the back seat. "Can't we go somewhere else?"

I roll my eyes at Riley's somewhat accurate definition of the ultimate luxury resort. "Fine, we can go somewhere else. What do you want to eat then?"

"A Key lime pie roll."

"Of course, you do," I say, thinking this will be the third time this week we have gone to the Flamingo café. "Fine, but just this once."

Chapter Ten

Counter-clockwise
Claudia

"Take this out, put in a Bordeaux wine color here, and bring in a deep moss green on that one over there." With my back to the computer and the zoom camera, I reach over to the pre-fall design board hanging on the wall and switch out multiple fabric swatches until I feel I have achieved the correct balance of mood and color.

"I love the linen caftan with the yellow and camel." A voice perks up from the computer behind me. "It's unexpected but yet stays true to the Claudia Caftan name."

I finish pinning a fabric sample to the board and turn to face my design team, who are gathered around a table, staring back at me from my computer screen. "Well, thank you, Lea. I'm particularly fond of that one as well."

"You're welcome. But that's just it." Lea takes a quick glance around the conference table she is sitting at, seeming to look for confirmation from the others before continuing. I see a few heads nod in her direction before she continues. "I think we need to do more of the unexpected. We need to start infusing some new life into the line." Lea pulls a piece of paper from her work portfolio on the table in front of her. "Our most recent statistics show people are looking for statement pieces.

They want that wow factor."

Slipping my reading spectacles on, I peer at the screen, trying to see the paper Lea is showing me. But I don't bother looking too hard. This isn't the first time I've heard this argument from Lea and the design team.

I suppress a sigh before addressing the team. "I understand what you are saying, I've heard you say it before, but I have already told you I have to stay true to what I do. I have and always will do the caftan. It is my signature. It is what I'm known for."

"Right, and we can continue to make the caftan, but if we don't start to infuse the pieces with something new, they will sit on the rack. If we want to create garments that sell, we need to consider some changes, is all I'm saying." Lea grabs her paper and shoves it back into her portfolio, crumpling the edges. "I'm just asking you to take it under advisement, do with it what you will, but I'd like to actually sell clothes this next season."

Even though Lea and I have gone around and around about this very topic, this is the first time she has taken to insulting me. Directly or not, I feel the sting of her words.

"So, let me get this straight, you think I'm designing pieces so I can just look at them hanging in the showroom?"

I watch as Lea shifts in her seat. When she addresses me again, it is with a much softer tone. "Sometimes I think you forget the pieces must be commercially viable. We need to sell to what the market is now, and it's much younger than it used to be." She pauses and looks around the table at the rest of the design team, seeming to ask a non-verbal question of everyone there. Once she has gotten the confirmation she is looking for, she readdresses the camera, looking at me head-on. "Maybe if you came to the New York office, we could sit down and go over the whole line. We could review the fabrics, see if we can infuse new life into the line, and get on the same page."

I continue to stare at the computer as a cold sweat starts to develop across my forehead. She is right. I haven't been in the presence of my team in a long time. And I have missed being surrounded by people with infectious excitement and passion for their work. People who love fashion and innovation as much as I do. And I know I should do what Lea is asking of me. I should get on a plane and head to the office. I should be present for the second proto review, interacting with my team in order to bring new inspiration to my work.

But I can't.

The thought of leaving the house, let alone the entire state has me trembling. I place my hands on the desk in front of me. "That isn't going to work this time. We have already agreed to send the proto garments down here, and we will reconvene with another zoom meeting to go through the pieces."

"I know we already decided that, but we could have the packages redirected. It would be so much easier if you came here—"

"Well, that's not going to happen," I say, abruptly cutting her off before she can make her case. "All I want to do is make beautiful, wearable, luxurious clothes. Why does it have to be so difficult? Please send the pieces here, and we will review them together when they arrive."

I watch as each team member shoots a glance around the table. I'm not usually so aggressive when speaking with them. So, my insistence must come as a surprise. Lea nods decisively, finally getting the message that I won't be joining them anytime soon. "Fine, we will continue to do this the way we have. But keep in mind, we haven't had a mention in *Vogue*, *InStyle,* or any of the other top fashion magazines in over two seasons. It's imperative we get something fresh out there. The industry is changing, and we need to be able to change with it."

I know Lea isn't going to let up on this, so I decide to change tactics. "You know my anniversary is tomorrow."

There is a smattering of "Congratulations" around the table, and I wait for them to die down before continuing.

"Yes, thank you. Well, what I'm trying to get at is Benedict gifted me with the most exquisite emerald necklace this year, and it did give me some inspiration."

I see the team perk up around the table, anxious to hear my suggestions, and I remember why I love doing this so much. The meticulous organization of creating and designing never fails to clear the constant fog of tiredness surrounding me. These meetings are what invigorate and energize me. I could never give them up as Parker has suggested I do.

"The green of the emeralds against my tan skin made me think, what if we did a chocolate silk with a gold leaf embroidery and emerald accents?" As the team takes notes, I continue to explain the concept of the garment inspired by Benedict's necklace. I don't bother to mention the necklace, meant for display at Palm Beach's most extravagant galas and balls, is currently tucked away, secure in our home safe where it will most likely stay. The chances of my wearing it to an event are nonexistent. It would mean I would have to leave the house.

Chapter Eleven

Millibar
Bri

"I can't believe you left without saying goodbye." Nick's voice crackles a bit on the speakerphone inside the Jeep.

"I told you I had to get to Orlando. Besides, from the look of things, you were a little preoccupied. I didn't want to interrupt your conversation with Zoe."

I am one hour into my drive to Orlando, and even though Nick sounds a bit peeved about me leaving without saying goodbye, his call is a welcome distraction from the monotony of the three hours of Highway 95 driving.

"My what?"

"You were talking with Zoe. I didn't want to get in the way of whatever you guys were discussing," I say.

Nick chuckles into the phone, causing more crackles to sound throughout the Jeep's interior. "And here I thought you weren't the jealous type. I guess I was wrong."

"I'm not the jealous type," I say, shifting in the car seat to relieve the pressure building up my backside for the last half hour. "I could care less about Zoe's fluttery eyelashes or the proximity of your face to them. That's not why I left."

Nick laughs again. "Right! Sure. Whatever you say.

But just for the record, I have no interest in flirting with Zoe. I was simply asking her to copy the keys for me so I could have a few minutes outside with you."

"You shouldn't have done that, Nick. Cassy asked you to take care of the keys."

"And I asked Zoe, what's the big deal? Either way, they get copied. Besides, the keys are for Zoe. This way, I'm just cutting out the middleman. Not that it matters. The person I wanted to spend that extra time with was gone when I turned around."

"Even if I had stuck around, you wouldn't be walking me to my car. You know we can't risk being seen together at the café."

"This again? Bri, listen to me. You're going to have to tell Cassy sooner or later," Nick says.

"I can't," I whisper.

"Can't or won't?" Nick's tone changes from playful to serious. "Because Bri, if we want to have any kind of future together, we are going to have to tell Cassy about us. I've told you how I feel. And I know you're not ready to say it back, but these feelings, these feelings have been growing for years. They're not going to just go away."

Chewing my lower lip, I change lanes to pass a slow driver in the fast lane. I know exactly what Nick is trying to tell me. We've known each other since high school. We've been in each other's lives through so much. The scandal that rocked his family's world, the accident that tore it apart, and the work it took to build his life back after it all. I was there every step of the way—a solid presence in his life. And while the physical part of our relationship didn't start until recently, our shared history has bonded us beyond anything that could tear us apart. But for all the times I was solidly by his side, I was also by Cassy's side. Was I willing to put our ride-or-die friendship in jeopardy for Nick? To risk one relationship for the other? The choice is an impossible one to make.

"You're asking me to make a choice I just can't."

"I think not making a choice is you making a choice."

I'm about to answer Nick's cryptic comment with one of my own when a knocking comes through from the other side of the phone. "Hold on, Bri. The vodka shipment just got here. I need to tell them where to put it. Don't hang up. I'll be right back."

I answer him with a weak "okay."

He persists, saying, "promise me you won't hang up."

"Fine, I promise. I'll be here—anxiously awaiting your return."

"Okay, I'll be right back."

"Not like I'm going anywhere anyways," I mutter to myself as I hear him call out to the vendor and shuffle out of his office.

Changing lanes back to the middle of the highway, I drum my fingers on the steering wheel and try to figure out why I'm all of a sudden so annoyed with Nick. He's had to dash off during our conversations a dozen times over. There is always something to unload, a shipment that needs to be put away, or a staff issue to handle. I know it's the baggage Nick comes with, and it's never bothered me in the past.

I've always understood THE NEST as Nick's savior. The responsibility that kept him focused after the accident. The sole reason he didn't turn to drugs and alcohol to soothe his depression. Even though the club scene surrounded him, he never wavered from his responsibility as the club owner and host. And he knew, better than anyone, that he needed to remain sober to do the job well.

It always amazed me how he took what could have been a disaster and turned it into a successful future. But that's just the thing. Nick's nights at the club were no big deal when we were just messing around and hooking up on the side. The excitement of having to steal moments because I was working during the day and he was busy at night made our rendezvous hot and steamy. But now he's gone ahead and changed everything by falling in love with me.

What does that even mean? He wants us to have a future, but what kind of future is available to us if I work during the day and he has to be at the club every night? How can we be together when we keep such different hours? A full-fledged relationship takes more time and effort than the occasional hook-up. And what if we do manage to make it work for a little while? What happens after? What about a family? I don't think I can bring a child into this relationship if Nick isn't even present for fifty percent of it. A shiver runs up my spine at the thought of children and my late menstrual cycle.

"I'm back. You still there?" Nick's voice cuts into my thoughts, reminding me I'm still on the phone with him.

"Yeah, I'm here."

"So…"

"So?" I say back.

"Come on, Bri, don't you have anything to say?"

"What I have to say you don't want to hear. You want me to agree to tell Cassy. But I can't just blurt it out like that. There's a lot for us to think about."

"Like what? Bri, you're overthinking this. Besides, whether we stay together or not, we should tell Cassy. Imagine if she found out about us without it coming directly from you?"

"There is no way that could happen. No one else knows about us."

"No one knows but imagine if she did find out. She would be more upset than if you just told her and got it over with."

So many thoughts are swilling around my head I'm starting to feel dizzy. And that is not a feeling I want to have while hurling a one-ton vehicle down a cement path, surrounded by other one-ton vehicles. "Look, Nick. I need to concentrate on my driving. Can we talk about this later?"

"Bri, you are literally running away from me right now. You realize that, right?"

"I'm not running away; I'm simply driving to a meeting. One that I need to kick ass on so the manatee babies," there is that twinge again, "can get the money they need." I clear my throat so I can speak clearly. "Which means I need to go and concentrate."

"Fine, but we will talk about this more later."

"Fine, goodbye."

"Goodbye. And, Babe?"

I can't help but soften at his term of endearment. "Yeah?"

"I still love you. Drive safe." And with that, he disconnects, not waiting for me to say it back.

It's not until I'm another good twenty miles down the road that I realize I forgot to tell him about almost being run over today.

Chapter Twelve

Vertical Stacking
Abigail

After pressing a few buttons to navigate the automated answering prompts, a nasal-sounding male receptionist connects to the line.

"Hello, and thank you for calling the Breakers. How may I help you?"

"Yes, this is Ms. Hernandez. I need to book a room for tonight." Situated above the courtyard, on the open-air balcony of the Flamingo café, I glance across the table at Riley, coloring in a manatee information packet she brought back from camp.

"Yes, of course, Ms. Hernandez. Will you require your usual suite for your stay with us?"

I can't help but feel validated at the instant recognition. Yet another perk of being Julian's fiancée that I'm not willing to give up just yet. I settle back into the plush pink velvet chair and contemplate taking the suite for the night, but at the last minute, I change my mind. Julian's words about the money going to my head making me switch directions.

"No. Not tonight. My daughter and I are having a girls' night out. A double room will suffice. But one with a view, of course." I glance out of the corner of my eye to see Riley looking at me expectantly.

"Of course, Ms. Hernandez. We have a beautiful

Atlantic Oceanfront double room that should please you and your daughter."

"Wonderful, we'll take it."

"Lovely, let me just enter your information into our system, and you will be all set. I'll need a credit card to secure the room."

"Julian Mendez is my fiancé. You can put the room on the card you have on file." I say, doing my best to project the confidence I always hear Julian speak with when making these reservations.

"Of course, let me just look up that account on the computer." There is a moment of silence before he's back on the line. "I'm sorry, ma'am, it appears all credit cards on this account have been suspended. I'd happily assist you with a new card over the phone."

Of course, they have. I can feel the heat rising in my cheeks. I can't believe Julian already froze the credit cards at the Breakers. Was I that predictable? Julian was undoubtedly making his point. My money might have been his money, but his money was most certainly no longer mine.

I grab my purse from the chair next to me and do my best to keep my voice calm, "Of course, let me just get that information for you."

Riley breaks into a massive yawn across from me as I rifle through my wallet for my Black Card. The one with my name on the front, but on autopay to Julian's bank account. I hold my finger to my mouth to *shhh* Riley as I mentally cross my fingers and read off the numbers for the reservationist on the other end of the phone.

A furious clicking of computer keys ensues as he types the numbers into the computer. When he comes back on the line, the change in his voice is palpable. A new faux-patience drips from his words. "I'm sorry, ma'am, but that card doesn't seem to be going through, might there be another card you'd like to use?"

"Oh, you know what? I totally forgot. We had to cancel that card. Being the victim of fraudulent charges is so inconvenient."

"Yes, I can imagine it is."

I sneak a glance at Riley, relieved to see she is oblivious to what is going on just across the table from her. I flip through my wallet for a second time until my fingers close around my personal credit card, which is not black in color and already over the limit. I do my best to keep my voice steady and say, "Try this one." I read off the numbers and hold my breath.

Again, our conversation pauses as he inputs the numbers, and again his demeanor changes when he comes back on the line. An absolute authority that wasn't there just a few minutes prior carries his words to my ear. "Ma'am, that card is coming back with the message of insufficient funds. I'm afraid we can't hold the room for you unless we have a credit card to do so."

Grinding my teeth together, I hang up on the receptionist. The sound emanating from my jaw causes Riley to look up from her drawing. I paste a smile on my face before she can notice my scowl. "All set. We just have to wait while they prepare the room for us."

"Okay, but can I have my Key lime pie roll now? I'm hungry."

I think of the last forty dollars in my wallet and try to swallow past the knot forming in my throat. With determination, I keep my smile firmly in place and reply, "Of course, *Mijà,* let's go."

As I rise from the table, Riley slips her hand into mine. I look down at our hands, her little one entwined with mine. Terror grips my heart as our situation starts to sink in. As of twenty minutes ago, I have no house to go home to. I have no access to money. I have a total of forty dollars in my purse, and I have a seven-year-old I somehow need to feed and shelter.

If ever there was a time I needed my *Mamá*, this was it. She'll know what to do. I won't even have to say more than her name, and she'll hear it in my voice. She'll tell us to come over right away. She'll feed us her famous empanadas. She'll tuck Riley and me into our guest room beds. She'll make all of this better. Sure, I'll have to eat my words and admit to her she was right all along, but if it means Riley and I have a place to lay our heads, I'm willing to do it. Besides, just because I say it doesn't mean I have to believe it.

As we walk to the top of the spiral staircase that connects the balcony to the lower café, I pull my phone from my pocket. Two quick swipes of my finger across the screen, and I'm listening to the ringing through the other end.

"Pick up, pick up," I mutter under my breath as I wait for *Mamá* to answer.

"*Hola, Mi Amore.*"

Relief floods through my body as I hear her pick up. "*Mamá—*"

"Thanks for calling, but we aren't home at the moment…" Voice mail. Of course, that just seems to be my luck right now.

"*Mierda*, what do I do now?" I say out loud as I end the call and step off the bottom of the staircase.

"*Mamá*! Language." Riley turns to look at me and

105

tilts her head toward the women sitting at a nearby table. All of whom are staring at me with a look of disapproval.

Ignoring the women, I slip my phone back into my purse. Unless one of them has a place for Riley and me to stay tonight, I could care less about what they think of my language.

Riley hits the main floor and immediately notices the dalmatian curled in his dog bed in the corner of the café. Releasing my hand, she races over to pet the spotted dog. As she goes, I'm left standing, reaching out for something that isn't coming back to me. A lady at another table catches my eye and gives me a knowing look. Like we are fellow conspirators against children growing up. I drop my hand to my side and follow Riley to where she is petting and cooing over the mangy animal.

By the time I make it to Riley, she is already standing back up and pointing to her favorite Key lime pie roll in the display case next to us, "This one, *Mamá*."

I turn to the girl behind the counter with the long blonde braid—Zoe, her name tag declares—and say, "That one." I point to the desert Riley wants.

"Sure thing," Zoe says, grabbing a plate and dishing up the Key lime pie roll. She sets the plate on the counter. "And for you?"

My stomach rumbles as I survey the display case full of lemon poppy seed muffins, Apricot Coffeecake, sugar cookies in the shape of flamingos, and a plethora of other baked goods.

"Nothing for me, thank you."

"Are you sure? The kitchen is closing, and doors close in half an hour."

"Yes, I'm sure," I say with too much force.

I hand over one of my last twenty-dollar bills from

my purse, pushing down the panic rising in my throat as Zoe retrieves the change from the register.

"Thank you," I respond with a tight smile while calculating in my head how long I can make thirty-odd dollars last. I have no idea. I haven't had to live on a budget for years now. Surely, I can remember. Lord knows, Julian and I did it before. It can't be that hard to do it again.

As I stuff the dollars back into my wallet, the coins slip out of my grasp and land with a rattle on the countertop. As I reach down to retrieve the change, the glint of something shiny catches my eye. Three keys are lined up next to the espresso machine, bright and shiny like they were cut today.

I stare at the keys feeling my body freeze up. Each key is labeled for an entrance; Side Door, Front Door, Back Door.

Automatically I take in my surroundings. Zoe has moved on to serve the next customer. The women sitting at the nearby tables have returned to their conversations and are no longer gawking at me. No one is paying me any attention. I look down at the counter once again. The keys stare back at me.

These keys might lack the same allure as, say, the key to the Breaker's hotel suite, but they are calling my name all the same.

Warning bells sound in my head, but I am decisive in ignoring them, pushing them down along with my conscience.

As casually as I can, considering my hands are shaking, I reach down and swipe my change off the counter, leaving the pennies behind in exchange for the key labeled Side Door.

I close my fist around the metal, grasp it tightly, and back away from the counter, retracing my steps up the staircase. In a daze, I pause when I reach the top and watch as Riley digs into her pastry.

She takes a big bite and looks up at me, still standing by the stairs. "Wanna bite?" she asks, with her mouth full.

Nodding my head, I leave my position at the top of the stairs and come to sit down at our table. I swiftly dump the contents of my hand into my purse before taking the fork from Riley and scooping up a hunk of Key lime pie roll, the bells still sounding in my ears.

Chapter Thirteen

A Drop in Pressure
Cassy

"Okay, it's official. I'm exhausted." I flip the *Open* sign on the door to the *Sorry, we are closed* side and walk back to Zoe, who is emptying the display case of the day's remaining pastries. I take a quick pause to pat Bo on the head before slipping back behind the counter.

"Oh, for sure! I'm so ready to go home and crash."

"No kidding," I agree. "But seriously, I couldn't have done this without you. Thanks for hanging in there today."

"No probs, boss lady," Zoe says, making me laugh. "You know I'd do anything for you, including serving about a million lattes in one day." She blows a kiss at me as I pull out the cash register log.

I grimace and then give her a megawatt smile at the reference to the breakneck pace we've held up since opening the doors. "Which is why I love you."

"And I, you, but you might want to hold that thought."

"Oh, no." I tense up. "Why?"

"Well…" Zoe breathes, "My parents are bugging out about this whole storm thing." She pauses to look me in the eye. "We're leaving tomorrow. The whole family is going up north to stay with my uncle for a few days. No way out of it for me, I'm afraid."

"So, I guess that means you're leaving in the morning?" I ask, hopeful she'll correct me and say she's not leaving until after working the morning shift.

"Afraid so."

I feel my shoulders sag. I'm so tired from today, but without Zoe to help prep tomorrow morning, I have no choice but to stay and prep tonight.

Zoe seems to sense my distress. "I'll be back after the storm." She offers.

I give Zoe a halfhearted smile. It's not her fault she has to leave. "Don't worry about it. You go home. Get packed up and stay safe. I'll see you when you're back."

"If you say so." She takes off her apron and pauses like she's remembered something. "What about you? Are you going to stay?"

"I always do."

Zoe gives me a quizzical look, but before she can say anything, I continue, "Now go on, get outta here. Call me when you're back."

"You got it, boss lady." Zoe makes smoking guns with her fingers, shooting them at me while making "pow pow" sounds as she disappears into the staff room.

I give her a smile that doesn't quite reach my eyes, only to have it disappear just soon as she is gone. I can feel the tension in my shoulders as I grab a rag from the bleach bucket and head up the spiral staircase to make one last swipe of the balcony.

Maybe it's because I'm completely caught up in my thoughts of making a "to-do" list. Or perhaps it's because I'm not expecting to see a person sitting at the table, or it could be the latent trauma from this morning's break-in. But, as I round the stairs and step onto the veranda, I can't help but let out a yelp of surprise when I see a lone silhouette sitting at the deserted tables.

The shadow of the woman whips her head around, her silky auburn hair flying behind her, and I find myself staring into dark brown eyes.

I don't get the opportunity to register anything else before I hear barking and a clatter below. Zoe and Bo are at the top of the stairs and by my side before I even realize what is happening.

"Are you okay? I heard you yell." Zoe, breathless from her dash, asks me while grabbing Bo's collar before he can advance past the two of us.

My cheeks heat at the commotion I've caused. I gesture to the dark-haired woman in front of me, who I now recognize as Abigail Hernandez, the subject of Bri's and my gossip session just a few hours earlier.

"I'm fine. Sorry. I was just startled." I say in the way of explanation.

"Well, I'm not fine. You nearly scared me to death." Abigail points her finger at Bo, who is still barking and recoils in her seat. "Control that thing."

I bend down to shush Bo and take him from Zoe. As I stand back up, I open my mouth to apologize, but Zoe cuts me off before I can respond.

"We announced closing half an hour ago," she says, planting her feet and folding her arms across her chest.

"That might be the case, but it still doesn't excuse startling your customers and *enviando al perro de ataque*." She huffs. "Oh, never mind. It doesn't matter. We were leaving anyway." She starts to gather her belongings, shifting in her seat.

When she turns to the side, I notice she's not alone. Her daughter, Riley, is lying next to her. She is stretched out along two chairs, asleep with her head propped in her mom's lap.

I bend down to pick up the rag I dropped earlier. "I'm sorry to have startled you. Honestly, I didn't mean to."

"Yes, well. Either way, we're leaving." Placing her designer purse on her shoulder, Abigail attempts to pull Riley up against her tiny frame. After struggling a moment, Abigail rises and carries her daughter past Zoe and me to the top of the stairs.

"Let me help you." I start to move forward to assist her on the stairs, but she turns and stares me down, her dark eyes boring into my green ones.

"We can manage on our own."

I don't move again until the two of them have disappeared down the stairs. Zoe and I continue to wait until the bell above the door chimes, and we know she's left before following down the spiral staircase and locking the door behind them.

"Well, she was a bit rude," Zoe says.

"Maybe." I pause. "But I did scare her. And I think she may have a few things on her mind."

Zoe smirks at me. "You mean like that football baller of hers? Yeah. I'm sure she's got more than just a few things she's dealing with."

I'm a bit taken aback by Zoe's comment. "You know about that?"

"Everyone knows about it. It's all over Hollywood Entertainment." Zoe says, referring to the television channel she watches in the back.

I nod in understanding as we walk back into the kitchen together. Zoe grabs her backpack and throws it over her shoulders. "Are you going to be okay, getting home?" I ask, glancing out the window. The sky had gone dark a while ago, the burnt orange sunset morphing into a starless sky.

"Yeah. Of course." Zoe inspects me with laser eyes, seeming to debate something in her head before asking, "Are you going to be okay? I mean, here, alone?"

"Oh, sure. Don't be silly. I have Bo with me, and Nick is coming to pick me up in a little while." I know Zoe is referring to my safety after the break-in this morning. And, honestly, I do have reservations about being in the café alone. But, as the owner of the café and her boss, my insecurities can't be Zoe's responsibility. So, I add, "Besides, Officer Jackson said it was a random break-in. He doesn't think they'll be back." I pause, mustering up the courage to finish my proclamation with the confidence Zoe needs to hear from me. "I'll be fine."

"Well, if you're sure. I'll see you in a few days then." Zoe blows me one last kiss as she leaves through the back kitchen door, pulling her helmet over her head as she goes.

I stand in the doorway as she mounts her Vespa scooter and points it in the direction of the bridge. I continue watching her until she is a block away before heading back into the café and locking the door behind me.

Despite what I had told Zoe, the silence in the café unnerves me. My skin prickles in unease.

"We're okay. Right, buddy?" I ask Bo as I flip the TV on and turn up the sound to a low hum. Bo cocks his head to the side but then retreats to his bed, where he does two circles and flops down with a huff.

"Right. You're obviously not worried, so I shouldn't be either."

Bo lifts his head and tilts it to the side.

"What's that?" I ask, "you think I should start working so we can get out of here and go home?"

Bo tilts his head in the other direction.

"Good idea." I walk over to the mixing stand, checking the clock on the kitchen wall as I adjust the settings. I still have half an hour before Nick gets here, which gives me just enough time to prep and bake the Key lime pie cookies before finally going home and ending this day.

Chapter Fourteen

Strengthen the system
Claudia

"Well, now, that was not how I hoped my meeting would go."

Pamela, who is wiping down the kitchen counters after our delicious dinner of *Midopilafo,* startles at my sudden entrance. She recovers quickly as I continue into the room, returning to her task of cleaning while seamlessly picking up her side of the conversation. "No?"

"No," I repeat. "The team wants me at the New York office."

Pamela stills her arm, holding the cloth against the marble countertop, and looks up to meet my gaze. "Oh."

"Right, Oh." Even though we've never spoken about it directly, Pamela understands my aversion to leaving the house. Probably even more so than Benedict does. "Honestly, I don't know why there is a sudden urgency. I've been overseeing the line from my office for some time now, and there's never been a problem. But now. Now, they want to change everything. They want new and fresh pieces." I explain as I walk to the counter, lowering my weary frame onto the bar stool. Pamela understands my wordless cue and abandons her cleaning to gather a late afternoon snack of *Kourabiethes* and *Amygdalota,* which she plates and sets on the counter before me. "What my team doesn't seem to understand, even though I keep telling them, is that I don't particularly want to change the designs. New and fresh. What does that even mean? I'm not interested in producing garments that will be discarded once the latest trend is abandoned. My desire has been and always will be to produce items that can withstand the test of time. Claudia's Caftans are classics a woman can return to time and time again and know she will look her best because it is quality clothing. Not some frumpy thing that fits the latest fashion and goes out of style in a matter of months."

"You be making the best clothes." Pamela smiles at me, encouraging. "But maybe you can find a way to do both? Classic with a style."

I blow a breath out of my nose in the form of a laugh. "I thought that was what I was doing. But apparently, that is not the case." I pause and drag my hand through my silver hair, from my forehead all the way down past my shoulders. "You know who would know what I should do?" I ask rhetorically, answering Pamela before she can respond. "Betty. It was Betty who planted the seed in my head to become a designer in the first place. All those years ago, when I was endlessly tired during the day but never able to sleep through the night. I would keep myself entertained while the rest of the house was silent by experimenting with the fabric samples my parents' business stored in their office. I loved all the colors and textures. Weaving the swatches together to create garments for Betty and me became one of my favorite pastimes. And Betty was my biggest fan. She wore everything I made her and then would turn around and demand that I make her more." I laugh at the thought of Betty's persistence. "She anointed me a style genius when I was seventeen and claimed fashion was my calling."

Pamela smiles at me. "She was not wrong."

I can't help but smile back. "I suppose so. She knew how happy I was when I was designing. And she had this way of getting people to believe in themselves the way she believed in them."

"So, if you be asking Betty. What would you ask?" Pamela questions.

I feel my face go slack at the thought of speaking to Betty one last time. Of everything I want to talk to her about and apologize for, my problems with Claudia's Caftans wouldn't make the list. "I'm not sure," I say, lost in thought.

Pamela waits for me to continue, but I'm unsure what to say next. The silence stretches between us until I reach for one of the almond cookies and take a bite. "Mm, these are delightful, Pamela. Just what I needed right now. Thank you."

Pamela smiles wide at the compliment and says, "You welcome. I made enough for your dinner tomorrow night. I know they be Parker's favorite."

I smile at Pamela's change of subject and the reminder of our anniversary dinner tomorrow night. "Yes, I'm sure Parker will love them." My gaze drifts to over Pamela's shoulder to where a collection of black and white photographs reside on the back wall of the kitchen, creating a collage of memories. I seek out my favorite and take a moment to savor the emotion it evokes. Parker, Nicholas, Cassandra, Betty, and I dressed in aprons, our hands coated in baking flour, smiling directly into the camera. Benedict's calling out,

"*Yasou*" as he stands opposite the five of us and takes the picture.

"Those were the days," I say, caught up in the memories of Betty and me baking with the children.

Pamela turns her head in the direction of the photographs. "Betty. She sounds very special. Yes?"

Pamela's choice of words to describe Betty sends a bolt of electricity down my spine. "Special doesn't even touch the surface of Betty."

Pamela turns back with a quizzical look, and I realize I've never fully explained to Pamela who Betty was to me. "Betty showed up during a very dark time in my life." I pause to put my thoughts in order before starting at the beginning. "You see, I was a teenager when my narcolepsy started. Of course, we didn't know what it was back then, let alone that it had a name." I look down at the countertop as the memories overtake me, and I can feel more than see Pamela leaning into the story I'm about to tell her. "It started as more of an annoyance than anything. A tiredness that I couldn't shake. I would be in the middle of a conversation with one of my friends or teachers, listening to the radio, or just sitting at the table having a nice dinner with my family, when out of the blue, a wave of sleepiness would overwhelm my entire body. I would have to find a place to lie down right away. I would fall asleep within minutes and not be able to wake up for at least half an hour, sometimes much longer.

"At first, my parents thought it was my way of seeking attention. When we first immigrated here, they had to work long hours at the textile shop. It wasn't that they didn't love me. It was just that they had to work hard to make money to put food on the table and a roof over our heads."

I look back to Pamela, who looks at me as though she knows all too well how hard a person must work to make ends meet when first coming to this country. She nods in understanding, and I continue.

"But it quickly became obvious to all of us. I had no control over my sleep episodes. They became increasingly frequent, and no matter how much I slept, I was still always tired. My mother had no idea what was happening to me, so her solution was never to let me out of her sight. Can you imagine that?"

Pamela giggles politely and says, "You not be liking that."

"You are correct there. I did not like that. *Mitera's* constant nagging, and incessant attention, became almost unbearable. To the point I couldn't handle it anymore. So, I did what any teenager would do. I started rebelling."

"Oh no," Pamela says, standing back as though placing a physical distance between us will make me morph back into an obedient teenager. "What did you do?"

I blow out a single laugh. "Well, because I was falling asleep almost all the time, there wasn't much I could do besides become a brat. I refused to do my chores; I spoke back to my parents. As my mother put it, I was simply miserable to be around."

"So, what happened?"

"Well, I continued to be a brat as my episodes became more frequent. Finally, it got to the point where I had to be taken out of school because I simply couldn't stay awake for a full day. My parents were at a loss and still working long hours at the textile business, so they devised the idea for me to stay home with a tutor. But, of course, when they said tutor, I heard babysitter."

I turn in my chair to face Pamela. "I was seventeen years of age. None of my peers had a babysitter. For goodness' sake, most of my friends *were* babysitters. You can't begin to understand the embarrassment I felt."

Pamela's eyes grow wide. "Oh no, you already be rebelling. Did it turn out bad? "

"It very well could have, but luckily for me, the tutor my parents hired was Betty." I pause and glance back at the picture. Betty's smiling face stares back at me. "She was only a few years older than me and so full of vitality it took my breath away. She was the one who taught me I could still live a life full of love and laughter, despite my condition. It didn't take long before Betty and I became inseparable. She would tutor me in the daytime, but we would take off as soon as my studies were complete. We never went far. Mostly stuck to walks on the beach, drives down to the local hang out, or just sitting around chatting and gossiping like teenagers." Again, I pause as visions of Betty and me in our youth dance through my head. "She became my best friend. Like a sister to me."

"So, Betty, not actually be related to you?" Pamela asks, cutting into my thoughts. "But don't Cassandra and Nicholas call you Auntie Claudia?" Pamela asks, and I can see she is still trying to put all the pieces together in her head.

"They do call me Auntie Claudia; you are correct there. But not because I am their aunt. They call me that as a term of endearment. You see, Betty and I became so close we felt like we were sisters. We grew up together. We were maids of honor at each other's weddings.

Betty's children became my children, and my children became hers. Cassandra and Nicholas became my grandchildren, and Parker became hers. Our children grew up together just as our grandchildren did. Generations of friendships and relationships have been nurtured in this very house." I hold up a hand to stop myself. "But I'm getting ahead of myself again."

Pamela leans over and takes my plate, placing it in the dishwasher and allowing me a moment to collect my thoughts before returning to the island and waiting for me to continue.

"Right. Well, as I was saying, Betty and I got on marvelously. Then—one day, as we were finishing my lessons and I was getting ready to lay down for a nap, *Mitera* came bustling through the door with the news of a referral to someone she described as the "sleep doctor." Apparently, she had been talking about me at the textile shop, and one of the clients had told her about this doctor, and while it was almost unheard of back then, this lady had sworn he was a miracle worker.

As it turns out, this doctor was studying what they called the characteristic features of excessive daytime sleepiness. And he was working with two other doctors at the Mayo Clinic, of all places. And get this, he just happened to have an office in Palm Beach!"

Pamela—caught up in the story, claps her hands in excitement.

"I know! It was the most hope I had felt in a very long time. So *Mitera* made an appointment. After a long consultation in his office where I had to answer dozens of questions, Dr. A suggested I sleep in what he called his 'sleep lab.' He had converted a room in his building to look like a standard bedroom. Only it wasn't just a bedroom. One side of the room was made up of one-way mirrored windows. He explained it was so I could be observed, undisturbed, while I stayed in the room for forty-eight hours. I must tell you," I say to Pamela. "I was beyond hesitant to stay in that room alone for so long. But Betty, always there to help, calmed my nerves. She talked me through my uncertainties and reminded me of the answers staying in the room would provide. And wouldn't you believe it, it worked!

The room was surprisingly comfortable, kept at an ambient temperature, and full of activities to keep me entertained. Finally, after I had slept and woken three times during the previous night but had to lie down two times during the subsequent day, the doctor announced he had a diagnosis for me.

I don't think I've ever been so happy in my entire life to finally hear there was something wrong with me. To hear I had something called narcolepsy, an actual disorder with a diagnosis and treatment, gave me a hope that had been absent from my life for the past several years."

"So, this be how you have your schedule?" Pamela asks, referring to my daily routine she is a part of controlling.

"Yes. It took months, but a schedule was created with Dr. A's guidance and my parents and Betty's help. I slept at the designated times, changed my diet, and started taking medications. The medications were a bit touchy at first." I shiver at the memory of the side effects. "Without knowing the correct dosage for my body, it took months to get it all figured out. But, when they did start working, I was a new person."

"Who was a new person?" Benedict's voice booms

through the kitchen, causing Pamela and me to swivel our heads in his direction.

"Well, I was, *glike mu*." I pause as Benedict walks over and places a gentle kiss on the top of my head. I smile up at him and say, "I was telling Pamela how Betty came to be a part of our family."

Benedict nods and slides his gaze over to Pamela, who stands up straighter under his appraisal. "Well, that must be a coincidence because I just got off the phone with the office." Benedict turns back to face me. "And I have some information for you regarding the Betty project you have me working on."

"Good information?" I ask, hopeful that Benedict's team has had a breakthrough on the legal case he has been chasing over the past ten years.

Benedict sneaks a glance in Pamela's direction before returning his attention to me and saying, "It's hard to tell at this point, but why don't we retire for the night? I can tell you more about it as we prepare for bed?"

Pamela graciously takes her cue and starts to resume wiping the counters. Over her shoulder, she says, "Good night, Mr. Castello. Good night, Mrs. Castello. See you in the morning."

I rise from the stool and take Benedict's proffered arm saying to Pamela, "Good night, Pamela. See you in the morning." But as soon as we leave the kitchen and are in the hallway, my grip tightens. "Tell me what you've found out."

Chapter Fifteen

Outflow
Abigail

Three little dots appear, blink in succession, and then disappear. "Seriously? Come on already," I mutter under my breath while staring at the phone. It was already dark outside when I left the Flamingo Café, and with the engine turned off, the interior of the SUV is pitch black except for the light illuminating my phone screen. The screen I have been staring at, exasperated, for the last thirty minutes while sitting in the parking lot of Currie Park.

The dots reappear, and a fresh wave of anticipation washes through my body. I try to fight the feeling into submission, but the knowledge that I have reached the end—of what I used to think of as an extensive list—of contacts takes over. My body involuntarily shivers as I lose the fight. I console myself with the idea that Suzy, the last person on my list, had been willing to help in her previous text, which was more than what I could say for the other WAGs.

The ghosting and denials leave no room for interpretation. Clearly, a concession already exists among the other WAGs and PBPs. I am off-limits. Not a single sister of this so-called sisterhood will take Riley and me into their home. But, of course, none of the ladies have come out and said it directly to my face. The rejection is more subtle than that. The denial of help is disguised in the form of "I'm sorry, but I'm already busy" or, my favorite, "If you had only asked earlier, I would've been able to do more for you."—like I could tell the future and I should have prepared for this. But seriously, how could I have possibly foreseen a future involving being homeless, penniless, out of options, and sitting in a parking lot in the middle of the night? Even if I did have a crystal ball, I'm certain it would never have shown me this scenario. It's absurd to think that, just a few hours ago, I was Abigail, soon-to-be Mendez—fiancée of Julian Mendez—sitting at home in my *castillo junto al agua* and in need of nothing.

The screen lights up with the incoming message, pulling me out of my self-depreciation. I read, desperate for Suzy's words and the chance to leave this god-forsaken parking lot.

—OMG—Sorry, Abbs but Travis and I have already left the house!—

Damn it. I blow out a breath laced with frustration and try to think. It's a Friday night, so the WAGs and their partners are most likely at dinner somewhere like Buccan or Imoto. I tap the phone against my chin and consider my next move. I can't come across as desperate or needy. One sure way to get a WAG to turn her back on you is to come across as desperate. Probably because deep down, we were all the same—afraid rejection will spread like a virus and we will be the next WAG to contract the disease.

No. I need to play it cool like I don't need her—even though I clearly do. I bring my phone away from my face and start typing a reply.

—Lucky you! Having dinner someplace epic, I hope!

Want to catch up after for a nightcap? I can totally come to you. I so need a drink after the day I've had.—

I congratulate myself for adding the tidbit about my horrible day. I'm sure it will spark Suzy's curiosity and make her think she can get all the dirty details from me with a cocktail or two. Admittedly, it is a cheap trick, but I'm reasonably confident it will work.

Immediately, the ellipsis appears, and I sigh with contentment at knowing exactly how to manipulate these women. My head flops back on the headrest as I await Suzy's drink invitation. As I'm resting there, my gaze drifts to the rearview mirror. In the light of the streetlamp coming in through the back window, Riley is illuminated in an orange glow. The top of her head and wild ringlets are the only part of her visible above the jacket covering her little curled-up body.

Shoot, how am I going to explain Riley to Suzy? It goes without saying, in this group, you don't bring your kid with you when you meet for drinks. I decide not to stress too much about it. I'm sure I can think of an excuse on my drive to Suzy's palatial mansion. I'm thinking about what that excuse might be when my phone lights up with another new message from Suzy.

—LOL-I didn't mean Travis and I were having dinner silly—I meant we have evacuated! You know, like, gotten the f*—out of town! We took the PJ to Aspen before the hurricane blows through. House is boarded up until we get back. Ohhh, I have an idea! You should totally come meet us! Why are you still in Palm Beach anyways?!!—

That is such a good question. *Why* was I still in Palm Beach? Oh, that's right, because I can't even pay for enough gas to drive out of the state, let alone fly to

Aspen. I am about to let my fingers fly with a text back to Suzy when my screen lights up with a second and third text bubble.

—*I'm sure you and Julian will get over this little bump in the road. You guys have been together forever. You belong together.*

Catch up when we get back?—

Okay, so obviously, Suzy isn't expecting me to show up at her doorstep in Aspen. Clearly, the invitation to join them was offered to appease me for now. And if I read between the lines as she did with my text, what she's really saying is. "Don't bother contacting me again until we can be seen in public as official WAGs."

I shoot off a quick text.

—*Yeah, when you get back.*—

And shut down my phone. I toss it onto the passenger seat, close my eyes, and try to forget about this God-awful day. But of course, I can't. The last line from Suzy's text plays on repeat like a ticker tape across my mind.

You belong together.

There was—once upon a time—when I believed the same exact thing. Before the lucrative endorsements and media appearances, before the sponsorship deals and the newspaper columns, Julian and I were a team all our own. It was Julian and me against the world. There was a reason I loved him.

I snuggle down into the seat's leather and pretend it is the warmth of Julian's body pressed against mine. We used to lie in bed for hours, stroking each other's bodies lovingly and talking about our dreams for the future. Him—being drafted and playing in the AFC. Me—attending design school and starting my own fashion line. We would envision ourselves accomplishing our goals and what that life would look like. God, we were so young and naïve. We didn't factor in what a child would do to our dreams. And while Julian went on to accomplish his, I was relinquished to becoming the caretaker and cheerleader.

In fact, it was only recently that we had drifted so far apart. Sleeping in different rooms and sticking to separate floors of the house was a new occurrence brought on by Julian's repetitive weekend binges with the guys. If I could just convince Julian to give up his Miami trips and all that went along with them, I'm sure we could rekindle that old flame. There had to be a way to get Julian back. I had to get him back. There was no other option.

Chapter Sixteen

Tropical Depression
Cassy

"We're almost done here, buddy," I say to Bo as he circles his memory foam dog bed and flops down with aplomb—like he knows he still has plenty of time left here in the café, and he's heard it all before. Once settled, Bo lifts his head in my direction and gives a snort of satisfaction before snuggling back down for his second evening siesta.

"Sure, fine. You take a nap. I'll keep doing all the work." I smile at Bo before surveying the cooling racks, taking in the rows of orange creamsicle pie tarts, coconut crinkle cookies, and apricot coffee cake bars. I mentally give myself credit for all I've accomplished in the last hour. I check my list and see the only pastries left to bake are the Key lime cookies.

"Right, well, let's get this done so we can get out of here," I mutter as I gather the butter and sugar and bring them to the mixing bowl. I add the ingredients to the eggs, vanilla, and pressed Key lime juice and beat it together with the paddle attachment.

I'm about to add flour and baking soda when the hair on my arm unexpectedly stands at attention. What was that? I turn my head to the side, waiting to see if the sound I think I heard comes again. Then, keeping my eyes locked on the swinging kitchen door, I inch closer to Bo.

As I approach, Bo lifts his head from the bed with sleepy eyes and looks at me. "Buddy, did you hear something?" I ask, knowing full well he didn't. Because if Bo had heard something, he would have shot out of his bed—teeth bared—and bolted to the kitchen door. As it is, he cocks his sweet head at me as if to say, "nope."

"You're right. I'm just jumpy from this morning. It was nothing." I pat Bo and move back to the island, determined to get through the next half hour so I can finally go home and put an end to this day. "You know what we need? A distraction," I say, reaching across the counter to flip on the television, setting the channel to WESH 2. Satisfied with the low hum of the nightly news to block out any imaginary sound I might conjure up, I turn and walk back to the mixing bowl. I'm about to take the bowl out of the stand when an all-to-familiar husky voice emanates from the television, causing me to drop my hands and stand at attention.

Abandoning the bowl, I retrace my steps back to the TV, lean over and turn the volume up on the remote. No matter how many times I see Parker Castello report on the weather, I still can't get over the shock of him being on actual television. Pride, awe and a sense of disbelief wash over me in the same way it does every time he appears on the screen. Even though watching Parker is a ritual the whole family participates in, it is still almost impossible for me to reconcile this Parker with the one of our childhoods. This Parker is poised, commanding, and possesses a charisma that demands attention—which is in strict contrast to the Parker I grew up with; goofy, rambunctious, and just the right amount of cocky.

Watching him on the screen, a world away, in his

new professional persona dressed in a navy-blue Canali suit—cut to emphasize his trim waist and broad shoulders—I try not to think about how long it's been since we last saw each other. Time and life have created an inevitable wedge between us. One that neither of us has dared to bridge. I can't help but wonder if this new Parker still has the spirit of the Parker of our not-so-distant youth. I shake my head at the idea of the boy with sand on his face and hair tousled from the waves and instead refocus my attention on this adult version of Parker. I lean my elbow on the counter, propping my chin in my hand, savoring every moment of his virtual presence.

He is talking about the tropical storm building off the eastern coast. Standing in front of the digital screen, he swirls his hand around, showing the storm's trajectory and how the arctic air is pushing the southern air, creating the funneling of the beginning of a hurricane. I'm enraptured as he explains how the low pressure and warm temperatures are a perfect recipe for a hurricane. Parker grows more serious and turns to face the cameras head-on, granting me and the thousand other viewers the opportunity to stare straight into those ocean-blue eyes—pools rimmed by swoon-worthy dark lashes. I'm locked on his face, all Greek god, muscular and chiseled, as he briefs us of the early signs of a hurricane.

I'm hanging on his every word when the camera suddenly cuts from Parker to the sports anchor sitting behind a desk, jolting me back to reality. I pull away from the island and stand up as Parker and the sportscaster engage in small talk. They chat about how the weather will most certainly cause a cancellation of the upcoming Miami Sting Ray's home game, allowing the female anchor, sitting at the podium between the two men, to segue into a story about the football team's quarterback, Julian Mendez. The camera cuts to her headshot as she begins the story of Julian being seen starting a fight at a local nightclub, causing him to get kicked out. Photos of him at the club with multiple women—all of whom were not his fiancée—have started to surface on social media. The anchor continues, speculating whether Julian will be benched for the next game due to his undesirable behaviors.

I sigh, uninterested in the lives of the overly privileged and underly mature and turn off the TV. Retracing my steps, I return to the mixing bowl and detach it from the mixer, carrying it back to the kitchen island.

I pull the container of graham crackers off the shelf in front of me and start pounding them into crumbs when my phone rings. I dust my left hand on my apron and grab at the phone, pressing the green "accept" button twice before it connects.

"I'm out back." Nick's voice bursts through the line.

"Okay. Coming." I hit the red button and head to the side door, passing Bo. He looks up at me with interest but does not leave the comfort of his bed. "You lazy bum, maybe I should trade you in for a real attack dog." I tease as I grab the door handle.

As the door swings open, I do a double take. Dressed head to toe in lime green golf attire, Nick resembles one of the Key limes I juiced only a few minutes ago. I laugh out loud.

"What?" Nick looks at me, clueless.

"I'm not so sure neon green is your color."

Nick glances down at his outfit and holds his shirt

out with his thumb and finger. "What's wrong with this? Rory McIlroy has the same one, and he wore it at the PGA National Resort last week."

"Maybe, but Rory doesn't have your red hair. You look like a leprechaun."

"So now you're picking on me because of my hair color? You realize you have the same fluff coming out of your head, right?" Nick bends down and pats Bo, who lets out a humph and snuggles deeper into his bed.

"Yes, I do," I say with amusement at Bo and Nick. "Which is why I don't wear neon green."

"That's right. You prefer hot-pink head to toe." Nick says, gesturing to my uniform.

I give him a look that I hope conveys my exasperation.

"Fine, you win. Hurry up so I can go change after I drop you off."

"Oh, don't change on my account. I'm sure you can impress at least one girl at THE NEST with that outfit." I say with a raised eyebrow.

Nick surveys the counter—settling on a handful of flour, he picks it up and throws it at me.

I laugh and dodge the plume of white dust dripping through the air. "You are so cleaning that up."

"For your information, I'm not trying to impress anyone, but I can't wear this now that you've made me feel like an oversized lucky fairy. So come on, let's go." Nick wipes his hands on a spare towel and heads toward the door to leave, ignoring my comment about cleaning up the flour.

"Hold on," I say as Nick pauses with his hand on the door. "I still have to finish these." I point to the batter in the industrial-sized mixing bowl and the graham cracker crumbs.

Nick glances at the amount of dough in the mixer and rolls his eyes before returning to the counter and leaning his hip into it. He stares at me with noticeable irritability as I reach below the island and take out multiple baking sheets. Ignoring him, I grab the ice cream scoop and get to work, taking my time pulling out a dollop of dough, rolling it in the cracker dust, and then placing the mound on the sheet, making sure to space the cookies evenly until all the sheets are full. Nick sighs audibly and drums his fingers on the counter.

"Cool your jets. I've got to wait ten minutes for these to cook, and then we can go, okay?" I say like I'm speaking to a toddler. "I have an idea; why don't you check the security cameras for me while you're waiting?"

Nick rolls his eyes again but obediently turns and exits the kitchen heading back into the café.

I place the baking sheet in the preheated oven and then busy myself tidying up the kitchen. I clean Nick's mess of a flour bomb before moving on to the bowls and pans. I'm just wiping down the counters when the timer goes off. Grabbing my oven mitt, I carefully take the cookies out of the oven and place them on the cooling rack before heading out of the kitchen and into the café to find Nick.

Bo dutifully rises from his bed, stretches, and yawns before following me through the swinging doors to where we find Nick standing on a chair, facing the wall, sticking his tongue out at the new security camera.

"Um, what are you doing?"

Nick stops making faces and clambers down from the chair.

"Here, give me your phone." He reaches out his

hand, making the universal "give me" gesture with his fingers.

I dig into my back pocket and hand over the phone, smacking it into his outstretched hand.

"Check this out."

I stand behind him, looking over his shoulder as Nick taps a few buttons on my phone. Seconds later, his face is illuminating my screen. The recorded image of Nick sticking his tongue out and crossing his eyes into the camera plays on my phone, making me laugh out loud.

"See, you can check the video anytime, and your phone will alert you of any movement." He flips through the settings, and I do my best to follow along. "Make sure you switch it on at the end of the day and switch it off when you open, so you don't receive like a gazillion messages. Easy." He flips the phone back to me, making me dive for it before it hits the floor.

"Sure, got it. Easy," I repeat after him while simultaneously making a mental note to review how to use the app when I have a free second. I put the phone back into my jeans and untie my apron. "Come on. Cookies are done. Let's go."

"Cool, lead the way."

Nick stands by the kitchen door and waits as I double-check the doors and windows, ensuring they are locked and secure. He follows me back to the kitchen, where I wrap the entire cooling rack in cellophane and confirm the ovens are turned off.

Nick, Bo, and I exit through the back kitchen. Again, I ensure the door is locked and secure before crossing the sidewalk and getting into Nick's Hummer EV.

He guns the engine, and we ride in silence as he pulls

onto A1A toward West Palm Beach. As we pass the uniform palm trees Nick gives a brief glance at Bo in the rear-view mirror before rolling down the window on the back-passenger side. Bo jubilantly perches himself on the doors edge and sticks his head out into the cool night air. In my side mirror Bo's ears flap and flail in the wind. A tickle of breeze circles through the Hummer's interior fanning my loose hair across my eye.

As we drive toward my apartment, my shoulders sag as the day's tension slowly starts to fritter away. I stare out the window as we pass over the bridge, watching the boats bobbing up and down in the dark water.

"Want me to pick you up before dinner with Auntie Claudia and Uncle B tomorrow?" Nick asks, breaking into my reverie.

"Hmm? Yeah, sure. That'd be great."

"It's their anniversary dinner, right?"

"Yeah, I can't believe they've been married fifty-five years."

"No kidding. That's a small feat, for sure. So, what did we get them?"

"You're serious? You didn't bother to get them anything?" It is so classic Nick. I'm not even surprised.

"What?" Nick asks, glancing at me out of the corner of his eye. "You're supposed to do all that shopping for the family stuff."

I shoot him a look. "Is that so?"

"Yup."

"I have an idea. Why don't you give them the balance on the loan they gave you?"

"Yeah, right. I wish. How about you do the same and we call it even?"

"That's not even close to being a possibility.

Especially now that I need to replace the inventory destroyed in the break-in." I pause and unbuckle my seat belt as Nick pulls up to the curb of my building. I grab Bo's leash and open the door as Nick rolls to a stop.

"Not to worry," I say as I hop out of the car and onto the sidewalk. "I'm way ahead of you. I did my research, and Auntie and Uncle are going to love their gift."

Chapter Seventeen

Rapid Intensification
Abigail

"Julian, pick up your damn phone," I hiss into Julian's voicemail.

I am officially pissed off. All those sweet nothings I told myself last night wore off the second I woke up and realized I was still in my car in the parking lot of Currie Park. Waking up with a crick in my neck and wearing the same clothes I wore yesterday had me seriously peeved.

Even when Julian and I were dirt poor and struggling to make ends meet, we were never reduced to sleeping in a car in a parking lot in the middle of West Palm Beach.

Still asleep and spread across the back of the Mercedes, Riley will be up any moment. So, naturally, this means I need to have some explanation at the ready for why she is in Currie Park and not tucked into her bed at home.

Of course, I have no clue what my explanation will be. Riley and I have never even gone camping, let alone slept in the back of a vehicle.

I jam my finger into my phone, hanging up on the voicemail and re-dialing Julian's phone number for the twenty-seventh time this morning. I am preparing to leave another seething voicemail when I'm caught off guard by Julian answering the phone.

"Woman, don't make me get a restraining order on you. You need to stop fucking calling me."

I clench my fist and fight my first instinct of laying into Julian with a litany of cuss words. I can't risk him hanging up on me now that I have him on the line.

If I have any chance of winning my way back into the house and Julian's good graces, I need to play this conversation strategically. Even though I've slept in a vacant parking lot overnight with our child, I'm willing to overlook this whole scenario if we can just get back into our home.

"Julian, wait. Can we talk this out?" I say, pushing away from the Mercedes while keeping my voice calm. Low and sultry, like how I used to talk to him when I wanted him to do my bidding.

"There is nothing to talk about." His clipped tone is like a slap in the face, and I bite my tongue from spewing foul language into the phone.

Okay, so sexy isn't going to work. Spontaneously I change my tact, deciding to appeal to his guilty conscience. "Julian, Riley and I slept in the Mercedes last night in a deserted parking lot."

Silence follows from the other end of the line. Crossing my fingers that I'm playing my cards right, I continue. "I know you're trying to make a point, and I hear it loud and clear. But I know you don't want your *mamacita* sleeping in the back of a car. Riley needs stability in her life, you know? You were supposed to be the person who provided that. Sleeping in the parking lot, not having a place to rest her head at night, that's not stability."

"I told you to go to your ma's place. Why didn't you

listen to me?" I don't miss the accusatory edge in Julian's voice.

"I tried calling, but there was no answer."

"That's never stopped you from going over there before."

More than anything, I hate it when Julian is right. I've never hesitated to barge in on my parents whenever it suited me. But last night, I stopped calling after getting *Mamá's* voicemail for the third time. My ego preventing me from showing up on their doorstep, proving *Mamá* right.

"It just wasn't an option." I don't bother explaining why it wasn't an option before continuing. "Come on, Julian. I'm bringing Riley back home. I'll be there in ten minutes. I expect the gate to be open for us when we arrive."

"Don't bother. You can't get in."

I stop walking in the circle I had been traversing in the parking lot, just a few feet from the Mercedes. "Julian. This is enough—"

"I'm not home." He cuts me off before I can lay into him.

"Where are you? Then call and have the staff open the gate for me."

"Not possible. I took the plane out last night. I had the staff board up the house for the hurricane. It's all locked up. There's no one left." He says it matter of factly, with no tinge of regret in his words.

The mention of hurricanes has me momentarily dumbfounded. In the drama of the past twelve hours, I had pushed all thoughts of a hurricane to the back of my mind. "What do you expect me to do, Julian?" I whisper, hating the hysteria creeping into my voice and hating even more that I cannot push it back down.

"You still have time. Go to your *Tía's* place.*"*

He is referring to *Mamá*'s sister, who lives in Georgia. The fact that Julian can still manage to think logically only serves to piss me off further.

"And how do you propose I get there? You've frozen all my credit cards. I can't afford last-minute plane tickets for Riley and me."

"Come on, woman, use your head. You don't have to fly everywhere." Julian says in exasperation. "You have the G-wagon. Get on the freeway and drive."

"You're seriously going to leave Riley and me to fend for ourselves."

"Look, you're going to have to get used to it. Now seems like a good time to start practicing. You'll be fine."

The anger I've been suppressing this whole conversation explodes out of me. "God damn it! Julian, who the hell do you think you are? You can't fucking leave your family in the middle of a hurricane with no place to go. Did you hit your head too many times out on the field? You can't be thinking logically. You are crazy!" I am screaming now, unable to control myself. "You're a no-good, cheating, lying ass. That's what you are."

I pause to catch my breath, giving Julian the opening he needs to respond. "I have to go now."

There is a click, and I'm left staring at a blank screen. I yell and throw the phone, which lands on the park's grassy lawn, mercifully not shattering to pieces.

I lean over and grab my knees, trying to catch the breath that has been knocked out of me. I don't understand who this person is. I can't even recognize Julian anymore. I'm trying to remember the exact moment he became so callous when I notice a rocking motion coming from the G-wagon. Immediately I stand up and wipe my eyes with the backs of my hands. A second later, the side door opens, and Riley steps out. Blurry-eyed, she squints at the sun and pushes her glasses up her nose. Hair tousled from sleep, she yawns and takes in the park and her surroundings, smiling when she finally notices me. *"Buenos días, Mamá."*

"Good morning *Mija*," I say and plaster a smile on my face. I walk over and hug Riley. "Did you sleep well?"

Riley nods and mumbles, "Mmhmm," into my stomach, where she has dug her head while hugging me back.

She pulls away from me. "What are we doing here, *Mamá?"* Riley asks, turning her head in the direction of the grass and water.

I'm relieved Riley isn't visibly distressed by waking up in a park. Just curious. Julian's words about driving to Georgia flash through my mind, helping me make a split-second decision.

"Surprise!" I throw my hands out at my sides, indicating the park. "We're camping."

Riley lifts one eyebrow at me, and I almost waver, but I keep my smile firmly in place until her own smile appears.

"Really? We're really camping?"

"Ah, huh, we are. Are you happy?"

Riley releases me and starts hopping up and down in place. "This is so cool. I love it." She stops bouncing to push her glasses back up her nose. "Can we sleep in a tent? Can I use a sleeping bag? Can we cook breakfast over a gas stove?" Riley is looking around us but stops when all she sees is the Mercedes.

"Where are all the camping supplies?"

"Well, this camping is a little different. We're going to sleep in the car while we camp. Then, we can go on a little road trip. It's safer that way."

Riley considers what I'm saying and nods in agreement after what looks like an internal debate. "Where are we going?"

"You'll see," I say cryptically.

"Okay. But I'm hungry. Is the food in the back?" Riley starts walking to the rear of the G-wagon.

"Uh, hold on a second," I call, holding up a finger. Riley stops and turns to wait for what I'm about to tell her. But I'm momentarily stuck. I had somehow managed to forget—for the second time in less than twenty-four hours—that I need to feed my daughter.

"Well, that's part of the surprise. It's going to be our first stop on the trip," I say, coming up with my explanation as the words leave my mouth. "We're going to go to the grocery store and pick up some munchies to take with us." Cheap snacks should hold us over until we make it to *Tía* Benita's.

"Can I get Cheetos?" Riley asks as I usher her back to the SUV, stopping to grab my phone from the grass as we walk.

I try to remember how much Cheetos cost the last time I went grocery shopping, which was over two years ago. "Maybe. We'll have to wait and see," I say, trying to sound playful and not panicked.

Riley buckles herself into the backseat while I start the engine. But as soon as I push the ignition button, I am met with the ping of the gas gauge, alerting me to an empty tank. Sweat prickles my forehead. Why hadn't I bothered to think of the gas gauge while driving around aimlessly last night?

It doesn't require advanced math skills to immediately calculate how much I have in my purse and realize I don't have enough money to buy groceries and enough gas to make it to Georgia.

"*Mamá?*" Riley calls from the backseat, causing me to let out a breath I didn't realize I was holding.

"Yeah?" I answer.

"Are we going?"

"Yeah. Yes. We're going now." I pull the G-wagon onto North Flagler Drive and head toward the nearest convenience store. "So, what do you want to do after we grab the food?" I ask, trying to calm my nerves.

"Can we stop by the Manatee Lagoon?"

Chapter Eighteen

Flying into the storm
Bri

Happy doesn't even begin to describe my current emotional state. Jubilant. Ecstatic. Euphoric. Sing at the top of my lungs to the radio, happy. Punch my fist in the air and shadow box along to the Rocky theme song, happy.

Call my boyfriend and share my latest accomplishment of being awarded the funds for the manatees happy. This is probably the better option than shadowboxing, considering I'm sitting in the tight confines of the jeep's interior once again hurtling down 91 toward home. I'm about to call out my instructions for the autodial on the Jeep Siri but stop when I catch a glimpse of the in-dash digital clock. 8:00 A.M. Okay, nope, never mind. I don't have to question whether Nick is awake at this early hour. I can just picture him splayed out across his unmade bed. Face down and naked, baring those adorable freckles splashed across his butt cheeks to an empty room. Heat pools low in my stomach at the thought of Nick's warm, hard body illuminated by the rising sun streaking in from the window. I shake my head—this line of thinking can't possibly be to my benefit. I need to change the subject fast.

I drum my fingers on the steering wheel and refocus on the view. I'm the only car on the freeway at this time of the morning. A few cars have passed me heading north, but no other vehicles are traveling south. There are cumulus clouds in the atmosphere, and if I squint my eyes, the sky and the road blend into a mirage of endless concrete. But at least this drive is in the daylight instead of the pitch black like last night.

After arriving at the hotel late, tired and depleted, the front desk clerk directed me to the nearest open café, where I picked up enough snacks and drinks to sustain me through the next eight hours and returned to my room. Re-invigorated by the room's fluorescent lighting, I rallied by putting on my pajamas and downing a triple espresso. Comfortable and with just the right amount of caffeine cursing through my veins, I practiced my presentation in front of the mirror until I knew it by heart and could spew my presentation facts without a single glance at my note cards—all with a smile on my face. It must have been around midnight when the caffeine officially stopped affecting my central nervous system because that was the last time I remember looking at the clock before waking up face down on my own bed at the unspeakable hour of six in the morning—the sound of my phone alarm barking at me to get up.

After a quick shower and blowout to get my heart pumping at the desired rate, I was headed back out the door. It was literally the crack of dawn as I made the trek over to the manatee habitat to present my case to the Marine Mammal Commission, who, as it turns out, appreciated my compulsive over-preparation. After a round of questions and answers, where I was able to provide clear and explanatory information to each question asked of me, the head of the Commission thanked me for my time and let me know that the proper paperwork needed to be filed. Still, I could expect the grant money within the next month.

So now here I am, jittery after coming down from my adrenaline rush, with no one to talk to, waiting for the sun to fully occupy the horizon. The thought occurs to me that the only other person ordinarily awake at this time of day is Cassy. I also realize she is the only other person I want to share my good news with. I take my eyes off the road in front of me for a second to glance at my phone when a ping comes from the dash.

I laugh out loud. The telepathy Cassy and I share is almost on the scary side. What are the chances she is calling me at the exact same time I'm about to call her? I'm about to press the button to answer the phone, but as I peer closer at the dashboard, I discover the gas light has pinged, not my phone.

Feeling foolish for thinking I could manifest Cassy contacting me with a single thought, I lean forward and peer over the steering wheel for closer inspection of the gas gauge. The estimated mileage shows my fuel consumption is rapidly approaching the zero mark, and as much as I don't want to take a detour this close to home, I take the exit for HWY-1. I pass Riviera Beach and the Manatee Lagoon before stopping at the closest Sunoco Gas Station. The station is tiny and only houses two pump stations, but they are both empty of customers due to the early hour. I pull up alongside the first one, hop out, and start pumping gas.

While the tank is filling up, I grab my cell phone from my purse in the front seat and text Cassy.

—*Hey! I'm almost home. I have good news! Are you already at work?*—

I replace the hose and move my Jeep to a parking

space adjacent to the gas station's convenience store. I might as well replace the caffeine my bloodstream is becoming dependent on and grab some coffee while I can.

The bell above the door chimes as I walk into the store and pause while searching the store's perimeter for the coffee station. I locate it at the back wall and walk down the nearest aisle. But as I'm casually scanning the merchandise on display, I realize I have chosen to walk through the personal hygiene aisle.

Heart palpitations set in as my gaze drifts from the shampoo and conditioner to the body lotion and on to the feminine products. I can feel my steps slow, and my breathing become faster as I try my best to avoid searching for the little pink life-changing rectangular box tucked in between the toothpaste and the condoms. But it's no use. As soon as my sight lands on Pandora's Box, my footsteps stop.

I don't even realize what I'm doing until I look down and see that I've reached out and plucked one of the packages off the shelf and am now holding it in my shaking hand.

"Bri!"

I jump in the middle of the aisle and watch in horror as the box clatters to the floor at my feet. I stoop down and sweep the evidence back into my arms, trying my best to position the box so the label is tucked against my "skip a straw, save a turtle" t-shirt.

Still crouched near the ground, I take a second to close my eyes and control my breathing. *I'm okay.* I coach myself. *This is fine. Whoever it is couldn't have seen anything.* I take one final breath and open my eyes as I stand and turn toward the person calling my name. I almost weep with relief when I see Riley, dark curls sticking out at all angles from her head, waving at me from the end of the aisle.

"Hey!" I say—even I recognize how overly cheerful I sound. I clear my throat and affix what I hope is a genuine smile on my face while she walks toward me. I try again. "Hey, kiddo. How's my favorite camper? You're up early this morning."

"Hi, Bri. I'm great! Yeah, I woke up with the sun rise because, guess what?"

"What's that?" I ask, taking a step closer to her.

"I went camping with my mom last night, and I get to do it again tonight." She pushes her glasses up her nose.

"Really? Well, that sounds like fun." I say, trying to keep my face neutral.

"I know. It's super cool. My *mamá* took me to the Manatee Museum when we woke up. Did you know manatees fart to control their buoyancy in the water?" Riley giggles with the relay of this particular fact.

I laugh along with her. "You know, I did know that. Here's another cool fact for you. They do something called unihemispheric sleep. Because they must come to the surface to breathe, they can't truly sleep underwater when they need to breathe air. That means half their brain gets to rest while the other half remains alert." I'm about to ask more questions about how they got onto the property when Abigail spies us from the end of the aisle and starts walking toward Riley and me.

It takes me a second to process that it is indeed Abigail. She looks so different. Her usually coiffed waves are pulled back into a messy ponytail, giving her a slightly disheveled look, and her daily wardrobe of designer labels have been replaced with jeans and a gray V-neck t-shirt.

As I observe Abigail, I notice she is also giving me the once-over. I watch her gaze travel the length of my body, and the skin around her eyes crinkle when she settles on the box half hidden in my arms.

Without missing a beat in Riley's and my conversation, Abigail says, "we also learned that after mating is over, the male leaves and never takes part in raising the child." Abigail looks at Riley and scoffs. "Go figure. Mammals of the male variety are all the same." She glances pointedly at the box again. "But I would bet you already know that little tidbit of information, don't you?"

I resist the urge to fidget or shift my arms. "I suppose I did." I search the recesses of my brain for something else to add. But instead of producing some witty comment or brilliant conversation, I trail off into silence.

Abigail stares at me silently until I can't take it any longer. "I was just on my way to get some coffee. I guess I'll be seeing you around." I back down the aisle, away from the two of them, with the box still firmly tucked in my arm, and give Riley an awkward wave. "So anyway, have fun camping."

Abigail regards me with a look I can't quite place, and I fear I've said something wrong, so I add, "stay safe out there. See you later, kiddo."

I make haste to the coffee stand and pour myself a steaming cup of French roast before taking my purchases to the counter. As I head out the door, I glance at Abigail and Riley. Abigail is shaking her head at Riley in the negative, and I wonder what she is saying no to.

I'm tucking my coffee into the cup holder of the Jeep

when Abigail and Riley exit the store. They cross the parking lot empty-handed and open the driver's side door of a black Mercedes G-wagon SUV. It takes me a few minutes to register the tinted windows, and it's not until they are pulling out of the parking lot and I'm staring at the Miami Sting Rays vanity license plate that it hits me.

"What the hell? It was Abigail?"

Chapter Nineteen

Organizing the System
Claudia

"Pamela, this looks simply marvelous!" I say with pride for my employee. Over the years, Pamela has developed quite the talent for envisioning and implementing artistically impressive tablescapes—this occasion is no exception.

"You be teaching me everything I know." Pamela blushes at the compliment.

"I might have taught you proper place settings, but this," I wave my hand to indicate the centerpiece in front of me. "This is outdoing yourself. It is simply beautiful."

"It be a special day for you and Mr. Castello. I be wanting to make you feel special." Pamela beams at me and reaches out to adjust the row of palm leaves sitting beneath golden candlestick holders, blush pink candlesticks poking out the top. The candles are encircled by glass hurricane tubes. And it looks as though Pamela was able to secure every color of pink peony available in Palm Beach to flank the tubes. Citrus fruits, cut on the diagonal, are expertly distributed among the flora for extra pops of color. Pamela plucks my favorite detail off the table and hands me the pink cabana striped paper drink umbrella "You say, always include a touch of whimsy."

"I do indeed. My dear, you have accomplished your

goal, I feel exceedingly special today." I stick the umbrella behind my ear and reach out to touch the Princess pink 1930s Depression glass goblets and green spiral glass salad plates. "Thank you," I whisper.

Pamela doesn't respond to the praise but nods and says, "I need be return' to the kitchen now. Dinner be ready at six." She turns to go, leaving me to inspect her work privately, but as she heads through the dining room door, she lets out an "Oh!" of excitement.

I turn my head in the direction of her outburst to see Benedict escorting Parker into the room.

"Parker!" Pamela and I declare in unison, prompting a genuine smile to break out across my *engonós* adoring face.

"Pamela, *Giagiá*," Parker responds, and since Pamela is closest to him, he tucks her under his arm for a bear hug. "It's so great to see you." He releases Pamela, who comes up sputtering, being caught off guard by Parker's overzealous affection.

"Boy, you be losing weight out there in the world." Pamela declares after being released and sizing Parker up with her laser stare.

Parker, who stands just as tall as Benedict at six foot two and is as solid as the day is long, laughs at Pamela. "Well, I guess you better start fattening me up then."

Pamela puts on a serious face and says, "That is exactly what I goin' do. You be eatin' the entire dinner tonight."

"Yes, ma'am," Parker says, with an equally serious face, but I can see the corner of his mouth twitching with a suppressed smile.

And with that, Pamela leaves for the kitchen, a renewed determination in her step. Once she is out of earshot, Parker breaks into a laugh and crosses the room to hug me. Benedict follows, right behind him.

"Parker darling, what a lovely surprise. We weren't expecting you for at least another hour or two." I say as Parker envelops me in his arms. His strong muscles cradle my frame gently like my old bones might snap in half if he applies too much pressure on them.

"Parker was telling me they finished up early at the station." Benedict chimes in behind us as I take my time relishing Parker's solid warmth before letting go.

"That's right," Parker says, looking over his shoulder at Benedict while still holding on to me. "We finished for the night. The station transfers to the national news in the evening, and with the hurricane, on its way, I know I will have to be at the station from tomorrow on. So, I wanted to come early and spend as much time as possible with you both."

"Well, we will take any time you can give us, won't we *Agápi mou*?" Benedict asks me.

"Of course! You're never too early for us. You can come any time, day or night."

"Ah, be careful. I might just show up at two in the morning, looking for some of that food Pamela's famous for." Parker teases.

"Well, you'd be more than welcome at that hour too." I squeeze Parker's hand and lead him over to the table. "Look how beautiful this is," I say as I adjust the palm frond printed linen cloth napkin situated between the bamboo dinner plates and green and gold chargers.

"It really is." Parker agrees, taking in the display before him before facing Benedict and me. "Oh my gosh, I almost forgot! Happy Anniversary!" This time Parker envelops both Benedict and me in a group hug. "Wow, fifty-five years! That is incredible." Parker leans into the two of us like he's about to ask us something important. "What's the secret to everlasting love?" He asks in a low voice, as though he knows we hold the answer to one of life's most pressing questions.

Benedict takes hold of my hand and gently kisses my knuckles in response. "We've made it this far because we've learned how to compromise and work together," Benedict says like it's the obvious answer.

Parker straightens back up and eyes Benedict and me. "You sure have. I can't even remember a time when you guys weren't together." Parker pauses and looks up to the right, pretending to search his memory before returning his gaze to meet ours. "Nope, no memory of you guys being apart."

"Well, that's because once I got ahold of your *Giagiá*, I never let her go." Benedict laughs and winks.

"You know it's crazy, but I don't think I know how you two met. I guess I just assumed you were always together." Parker chuckles to himself.

I smile at the men and try to search my memory for the first time Benedict, and I met. "Oh, I remember," I say, snapping my finger. "It was the first time Betty and I went to the Paramount Theater." I sneak a glance at Benedict, who smiles at me in answer, and nods for me to continue. "Oh, we were so excited. After months of begging, my mother finally let us girls attend a movie without a chaperone. Of course, *Mitéra* was beside herself with worry, but she always was in those days.

"The theater was showing a replay of the 1942 comedy *The Palm Beach Story* with Claudette Colbert and Joel McCrea. It wasn't a new release like *The Sound of Music* or *The Great Escape*, but Betty and I were excited nonetheless to be granted this tiny taste of independence. It didn't matter what we were watching.

We spent hours choosing our best sundresses—hand-sewn by me, of course—and rode our beach cruiser bikes down to North Country Road. Unfortunately, in our excitement, we misjudged how long it would take us to ride to the theater. We arrived twenty minutes early, which was good because we had to stand in a line wrapped around the block to buy our tickets."

I laugh at the memory, adjusting the silverware at the place setting in front of me before continuing to the next arrangement, leaving Benedict and Parker to pull out chairs and make themselves comfortable as I continue my way around the table. "I can still remember what it was like entering that theater for the first time. It was magnificent. A mural of fish was painted on the walls, their tails flowing as if underwater. The orchestra held over a thousand seats, but only about a hundred and fifty were on the balcony. Of course, everyone wanted to sit on the balcony, so once we were inside, Betty and I hurried to the concession stand for our popcorn and cola, then raced up the stairs, pushing and shoving the other teenagers out of our way to get the good seats."

"It sounds like it was a popular place," Parker says, crossing his ankle over his leg and leaning back.

"Oh, you wouldn't believe how popular it was. It was always crowded with boys and girls. Some would call it lip lock heaven, up on the balcony."

Parker blushes, and Benedict chuckles. "Ah, those were the days."

"But not for Betty and me," I say, pointing at Benedict, who laughs harder. "We were there purely for the entertainment."

"I like to remember it as it was in its prime. As a place of grandeur. A place to see and be seen." Benedict chimes in.

I nod at Benedict in agreement. "Which is why I was determined to conduct myself in a manner worthy of the theater." I pause, "But those balcony chairs were so comfortable. Too comfortable."

I glance at Benedict, who gives me a knowing look.

"I don't think I made it past the wedding scene—the one at the beginning of the movie—before I fell fast asleep." I pause, picking up a spoon to inspect it. "Come to think of it. I don't believe I've ever made it through that entire movie." Regret courses through me immediately followed by acceptance. And it strikes me as ironic that even, after all the years of therapy I've been through to accept my disability, it is a sense of self-reproach that still boils to the surface first.

I place the spoon on the table and continue to the following setting. "Anyways, the lights came up, and everyone exited the theater. That is except for poor Betty. She hadn't noticed I'd fallen asleep until the lights came up. She shook me, pinched me, and even tried lifting me. I think she tried everything she could think of to wake me. But nothing worked. There I was in the middle of the Paramount Theater, having a narcoleptic episode. Betty thought she would have to wait it out on the balcony. But eventually, with the help of a dashing theater attendant…" I smile at Benedict.

Benedict locks eyes with me. "I *was* fairly dashing in my day."

"Dashing indeed," I repeat.

"Wait, *Pappoús,* you worked at the Paramount?" Parker asks, now fully invested in the conversation.

"I sure did. I remember it like it was yesterday. The boss had a hot date and wanted to close the theater as soon as everyone left. So, he sent me to the balcony to clean and ensure it was empty before we locked up. So, I headed up to get started. Well, you can imagine my surprise when I walked up the stairs and saw Betty looking bewildered and slightly frantic." Benedict says. "I thought something was terribly wrong."

"Yes, well, eventually, I came around," I interject, coming around to stand on the same side of the table as Benedict and Parker.

"But not before I had to carry you down the stairs and call your parents."

"Yes," I sigh. "*Mitéra* was not happy that night."

"Oh my gosh, *Giagiá*, I bet you were so embarrassed." Parker wrongly assumes.

"Not in the least, *Agápi mou*. I was just happy the theater manager didn't call for the medic. Now *that* would have been a disaster."

"You might have avoided one disaster, but you also created another one," Benedict says, rising out of his chair to stand by me. "I couldn't get the black-haired sleeping beauty out of my mind. I thought about her every second of the day. Whenever I went to work, I would keep my fingers crossed that my mysterious beauty would reappear."

I laugh at Benedict's description of me as he takes my hand. "Of course, I had no idea I'd made such an impression until my mother made me return to the theater and apologize to the manager for making a scene and thank the boy who had helped me."

"The second she walked through that door, I knew it was over. I was a goner. So, of course, I did what any man who experiences love at first sight would do. I asked her out." Benedict lifts my knuckles to his lips and brushes a chaste kiss on them. "Do you blame me?"

"Can't say that I do," Parker says.

Benedict lets down my hand and turns to Parker. "And as they say in show business, the rest is history."

Parker reaches across the table, grabs one of the empty water goblets, and holds it to us in a mock toast. "To history!"

Benedict and I laugh and follow Parker's lead, leaning over the table and collecting an empty goblet each, repeating "To history!" as we clink glasses.

"You guys are what stories are made of," Parker says as I collect the goblets and replace them in their exact spots on the table.

"Well, don't let us fool you too much. Marriage takes a lot of work and compromises on both parts," I say as I take Benedict's arm and direct our little party toward the hallway. "Not to mention learning how to communicate."

"I can only imagine," Parker says as he follows us.

"Speaking of communication," I stop walking and turn to face Parker. "Have you had any with Cassandra yet?" Benedict squeezes my arm, and he doesn't even have to say anything for me to know he is telling me to let it rest, not to force what we both know to be inevitable.

Parker looks sheepish and glances down at the polished hardwood floors under our feet. "Not yet, I was planning on calling her, but I was so busy. I wasn't able to fit it in."

"Mmmhmm, Well, I guess you'll get the chance to do so tonight," I say, taking Benedict's suggestion and letting the conversation die out naturally. "Mentioning tonight, I must lie down for a nap if I'm going to make it through dinner. Parker, make yourself at home. You know where your room is. It has already been made up for you."

Parker looks relieved to be let off the hook for now. "Thank you, *Giagiá*. You know, after the last few days I've had, a little *ypnáko* sounds like just what the doctor ordered."

Benedict squeezes my arm again before letting go and placing a soft kiss on my cheek. "Well, my love, I guess that means I can keep myself entertained with a little paperwork. So, I will bid you both *antio sas* and see you in an hour or two."

I watch both men start down the hallway in different directions, taking a piece of my heart with each of them.

Chapter Twenty

Perfect Conditions
Cassy

Nick pulls off Ocean Boulevard with a flourish, swinging his Hummer EV under the Porte-cochere and abruptly stopping at the cusp of the double French doors.

"Geeze, Nick. How you got your driver's license is beyond me," I say, placing both hands on the dashboard in front of me for stability.

"Well, at least I have a license," Nick says, slipping the vehicle into park and shutting down the engine.

I decidedly ignore Nick's rib about my choice not to get my driver's license. A topic that has been one of contention between us for years now. And one that I refuse to budge on. Nick hadn't been there for the accident. I know if he had seen what I had at the age of sixteen, he wouldn't be pushing me to drive. As it was, Nick only heard about the wreckage of our life second-hand. He wasn't there to witness the Jaws of Life extracting our parents from the car wrapped around the light post. He never had to see the pools of crimson staining the sun-bleached concrete beneath their limp bodies. He has never had to block out the memories of white sheets draped over motionless mounds being carried away on stretchers. So no, Nick will never get the shakes when he hears a siren approaching from the opposite direction, and he will never suffer a blackout while driving if he sees police cars with their lights flashing, which is why Nick should be the one to have a license, not me.

"You know why I don't drive," I say quietly and shake my head to prevent the memories from seeping in further. I release my seatbelt and reach for the door handle, desperate to remove myself from this death trap of a vehicle before Nick tries to press the issue further.

"This really is a prick car." I shout at Nick as I hold the door open for Bo to follow me. Even Bo looks shocked from the ride over.

"So you've mentioned before, and no, it's not," Nick says, either oblivious to my trip down memory lane or choosing to ignore it, like he does every time a person refers to the past. "It's electric, which gives me cred for doing my part to save the earth."

"Well, I bet Bri would be happy to hear you're out there saving the wildlife from dangerous fumes and pollution," I say absent mindedly placing a correlation between Bri and anything that has to do with saving the environment.

"Oh, she is." Nick says, causing me to take pause at his quick comeback. But before I can process it any further, he continues, "And besides, she looks good on me." He leans against his prized possession, the "she" in his comment, and strikes a pose like I'm about to take his picture and post it to my Instagram. And even though he is dressed in a fresh pair of black jeans and a white polo shirt—a vast improvement from last night's outfit—he still looks ridiculous.

Bo and I tilt our heads to the side. I grimace and turn to Bo. "He is too much."

Bo cocks his head to the other side as if to say, "No

kidding," and strides right past Nick, ignoring him, heading for the front entrance.

"Hey, not cool," Nick calls after me as I follow Bo to the front door. I laugh, feeling much more lighthearted than just a moment ago, and place my finger on the doorbell. Instantly the familiar chimes announce our arrival by rippling throughout the manor. Nick hurries from the beastly SUV and takes his place beside me as Pamela's friendly face greets us upon opening the door.

"Cassandra. Nicolas. Bo. Come in, come in." Pamela, dressed in her pale blue polo shirt and khaki pants uniform, steps aside to let Nick and me enter the grand foyer. Forgetting his manners, Bo bounds straight past us and into the house. Surprisingly light on her feet, Pamela deftly grabs Bo's collar before he can race past her.

"Hey now, boy, you be coming with me. It's your lucky day, ya know? I just might have a bone left over from tonight's dinner with your name on it."

Bo, recognizing the word "bone," gazes at Pamela like she's his new best friend, his tail whipping the air at megawatt speeds.

Still bent over at the waist and holding onto Bo's collar, Pamela turns to address Nick and me. "Mr. Castello be in the den, and Mrs. Castello be upstairs in her drawing room. I be takin' Mr. Bo and make sure he be takin' care of."

I bend down and rub Bo behind the ears before untying my work shoes and slipping them off, leaving the hot-pink high-tops by the front door.

"You be a good boy now, okay?"

Bo gives a quick "Yip" as I stand back up.

Pamela gives me a wink and skillfully guides Bo

down the hall toward the staff quarters.

I slap Nick on the back. "I'll be upstairs with Auntie. You go do your guy thing with Uncle B."

Nick doesn't bother with an answer. Instead, he just huffs and heads down the hallway in the direction of the den.

Taking the stairs two at a time I make my way up the winding, double staircase to the second floor where the primary bedroom and Claudia's drawing room are located.

"Auntie Claudia?" I call softly as I enter the bedroom, keeping my voice low in case she is still sleeping. But as I enter the room, I see she isn't in bed. "Auntie?" I call again, louder this time.

"In here," comes her muffled reply.

I follow her voice through the bedroom into the en-suite bathroom, pausing as I step onto the marble tile. The floor is cool under my socked feet. Memories of watching Aunt Claudia applying "her face," as she calls it, float into my mind as I pass her vanity, lined with glass bottles and golden compacts.

I search the spacious area but continue walking when I come up short of finding Auntie Claudia at the table. I'm almost completely across the bathroom, having passed the shower, sauna, and Jacuzzi tub, when an unexpected silhouette of Parker pops up on the built-in television suspended over the double sinks causing my heart to suddenly jump into my throat. My breath catches at the sight of him and the sound of his deep baritone voice echoing off the marble walls surrounding me.

"Hurricane Odette is strengthening and taking aim for Florida, where residents are bracing for a possible Category Three landfall expected in the early hours of

Monday morning." His words reverberate in my eardrums, vibrating all the way down my spine.

"Odette is forecasted to make landfall somewhere between Melbourne and Miami. Everyone on the east coast of Florida is urged to be prepared for a possible life-threatening storm surge, devastating hurricane-force winds, and over a foot of rain. All indications are showing this hurricane is going to hit fast, and it's going to hit hard."

I'm still trying to recover from Parker's sudden appearance when Auntie Claudia's lyrical voice sounds atop Parker's, dulling the vibrations in my body, "Cassandra? *Agapitós?* Are you there? I'm in the closet. *"*

I take one last glance at Parker, once again committing his face to my memory, before calling out, "Yes, Auntie. I'm coming."

It takes me another minute to pass the threshold from the bathroom into the luxurious white-carpeted, two-story dressing chamber. But when I do, I'm instantly transported back to my childhood. Back when Nick, Parker, and I would sneak up here while our parents and all the adults would hold court downstairs, drinking and socializing. We would huddle together in the built-in racks of clothes, shoes, bags, and jewels—all designer, all sparkling, and all vintage—whispering and laughing until one of us would inevitably suggest a game of hide-and-seek like it wasn't what we came up here to do in the first place. A lively round of rock-paper-scissors would ensue, after which whoever was appointed the counter would have to sit in the middle of the room on the tufted white chaise lounge, hiding their eyes in the cushions and counting to fifty.

Under the stained-glass skylight and antique white

crystal chandelier, the other two would dash up the short staircase to the terrace encircling the room below it. Then, stealth-like, we would enclose ourselves in one of the twenty identical built-in closets, stuffing our bodies between racks of clothes smelling of violet and lavender, holding our breath as the countdown descended closer to zero. I always loved it when Parker was the counter. He had the loudest voice, so I would know when he was on the move. And when he did find me, he would fling the door open and yell, "gotcha!" before reaching in with both hands and tickling me until I would squeal with laughter.

I smile at the memories as melancholy for the old days washes through me.

"Auntie?" I call out, not immediately seeing her among the racks of clothing.

"Up here, *Agápi mou.*"

I look up to see Claudia closing one of the mirrored French doors. She waves at me over the balcony railing and begins descending the stairs to greet me.

"Hello, darling," she coos when she reaches the bottom step, enveloping me in a warm hug. "Oh, I'm so glad you're okay." She holds me out at arm's length to look me over from head to toe. I'm a little confused about what she's talking about until she says, "I don't know what I would have done if something happened to you. Are there any new developments on the break-in?"

"No, nothing new," I say, slightly defeated but not wanting to upset Auntie Claudia I add, "I don't think we'll find out who did it. And besides, I'm fine. But enough about that." I continue, purposely changing the course of the conversation. "I'm here to celebrate you. Happy Anniversary."

"Thank you, dear. I can always rely on you to be so kind." She brings me in for one more hug before releasing me.

"And how are you feeling today?" I ask, following behind her as she walks to the built-in cupboard housing neatly folded shawls in a rainbow of colors.

"I'm fine, but I always wonder why people start a conversation with me by asking how I'm feeling?"

I laugh. "Well, I can't speak for anyone else, but I can assure you I didn't mean anything by it. I was simply asking how you were doing today."

Aunt Claudia pulls out an emerald green wrap that matches a stunning necklace she is wearing, one that I don't remember seeing before, and turns to study me. "No, you weren't. You might have asked, 'how are you feeling today?' But what you meant was, 'Have you had an episode?' " She tsk-tsks, and it's only after she's said it that I realize there might be some truth to her statement. "You do realize narcolepsy isn't a death sentence, don't you?" She raises her eyebrow at me.

"Of course, I know that," I say, raising my hands in defeat, "but you know I only ask out of love and concern."

"Love is fine. Reserve your concern for better things. I'm taking care of myself, following my routine, and taking my medications. I'm not going to be signing off anytime soon. So, you can save your worries for another day. Now come here and let me have a look at you."

I step closer, knowing, without a doubt, I will not pass her inspection.

"All these years and have I taught you nothing? You don't come to a dinner party dressed in jeans and a t-shirt,

Agápi mou."

"I promise you have taught me," I say as the image of my forgotten change of clothes on my bed flashes through my mind. "It's just that I came from work. I didn't have a change of clothes with me."

She snaps her fingers with renewed determination. "Well, we will be fixing that." She sweeps her hand around the closet. "I think we might have a thing or two you can choose from."

I know, better than anyone, that once Auntie Claudia gets an idea in her head, there is no changing her mind, so I nod in agreement, taking in the hundreds of garments and caftans surrounding us. After all, if there was ever a place for a wardrobe change, this was it.

Claudia walks over to one of the mirrored French doors and pulls it open with a flourish. A fashionista's dream of silks, linens, and cotton in various shades and colors are suspended uniformly on their hangers, brushing the floor beneath them.

"I know I have something around here." Claudia reaches one arm into the plethora of garments and emerges holding a column of white silk. Shiny threads of rose-gold run through the fabric in an intricate pattern of flowers and ivy. It is sheer bohemian perfection. "Now, here we are. This will do just fine," she says.

"Oh, it's so beautiful." I gush as Aunt Claudia motions for me to extend my arms, laying the cool fabric across them. She turns to the closet next to her, housing shoes and sandals of various designer labels. I recognize the names on a few soles—but there are some so fashionable I have no idea who they are.

Claudia rummages around for a few seconds before pulling out a pair of knee-high, rose-gold gladiator sandals and adding them to my pile.

"Auntie Claudia, I couldn't." I start to protest.

"Nonsense, child. Tonight, we dress up. These are from my vintage collection. In fact, I believe your grandmother used to wear that very dress to our parties. So, it is only fitting that it belongs to you now. Betty would have wanted you to have it."

I feel the heat touch my cheeks as I accept the dress, holding it up in front of me as I gaze in the mirror, imagining what my grandmother might have looked like wearing it at my age.

Claudia abruptly claps her hands together, breaking my trance.

"Go on and change, and when you are done, come downstairs. I'll meet you in the den, and we will have proper drinks with the men before dinner."

"Yes, Auntie." I nod at Claudia as she drifts out of the dressing room. "I'll just be a minute."

Chapter Twenty-One

Tropical Storm
Abigail

Seriously, what kind of woman takes her daughter camping right before a hurricane? Bri must think I'm either crazy or have more money than sense.

Ha.

She might have had more to say about this brilliant camping nonsense if she knew how lacking both of those little gems were from my life right now.

But, whatever. It looked like Bri had some drama of her own to deal with anyways. Not to mention I should probably be thankful she didn't recognize me from our little run-in at the crosswalk yesterday. At least, that's one thing I can count as going my way because it's obvious the rest of my life has gone to complete shit.

In my wildest dreams, I never predicted I'd be sleeping in the back of my SUV in the deserted parking lot of Currie Park. And not for just one night of novelty and excitement, but for two nights in a row.

Please.

The flags of the Martin Luther King Memorial flap in the breeze as I stare across the channel at the houses lit from within, a few blocks removed from my own home, and I can't decide if I'm more comforted or freaked out by how empty the park is at this time of night.

The playground grew silent hours ago. All the

responsible mothers were shepherding their children home, tucking their precious little darlings into warm beds before kissing their foreheads and wishing them goodnight.

I turn to stare at Riley. Her body sprawled across the flattened back seats, her head resting on a pile of folded t-shirts, and I realize I never got around to kissing her goodnight.

I had let Riley run wild after pulling into the parking lot of Currie Park, watching blindly as she sprinted between the piers, playground, and boat ramps for over two hours. Dutifully following behind her, pretending to be watching as Riley explored the whole park.

The longer we walked, the harder I tried to come up with a solution and the more paralyzed I became. Eventually, the sky grew dark, and Riley came trotting back to me to ask if it was time to "camp."

I had simply nodded and ushered her back to the Mercedes, pulling a fresh t-shirt from the duffle bag to sleep in before lying down in the back seats and watching as she climbed in and got comfortable.

Now, I let my gaze leave Riley's tiny face, all scrunched up in sleep, and let it drift down to her feet, still dirty from playing outside. How long can I keep this little charade up before she starts to catch on? Camping in the car is fun for now, but what will happen to us when the storm rolls in?

I turn back around in the seat I've been sitting in for the past hour, rotating my phone in my hand. Circling it as if it is a compass, and if I point it in the right direction, it will lead to the answers, and try again to come up with a solution.

It was only a few days ago this very phone was

amassed with text messages from my so-called "friends" eager to share the latest gossip or check what I was wearing to the next event. But now, when I need a friend, the screen remains blank.

Where are all the women who declared themselves a part of this WAG sisterhood? The ones who promised to be there for Riley and me when we needed them?

I don't have to think about the question for too long before I come up with the obvious answer. They are in the same place Suzy and Julian are. On their private jet streams, they are evacuating the storm to posh destinations like Aspen, L.A., or the Hamptons. Texting each other their locations and comparing thread counts or how many pieces of luggage they brought, not wasting their thoughts on poor Riley and me.

The realization that Riley and I are truly alone, abandoned by the people I thought I could depend on, hits me so hard I literally gasp for breath, like the wind has been knocked out of me. I want to scream with frustration but stop myself before waking Riley up.

Instead, I squeeze out the door and shut it gently behind me, leaning my back against the cool metal of the car. I take greedy breaths of thick salty air into my lungs until I'm able to get myself back under control.

What am I going to do?

The wind cuts through my shirt's thin fabric, causing me to shiver and cross my arms around my waist. If only I could go back home and crawl into bed, pull my duvet up to my chin, and stay tucked beneath it until the storm passes and Julian comes home. Or better yet, climb into the guest bed at *Mamá's* and have her care for Riley until I figure this out.

And just like that, I know what needs to be done.

The only problem is that pressing the numbers on my phone and making *Mamá* magically appear is the rough equivalent of admitting I was wrong in almost every argument *Mamá* and I ever had.

All those lectures I fought against during my long, drawn-out engagement will be null and void. I'll have lost. Like when she said I needed to find a way to support myself. Or, I was foolish to put all my trust in a man. Or, when she insisted I have more potential and natural talent in my little finger than most people have in their whole body, and I was sitting there, wasting it away. All those times I dismissed her as arrogant and nosy are about to come back and slap me in the face.

The second I tell *Mamá* about Julian will be the moment I say, "you were right, and I was wrong." And that realization hurts almost as badly as Julian shutting his daughter and me out in the middle of a natural disaster.

The stars peek through the clouds as I pull out the phone and press the screen. Knowing there is no other way around it, I have to call.

"*Hola, carino, como estas?*"

A mixture of relief and dread wash through me at the sound of *Mamá's* voice cutting through the silence of the night.

"*Hola Mamá,*" I pause, "am I interrupting your supper?" realizing too late that I am calling in the middle of their dinner time.

"*Oh querida*, didn't Julian tell you? We left a message at the house earlier today. We decided to drive up to *Tía Benita's* house, you know, to get out of the storm. We decided to drive at night to beat the traffic. But I'm glad you called. *Papá* and I planned on trying you again when we got to the house."

As *Mamá* talks, my throat starts to close up, making breathing hard. "So, you've left already?"

"*Sí Mija.* We decided to evacuate before the order. You know how it gets when everyone waits until the last minute. The interstate gets so congested. Anyway, we are heading up there now. Going to stay until this thing passes and then come back to evaluate the damage—" She interrupts her own conversation to yell. "No. No. Turn here. Hold on*, Mija.*" I hear her giving *Papá* directions in rapid Spanish while she holds a hand over the speaker before removing it and returning to our conversation.

"Sorry, your *Papá* isn't the best with this GPS thing. Anyways, how about you? Are you all prepared? Oh, who am I kidding? You and Julian probably have all your little worker bees running around doing everything for you." The condescending tone of her voice is not wasted on me.

I decide to ignore her snide comment and focus on the one thing that has been running through my head this whole conversation. "So, *Mamá,* you're saying the house is empty?" The plan is forming as I talk. If the house is empty, Riley and I can go there and stay until the storm is over. I won't have to tell my parents about Julian until after deciding my next move.

"Well, yes, it's empty but don't worry, your *Papá* and I hired a board-up service to come and secure the house. They started before we left and texted us a few hours ago to let us know they have completed the house. They sent us some pictures of their work over the phone. They did an excellent job. I don't think a fly could get into the place."

My heart sinks as she keeps talking— no way into the house —parents halfway out of the state, no place for Riley and me to go.

"That's great, *Mamá*. I'm glad you got somebody to take care of it." I pause, trying to sound sincere. "So, you're saying there's no way anybody could get into the house. Do you think it's really that secure?"

"Oh s*í*, they assure us the house is quite protected. You would need a toolbox to get into it. And even then, all the doors are locked and sealed shut."

"What about the key you leave out under the rock?"

"Oh no, we took it with us. We didn't want to take the chance of the wind blowing it away. How about you? When do you plan on leaving?

"I don't know. We're still discussing the plan. I'm sure we'll figure it out soon enough."

"Don't wait too long. You know how the roads are when people wait for the mandatory evacuation. They move at a snail's pace. I'd hate for you to get stuck in traffic."

I lean my head against the door behind me with a *thunk* and shut my eyes. I need to tell her. Just spit it out and say, "Julian kicked me out with no money or resources." I must tell her I spent my last forty dollars buying potato chips and Gatorade to feed my daughter.

Of course, I need to tell her.

There is no way my situation can improve without asking for her help. I scrunch my eyes tight and pinch my lips together, biting them with my teeth. All these years of hearing *Mamá* tell me this is where I would end up crashing through my brain. She was right. It was like she could predict the future. She was the one with the crystal ball, not me. Whenever I shot back some smartass remark or came up with an excuse to keep the status quo where it was, I was in denial, not her. But the look I imagine on her face when I finally admit she was right all along is enough to stop me from opening my mouth and regurgitating every sordid detail.

I rotate my body, so my forehead rests on the window, and I'm looking through the SUV's tinted glass. The duffle bag is still on the passenger seat, where clothes are spilling out of it. The empty potato chip bag is on the floorboard, along with the half-full Gatorade. My gaze travels along the car's seats and finally rests on Riley. She has kicked my makeshift blanket off in her sleep, so she is bare except for her mermaid t-shirt. Her hair, curly and wild, surrounds her face like a halo. Dark skin shiny from sweat glistens in the dim light of the parking lot. Looking at my daughter, I suck in my breath and force out the word.

"*Mamá?*"

"Yes, *Cariño?*"

I open my mouth, determined to get it out, but she cuts me off before I can continue.

"Hold on. Your *Papá* is yapping at me about the directions again." She covers the mouthpiece with her hand, engaging in a muffled exchange as they try to navigate the roads.

Frustrated, I start bobbing my head against the side of the car door. It emits a *Thunk, Thunk, Thunk*.

I need to tell her now, or I'm going to lose my nerve.

"Abigail?" She says, cutting into my thoughts. "Abigail, is somebody at your front door? I hear knocking."

I stop pounding, realizing the rhythmic banging of my head against the car must sound like somebody knocking on my front door. "No, *Mamá*, it's actually—"

But again, *Mamá* cuts me off mid-sentence when she shrieks into the phone, "No! Don't take that exit!" Causing me to pull the phone away from my ear in an attempt to salvage my eardrum. When I return it to its original position, *Mamá* speaks to me again.

"*Cariño*, I have to go. Your *Papá* took the wrong exit, and now he's put us on the entirely wrong freeway. Oh, what a mess. I must redo the navigation system to get us out of here. Anyways, it sounds like you have somebody at the front door. Make sure you call and let us know where you'll be staying. Talk to you soon. *Adiós cariño.*"

A click, and before I can respond, she is gone. I push off the side of the car, dropping the phone to my side, and stare up at the stars in bewilderment. How did I lose all control of the conversation? That was not how it was supposed to go. What am I going to do now? *Mamá* and *Papá* are gone. I have zero dollars to my name, and a storm is expected off Florida's coast within hours.

"Damn it." I bury my face in my hands. "I need a drink."

I turn around and look through the tinted windows at Riley again, but my thoughts are obscuring my vision to the point that I can't process what I'm seeing. Not allowing myself time to think, I open the driver's side door, climb behind the steering wheel, shut the door, and start the engine.

Chapter Twenty-Two

Early Gusts
Claudia

"Was that Parker's voice I just heard in the hallway?" Nicolas asks me as I enter the den. Benedict rises from the brown leather chair, careful not to slosh the clear liquid in his highball glass as he saunters over to meet me in the middle of the room, brushing my cheek with a kiss.

"What's that now?" Benedict asks a little too loudly.

I glance at Nicolas, who makes a grimace and shrugs his shoulders. I let out a soft guffaw, reach up while Benedict's face is still close to mine, and switch his earpiece to the *ON* position.

"I see that smile on your face," Benedict whispers, his breath warm against my ear and the smell of *Tsikoudia* touching my nose. "What have you done now?" He catches my eye as he pulls away, a twinkle of conspiracy reflecting back to me.

I try to hide my smirk and whisper back, "Why? Whatever are you talking about?"

Benedict pulls away but leaves his arm around my waist. I give him a quick wink before addressing Nicolas's question. "Yes, *Agápi mou*. I mentioned it to Cassandra earlier. Did she not tell you that Parker was joining us for dinner?"

"She didn't mention it. It must have slipped her

mind. But that's great news." Nicolas amends. "It's been ages since I've seen him."

"Yes, well, I figured since he was going to be in town, it was the perfect chance to reunite everyone for dinner." I rub my bare arms with my hands. "I just sent him upstairs to grab a shawl for me before joining us. I forgot it in my drawing room before coming down to meet you. He should be down shortly."

Benedict grunts. "Yes, I do feel a slight drop in temperature."

I give Benedict a gentle elbow in the side, and he stifles a laugh.

Nicolas nods in obedient agreement, oblivious to the ambient temperature but not bothered by it either way.

"By the way, Happy Anniversary," Nicolas says, redirecting his attention to Benedict and me. "I'm honored to celebrate your big day with you."

"Well, my darling, we are also delighted to have you with us. These hallways are so quiet now that you children are all grown up and living your own lives."

Nicolas studies the carpet looking bashful, and I realize I must be making him feel guilty for not coming over more, which was not the intent of my comment.

"From what I understand, Parker will be in town for the next few days," I say, trying to make amends for my misstep. "Maybe you young kids can go hang around together," I turn to Benedict. "Is that how they say it?"

"I think it's 'hang out,' *Agápi mou*." Benedict offers.

"Yes, yes. Maybe you can hang out together while Parker is here."

Nicolas takes a sip from his Collins glass and nods before replying. "That would be great."

Benedict smiles and whispers in a faux conspirator's

voice, "A night on the town sounds just like what us boys need. How about you show us a good time at THE NEST, I'm sure you know plenty of young ladies you could introduce us to."

"Hey, now. Slow your roll there, big guy." I say pointedly to Benedict, proud of myself for once again being able to produce the slang the kids are using nowadays.

Nicolas chuckles good-naturedly and winks at me before turning to Benedict. "I'd love to show you and Parker a good time, but I'm afraid my days of wining and dining the PBPs and introducing young ladies are over."

My ears prickle at Nicolas's unintended admission. "Why's that, *Agápi mou*?" I ask while trying to sound as nonchalant as possible.

Nicolas colors at the cheek and glances down at the floor for a second before he says, "I think I'm just growing a little tired of the nightclub scene, that's all." Then, he looks up quickly and says almost apologetically, "It's not that I don't appreciate the opportunity you've given me. I do. I couldn't be more grateful."

"But," Benedict says, encouraging Nicolas to continue.

"But, well, I guess I've just been thinking about other possibilities that might be out there for me. You know, maybe going back to school and getting a degree in business," Nicolas looks at Benedict, "or even going to law school." He shrugs his shoulder and looks down again. "I guess I'm just getting tired of the party scene. All the fakeness and slick palms, it gets old after a while." Again, Nicolas lifts his gaze, this time settling on my face. "I think I'd like to settle down a little. Take on a calmer lifestyle." But before I even have a chance to declare my approval for his newfound desires and interrogate him further as to where all this is coming from, Nicolas dissolves everything he's proclaimed by saying, "But it's just something I'm thinking about. I know I still have a loan to pay back. And I have no idea where I'd get the money to go to school anyways. It's nothing. Don't worry about it."

A quick glance at Benedict and I can tell he is just as baffled as I am at this new Nicholas—still not an emotional guru by any means, but a more mature version, nonetheless. I step closer to Nicolas and place my hand on his arm. "Darling, I'm not entirely sure where this is coming from, but I'm so proud of you for telling us. I don't want you to ever disregard a dream simply because of a financial barrier. You know you have our support in that area."

"I know Auntie C," Nicolas places his hand over mine, and the warmth travels deep into my bones. "But like I said, you've done so much for me already. And I haven't even looked into the details, so there's really nothing to discuss. I was thinking out loud."

"Yes, well. I like listening to your out loud thoughts. I suggest you do some research, and when you have more information, come back and tell Benedict and me what you discover."

Nicolas looks at me thoughtfully, and I can tell a lot is going on inside that head of his. "Okay, sure," he says. But I don't know if he really means it or if he only agrees to appease me for the time being. Either way, I get the notion he is done with this part of the conversation when he turns back to Benedict and says, "Besides, I'm closing up THE NEST for the hurricane. A few of us were planning on boarding the place up later tonight. She'll be closed until after Odette."

"Ah, yes. I suppose you do need to secure the old girl before the winds blow through. Who are you meeting?" Benedict asks conversationally as he takes another sip of his *Tsikoudia.*

Nicolas looks sheepish as he admits, "Well, most of my staff have already taken off, so it's just Cassy, Bri, and I tonight."

"That's a small crew you got yourself. Why don't you see if Parker will join you? You can go after dinner. I'm sure he wouldn't mind lending a hand."

"Yeah, that's a great idea. I'll ask him." Nicolas says.

"How is Bri? I haven't seen her around here lately." I say, watching to see if I can catch the glint I thought I saw in Nicolas's eye earlier when he had—oh so casually—said her name.

Nicolas coughs into his fist and says, "She's good, you know, just busy with her job and all."

"Oh yes, she is so brilliant. I'm sure she is kept very busy with her research and manatee work." I pause before focusing my attention entirely on Nicolas. "Now she's not one of those PBP's at all, is she?"

Nicolas's cheeks color and he quickly sips his cocktail before replying, "No, she most definitely is not."

"Hmmm." I study Nicolas for a second longer, waiting to see if he will expand on the topic, but when he doesn't add any more, I already feel like I've gained all the knowledge I need. So, finally, I smile and turn away from Nicolas, addressing Benedict. "I think it might be time for dinner. Shall we call the children down?"

Chapter Twenty-Three

Slow Crawl
Cassy

"Gosh darn it! This is exactly why I don't play dress up." I rummage around, tented inside the caftan, with no apparent way out. Silently, I curse the buttons I must have forgotten to undo before slipping the silky fabric over my head.

"Auntie?" I call out, hoping she is still within earshot. "Hello?"

I stop pulling at the delicate fabric for a second, eager for a response. But when I'm met with nothing but silence, I go back to twisting the vintage garment around my head. In my panic, a light layer of perspiration has appeared on my skin, causing the caftan to stick to me, only working to increase my desperation. I keep working to untangle myself from the jumble, all the while being cautious about ripping a seam or tearing the precious material.

The more I work to untangle myself, the more twisted I become, to the point that I've now managed to add my arms to the mess of fabric above my head.

I'm about to call out for help again when footsteps sound on the bathroom floor, and a wave of relief washes through me. "Auntie? I'm having a little difficulty. Can you come and help me?"

The footsteps grow closer, and I start blindly

walking toward them, my arms still suspended above my head in a mass of silk fabric.

It's not until I am at the entrance to the dressing room that I realize the sound of the shoe on the bathroom tile isn't the click-clack of Aunt Claudia's kitten heel but rather a firm and robust stride.

I shake myself out of my momentary stupor and back away from the entrance, frantically increasing my efforts to untangle myself from the caftan while at the same time bumping into the chaise lounge with my bare leg.

I'm on the verge of letting out a string of very un-lady-like cuss words when the footsteps stop, and I know whoever is here has crossed the barrier from the marble floor to the lush carpet of the walk-in closet.

I hold my breath and stand completely still, realizing I'm half-naked from the waist down except for my white briefs. I pray that the island housing Claudia's jewels blocks the lower half of my body from view.

"Um? Nick? Uncle B?" My voice betrays me by cracking on the second syllable. I clear my throat.

There's a low chuckle, and I know right away whoever is in the dressing room is not Nick or Uncle B. Panic shoots through me, and for the briefest of moments, I'm transported back to the break-in at the café.

The air in my lungs is stuck, so I clear my throat again, finally choking out, "um, just a minute."

I give one last-ditch effort to struggle into, or out of, the mass of fabric suffocating me, causing a mad sweat to spread across my lower back. Despite the temperature and humidity-controlled closet, I'm dying.

Even though I can't see him, and he has yet to say a word, I know he's made his way across the space separating us. I stand perfectly still until his breath is directly behind me. I try not to flinch when I feel his fingers, gentle at first and then more urgent, searching for the buttons.

"Now, hold on a second." He finally finds the buttons and unlatches them. Then, mercifully, he opens a hole, so the caftan floats down over my head, encircling my body in a soft billow of air.

The heat touches my cheeks as I comprehend the baritone voice I know by heart, the same one I listen to every evening on the television. Willing myself to open my eyes, I blink twice, only to realize I'm still facing a row of garment bags.

"Here," I feel him sweep my hair to the side, and I have to prevent myself from visibly shivering at his touch. "Let me do that for you." He re-attaches the buttons he had just released seconds earlier. "There we go. All better now."

I take my time turning to face Parker, standing before me, flashing his famous too-white smile and staring at me with those ghost blue eyes crinkled at the sides with amusement. "Hi, Cassy."

"Hi." I'm able to whisper back. In the past, I would be ecstatic to see Parker, not hesitating to jump into his arms for a hug, but that was years ago. Before the accident and before we lost touch. "What are you doing here?" I ask before thinking, my voice hitching on my words.

The lines around his eyes deepen as he laughs his deep baritone. "It's good to see you too."

His familiarity helps to shake me out of my stupor. "Sorry, that's not what I meant." I backpedal while trying to regain some dignity.

"Then what did you mean?"

"I wasn't expecting you. Here. Now. I just saw you." I point to the bathroom just over his shoulder. "You were on the TV."

Parker glances behind him, catching sight of the newscast still playing on the hidden TV. "That segment is prerecorded. We taped it earlier today, so I could have dinner with *Pappoús* and *Giagiá* for their anniversary before returning to the station."

He turns back around, looking at me like that explains everything.

When I don't say anything, he leans over to touch my elbow, causing another fever to course through me. "Come on. I can't wait to catch up with everyone, but not in here."

He leads me to the dressing room door, and I grab the sandals as we walk by the counter. "Yes, everyone is probably waiting for us." I agree, trying not to flinch at the warm touch of his hand on my skin, and thankful for the opportunity to leave the closet behind.

He moves his hand from my elbow to my hand and pulls me after him, leading the way back through the bathroom. "That, and I want to give *Pappoús* and *Giagiá* the gift I got. They're going to love it."

Chapter Twenty-Four

Low Tide
Bri

My mouth feels like the Sahara Desert. I smack my lips together to try and activate my salivary glands, but they remain stubbornly dormant. I remember placing a glass of water on my bedside table right before succumbing to the exhaustion of the last twenty-four hours. Now I just need to wake up enough to locate it.

After arriving home to the empty apartment, my plan was to lay my head on the pillow for only a quick rest. But from what I can gather in my foggy state, I have been asleep for more than just a few minutes. I attempt to blink my eyes but see nothing but darkness, so I close them again and try to decipher what woke me in the first place.

Was Cassy home from dinner already? I strain to decipher if any noises are coming from inside the apartment, but all I hear is the wind whistling as it whips past my bedroom window. I have no clue what time it is. The only thing evident from my prone position under the covers is that I have slept through the last few hours of daylight and that the weather has taken on a more sinister mood.

I really should try and figure out what time it is. Through blurred vision, I reach one arm over to the nightstand and root around for my discarded phone, careful not to knock over my water cup. Once my fingers brush the smooth metal, I grasp it and bring it closer to my face.

I tap on the screen and instantly regret it. The light that assaults me is the equivalent of taking a flashlight straight to the eyes. My automatic reaction is to squeeze my eyes shut and angle the phone so it faces away from my pupils until they contract to the appropriate size.

Once recovered, I try again. The first thing I notice is the time stamp declaring it is now well past seven in the afternoon. The second is that I have at least three missed text messages. I quickly scroll through my phone, curious to see who I've missed connecting with while playing the part of sleeping beauty. It comes as no surprise that the first text is from Nick.

—Hey babe, meet me after dinner. Cassy, Parker, and I are heading to THE NEST. Need to board up. Where R U? I miss you. We can all hang out. I miss you. I could use extra hands boarding up (and for other things). Did I mention I miss you?—

I try to ignore my heart's flutter upon reading Nick's message. I'm still too groggy from my nap to process all my emotions. With so much to unpack between Nick and me, I can't possibly solve that puzzle right now. Deciding that procrastination is the most desirable option, I scroll to the following text. A message from the Marine Mammal Commission board requests information for the paperwork they need before I can receive the grant. I shoot off a quick answer and continue down the list. The final text is from Cassy.

—Change of plans for tonight. Nick needs help boarding up THE NEST and since I'm going to make him help me board up the café in the morning, I figured I'd

get ahead of the curve and just pay my penance tonight. Can you come? Having you with me would make it slightly more bearable. Oh, and Parker is here! It might be fun to hang out together—like old times—.

Like old times.

Before I can even process Cassy's request to meet up at THE NEST, flashes of Cassy, Parker, Nick, and I in high school parade through my mind. Grabbing burgers from Grease Burger after school and riding our beachcombers to the Municipal Beach. Is Cassy really naive enough to believe those events can be recreated? It's been years since we were that young and carefree, not to mention all in the same room at the same time.

After our senior year of high school—two years after everything fell apart for the Greene family—our four-leafed clover friendship crumbled like a wave washing over a sandcastle. I left for Eckerd, only coming home on the weekends. Parker left for the University of Miami to get his graduate degree in atmospheric science and Cassy and Nick were left here, broke and alone, to pick up the pieces of their shattered family. We were all forced to grow up. None of us are the same anymore. I can't possibly comprehend hanging out like the old times.

A ping comes from my phone, startling me from my thoughts. I glance at the screen.

—Don't overthink this. Just come and meet us.—

I laugh out loud into my empty room. This is why Cassy is my best friend. I don't know anyone in the world with whom I share this kind of telepathy. Following her directions, I obediently sit up, throw the covers to the side, and rotate so my legs dangle off the bed. As I wait for any lightheadedness to pass, I shoot off a quick text to Cassy,

—Fine, I'll meet you at THE NEST for a few hours of free labor.—

I make my way into the bathroom, intending to splash some water on my face, but as soon as I flip on the light, I am confronted with the little pink box I picked up earlier—and all that it represents.

The circle of life.

The result is one of nature's most rudimentary phenomena. For a species to be born, create a genetic replica of themselves, and leave behind indisputable proof they existed in the first place.

I study these miracles daily, from phytoplankton to marine mammals. But if it's the backbone of our species, why then do I feel nauseous at the mere vision of pink?

Never once, until this very moment, have I felt the elusive "biological clock" ticking inside me. And even now, I'm not confident it's the ticking clock I'm feeling. But rather a certain pulsing inside my body as adrenaline is released by intense fear, not a maternal yearning.

I try to control my rapidly increasing heart rate while contemplating what a positive result would mean. It would mean the responsibility of keeping another human being alive. A tiny entity that would rely on me to feed, bathe, love, and keep it safe. It would mean any semblance of my independence would be gone. A baby would forever link me to an endless stream of car seats, baby food, diapers, play dates, homework, and after-school activities.

I step forward and place my hands on the counter, not daring to pick up the box. As I avoid the mirror in front of me and stare at the accusing piece of cardboard, I search my memory for a reason or some traumatic event to connect me to my lack of maternal instincts. It would be so much easier if I had some obvious explanation for not having the desire to replicate my genetic code. But try as I might, I can't come up with a single justification.

I was blessed with a loving family. I'm a product of two well-adjusted, mature parents. High school teachers by profession, who were dedicated not just to each other but to me, their only daughter. Whose only crime was providing me with a comfortable life and encouraging my love for learning. There wasn't a book I couldn't ask for my parents wouldn't get for me. They always told me, "knowledge is power," and "science holds all the answers to what we humans seek to understand." If only they could give me a book to answer my concerns now.

At least they had each other when they were raising me—working as a tag team, they passed the baton seamlessly between work and life. I'm not so sure Nick and I will be able to recreate that kind of baton passing. I try to imagine Nick as a father. Nick, as the father of my child.

Is Nick the person I envision as the father of my child?

Images of Nick making the rounds late into the night at THE NEST invade my mind. But, him shaking hands with the guys and whispering secrets into the girl's ears that make them titter with laughter doesn't hold the same appeal as, say, the memories of my parents, sitting out on the back porch, in their rocking chairs, book in one hand, ice-tea in the other.

Nick might say he loves me, but does he love me enough to change his whole life? To put family first. As if he can sense me thinking about him, a text from Nick pings my phone, shocking me back into the present.

—Cassy says you're coming. I'll text you when we leave Auntie C and you can meet us at THE NEST. Thank you—

I take a deep breath and try to clear my mind of my earlier thoughts. Without the answers the little pink box can provide me, there isn't any reason for me to be lingering on "what ifs." And since I obviously don't have time to find out now, I pick up the box between my finger and thumb and place it inside the medicine cabinet. I close the mirrored door on the cabinet and regard my reflection staring back at me.

"Don't look at me like that. I'll do it later. Besides, it's fine. It's all going to be okay." I tell myself, willing what I'm saying to be true. In some deep recesses of my consciousness, I'm hoping I'll have my answers once I see Nick again. So, I pick up my phone and send a reply.

—Thank your sister. She convinced me to come.—

Nick's response is immediate.

—Ah, so you're saying she's finally useful for something—

My frown muscles experience a momentary relief when I crack a smile at Nick's sarcasm seeping through the message.

—Ha ha. She's useful for a lot of things and you know it. Besides it sounds like you're getting her to do your boarding up so you're getting free labor all around. Let me know when you leave, and I'll meet you there.—

With renewed determination, I set down my phone, quickly brush my teeth, and comb my hair. Once deeming myself presentable, I turn my back to the mirror and turn off the light to the bathroom, closing the door on my little secret one more time.

Chapter Twenty-Five

Heed the Warning
Abigail

The sticky sweet smell of mixed cocktails combined with the sharpness of stale beer invades my nostrils as I traverse the catwalk from the bar's entrance to the serving counter. The familiar scent soothes my nerves and gives me a sense of home. Of course, this dive of a bar is no comparison to THE NEST, but it will do for now.

I pull the elastic band from my hair and shake it out, letting the tangled strands land on my shoulders in what I hope is a tousle of waves. I give my head a quick shake for good measure and catch sight of one of the many televisions dotting the walls. This one is turned to the non-stop hurricane coverage and evacuation warnings that are doing nothing to deter the bar patrons from ordering another drink and hanging around a little longer.

I decide to follow everyone's lead and ignore the broadcast, instead focusing on why I came here in the first place, which is to become fully and entirely numb to my circumstances.

I'm entirely aware the amount of cash in my purse has not suddenly and magically multiplied. This means I will have to get creative and rely on some old tricks. For example, I've removed the engagement ring from my left hand. And if history serves me right, I should be able to get some lug at the bar to buy me a drink within the first five minutes of sitting down. All it should take is showing a little leg and twisting my hair around my finger.

With renewed determination, I scan the options at the bar, dismissing the tall blond picking his teeth with a toothpick. He can't be much over the age of twenty-one, and while he would most likely be a willing participant, there is no guarantee he can cover our combined tab. The dark-haired guy with two empty beer flasks in front of him is most likely too far gone to be of any use to me. I keep scanning until I settle my sights on a tall, dark, and handsome guy seated to the left of the bar. He is nursing a beer and leaning one elbow on the counter in front of him. Dressed in a business suit, he has loosened his tie and undone his shirt's top button—the universal signal of relaxed and open for conversation.

My cheeks tighten into a smile when I spy the empty stool next to him. But I've only taken two steps in pursuing Mr. Perfect when I feel somebody grab my wrists and place something smooth in my hand. With a start, I look down and realize I'm holding a twenty-dollar bill. I follow the hand attached to my wrist and look up to see a man staring at me.

"Hey, darlin', if you're headed to the kitchen, can you grab me another one of those hurricane drinks? Keep the change," he slurs through yellowish-white teeth before turning back to the table full of his companions, all similarly dressed in jeans and t-shirts, as they had just come in off the boats.

I look from the man down to the money and back up to the man. Could it seriously have been so easy? I mean, it's not my fault this half-wit assumes I work here. But, on the other hand, if he's so ready to hand out cash blindly, who am I to deny him? A smile creeps onto my face. "Coming right up."

I start to leave when my gaze travels to the front window. Catching sight of the Mercedes, visible from inside the bar, I pause to study the vehicle. I had angled it in the nearest parking space to the window before I left. Fluffing up clothes around Riley in the backseat, so if anyone tried to look in the back window, they would see a messy backseat but nothing else.

Twenty bucks won't get Riley and me very far, but it is a start. Deciding to press my luck, I return to the table, "Can I get anything for anyone else?"

One guy holds up another twenty, so I can pluck it from his grasp with my thumb and forefinger. "I'll take one too."

I nod as I palm the cash and point my shoulder toward the bar. "I'll be right back with those."

I scurry away from their table before they can say anything else, glancing over my shoulder as I stuff the forty dollars into my purse.

I make my way toward the bar, watching to ensure the men have returned to their conversation before veering to the left and heading toward the open bar stool.

Still wanting the drink I came here for, and emboldened by my recent windfall, I take the seat next to Mr. Perfect and order a mojito from the bartender. Mr. Perfect gives me a curious glance but doesn't comment when I give him my most seductive smile.

"Hey." I try again.

"Hey." He replies, this time turning his body toward me on his stool, which I interpret as an invitation.

I'm about to ask him if he comes here often when a slender hand wraps around his shoulder from behind. Mr. Perfect reaches up and touches the long fingers caressing his chest, continuing to rotate in his chair, revealing a perfect pert blonde standing behind him.

"Hi, love, have you been waiting long?" she purrs, addressing Mr. Perfect.

"You know I'd wait all day for you," he says, echoing her purr.

I'm about to throw up in my mouth from their public display of perfection when Mr. Perfect's new companion glances my way. I know as soon as she locks eyes with me that she recognizes me. And when she risks a quick sneak at the television, the one tuned to the Hollywood entertainment channel, my suspicions are confirmed.

"I know you," she says, coming closer to me while still leaving her hand on her companion's shoulder. "You're Abigail Mendez."

"No, I think you must be mistaken," I reply, which causes her to tilt her head to the side. "I'm Abigail Hernandez." I don't bother to correct her about Mendez being Julian's last name. And I really don't want to explain how it will never be mine.

But just as I think I've put a pin in the conversation, Mrs. Perfect lets out a little squeal and points at the television. "No, I was right. It is you!"

I follow her finger, pointing at the screen, and sure enough, a high-definition image of my face, taken from one of the Miami Sting Ray games and showing every pore and imperfection, is staring back at me. I'm dressed in Julian's jersey and cheering for him as the clock counts down to the final seconds in the fourth quarter of the playoff game.

I'm rooted to my stool at the bar as I take in the image of my former self. A self that looked like I had it all from the outside. But, now that I really look at the image, I realize I was a shell of a person on the inside, trying my best to fit the mold of the football player's wife. Only, at what cost? I gave up all my independence only to have it all backfire in my face.

"So, what are you doing here?" Mrs. Perfect asks, shaking me out of my trance and bringing me back to the room.

What *am* I doing here? I don't have to think about the answer for too long. I'm doing what I always do. I'm running from my responsibilities, drowning them in liquid courage. Or rather, in this case, I'm just trying to drown. I'm perpetuating the cycle my life has been on for the past seven years. And look where it has gotten me. Even though I have yet to take one sip of alcohol, my head feels like it's a top spinning across a concrete floor, thoughts swirling around at warp speeds. I can't do this anymore. I have to start taking care of myself and Riley. No one else is going to be taking care of us. It has to be me, and I can't take care of us if I am drunk and hitting on a random guy in some dive bar.

All of a sudden, I can't get out of here fast enough. Not bothering to respond to Mrs. Perfect, I reach into my purse, intending to leave one of the twenty-dollar bills on the bar to cover my tab, when my fingers brush against something hard with sharp edges. It takes me less than a second to remember what I had taken from the café yesterday. My fingers wrap around the key just as my brain wraps around a single thought.

Shelter.

Chapter Twenty-Six

All Hands-on Deck
Claudia

I glance around the table as I take a bite of my baked cod soaked in a creamy white wine sauce and am pleased both by the tang on my tongue and the captive audience I have created by reminiscing about the movie nights we used to have here at the house out on the pool deck, a memory we all shared together.

"I still remember your tiny little toes wiggling as you sat in your moms' laps and munched on popcorn— all of us sitting under the balmy summer sky. The three of you would giggle and laugh until it grew dark, and a million stars would be twinkling above us. Then you would each fall fast asleep, the soft breeze stirring the palm leaves and creating nature's lullaby."

I glance around the table, filled with my family, and I can't help but feel a sense of satisfaction wash over me. I smile as my eyes involuntarily dart from Parker to Cassandra who is seated next to him.

Dressed in Betty's favorite caftan, Casandra resembles a blushing angel. "You look just like your grandmother. Beautiful, just as she was." I blurt out, causing all eyes in the room to focus on Betty's reincarnation sitting across the table from me, who blushes red from the sudden attention.

"Thank you," she mumbles and takes a sip of her

wine.

"She would always do her hair up in a bun. Bright red ringlets would fall out, framing her face. She was simply luminous. Just as you are illuminated now." I continue, completely aware of the conversation I have halted by falling into my reminiscent ways. "She had the same coloring as you do."

I smile at the memory Cassandra has conjured up in my head. Betty always claimed her hair had been her gift to Cassandra and Nicholas, implying that the children's genetics were purely her doing, despite the generation separating them. Cassandra, aware of this link to her grandmother, has always taken considerable pride and care of her own tresses, keeping her hair long and natural.

"Thanks, Auntie. I miss her."

"As do I. Every day." I take a bite of my *Spanakorizo*, savoring the flavors of lemon and dill before chewing and swallowing.

Nicolas, impartial to emotions, and his sister's attraction, brings the conversation back to the topic at hand. "Those movie nights are one of my favorite memories of growing up here."

"Me too," Cassandra agrees with her brother. "It is one of the things I miss most…" A darkness covers her lovely features for a fraction of a second before she shakes her head and continues. "We should do them again sometime."

"I'd love that," I say kindly, assuming she is remembering the reason we stopped recreating the family movie nights.

"That is lovely idea, *Agápi mou*. But we might have to postpone those plans of yours," Benedict says, cutting into the conversation.

I look at him quizzically as he nods his head in the direction of the terrace just outside the closed French doors. Patio lights blow back and forth illuminating the dark courtyard in dancing shadows, providing pulsating light for the multiple staff who are bustling around, moving the potted florae and furniture into the pool house so they don't become projectiles in the storm.

Nicolas, taking notice of the change in weather, turns to Parker. "We were just saying earlier how you're probably going to be busy, with this storm coming our way and all."

Parker's eyes lock onto my own as he addresses his comment to Nicolas. "You can't even imagine. The station is letting me off the hook for tonight, but I'll be right back in the studio early tomorrow."

"Are you going to be doing any 'live at the scene' reporting?" Nicolas asks in a faux reporter voice.

Parker breaks eye contact with me and chuckles as he turns to Nicolas. "I sure hope so. When a storm like this comes through, it's all hands-on deck in the studio. You know what I mean?"

"Isn't there some kind of saying, 'only the crazy ones go out in the storm'?" Benedict interjects from beside me.

"Oh, Parker darling, please do be safe. I don't like any of this 'being crazy' nonsense."

Parker slides his hand across the table and takes my hand in his. They are large but callus-free, and his nails are clean and trimmed. "*Giagiá,* I'll be safe, but honestly, I'm more concerned about you and *Pappoús,*" He turns to face Nicolas and Cassandra. "And you guys."

I can't help but notice Cassandra duck her head as

she says, "we'll be fine."

Parker's mouth twitches into a half frown. "You say that, but I happen to know they are going to start broadcasting recommendations for Zone A evacuation in just a few short hours." Parker re-directs his attention back to Benedict and me. "Why don't I call Dad. I'm sure he'd love to have you visit him in New York. You could pop in on the flagship store while you're up there."

I shake my head at him, his words sounding all too familiar.

"Really? Won't you even consider leaving? I don't understand what the big deal is. It'd be like a little vacation for you. A quick trip to New York, I'm sure the team would love to see you. You'll be back as soon as this whole thing blows over."

Nicolas snorts next to Parker and claps him on the back. "Blows over. That's a good one. Did you make that up right now, or is that one of those meteorologists' jokes you guys tell?"

Parker looks at Nicolas out of the corner of his eye, only managing a half-smile. "Uh, just came up with it, I guess."

"Nice, nice," Nicolas says and bites into the *Galaktobureko*, the crispy filo dough cracking between his teeth and leaving a spot of custard on the corner of his mouth. "Mmm, oh man, this is good."

I smile at Nicolas—happy he is enjoying his food.

"*Pappoús,* what do you think?" Parker says, doing his best to engage Benedict into joining his side of the argument. "You know she's stubborn, right?"

Benedict clears his throat and takes a sip of his wine before starting. "I know you take your job seriously, son, and I think that is great. You should. But you have to remember, your *Giagiá* and I have been through dozens of storms, maybe even two dozen in all our time living here, and we've always managed. We've only evacuated once, and that was for Hurricane Irma, a category four."

"And thank goodness you did. That was one of the worst storms ever to hit the East coast of Florida." Parker says.

Benedict shakes his head in the negative. "You might say that, but honestly, it was just a hassle. We had to pack up everything, let the staff go, find accommodations, and in the end, this house was still standing. A few downed fences, a little water damage, but we ended up surviving just fine. I'm just not feeling it this time. I think if your *Giagiá* wants to stay…" Benedict turns to me, smiles, and shrugs his shoulders. "We stay."

"It was more than just a little water damage." Parker, in an unusual show of defiance and disrespect, rolls his eyes at the table.

"Parker, that is enough," I say, growing tired of his implicit insults. "Besides, I'm not going to be convinced it's so imperative to leave while you are still here, storm chasing, as you say."

Parker sighs and purses his lips together, seeming to want to say something but thinking better of it. Instead, he turns to Cassandra and Nicolas.

"Well, you guys will be evacuating, right?"

Cassandra and Nicolas stop chewing and glance at each other. I silently snicker to myself. Parker is about to be rebuffed for a third time tonight.

Cassandra swallows her mouthful and wipes her hands on her napkin before finally responding. "Not exactly."

"What? You can't be serious?" Parker dips his chin at her like he thinks she's crazy.

"Well, you know. If Auntie and Uncle B are planning to stay…" She looks at me, and I nod at her in support of her decision. "…Besides, Nick and I don't really have anywhere to go." She turns to her brother and bites her lower lip.

Nicolas nods in agreement. "Sorry, dude, our businesses are here, our life is here. Not planning on leaving."

I watch Parker closely, to see just how dejected my grandson is feeling right now. I know he only wants what he thinks is best for us, but I also know we will be perfectly safe in this house if we stay. There is no reason to leave.

I clap my hands together. "*Arketa*, that is enough. Your *Pappoús* and I invited you here to celebrate and enjoy dinner with us. Let us leave this conversation for later." I survey the table. "Now, what can we do to bring this party back to life?"

Parker clears his throat. "Well, if you're sure I can't talk some sense into you guys—"

"You can't," I say pointedly, ending that conversation.

"Fine. Fine. Then how about you open this?" Parker digs into his jacket pocket and produces a thick envelope, which he hands across the table to Benedict.

"What's this, son?"

"Go on and open it." Parker nods to Benedict. "I did my homework, and it turns out, on the fifty-fifth wedding anniversary, it is traditional to gift the couple emeralds."

I touch the necklace Benedict gifted me, and I'm about to protest, but Benedict rips into the envelope with abandon before I can say anything.

"Tickets." Benedict declares as he starts to thumb through the packet of papers. "To the Emerald Isle."

Parker smiles broadly, clearly proud of himself. "I thought it could be a chance for both of you to relax. Get away for a while and really enjoy each other's company."

It takes a moment of processing before an understanding of Parker's words dawns on me. He is gifting Benedict and me a trip. An obligation to leave, to travel away from Palm Beach. With his gift Parker intends for us to take an adventure—away from the safety of our home.

As the information permeates further, my breath becomes thinner. My chest is tight and the walls surrounding our once pleasant meal are starting to close in around me. Benedict's profession of appreciation hits my ears as a muffled garble of words that don't make sense. How can Benedict be in support of this idea?

"Parker?"

"Yes, *Giagiá?*" He smiles at me, no doubt, waiting for my own profession of gratitude.

"We can't possibly accept this."

"Oh, *Giagiá* you don't have to worry. Since my promotion at the station I can afford this. It's not a hardship on me at all."

"That's not what I meant, darling," I say, trying to come up with an excuse for not being able to accept his gift. "You know I can't leave. I have too many responsibilities, what with the business, and…and…" I trail off desperately racking my brain for another reason that would make perfect sense as to why Benedict and I must stay put and not leave.

Benedict, now fully engrossed in the packet, starts

listing the itinerary. "Two tickets to Ireland, a driver, a stay at the five-star Ashford Castle overlooking the shores of Lough Corrib." He raises his eyes to glance appreciatively at Parker before continuing. "Planned tours, golf, spa, Michelin restaurants." Benedict turns to me and my heart sinks. "Wow, this sounds amazing."

Parker, sensing the opportunity, chimes in. "*Giagiá,* I just wanted you to have a taste of what life could be like if you took some time to focus on each other. This is my gift to both of you." Parker turns to Benedict. "You should have a chance to enjoy life. Travel the world together. You've worked so hard to get to where you are. I just think it's important you get a chance to appreciate it."

"Claudia, I do think we can make this work. The business can survive without you for a little while. It has before. And I don't have any cases that need my attention at the office except for the one you have me working on. Our grandson is just trying to give us a gift. A generous one at that." Benedict stares at me with a look he reserves for when he wants to make his point made. "I believe the proper thing to do in this situation is to tell him thank you." He softens his stance before adding, "Besides, don't you want to take an adventure with me? I know I'm ready to take one with you." He reaches out and encloses my hand in his, speaking softly, "And I wouldn't mind if we kept taking adventures. Don't you think it's time to start getting out and seeing the world again?"

"No, I don't." I remove my hand from Benedict's, and his face falls at the very same time my heart shatters.

Chapter Twenty-Seven

Early Gusts
Cassy

Across from me, tears glisten in Auntie Claudia's eyes as she regards Uncle Benedict's bewildered face. Her breaths are coming in fast, shallow spurts, causing her chest to quiver in an effort to breathe normally. Auntie Claudia is the rock of our family—the one who always remains levelheaded and in control of her emotions to get problems solved. So, when I notice her hands are also starting to shake, it takes me a minute to realize why Auntie Claudia is acting so differently. She is showing signs of the beginning of a panic attack.

Since the accident, I've suffered my fair share of panic attacks, sneaky little buggers that come on slowly, only to consume my entire being within minutes. It's the reason Auntie Claudia got me Bo. He can detect when I'm about to have one and can stop the attack before it has a chance to progress. I have yet to figure out the exact trigger for my panic attacks, but I do know that this dinner will take a disastrous turn if I don't change the current conversation's direction.

"Hey!" I practically shout, causing everyone at the table to jump in surprise. The fire builds up my neck as Parker, and everyone else turn to stare at me in unison.

I clear my throat and try again, this time keeping my voice at a more acceptable decibel. "Um, it's just we brought a gift too." I gesture to Nick and myself. "Hold on one minute." I glance at Auntie Claudia before making a hasty exit from the dining room and into the hallway. Once I'm alone, I take a moment to calm my nerves before gathering the square box covered in gold wrapping paper into my arms. It's a large box, so I must raise my chin not to smash the gold bow attached to the lid.

Affixing a genuine smile, I re-enter the dining room and head toward the table where I set the gift down between Uncle Benedict and Auntie Claudia.

"This is from Nick and me. Like Parker, we also wanted to do something for the two of you on your special day. It's not quite a trip to the Emerald Isles, but we hope you like it all the same."

I am relieved when I notice Auntie Claudia's breathing has returned to a regular rate, and her hands no longer shake as she wordlessly lifts the lid off the box. The four remaining sides float gracefully to the table, revealing a golden oak tree sculpture. Perched upon a slab of rough marble, the tree stands a foot tall, and in the glow of the candlelight, it gleams as if it's lit from within.

Auntie Claudia clasps her hand to her mouth. "Oh, Cassandra." She removes one of her hands and reaches out to grasp my arm. She squeezes it, and I know I've succeeded in shifting her mood. "It is simply perfect, *Agápi mou.*"

"I'm so glad you like it," I say, turning to Uncle Benedict, who has moved on seamlessly from the earlier conversation and is now inspecting the tree closer. "It's a family tree," I explain.

"Oh yes, I see that." Benedict squints and moves his

nose even closer to the tree. "It's wonderful. I'm just trying to decipher what it is that's on these leaves."

"Names, Dear." Auntie Claudia touches the paper-thin gold leaves, turning them over. The smooth gold slips easily between her fingers. "See, this one says *Andrew*."

I reach between Auntie Claudia and Uncle Benedict and point to the leaves closest to the top. "There are leaves for each family member, starting with the both of you."

Auntie Claudia leans in, inspecting the inscription of *Claudia* and *Benedict* engraved in fine gold.

"There's a leaf for your son, Andrew, his wife Joanna." I continue touching each leaf as I talk. "Below that is a leaf for your grandchild." I point to a leaf in the middle and look up. "Parker, that's your leaf."

"Awesome." Still seated across the table, Parker stands and moves closer to where we are all gathered. "Let me see that."

He slides in next to Auntie Claudia, scooting me out of his way. "Hey, you're right. There I am."

I roll my eyes but feel encouraged when Auntie Claudia smiles, indulging Parker's ego, and says, "Of course you are, dear." She touches his arm before turning my way again. "Go on *Agápi mou*."

I make my way through the rest of the tree, pointing out other cousins and more distant relatives before pausing and pointing to a branch coming off the side of the tree, not connected to the other branches. "I hope you don't mind, but I took the liberty of adding a branch for Betty." I bite my lip and look at Uncle Benedict. "I know we aren't related by blood or marriage, but—" I pause and scan the faces surrounding the table, finally locking eyes with Auntie Claudia. "Well, you were like a sister to our grandmother and to us, you're family."

The emotions the tree has evoked are unmistakable on Auntie Claudia's face, but before she can say anything, Uncle Benedict pushes his chair back and stands, enveloping me in his arms, hugging my body close to his. "Of course, you're family. You and Nicolas belong on that tree just as much as anyone else."

"Thanks, Uncle B.," I murmur against his chest before extracting myself from his grasp. I try to play it cool, but Auntie Claudia notices as I wipe a stray tear from my eye.

I sniff, clearing away the moisture, and turn back to the tree, "So, there's Betty and our mom, and then there's Nick and me." I point out the last few leaves, not lingering over mine or Nick's.

"Cassandra, my heart is full. Thank you." Auntie Claudia turns to Nick. "And thank you," she says, adding him to her appreciation.

"You're welcome. I knew you'd like it, didn't I, Cassy?" Nick says, causing me to raise one eyebrow in dismay.

"Yeah, right. Something like that."

"Oh, how I wish Betty could be here to celebrate with us and see this lovely gift. She would have been so proud of how the two of you turned out." Auntie Claudia says. I watch as she turns into herself for the second time tonight, caught up in her own thoughts. "If only life had been kinder to you children." She pauses and shakes her head. "I'll never forgive myself for what I did."

I'm about to interject and remind Auntie Claudia that the only thing she did was save our lives by taking the two of us in after our parents died.

But before I can say anything, Uncle Benedict says, "You could have never known introducing Betty to Ernie would end up the way it did." He wraps an arm around Auntie Claudia's shoulders, creating a tiny bubble of privacy between them.

It takes a few seconds to process the significance of Uncle Benedict's words, and even as I think I understand them, I'm not entirely sure I do. "What did you just say?" I ask, conscious that I'm breaking into their moment but wanting to ensure I haven't misunderstood.

Auntie Claudia and Uncle Benedict look up with a start like they have been pulled abruptly from some kind of trance, only to notice three bewildered young faces staring at them for the first time.

"Oh, no. It was nothing *Agápi mou*." Uncle Benedict says, standing up and stiffening his posture as though he can erase what he just said with a taller stature.

"No…You said Auntie Claudia was the one who introduced Ernie to Betty." I turn to Auntie Claudia, "but you've never told us that. Did you? Did you introduce them?"

Nick and Parker observe the exchange between me and Auntie Claudia and Uncle Benedict like they are watching a tennis match, their heads shifting back and forth. But I notice the second the dawning of understanding lights Nick's eyes as he observes our conversation.

"Darling, that was not a piece of information we felt was important to disclose at the time. You were both so young and fragile. The only thing you needed at the time was stability. We saw no need to complicate things for you further." Auntie Claudia says, rising out of her chair and stepping toward me.

But before she can get closer, I take a step back. Hurt shines in her eyes as I keep the distance between us, but I need space to understand this new piece of information. Information Auntie Claudia has been keeping a secret all these years. All the years I've spent trying to put the puzzle pieces of the accident together.

Years of therapy and discussions of depression start to swirl my thoughts around, making it hard to think straight. "You lied to us," I say, looking up at Auntie Claudia, whom I've idolized for the past decade.

"No, *Agápi mou*. We did not lie. We omitted a piece of information that wasn't pertinent at the time. There is a difference."

"Actually, I don't think there is a difference. Not telling Nick and me that you were the catalyst for everything that happened to our family is not just an omission of a fact. It's the omission of the truth." I pause and close my eyes as flashes of the past race across my memory. It was December, and I was excited about the upcoming winter holiday. I had rushed home to pack for our vacation from school when our dad sat Nick, Mom, and me all down at the table and, with shaking hands, explained to us he had lost our family's entire savings. He, along with a thousand other investors, had been the victim of a Ponzi scheme. He had explained how he had invested our family's money with someone who lived here in Palm Beach, how he had been assured over and over again that this was a safe investment that would garner unbelievable returns. I remember Dad slamming his fist down on the table, making us all jump, and saying, "Unbelievable is right!" before breaking into tears. I had never seen my dad cry like that, and it scared me. But as I learned later, I had a right to be scared because our life was never the same after that day.

"Wait a minute, Cassy," Nick says, breaking into my thoughts and returning me to the present. "Let's give them a chance to explain." Nick looks at Auntie Claudia and Uncle Benedict almost pleadingly. "There's an explanation, right?"

Parker, Nick, and I turn and wait for Uncle Benedict or Auntie Claudia to answer, but when Auntie Claudia opens her mouth and then closes it again, I know she has nothing she can say to defend her actions. And just like that, the pedestal I placed her on topples over and shatters into a million pieces.

"I have to go." I turn toward the hallway and tell Nick, "Get your keys. We're leaving." I don't bother to pause as Auntie Claudia calls after me to stay, begging Nick and me to give her a chance to explain everything. Unfortunately, nothing she can say now can change the past or her part in it.

Chapter Twenty-Eight

On Your Own
Abigail

The air conditioning of the G-wagon hums and blows a stand of hair across my forehead, but I don't bother to brush it away. Instead, I let my auburn waves dance in the artificial breeze as I stare straight ahead into the dark, deserted street.

It's hard for me to comprehend that I was walking up and down this very road, shopping without a care in the world, just a few days ago. Laughing and chatting with Suzy and the others, our hardest decision of the day was where to stop for happy hour. How could I have known I would be back here, wishing for the opportunity to go back in time and re-do everything?

Giving my head a quick shake to snap me out of my reverie, I reach into my purse and pull out the key that has been sitting in the bottom of my bag all this time. Pinching the key between my thumb and finger, I allow my eyes to gaze upon the shiny piece of silver metal in front of me.

My breath catches in my chest, and for one horrific moment, I think I might cry from a mixture of relief and sorrow. But, if I start crying right now, sitting in the SUV, it won't be a little damsel in distress kind of cry. No, it will be the kind of body-shaking, sobbing, soul-sucking type of cry that will take me under. And as tempting as it is to give in to the notion of giving up, I don't have time for that kind of self-pity right now.

I lift my gaze to the rear-view mirror, where Riley is still asleep on the folded-down seats. The realization that Riley's future is now solely in my hands sends a shiver up my arm. Or maybe it's from the air-conditioning? It's hard to tell which of my senses are firing through my fog. What am I going to do? I can barely care for myself on a good day. And now it looks like Riley and I only have bad days ahead.

I don't realize how hard I'm gripping my hands until I unfurl my fist, and a red imprint is burned into my palm in the shape of the key. The key is the answer to at least two of my current problems—food and shelter.

Not letting myself have second thoughts, I gather a change of clothes for Riley and me and stuff them into the duffle bag with shaky hands. I grab the bag and my purse and throw them over my shoulder before exiting the SUV. Once in the street, I round to the Mercedes' back and open the tailgate with the button on the key fob, leaning over the edge of the bumper into the G-wagon and gathering Riley into my arms. She is only half my size, but I still struggle to lift her body.

"*Mamá?*" Riley's eyes are still closed, and the word comes out slurred.

"Shh, baby. *Mamá's* got you." My whispered words do what I hoped they would, and she wraps her arms and legs around my body, making it easier to lift her.

Using one leg, I shut the back door and press the fob button to lock the Mercedes. Then, keeping my head ducked, I carry Riley across the street and to the side door of the Flamingo Café.

My hands are sweaty, and I'm afraid I will drop the

key on the ground. I try to steady my breath and nerves as I slip the key into the lock. A "click" sounds through the silence surrounding us as the lock is released and the door drifts open.

Glancing to the right and left, I slip through the door, locking it behind us and shutting out the light from the sidewalk.

It takes a moment for my eyes to adjust to the darkness inside the café. Re-adjusting Riley in my arms, I try to gain my bearings. Without the customers' bustle or the coffee machine's hiss, the café seems hollow and empty. I glance left to where the winding staircase leads to the veranda Riley and I had patronized only two days ago. But I don't let my gaze rest there for too long because I remember there is an alcove past the stairs, a few feet beyond the coffee stand, made to resemble a comfy library, complete with a pink velvet couch and leather chairs.

I head in that direction, careful not to disturb Riley as I go. It's not until I have deposited the duffle bag and my purse on the leather chair and laid Riley down on the pink velvet couch that I allow myself to comprehend what I have done. Breaking and entering is right on up there with "things you can get arrested for." I could go to jail for this.

I lie down behind Riley and gather her into my arms, running my hand over Riley's hair, repeating the motion over and over. I tell myself it's Riley I'm soothing, but the tears eventually break free, silently streaming from my eyes, blurring my vision of the neon pink flamingo in the window.

Chapter Twenty-Nine

Batten down the Hatches
Bri

"Hello?" I pause and wait for a response as I enter the seductive interior of Nick's pristine nightclub. An establishment I rarely visited in the past, only showing up to partake in the occasional get-together with Cassy on a rare night she felt like staying up late. But over the last year, THE NEST has become more familiar to me as I've met up with Nick in the dark hours of the night, feeling the safety of our secret in the absence of daily activity.

Nick texted me just a few minutes ago and let me know that dinner was over early, and I should come to meet them here, but as I pass the hostess stand and proceed farther into THE NEST, silence is the only greeting I receive. A soft orange glow lights up the back of the bottle display wall, casting moody shadows over the plush velvet VIP couches, revealing an empty bar and dance floor.

"Hello?" I swerve toward the left and call out again as I make my way onto the open-air patio.

"Bri! Over here!" Cassy, dressed in her work uniform and standing with Parker, breaks from what looks to be a deep conversation. Her face, previously serious with frown lines, breaks into a slight smile as she waves at me from the far corner of the waterfront porch.

I wave back and head in their direction. A salty breeze from the Atlantic blows my hair across my face, obscuring my vision so I don't notice the pile of artifacts I trip over en route to Cassy. I stumble and catch myself, regaining my balance quickly.

"Careful!" Cassy calls to me. Using the same tone she does every time she perceives me as being distracted and clumsy.

Irritation bubbles up at Cassy's automatic assumption that I'm to blame for my misstep. Waving her off, I don't bother with a response as I right myself and resume my path. As I move closer, I notice teak tables, wicker sectionals, and several other objects not physically built into the concrete porch have already been stacked to the side, waiting to be taken in and out of the storm. I grab an oversized lantern and add it to the next pile.

"Wow, you guys move fast," I say, looking over Cassy's shoulder at the remaining furniture. The gently swaying Malia Hanging Daybeds have already been stripped of their luxurious pillows and cushions, as have the built-in bench seats.

"Well, it helps when you have an extra set of hands." Cassy nods toward Parker.

"And now you have two more." I surrender my hands, palms up, as my gaze glides over to Nick, who is across the patio, lifting one of the day beds over his shoulder like it's as light as a feather. I watch in ardor as he ferries it through the open-air lounge and to the bar's back wall. My attention is brought back to the patio when Parker coughs into his fist, and I realize belatedly that I have been staring.

To cover my indiscretions, I fling open my arms.

"Parker, long time no see," I say, and to my delight, Parker walks right into them without a hint of hesitation, giving me the kind of hug only found when two lifelong friends are reunited.

"Hey there, kiddo. Long time."

"Who you calling kiddo? You do realize you're only three months older than me, right?" I laugh and hug him back.

"Is that all? I could have sworn I was at least five years more mature than you."

I give a mock gasp of offense and pull away to sock him in the arm.

Parker lets out a wounded "ow" and rubs his arm where I punched him, causing me to reach out and stroke the affronted spot in apology.

"What now? Can't I leave you alone for one minute without the ladies hitting on you? Oh, wait, not hitting on you, just hitting you." Nick says as he approaches us, stopping to stand between Parker and me in a clear demonstration of male territorial dominance. He is so close I can feel the heat of his body on my arm. I immediately glance at Cassy and am relieved when I see she is too preoccupied to notice her brother's testosterone-induced preening.

Taking a step to the side, I deliberately increase the space between Nick and me. His face falls as I place enough distance between us to quell what I can only perceive as an inferno burning in the open space. But as Nick continues to stare at me, a glint of something else, mischief maybe, replaces any injured ego he may have suffered as he says, "Now, you can't be beating this guy up." Then, as if taking it all in stride, Nick brushes past me and throws a sweaty arm around Parker. "He has to be presentable for the camera tomorrow. No bruising allowed."

Able to think clearly again now that Nick is not invading my personal space, I smile playfully at Parker. "I wouldn't dream of defacing a national treasure."

Nick narrows his eye and curls his lips into a pout. "Now, I'm not sure I would go that far. He's just the weather guy."

Parker, the brunt of another joke, decides he's had enough and slips out of Nick's grasp, but not before reaching out and mussing Nick's red hair. "Hey, at least I have a respectable job. I don't just hang around and take shots all day." Parker takes a step back as Nick lunges for him. But Parker isn't fast enough, and Nick grabs Parker, attempting to put him into a head lock. Cassy and I look on, watching the boys wrestle like they are back in grade school, until Nick finally gives up and let's go of Parker.

I roll my eyes at the immaturity of the two boys before turning to Cassy, intending to ignore Nick and Parker until they can act like adults again.

"So, how was dinner?" I ask, focusing my question on Cassy. But as soon as I ask the question, I realize it is the wrong one because, within seconds, somber faces replace the carefree moments of before.

Before anyone can answer my question and shed some light on the sudden mood shift, Nick clasps Parker on the back and says, "I still need to close the accordion wall and nail some CDX plywood over the glass to protect it from the wind and flying debris. Give me a hand so that we can seal this place up."

The guys turn to leave, but Nick calls out one more directive as he moves away. "Since us guys are going to focus on the heavy lifting. Why don't you ladies do a final sweep and ensure all the small objects are taken in? You know, lanterns," he points to the one I just added to the pile as an example. "Pots, cushions, anything else that will take flight in heavy wind."

Cassy nods in agreement. "Got it. We're on it."

She takes my arm and directs me to a seating pod where we gather more pillows.

"Okay, what was that all about?" I ask as I wait for Cassy to gather the tea candles off the built-in concrete tables and stand up so I can have her full attention.

When she finally looks at me, tears are gathering in the corners of her eyes.

"Oh my God, Cassy!" I reach out, take all the trinkets gathered in her arms and set them on the table before leading Cassy over to the built-in bench and sitting her down. I sit beside her, angled to see her face, our knees touching. "What's going on?"

"Dinner was a disaster," Cassy says, brushing away her tears as she stares at the table before us. "I left without letting Auntie Claudia explain, and now Nick's mad at me for being so reactive. But I don't see how she could say anything to make what she did any better."

I take Cassy's hand and nod along in encouragement because that seems to be what she needs right now, but I'm desperately hoping she will say something that will make me stop feeling like I'm taking a test from one of my Ekard classes without having read the book. I try to form a hypothesis of what she might be talking about in my head, but I'm still at a loss without some key details. So I ask, "And what was it that she did?"

"She introduced Betty and Ernie," Cassy says, as though this explains why she is in tears.

"Right, and that's bad because…" I trail off, waiting for Cassy to realize she still needs to explain more clearly.

Cassy shifts her gaze from the table and meets my eyes. She sees the question on my face because she sniffs, straightens up, and says, "Ernie Mastiff killed my parents."

I open my mouth to say something and then close it again. I wasn't there when the car accident happened, but I do know that the only two people in the car were Cassy and Nick's mom and dad. "I don't think—"I start, but Cassy cuts me off, already knowing what I'm about to say.

"He didn't cause the car accident. I know that. But they wouldn't have lost their entire life savings if my grandmother hadn't invested with him and convinced my dad to invest with him. My dad wouldn't have fallen into the deepest depression I've ever seen, and he wouldn't have thought ending his life and my mom's life by running his car into a telephone poll at seventy miles an hour was the only solution."

I take Cassy's hand in mine as tears run down her cheeks. I know how hard it is for Cassy to talk about her past and that reliving it now must be killing her. I look around for Bo but don't see him anywhere, so I turn back to Cassy and say as gently as I can, "I appreciate the circumstances of the accident are beyond tragic, but Cassy, your Auntie Claudia didn't cause the accident to happen. People introduce people to each other all the time. There is no way to know what the outcome of that would be. You can't blame her for something she didn't do."

Cassy wipes her tears away with the back of her

hand and then wipes them on her jean shorts. "I know that. That's not why I'm mad at her."

"It's not?"

"No, I'm mad at her because she kept it a secret all these years. Like she thought I was too weak to know the truth. I can handle the fact that she introduced them. You're right. She couldn't have known what would happen. But she lied to me, to Nick and me, for years. She kept a secret, and that's what hurts the most."

As Cassy is talking, I can't help but look over to where Nick and Parker are working to take the daybeds into the club's interior. "Sometimes people keep secrets to protect the people they love from getting hurt." I turn back to Cassy. "What if she was just trying to protect you?"

"I don't need to be protected. I'm an adult."

I look at Cassy, trying to decide if her declaration is indeed true. What if Claudia and I are doing the same thing? Keeping secrets from Cassy with the intention of not hurting her further. But in actuality, Cassy is much stronger than we give her credit for. After all, she did survive the death of her parents. Sure, she had support and still has the minor lingering issues of her panic attacks, but maybe we are tip-toeing around her too much. Perhaps she can handle more than I think she can. And if that's indeed the case, then I'm the one in the wrong for keeping a secret from her.

"I can't speak for your Auntie Claudia, but have you thought about the possibility that she was just keeping the secret out of love for you? You and Nick have been through so much. I can't see any other reason than her wanting to keep you from hurting anymore. I know you're an adult, but you were only children when you were forced to deal with the death of both of your parents."

Cassy slowly shakes her head like she can't let it go yet.

"I think you should talk to her again. Give her a chance to explain."

"I'll think about it."

I smile, knowing full well that Cassy will pretend to think about it, but in the end, she will give Claudia a chance to explain her side. I'm about to open my mouth and tell Cassy as much when Nick calls out from across the patio.

"All done out here, come on in, and let's have a pint together before this one here has to go back to work." Nick grabs Parker in a headlock and smiles like a goof, causing Cassy and me to laugh out loud, lightening the mood.

Cassy stands up, gathers the décor we set on the table earlier back into her arms, and heads toward THE NEST interior, where Nick and Parker just disappeared.

"Hey, how was Orlando? I totally forgot to ask." Cassy asks over her shoulder, clearly changing the subject and letting the other one rest.

"Successful!" I pronounce proudly.

"Nice. I knew you'd get the money."

"Thanks for believing in me." I joke but then remember something I know she'll be interested in. "Oh, and there's something else. You'll never believe it. I was at Sunoco gas station, and I ran into Abigail and Riley."

"Oh yeah?"

"Yeah, Riley spied me from across the aisle and came over to tell me that Abigail was taking her camping."

"Camping? You can't be serious. What is Abigail thinking?"

"Right?! That's what I thought too. But that's not the part I wanted to tell you about. I watched Abigail and Riley leave the store and get into their car, a black Mercedes. With tinted windows. The same car that almost ran me over yesterday."

Cassy stops short in front of me, and I almost walk into the back of her.

"What?!"

"I know. Can you believe it?"

"No way. Are you sure you didn't mistake it for another G-wagon? I mean, Palm Beach is crawling with those ostentatious vehicles."

"I'm positive. The car that drove away had the same Miami Sting Rays vanity plate as the one Abigail was driving."

"But that makes no sense. Why wouldn't Abigail stop to check on you? You're her daughter's camp counselor, for goodness sake."

"I know." I shrug my shoulders and keep walking past Cassy, who hurries to catch up as I enter the interior, now glowing with soft orange light from the bar. "I guess she's more of a bitch than I gave her credit for."

"You know, she was at the café past closing the other night. It doesn't make any sense. Why would she return to a place where she almost ran someone over?"

"And why would she stay so late?" I add.

"I have no idea, but next time I see her, I'm going to give her a piece of my mind," Cassy says, dropping her armful on top of another pile. "Only a crazy person runs someone over and then leaves the scene."

"*Almost* runs someone over." I hold up my index

finger, correcting Cassy on the details.

"Same difference," Cassy says, waving me off. "She's still crazy."

Chapter Thirty

Purple Skies
Cassy

"Who's crazy?" Nick asks as he walks behind Bri and me as we park ourselves on two stools. Rounding the counter so he stands across from us, Nick takes down four pint glasses and throws a towel over his left shoulder.

"None of your business," I say, pointing to the tap. "I'll take one of those, please."

"Make that two." Parker appears by my side, causing goosebumps to rise on my arms. As Nick pulls on the tap, skillfully filling a pint, Parker bends his head closer to mine and, in a low voice intended for my ears only, asks, "Hey, are you okay?"

Parker's concern touches me, but the last thing I want to do is re-hash the drama from tonight for a third time, so I give Parker what I hope is a genuine smile and say, "I think so."

Parker nods, accepting my response for what it is, and turns to take his pint from Nick—who, in true Nick fashion—is oblivious to what is happening around him and brings the conversation right back to tonight's dinner.

"I can't believe the way Auntie Claudia reacted to Parker's gift," Nick sets another beer at the bar, and I sigh in resignation as I take it from him, and he continues, "I mean, I'd take a free trip to Ireland any day."

"Ireland?" Next to me, Bri raises an eyebrow in puzzlement, so I quickly fill her in on the trip Parker gifted Auntie Claudia and Uncle Benedict and how they had each reacted to the gift so differently.

"I'd take a free trip any day of the week, too," Bri says thoughtfully. "But we don't travel the world for fashion shows like your aunt does. Maybe she's over it? I mean, I know narcolepsy is a big part of her life, and she's managed fine with it, but maybe she's just ready to relax and stay home."

There is logic in Bri's point, and I'm about to say as much, but Parker lets a puff of air out of his mouth, cutting me off as he says, "I do see your point, Bri, but that's the thing. She doesn't relax when she's at home. She's constantly working on the business. I want her to have a chance to take a break, a real one. Ya know?"

I think about the arguments Bri and Parker are each making and, in my head, try to reconcile it with my ebbing emotions of tonight. Auntie Claudia does indeed work an awful lot of hours, but I'm struggling to find the sympathy required to believe she has no control over the decisions she makes, in turn creating her own fate. But I don't get to think about it for too long because Nick changes the conversation on a whim as he reaches for the next glass, "Did you guys catch the sunset tonight?"

Bri interrupts him before he can pull on the tap, "Just water for me."

I catch the look Nick gives Bri before shrugging and placing a glass of water on the bar. Her fingers brush against his as she pulls the glass in front of her, and for a split second, I feel like I'm an outsider looking in, watching a silent conversation unfold before me. I tell myself I'm still tired from tonight's drama and let it go.

Once we are all served, Nick pulls a pint for himself, leaves the bar, and walks over to the DJ stand, where he flips on the sound system. "Summer in the City" by the Lovin' Spoonful starts blaring from overhead speakers.

"What was up with that color? I've never seen anything like it." Nick yells over the blaring music before turning the knob on the system, returning the volume to a more bearable decibel. With the music settled, Nick returns to the bar, where he slides onto a stool next to Bri.

"I love those sunsets," Parker says.

"Me too," I say, smiling at Parker before taking a sip of my ale, relieved the conversation has returned to a more benign topic. I'm about to comment on the purple explosion of color in the sky when Nick calls out, "Hey, Cassy, you got something there!" Nick points at his upper lip while Parker chokes on his beer, trying to stifle a laugh.

Feeling the blood rush to my face, I grab a napkin and wipe away the foam. "Real mature, you guys," I say to cover my embarrassment before abandoning my drink on the bar and hopping off my stool, suddenly in need of some space.

Blessedly, Parker resumes the conversation as he winks at me as I walk by him.

"I know. It was a wild violet sky tonight." He takes a perfectly spotless drink before continuing, "You know, the colors result from something called the Raleigh effect. It's when molecules and small particles in the atmosphere change the direction of light rays, causing them to scatter. Usually, only the longest wavelengths of light on the color spectrum are visible through the clouds—that's why sunsets often appear gold, pink, and orange." Parker takes another long drink before continuing, not bothering to check if we are still engaged in his explanation.

"Our eyes have limitations. They can't normally detect the violet wavelengths—the shortest on the spectrum—so the sky tends to appear blue because these waves are scattered in all directions." Parker spreads his hands and wiggles his fingers. "But hurricanes can bring a unique mixture of conditions which allow us to see the scattered violet light already present."

Parker looks at us all expectantly, but silence meets him, and his poise falters, "but that's probably just boring details to you guys. It was a cool color." He looks down at the wooden planks of the bar floor, and I can feel his unease as if it's my own.

"Are you kidding me? I love that stuff." I say, circling back to stand next to Parker.

"Yeah, me too." Bri chimes in from her stool. "You can riddle me with science trivia any day of the week. I mean, come on, you're really just speaking my language."

Our encouragement elicits a smile from Parker, and the room lights up again from the flash of his white teeth. "That's right. I forgot I was in a room full of nerds."

I smile, happy to have saved Parker from any embarrassment, but Nick, not feeling as gracious, balls up the towel over his shoulder and throws it at Parker's head before saying, "I only see three nerds in this room. Talk for yourselves. I have always been the stud of this group."

Parker ducks as the towel sails past his head, and before we know it, we are all laughing, talking over one another about who earned the outdated labels of nerd, jock, prep, and bad boy back in high school.

"Those were the days—when we were always together." Bri sighs as we wind down, and there is a natural lull in all the teasing. "I wish we could go back in time and relive it."

"I don't," I say, barely loud enough for anyone to hear as the unbidden memories of our last few years of high school sweep through my head. I close my eyes and take a deep breath, determined not to ruin this fun time for all of us. When I open them, Nick is staring at me. Etched across his face is a sadness he seldom displays.

But before I can say anything, Nick blinks at me and rearranges his face into his customary good cheer. I recognize this transformation as his way of pushing his feelings down, a talent he has perfected over the years, and I can't help but wonder how long he can keep ignoring his emotions before they erupt out of him.

With a firmly fixed smile, Nick walks over to Bri and throws an arm around her shoulders, playfully pulling her in for a side hug. "Hey, ignore her. I know what you were trying to say. We need to live for the moment. Enjoy the time we have together." He throws his other arm around Parker's shoulders, sandwiching himself between them. "We've missed you around here, buddy."

"We have." I agree, letting Nick's dismissal of me slide this time. I decide instead to focus on relishing the sight of my three best friends from childhood all together again, standing in front of me.

"I've missed you guys too," Parker says, directing his attention to Nick and Bri. "To tell the truth, it's lonely sometimes. I work crazy hours, which makes it a bit hard to have a social life." Then, he looks at me and adds, "Not that I've met anyone or anything."

I pinch my lips together, not daring to let myself hope or believe that Parker could have been thinking of me—in the same way I've been thinking of him—all this time we've been apart. Luckily, I'm saved from any unproductive internal debate when "Born to be Wild" by Steppenwolf comes through the speakers. Taking advantage of the chance to pump us up, Nick rushes to the DJ stand and turns up the volume.

It only takes us until the first chorus before we are all singing the lyrics and dancing around the room. By the time the refrain hits, we are yelling born to be wiiillddd at the top of our lungs, laughing, and jumping up and down in a circle.

I have to grab my knees to catch my breath when the song ends, and "I Don't Want to Miss a Thing" by Aerosmith starts up, instantly changing the atmosphere in the darkened nightclub yet again. Before she can protest, Nick grabs Bri's hand and starts waltzing her around the room in a grand display.

"Hey, who said I wanted to dance with you?" she laughs as Nick guides her expertly around the dance floor.

Nick pushes Bri out for a twirl and puts on a sad puppy dog face. "It's not like I can dance with my sister. You're my only option here, so get steppin'."

Bri laughs again and salutes Nick as she spins back into his arms. "Yes, sir."

"Now that's what I like to hear." Nick teases and continues his march across the floor. As they glide past Parker, Nick stage whispers, "Come on, man, get your game on, or can't you do the two-step?"

Parker scoffs at Nick, clearly accepting the challenge. Then, with a look of determination in his eye, Parker saunters across the floor and grabs my hand, practically pulling me along the dance floor as he calls out to Nick, "Well, I'm not as Fred Astaire as you are, but I think I can move a lady around a room."

Bri catches my eye, and we laugh at the same time. She winks at me, and I shrug my shoulders helplessly in return before refocusing on not stepping on Parker's feet as he whisks me to the other side of the room.

Once we are out of Nick and Bri's path, Parker slows his steps so I can catch up.

"I don't know. I think you're more Fred Astaire than you give yourself credit for," I say as Parker pulls me closer to him, and I have to readjust my arms, so they wrap around his neck.

"Well, *Giagiá* used to make me take dance lessons with her back in the day."

"You're kidding! I didn't know that."

"Yup, said I would need to know how to dance one day. I guess she knew what she was talking about."

"She usually does," I reply, confusion creeping in.

Parker regards my face and then bends his head down so his lips are close to my ear, causing heat to travel down my back and my knees to feel weak. "I meant what I said earlier. It's good to see you again. I've missed you."

I pull back so I can look up at him. I want to ensure I've heard him correctly, but I know I have when I see his eager face. "We've missed you too," I say.

Parker smiles down at me, and my knees almost buckle in response. He must realize my instability because he pulls me even closer to him, his body radiating heat. "I said, '*I've* missed *you*.' But then you said '*we've*' missed you." Parker pauses, his face dangerously close to mine. "But I want to know if *you* missed me, Cassy?"

My breath catches in my throat. Of course, I've missed him. I've watched him every day on television for the past five years missing him. Missing his laugh. Missing his friendship. Missing his familiarity, but most of all, missing what could have been between us. I wonder if Parker still thinks about the failed attempt at a kiss we shared after the accident—after my world caved in on itself and I lost the capacity to open my heart to love. But it's been eight years since that night and about half that time since I started to embrace emotions again. Could it even be possible that Parker has thought about that kiss as many times over the years as I have?

"Parker, I've—"I smash right into Parker's chest when he stops abruptly, avoiding a collision with Bri and Nick, who have waltzed their way over to our side of the room. "Ow." I pull back and rub my nose, where it collided with Parker's clavicle.

"Oh my gosh, Cass, are you okay?" Bri asks, breaking away from Nick to come to check on me.

"Yeah, I'll be fine." I rub my nose more, adding, "It's like running into a brick wall."

I'm satisfied when it's Parker's turn to have his cheeks turn pink. "I'm sorry. I was just trying to avoid Mr. Twinkle Toes over there." Parker takes hold of my face between his hands to look at my nose.

I hold my breath at the closeness of Parker's face to mine and the intimate way he cradles my head. "I'm okay," I say, managing to put together two words to create a coherent sentence.

Parker drops his hands while Bri says, "Well, I think that's our cue to call it a night. Cassy, want to ride home with me?"

Parker looks closer at me, asking, "Are you sure you're okay?"

I manage a laugh as I take a step away from Parker, increasing the space between us and severing the intimacy of the moment. "I'm fine, but on that note, Bri's right. We should probably get going. I need to be at the café early tomorrow."

Parker checks his watch. "Wow, yeah, me too. Need to be at work early, I mean."

Bri nods and looks over to Nick. "You all set here?"

Nick takes a step toward Bri but then stops and takes a cursory glance around the place. "Yup, we got the old girl locked up nice and tight. Nothing else we can do now but wait and see how bad this thing will get."

Chapter Thirty-One

Give it a Name
Claudia

"Good morning, ma'am." Pamela greets me as I wander into the kitchen. "You sleep well?"

"Not at all," I grumble, greedily taking the mug of herbal tea Pamela hands me.

Pamela doesn't respond but instead gives me a sympathetic nod and heads back to the stove to finish plating eggs benedict, the same meal I eat daily for breakfast.

Taking my tea, I shuffle my slippered feet as I enter the atrium. Benedict and I decided long ago that the cavernous dining room was too apathetic for breakfast, instead creating a cozy nook in the brightest part of the house for the day's first meal. I settle into one of the comfortable wicker chairs and sigh, marinating in my somber humor. The minty steam billows and fills my nostrils as I hold the mug to my lips and blow over the liquid, cooling it down. I blow once more as I reflect on the last twenty-four hours.

After the children left so abruptly last night, Benedict and I had no other option but to abandon the rest of our meal as we no longer had an appetite following such an upsetting evening. Climbing the stairs and entering our bed chamber, I asked Benedict if he thought we should have confessed to Cassandra and

Nicolas about my connection to Ernie earlier. It was a rhetorical question, of course. Even though Benedict and I had never discussed it outright, I knew we were on the same page. No good would have come out of rehashing the details of what happened when the children were so young.

But Benedict surprised me by saying, "I don't know. Maybe we should have told them. But, on the other hand, Cassandra does make a point. The children are no longer children. They are adults now."

"But that's my point exactly. The children have grown. Rehashing the past would only upset them again," I said.

"You mean like how they got upset tonight?" Benedict sighed. "Besides, the kids might have grown up and moved on, but darling, I think it's pretty obvious to everyone you haven't been able to."

"What's that supposed to mean?" I said.

"It means if you weren't so consumed with the past and your guilt, you wouldn't have been so cavalier in saying something about it tonight. It even affected how you reacted to Parker's gift. You've been paralyzed with guilt. I know you don't think I see it, but I do. We all do."

"Don't be ridiculous. I'm not paralyzed. See." I waved my arms through the air to emphasize my point.

Benedict had scowled at me, saying, "Fine, if you're not willing to admit it. There really isn't any reason to further this discussion." and turned away, in essence dismissing the conversation. I watched in dismay as he disappeared into his closet to change into his pajamas. Without another word on his return, he climbed into his side of the bed and picked up a book.

Humphing dramatically, I turned to deposit my

necklace in the wall safe. After changing into my dressing gown and washing my face, I joined Benedict in bed, who was still awake and reading. I had tried to wait patiently for him to acknowledge me, but with my energy levels finally declining, I hadn't stood a chance against his silence. I was asleep within seconds of getting into bed.

I had missed any opportunity to make things right. And when I had woken up at two in the morning due to my ever-malfunctioning REM cycle, I instinctively knew I had lost that round. Going back to sleep was a pointless endeavor, and as experience has taught me, the only way to pass the time was to get some work done. So, I had crept out of bed, leaving a snoring Benedict behind, and made my way to my worktable.

Hovering over my designs, I had spent the early morning hours restlessly tweaking garments, trying to come up with something fresh and new for the New York team. I was about to give up on the whole endeavor when I heard Pamela enter the kitchen, starting her day by preparing breakfast.

I could already predict my morning schedule was going to require a nap. I would have a narcoleptic episode if I tried waiting until the afternoon to rest. Yoga alone wasn't going to cut it this time.

Pamela sets my plate on the table in front of me. "Mrs. Castello, I be meaning to talk with you. Is now a good time?" She asks.

I fight the urge to rub my temple and say, "Yes, of course, Pamela. What is it you need to speak to me about?"

Pamela glances out the window at the palms blowing in the wind, hesitating before saying, "My husband be wanting to go to Maryland. Ya know, to get out of the way of da hurricane. He be wanting me to go too. He say we leavin' tomorrow." Pamela wrings her hands together as she talks and looks about to cry. "I'm so sorry. I know you gonna be in this house, and I don't want you to be all alone."

Pamela is chattering without stopping to breathe, so I take one of her hands in mine and pat the top of it with my other hand. "No, hush now. Of course, you have to be with your family."

She wipes a tear away with the back of her free hand and gives a little sniff. "I'm sorry. I don't mean to be cryin'. It's just that I worry 'bout you. If I'm gone, who takes care of you?"

"Well, Benedict, of course," I say, eliciting a smile from her.

"Yes, I forgot. But, of course, Mr. Castello will take care of you and you of him."

"That's right, now don't you worry about this anymore." I let go of her hand and pick up my fork and knife, returning my attention to the eggs. "I'll expect you back here as soon as possible."

"Oh, yes. Thank you, Mrs. Castello. Thank you."

The clicking of nails on the hardwood floors puts an end to our conversation as Bo comes trotting into the atrium alongside Benedict, who doesn't look up as he pulls out a chair across from me at the table. Bo continues, finds a spot in the corner of the room, and lies down, stretching out his hind legs behind him.

"Bo's still here?" I ask, surprised Cassandra would leave her trusted companion behind.

"Yes, ma'am. Cassandra left him here last night." Pamela looks at me sheepishly and says, "She be in a hurry to leave and did not collect Bo on her way out. Mr. Parker be returning Bo to her this morning."

"Wait, Parker's here too?" Benedict asks as he sits across from me at the breakfast table. His hair is combed back and still damp from the shower.

Pamela turns to the side table where a second covered dish is waiting. She removes the silver dome and picks up the serving platter, placing a bowl of Greek yogurt and granola in front of Benedict before replying, "Yes, he sleep here last night. He wasn't wantin' to wake you when he came in, so he be in the West Wing guest room."

Benedict nods and picks up his spoon. "I see. And are there any other stowaways in my house I should be aware of?"

Pamela looks at me over Benedict's head, her eyes wide. "No, Mr. Castello. That is all." She backs away, leaving me to deal with my moody husband.

Benedict and I hover over our plates for the next few minutes. The only sound punctuating the silence between us is our silverware clinking against our bone china.

"You were quiet last night," I venture to say.

"Hmm," Benedict mumbles as he chews.

"Is there anything you would like to talk about?" I try again, this time with a different angle. After fifty-five years of marriage, I know our argument's route. Last night was Benedict making a point. Now this is the teasing out portion where I will need to encourage Benedict to use his words. Because, as he and I both know, a disagreement cannot be settled until Benedict starts talking to me.

"It's time things change around here. We can't keep

pretending the rest of the world doesn't exist. It's time for us to let the past go and move forward, and I think one way to do that is to accept Parker's gift." Benedict finally blurts out.

While his words are upsetting, I do not find them surprising. I expected a comment of this variety to eventually make its way to the table. And even though I thought I was prepared to consider his words, leaving the house and traveling halfway around the world makes me break into a cold sweat.

I place my fork down and lay my napkin over my half-eaten meal, trying to keep my hand from shaking. "I'm not sure I'm ready for that," I say.

"Not ready?" Benedict explodes. "What will it take for you to be ready for an all-expense-paid vacation to one of the most picturesque places on this planet? What could you possibly need to do to become ready?"

"I'm not sure you would understand."

"Well, why don't you try and enlighten me." Benedict wipes his mouth with his linen napkin and throws it on the table. "Actually, no. That's where you're mistaken. I do understand. In fact, I have perfect clarity. We have survived fifty-five years of marriage, kids, grandkids, and the explosion of your business. And you know why?" He holds up his hand before I can respond. "Because I have bent over backward to support you. Despite your condition, I have encouraged you and stood by your side while you've decided to give up on life."

"I can't do anything about my condition."

He yields a touch before continuing, "I know. I understand you have the condition, but it affects me too." He pauses, and I know he is trying to come up with the right words in his head—like he is concocting his closing argument in court before proceeding. "But when coupled with your love and devotion of someone who isn't even here anymore, it leaves me feeling like I'm left towing the rope. Like I'm the last one on your list. And when our dear grandson gives us a gift, one where we can spend time together and enjoy each other's company uninterrupted, I hope my wife will be beside herself with joy. Not offended at the very idea of having to spend time with her husband."

Benedict stands up and pushes his chair into the table, scrapping the legs against the wooden floor and heading toward the door.

"Wait. I don't think we are done here. Where are you going?" I ask.

Benedict pauses and lets out a breath as he runs an erratic hand through his hair. "I have a meeting this morning, so we will have to shelve it for now. I'm seeing some people about our little situation you've had me chasing for the past ten years."

I find myself leaning forward in my chair at the mention of the ongoing lawsuit Benedict has been working on.

"Yet another example of my devotion to you," Benedict mumbles as he exits the kitchen, leaving me to wonder what I can do to bring my husband back to me.

Chapter Thirty-Two

State of Evacuation
Abigail

"Starting at three o'clock today, all city services will be suspended. Palm Beach officials cite the path's uncertainty and the heightened intensity of Hurricane Odette as the reasons for issuing the mandatory evacuation order.

It is imperative that residents take all the necessary precautions to protect and secure their homes. It is highly recommended to move to safety off-island. Police and fire services will not be available once winds reach tropical storm strength. Those not following the evacuation order should not expect public safety services once conditions worsen."

The live broadcast, illuminated by the small television, sends shivers down my spine as I pull my hair into a haphazard ponytail. I glance out the small window while passing the stainless-steel island, making my way to the cooling racks at the far end of the kitchen. It is just becoming light outside, but I can tell the wind has picked up during the past few hours Riley and I have managed to get some sleep.

A far cry from the king-sized four-poster bed I had been lounging in less than forty-eight hours ago, the velvet couch sufficed for only so long before Riley started tossing and turning. Ultimately making it impossible for us to fit on the bench-sized furniture comfortably.

Of course, I knew it was only a matter of time before Riley woke up and asked questions. "Where are we? Why are we here? What happened to camping?" She fired at me in rapid succession, forcing my sleep-deprived brain to work overtime to come up with a plausible explanation. Finally, I managed to slap together some fuzzy limerick about getting a text in the middle of the night from the owner of the Flamingo Café, someone who was *Mamá's* friend and needed us to check to make sure she had turned off the ovens. It was a ridiculous fabrication, but it worked because Riley rubbed the sleep from her eyes and said, "Okay," before asking, "Does that mean I can have a treat?"

"*Cariño,*" I call through the swinging partition door, now fully awake, "What do you want to eat?"

I know, technically speaking, what I'm doing is considered stealing. But it would be impossible to convince Riley of the story I fabricated about "*Mamá's* friend" without allowing Riley free access to all the delicacies inside. Besides, I'm certain Cassy won't miss the food, especially now that Odette is set to make landfall in mere hours.

"Can I have a cookie and some milk?" Riley calls back to me.

"Of course." I turn to gather milk and cookies for the both of us while the hum of the weather anchor's voice continues to warn us the hurricane is set to make landfall in less than a few hours. I glimpse the television as the screen pans to a wall of rain passing over the ocean, traveling surprisingly fast toward land. The camera cuts back to the anchor, warning anyone who decides to stay on the island to find shelter and stay inside.

A chill passes through me as I look around at my only option of shelter—obviously not my first choice, but miles better than sitting in the G-wagon in the parking lot of Currie Park. I know Riley and I should leave soon. Of course, I intend to return here to shelter from the storm, but my instincts tell me that until the food has been stored properly and the café has been boarded up, Riley and I are still in danger of Cassy walking in on us. I check the clock on the kitchen wall and decide a free meal is worth risking a few more minutes inside the café. We will leave just as soon as Riley eats something.

I mentally cross my fingers and grab the portable television taking it, along with the tray of milk and cookies, as I exit the kitchen and return to the café.

Riley glances up and smiles when she eyes the Key lime, white-chocolate-chip cookies I've brought her. She is tucked into the pink velvet couch, playing a matching game with a deck of cards she must have found tucked among the bookshelves lining the palm frond wallpaper behind her.

I set the tray on the table and reach out to run my hand through her wild hair. My fingers get lost in her soft and silky curls. I repeat the motion watching as my chipped nails sink into the black pillow surrounding her angelic face.

"We should leave soon, but do you want me to braid your hair before we go?" I ask.

"Really?"

"Sure, but we have to do it quickly, okay?"

"Okay." Riley bounces around on the couch, sitting

between my legs. I use my fingers to comb her hair into sections and start twisting her hair into two French braids, realizing the last time I braided Riley's hair was over a year ago. An uncharacteristic and uninvited tear slips from my eye. I reach up and push it away, steeling myself from allowing anymore. Last night was a one-off. I can't be letting myself cry at the drop of a hat. No good can come from letting my emotions run wild.

We sit this way, me working her hair and Riley munching on her cookie, listening to the news report for a few minutes before Riley breaks the silence.

"*Mamá?*"

I clear my throat. "Yes?"

"Are we going to go home when we're done here?"

My hand freezes in Riley's hair, and I squeeze my eyes shut behind her back. "No, sweetheart."

"They're still painting the house?" Riley asks in a horrified voice.

For the briefest moment, I have no idea what she is talking about, but then I remember the story I made up when we first left the house. "No, *Cariño*, they're not painting the house now. That would be too dangerous."

"But why aren't we going home then? *Papá's* probably waiting for us, so we can all e-vac-u-ate," Riley says, pronouncing the word slowly to ensure she says it correctly.

I stall, trying to decide how to answer. I might not be a stellar mother, but I am reasonably sure the truth is not what I should lead with. I still haven't figured out how a person tells their daughter their own father has tossed them out of their house. But I'm starting to lose my grasp on all the lies I've told. I can't keep leading her on forever. "Camping" in the car and "borrowing" the café are excuses I can only use so many times before she will know this isn't just for fun. I can't keep this charade up forever. So, deciding to reveal a slice of the truth at the last moment, I take a deep breath and say, "*Papá's* not at the house, darling."

Riley stills under my hands before asking, "Is *Papá* at an OTA?"

It takes me a second to understand she is referring to the football acronym for Organized Team Activities, and I can't help but wonder what other slang she has picked up over the years. I consider how wise my seven-year-old daughter is, and I realize I have played her as a baby this whole time. All the while, she's proven over and over again that her reasoning skills are far more advanced than I have given her credit for.

Riley must sense my hesitation because she turns to look at me. The question in her eyes, *Why are we really here?* pierces right through me. And, even though my body has turned cold, I know I must tell her. It became evident long ago. Julian is not coming back for the two of us. We are on our own. And I now must explain this to Riley.

But when I open my mouth, no words come out.

I gently turn Riley so she is facing away from me and resume my braiding, racking my brain for an answer to Riley. "No, *Cariño, Papá's* not at an OTA this time." I place my hands on both sides of her head and adjust it so it's tilted to the side. Once she is situated to my liking, I continue the rhythmic twisting and tucking of her hair.

"Where is he?" Riley asks through a bite of her cookie.

How I have no words to explain this to Riley is beyond my comprehension. I should have planned this out better. I curse myself for not putting together a way to describe our situation to Riley long before now. It should have been the only thing I focused on while we were "car camping." But instead, I had been alternating between feeling sorry for myself, coming up with lies, and falling into a deep denial of how this is where life has led me.

But I can't deny where I've ended up anymore. Reality is sitting in front of me, demanding answers. I've always had two paths to choose from, and I now realize I have been taking the path of least resistance.

Did I give up my dreams of fashion design and attending Parsons in New York City, or did I follow my high-school boyfriend and his ride to football royalty? Did I learn how to support myself to be one of those fiercely independent women Beyoncé is always singing about, or did I give up my entire identity to become a proper WAG, fitting into the prerequisite role assigned to me? Did I wait for marriage to have children with my man, or did I get pregnant to trap my boyfriend into marrying me?

I try to still my shaking hands, already knowing the answers. Every hasty choice I made over the years has led me here. I let go of my identity long ago. I took the easy road, and now it's my turn to reap the rewards for taking the path of least resistance. I need to wake up and realize that being penniless, alone, and solely responsible for my child is the making of my own destiny.

I have no more choices to make, and I am fresh out of easy paths to take. There is only one road ahead of me now. The awareness of having to be the adult in charge is enough to knock the breath right out of me.

I close my eyes and vow to do better, to take

responsibility for my actions. To pay more attention to Riley and to start planning for our future. One where I can take care of not just myself but Riley too.

A tingling starts in my fingers as I silently pledge to the future, and I almost believe myself. Still, within seconds shame slams into my consciousness knocking down my determination as I realize my first instinct is to tell Julian about my plans. There is seriously something wrong with me. Why can't I comprehend that he's not here and he doesn't care?

Well, if Julian doesn't care, maybe I shouldn't care as much, either. I finish the braid, wrap a hair tie around it, and turn Riley to face me on the couch.

"*Mamá?* Why are you looking at me like that?" She asks with wide eyes.

"Like what, C*ariño?*"

"I don't know, like your eyes are about to pop out of your face."

I blink rapidly, trying to disguise whatever face I'm making—doing my best to change my features into a more neutral state.

I must not be doing such an excellent job of it because Riley asks, "What's wrong with you, *Mamá?*"

"Nothing, baby. Nothing is wrong." I tell yet another lie and immediately chastise myself for the action. If I am going to follow through with my resolve to make a better life, then the lies need to stop.

"So, can we go home then?" Riley repeats.

"No, baby, we can't." I bite my lower lip while simultaneously eliminating the multiple choices of how to tell Riley I messed up. When I made my life decisions, I wasn't just putting my well-being in danger but also jeopardizing Riley's. The harder I try to find the perfect way to tell her, the fewer options there seem to be.

I stall until I can't any longer. I decide to do it like a Band-Aid, rip it off quickly, hoping the sting won't hurt as bad. "*Papá* has already evacuated." I look at Riley closely to ensure she understands what I am telling her.

She squints one eye at me like she wants to ask a question but isn't sure what that question is. "He already left?"

I nod, still trying to put the words together, waiting for the epiphany to make this explainable to a seven-year-old.

"Without us?"

"Yes. *Papá* left yesterday. Without us.*"*

"Where did he go?"

"I'm not sure." God, I wish I could make this torture go faster. I scan the palm frond wallpaper behind Riley's head, searching for something that will help me.

"But he's coming back, right?"

Giving up on finding answers on the wall, I return my gaze to Riley. "No, he's not."

"But then we should just go home. If *Papá's* left, we can just go stay at home until he gets back."

I take a deep breath, and when I exhale, it all comes falling out. "Sweetheart, *Papá* has decided he and *Mamá* aren't going to be a family anymore. You and I can't live in *Papá's* house without his permission. And right now, *Papá* says no."

"Why would he do that? He can't do that." Riley is looking at me for confirmation of her statement. Like I'm supposed to say, *"You're right. He can't. I've paid just as much into the house as he has, so I own half, and we can go home. He can't just kick us out."* But I can't say what she wants me to. I don't know how Julian could be so heartless to do this to his daughter. And I can't tell her he can't keep us from going home because the truth is I didn't contribute a single penny to pay for the house. Nor did I contribute in any way to our lavish lifestyle. I didn't bother to save a single penny Julian gave me. And now I'm in this position, having to explain to my daughter not only did her father no longer want her, but her mother's lack of planning has placed them squarely in the category of homeless and broke.

"Unfortunately, he can."

Riley doesn't say anything for a few minutes, seeming to think this all through, then she says, "*Papá* cannot love you anymore, but he's not allowed not to love me. I'm his daughter." Riley looks into my eyes, and my heart cracks right down the middle. "Right?" She asks.

I want to murder Julian for putting me in this position. I want to tell Riley precisely what I think of her father and exactly how I plan on making him pay for what he's doing to us, but instead, I gather her in my arms, hugging her to my chest, and say, "I'm sure your *Papá* loves you very much. *Mamá* and *Papá* just need time to work out what happens next, that's all."

"But what *does* happen next?" Riley pushes her arms against my chest, forcing me to hold her at arm's length and not close to my body, where I can comfort her.

Riley looks around the café as if seeing it for the first time. "And if *Papa*'s gone, that means you can't talk to him." She narrows her eyes at me. "You're lying. *Papá* didn't say those things.*"

And, as inappropriate as it is, I can't help but burst out laughing. Of everything I have lied to Riley about in the last few days, she chooses my one truth to call a lie.

"No, C*ariño,* I'm not," I say once I've gained control of myself.

"You're laughing at me?" Riley asks, and I instantly know how big a mistake I've just made.

She shoves me away as I try to gather her back into my arms. "No, I'm not laughing at you. I'm sorry." I try to apologize.

Riley stands up and starts backing away from me. "Sorry for what?" she asks, wide-eyed. "You're lying. Otherwise, you wouldn't say you're sorry. You're lying. Stop saying *Papá* doesn't want me. He does want me!" She's practically yelling. "He's probably at home right now, waiting for me, and you're just trying to keep me from him so I can't see him."

The venom in her words stings as if she had hauled back and slapped me.

"I'm not lying." I manage to get out through clenched teeth. "Your father is long gone. He's the one who kicked us out. He's the one who decided to walk out on us. Not me. He hasn't even bothered to call. Not me. Him."

A black fog disorients my vision as I spew the frustration building up over the last two days. The release of the truth tumbles out of my mouth, but as the last word leaves my lips, my vision clears to reveal Riley still standing in front of me. Tears are streaming down her cheeks, and her face has crumpled in on itself.

"Oh, baby." I reach out to touch her, but she bolts out of my grasp.

I run after her and catch her right before she reaches the side door of the café.

"No. No." Riley tries to push me away again, but

this time I hold her tight to me as I used to when she was a toddler and needed soothing.

"I'm so sorry, *Cariño*. I was wrong to say those things." I shush her, rocking back and forth until her cries turn to whimpers. I stroke her hair as she ducks her head under my chin, burying her face into my skin.

"It's okay, *Cariño*. I promise we are going to be okay." I repeat over and over as we stand in the middle of the café.

Now all I have to do is figure out how I'm going to keep my promise.

Chapter Thirty-Three

Here Comes the Rain
Claudia

The silence in the atrium is interrupted by whining from under the table. I scoot back in my seat and bend to see Bo watching me from his spot on the hardwood floor.

"Well, what are you looking at?"

Bo, ever the affectionate one, mistakes my question as an invitation for a pat on the head. Resting his head in my lap, he lets out a snort of contentment as I pat him accordingly.

"What do I do with you now?" I ask.

Bo tilts his head and sets his haunches back down on the wooden floor, transforming himself into my own personal Molossian guard dog.

"How about I take him off your hands?" Parker's deep voice elicits a thumping of Bo's tail against the wooden planks. "I'm heading over to the café to help board up after I grab a bite and before I head to the station."

Despite our little squabble last night, I smile at Parker as he gently kisses my cheek before sitting beside me at the table.

Pamela reappears from the kitchen, this time carrying a stack of pancakes covered in fresh berries. She sets the plate in front of Parker, along with a carafe of orange juice and a ramekin of maple syrup.

"Thanks, Pamela," Parker says before digging into his meal.

I let him eat a few bites before asking, "How are you this morning, *Agápi mou*? Did you sleep well?"

"Mm, yeah." Parker manages through his mouthful.

"Did you kids have a nice time last night?"

Parker swallows and replies, "We did. It was great to catch up with everyone. You remember Bri, right? She came out to help board up THE NEST. It was like the old times."

"Oh, yes. Bri is a lovely girl. It's so nice to see Nicolas finally settling down with someone who can hold a conversation." I muse.

Parker chokes on his food and reaches for his orange juice. Once he has regained control, he turns to me. "Um, *Giagiá.* I think you might be mistaken. Nick isn't settling down with anyone, let alone with Bri."

"Well, of course, he is. It's as plain as day to anyone who sees the two of them together. After spending time with everyone last night, I thought you would know."

"Nope. They certainly did not act like a couple last night. I'm sure I would have picked up on it if they were together. What makes you think they are? Together—I mean."

I look long and hard at Parker. "My dear boy, I know when I see the love between two people. And just as I see it between you and another person dear to my heart, do I see it between Nicolas and Bri."

Parker blushes and returns my stare. "Right. Well, I think you might be the only person who sees it." He picks up his fork and shovels another bite of pancake into his mouth, not furthering our conversation.

I let him chew in silence for a few minutes, but I can

tell he has become uncomfortable with the idea I've placed in his head, which is why it is no surprise when he switches the subject.

"How about you? Did you sleep well?"

"If you are looking for an honest answer, no. I did not sleep well. But that is nothing unusual, now is it?" I give him a weak smile he does not return.

He studies me intently, and I sit patiently, waiting while he gathers his thoughts. "*Giagiá,* you know I didn't mean anything by my gift. Don't you? I just wanted to give you something that would make you and *Pappoús* happy. I'm sorry if it didn't come across that way."

I can feel the sincerity coming off Parker, so I surrender and say, "I understand what you are saying, and I hear you. It is a lovely gift, and I apologize for how I reacted last night." I place my hand over his free one, and he turns it over so he is holding mine. I am aware of how he must regard me. As a frail older woman, he must protect.

"But Parker, *Agápi mou,* you know caring for me isn't your job. I am a strong woman who has survived and thrived even with this condition since my sophomore year of high school."

"And I realize you're strong. I do. But you've worked so hard for our family, and you've been so alone, *Giagiá.*" Parker squeezes my hand in his. "Can't you see why I think you deserve a vacation?"

I squeeze his hand back. "I can. But you know I was never alone. Even after I fell in love and married your *Pappoús,* Betty remained by my side. She never grew tired of looking after me and never got upset when I needed to rest instead of having a good time. She was my guardian angel." I pause, thinking of my dear friend. The guilt sneaks up on me, enveloping me like a cloak I can't shrug off. "Which is why I can never stop. I can never forgive myself for providing her the advice I did."

"I don't follow," Parker says, adjusting in his chair, sitting up straighter.

"Oh, *Agápi mou*. It all started when I was introduced to Ernie Mastiff. Benedict and I met him through friends at the Palm Beach Country Club. He was so charismatic and charming. And most of all, he was persuasive. Talking to him was like talking to my new best friend. He made me feel like he was sharing his secrets with me. Like he trusted me with his private information.

"He was never brash enough to ask us to invest with him. It was simply implied that if we wanted to make a fortune, we should, and we were fools if we didn't. But quite frankly, Benedict and I couldn't afford to. We were sinking every penny we had back into the business. Claudia's Caftan was starting to take off. We had faith the company would succeed, so we chose to invest in ourselves instead."

Parker interrupts me. "And it was a good thing you did. Look at what you've created!"

"Yes, well, I wasn't so sure I was making the right decision at the time. I wish I had been as cautious with Betty. But, you see, I encouraged her to invest with Ernie. I thought, just because I couldn't reap the rewards, there was no reason Betty couldn't.

"She was a recent widow, responsible for supporting her only daughter and grandchildren. Benedict and I thought, wouldn't it be great if Betty could surprise Nicolas and Cassandra with a hefty inheritance?"

"So that's how Nick and Cassy's parents ended up investing too?" I can see Parker starting to put all the pieces together in his head.

How I had been the one to introduce Betty and Ernie. How Betty had, in turn, encouraged her daughter and son-in-law to follow her lead and invest. How, for Cassandra and Nicholas' parents, the prospect of turning their hard-earned savings into a true fortune was too much of a temptation to pass up. How, two years after Betty's passing, Betty's daughter and son-in-law, along with the rest of America, had learned Ernie's investments were all a scam and their entire life savings was gone. And how I had been the one who put the chain of events into motion, ultimately leading to the death of Cassandra and Nicholas's parents.

The demise of an entire family rested in my hands.

"But *Giagiá,* you never could have predicted Ernie was the ringleader of the biggest Ponzi scheme in American history. It's not your fault. You could never have foreseen what would happen to them and thousands of others who chose to invest with him."

I shake my head in the negative. "No. I owed my life to Betty, and what did I do? I failed her. I led her and her family down a path of no return." I wipe my face, push the tears away, and look Parker dead in the eye. "I thank God Betty passed away before she could see what happened to her family. She would never have forgiven me."

"That's not true. You're being too hard on yourself, *Giagiá.*"

"Am I? I don't think so. How could anyone forgive someone for destroying their family?"

"But Giagiá, you were only trying to help Betty and her family in the first place. And ever since the accident, you've done nothing but work to improve Cassy and

Nick's life. Betty isn't here anymore. She can't be the one to forgive you for what you believe you did wrong." Parker looks over my shoulder out the wall of glass behind me. I follow his lead and gaze out the window as well. The sky is getting darker, and the wind is picking up. Parker squeezes my hand before letting go and pushing back from the table. He bends down, kisses my forehead, and says, "I hate to leave you like this, but I need to get going." He pats his thigh, and Bo springs to attention. "It's never too late to put things right, *Giagiá*, but first, you must forgive yourself. Otherwise, no matter what anyone says, it won't be enough for you to live freely." He starts to head toward the hallway with Bo tight at his heels, but before he is gone, he turns one last time and says, "You are the pillar of this family. It's time to accept the past and let it go so you can stand strong for yourself again."

Chapter Thirty-Four

Feeder Bands
Cassy

I watch, with ill-contained horror, as I swing the hammer through the air and nearly miss my finger for the third time in under an hour. "Damn it," I mutter under my breath while I try to line up the hammer with the nail for yet another attempt at boarding the window.

"Whoa there, easy with that thing. We don't need to add fingers to your list of injured extremities." Parker calls out from somewhere behind me.

I bite my lower lip, embarrassed I've been caught swearing to myself while hammering a large piece of CDX plywood to the front café window, and peer into the sun above me. I release my lip from between my teeth and break into what I hope passes as a welcoming smile when I see Parker and Bo walking down the sidewalk toward me.

Setting the hammer on the step of the ladder, I release my hold on the plywood, which hits the ground with a loud smack. Undeterred by the noise and eager to have Bo back with me, I bend to pat my knees, calling, "Come here, boy!"

At the sound of my voice, Bo's ears perk up, and he strains on the leash Parker holds. Then, with one powerful burst, Bo breaks free from Parker's grasp and bounds into my outstretched arms as I kneel on the pavement, knocking me over in a show of enthusiasm. "That's right, buddy, I've missed you."

I'm so used to Bo being my constant companion, always underfoot, that getting him back has the equivalent sensation of reattaching a lost appendage. I embrace his wiggly body and laugh as Bo pulls his head out of my grasp and covers me with slobbery doggy kisses.

"All right. All right," I say, gently pushing Bo away.

I glance up as Parker joins us. His face crumpled in disgust. "You do realize where that tongue has been, don't you?"

I roll my eyes and stand up. "Dog's mouths are supposedly just as clean as yours, you know."

Parker lifts an eyebrow in question. "Um, no. I'm fairly sure that is not correct."

As if to prove Parker's point, Bo drops his bum to the sidewalk and starts licking between his legs.

I bring my hand to my face, covering my eyes. "Okay, fine, you win."

Parker lets out a deep throaty laugh, indicating victory. The desire to share in his obvious delight outweighs my mortification. Spreading my fingers, I peer at him through the opening.

He catches me staring at him and stops to smile at me. "You know, last night was fun."

I nod my head and drop my hand back to my side. "It was." A deep heat breaks out along my collarbone and travels up my neck, eventually taking up residence in my cheeks.

It would be so easy to try and place the blame for the distance between the two of us on Parker. To use the excuse of him moving and starting a new life that didn't include me as the reason we lost contact.

But that would be a lie.

We both know what the truth is. As strong as my desire to see Parker has been, I was the one to push him away. It was like after my parents died, my heart turned to stone. There wasn't a single piece of it that was available for a relationship. The mere thought of loving someone again was incomprehensible to me at the time. But as the years went on and the pain subsided to a dull ache, I couldn't help but return to the memory of my one kiss with Parker. Frequently playing the game of "what if" only to reprehend myself for thinking Parker could still have feelings for me after so many years of dismissal on my part.

Parker stares at me, and I feel he's about to say something. I mentally will him to call me out on my self-sabotaging ways. To make me acknowledge my inability to face the emotions bubbling inside me for so long, preventing me from letting anyone get close again.

But instead of addressing the obvious tension between us, Parker clears his throat and looks away, scanning the exterior of the café. "Where is everyone? Didn't Nick say he would help you board up today?"

Letting my fantasies of Parker and I engaging in a deep, meaningful conversation evaporate like steam on the sidewalk after a Florida rainfall, I follow Parker's lead and glance around the exterior of the café. As though, if I look too, Nick will suddenly and magically appear.

I pick the hammer up off the ladder, still scanning the exterior of the café littered with piles of boards and nails. "Bri and Nick were here earlier, but Bri said she wasn't feeling well, so I sent her home." I shrug my shoulders and pick up a nail off the ground. "And as for Nick, he wanted to go to the hardware store again. He mentioned something about needing more supplies."

Parker takes in the disarray surrounding my feet. "Well, you'll never get all the windows covered at this rate." He rolls up the sleeves of his button-down shirt, exposing his muscled and tan forearms, and walks toward the pile of tools Nick left behind. "You need help."

My first instinct is to tell Parker I don't need any help. To say to him I am completely capable of boarding up the café on my own. But one look at the piece of plywood before me, and I know I'd be lying. If I insist on doing this by myself, I will end up with a swollen thumb, or I'll still be here hammering these stupid nails into the walls when the hurricane finally hits. And despite my desire to prove I can do it all on my own, I know now is not the time to try and make my point.

So, instead of arguing with Parker more, I gesture to the pile with my hand. "Be my guest."

Parker saunters over and bends down, surveying the pickings.

"Oh, now here we go." He dives in and emerges, holding an electric drill. He points it in the air and squeezes the trigger making a zing-zing sound. "Now, we're talking."

I can't help but chuckle at his childlike joy of playing with a power tool. "You obviously spend too much time in a suit and tie."

Parker winks at me. "You're probably right. Unfortunately, I don't get to play handyman very often. But that doesn't mean I don't know my way around an electric drill."

He squeezes an adjustment on the front of the drill and sticks an attachment into the hole. Then, he flips something on the side and presses the adjustment again. "That's it, good to go."

He points to a pile of screws near my feet. "Grab those and come on over here."

I obediently grab the screws after I fasten Bo's leash around my waist in a makeshift belt.

Once I'm standing next to Parker, he begins giving me directions. "You hold the board over the window." But then he pauses, seeming to think better of his first directive. "Do you think you can handle the weight of it? It's not too heavy for you, is it?"

I raise one eyebrow at him. "I was doing it by myself before you got here. So yeah, I think I can handle it."

Parker gives me a dubious look. "I'm not going to say anything about your progress before I got here."

I lift my hand and make a fist like I'm going to sock him in the arm, but he just laughs again and moves out of my reach.

"Okay, fine. Now that we've established, you do indeed possess super-human strength. You hold the board."

I give him my cockiest eye-roll but decide to grab the board anyway. I position it over the window so the panel is flush with the windowpane. "This good?"

"Yup, just like that. Hold it right there."

Parker takes a step closer so he is directly behind me. A lightning bolt shoots up my spine as he reaches over my shoulder to drill in the first screw, brushing my back with his front. The heat of his body passing between our shirts. And just like last night when we were dancing together, my heart starts pounding.

As we work in tandem for the next hour, brushing and pressing up against one another in an effort to board and secure the café, I do my best to ignore the touch of his body against mine.

By the time we've placed the last piece of plywood, we are both breathless, but I'm not sure it's for the same reasons.

Parker wipes his brow and takes a step back to survey our work. "Looks good to me."

"Except we ran out of wood for the side door," I say, indicating the side of the café.

"You don't need to board up that door. It doesn't have any glass." Parker glances around us. "Do you have any sandbags left?"

"There's a few over there." I point to the seven bags left on the side of the café wall.

"Perfect. It's the flooding you need to worry about, but these should do the trick." He lifts one of the bags over his shoulder and heads to the side door. "Let's get these in place. Then it's officially time to get you home."

"Are you sure?" I ask, trying to keep the skepticism out of my voice. "About the door, I mean. I can call Nick and have him bring me more boards. I totally understand if you need to get to the studio. I've kept you long enough. I can wait here. It's no problem, really."

Parker looks at me like I've grown a second head. "You do realize a mandatory evacuation has been implemented, right?"

I shrug my shoulders and mumble, "I might have heard something to that effect."

"Which means you can't be hanging out on the sidewalk, waiting around for absentee brothers who might or might not show up with more supplies." Parker gives me an exasperated grunt and grabs my hand, dragging me toward the leftover tools and supplies.

"You're just as stubborn as *Giagiá,*" he says under his breath. "Come on," he says louder for my benefit. "We are packing up, and I'm taking you and Bo home. Where you'll stay, so I know you'll be safe. No more arguing."

Chapter Thirty-Five

Shelter in Place
Bri
One line or two.

All I have to do is pee on this little white stick, and if my body has produced and released the chorionic gonadotropin hormone, my urine will cause the second blue line to appear.

The explanation is simple enough, yet the resolution required to pee on the mystifying stick has been evading me for the past hour, preventing me from completing the easiest of tasks.

I double-check the back of the box, searching for the details in the directions that aren't there. Because the thoughtful people at the First Response packaging factory have conveniently forgotten to include "ignore your rapidly beating heart rate" and "just pee on the damn stick" in their hard-to-read yet effortless-to-follow instructions.

Irritated, I shut the toilet lid with a loud *smack* and flop down on top of it. Then, resting my elbows on my knees, I twirl the stick between my hands, creating a flap, roll, flap rhythm as I rotate it from one side to the other.

How did I get here?

Of course, I don't mean how did I drive my Jeep from Cassy's café back to the apartment after fighting a bout of morning nausea so intense I thought I was going to blow chunks outside the café, right there on the pavement.

No, I mean, how did I get *here*?

My mind automatically rewinds to a few nights prior. My naked body pressed against Nick, our appendages tangled in the sheets, and our skin flushed from exhaustion, and I know I've found my answer.

It doesn't take a rocket scientist to see the correlation between being sick in the morning, my copulation with Nick, and my gut feeling to know what the stick will tell me. So why is it so hard to confirm the inevitable?

Because once I confirm a pregnancy, I can no longer hide from all the secrets I've been keeping, and the thought of losing my best friend is more terrifying than being pregnant.

Last night Cassy had made it perfectly clear what she thought about being lied to. And according to Cassy, omitting the truth is the equivalent of being lied to.

I stand up again and pace from the toilet to the sink and back to the toilet again.

The problem is I don't know how to approach the topic with Cassy without letting on just how long I've been deceiving her. If Nick and I were starting a relationship, she might have a little more understanding. I could play it off as wanting to ensure we were solid before telling anyone. But Nick and I are anything but new.

I sit on the toilet lid again and let out a "grr" of frustration. All I want right now is my best friend.

If this were anyone else's baby besides Nick's, Cassy would be, without a doubt, the first person I would tell. And she would look at me and know, without me having to say a word, just how terrified I am. She would throw her arms around me and say, "We can do this. I'm here for you" or "You don't have to be afraid. It's all going to be okay."

But she can't do any of those things because I've been so incensed about keeping Nick's and my relationship secret that I've taken away any opportunity for Cassy to be there for me.

Surely, I must have known, on some unconscious level, that I couldn't keep this big secret from Cassy forever. What did I think was going to happen? I would just have a good time with Nick and then kick him to the curb when I was done with him. Or was it the other way around? That I was more afraid he would do that very thing to me? I never stopped to think long-term with Nick because I just assumed he wasn't capable of long-term. I certainly hadn't predicted he would fall in love with me. But the more I think about it, the more I realize the risks always existed. I should have known it was coming from the first time Nick kissed me behind Wallace boathouse at Eckerd College on his routine visit with Cassy, acting as her devoted chauffeur so she and I could see each other regularly even while I was away.

A kiss that had both surprised me and taken my breath away. I had found myself melting into Nick, letting my hands roam his biceps, traveling from his shoulders to his back and hair. I disregarded all my senses and kissed him back as he mumbled into my mouth how he needed my stability and security.

I hadn't given a second thought to Cassy as he told me how damaged he was, and when he confessed, "All I do is pretend anymore, Bri. I'm so over it. I'm tired of pretending that hooking up with random girls is what I want. I'm tired of pretending I'm a whole person when so many parts of me are missing. I'm tired of pretending like all the shit that happened to our family didn't affect me. I'm tired of pretending that the thing I want most in the world isn't to return to the way things used to be."

It was at that moment that I knew, just like I had been there for Cassy to help her pick up the pieces, I would be the one to help Nick become whole again too.

All I ever wanted was to take the pain away. After watching Nick and Cassy have their lives ripped apart by the accident, I only ever wanted what was best for them. I never wanted to give them more chaos, stress, or anything else to worry about. But now, here I am, potentially saddling Nick with more responsibilities than he can handle and giving Cassy a reason to hate me forever.

Chapter Thirty-Six

Water at your Feet
Claudia

My entire body aches with a tiredness that is all too familiar. Nevertheless, I can't get my mind to settle long enough to sleep. Every time I lay down, my thoughts drift back to my conversation with Parker. He had called me the pillar of the family, and in the same breath, suggested that I am not able to stand strong for myself. Could it be that he is correct in his observation? I have remained strong in my convictions to my vow to make up for my mistake all those years ago, but in that show of strength, am I also creating weakness? Unfortunately, the answers remain out of reach, keeping me from achieving a desperately needed rest.

So, here I am back in my studio, attempting to get work done but really staring out the French doors at the ocean cresting on the far side of the great lawn. Marveling at the waves as they crash against the sugary white sand, I can't help but contemplate how the water can simply suck the ground out from beneath it, carrying it away into the blue abyss beyond.

The rhythm of the frothy peaks lapping the shoreline provokes a memory to flash through my mind. One of another time, many years ago, on another beach many miles away. When Betty and I traveled to Greece after my high school graduation, staying in a little hut on the island of Santorini.

After following a winding path from the ancient site of Akrotiri, Betty and I stumbled onto Kokkini Beach— a combination of flaming red rock and turquoise waters. As soon as our toes touched the sand, we dumped our belongings on the glistening terracotta beach, stripped down to our bathing suits, and ran into the water, shrieking with childlike glee.

We lost ourselves in the water's embrace, diving down and touching the bottom of the ocean, scooping up handfuls of sand and letting it siphon through our fingers back to the bottom. We chased fish and searched for marine life until we eventually grew tired and flipped over to float on our backs. Then, drifting on the tide, we allowed our bodies to be tugged gently toward the shore only to be pushed out once again with each passing wave.

Floating on my back in the crystal-clear turquoise waters of the Aegean Sea, with my inky black hair splayed around my head, thoughts drifted in and out of my mind. Being able to hold on to an idea for only a moment before moving on to the next, appreciating the blue sky above me and the tiny grains of sand below me, I thought about how many centuries this beach had been here before us.

"What do you think we'll be like as old ladies?" I asked Betty, breaking the silence between us.

"Well, we'll be fabulous, of course," Betty responded, taking my hand so the waves couldn't separate our floating bodies.

"That goes without saying." I laughed. "But, really, what do you want out of life? When we're at the end of this journey, looking back on our time here on earth, what do you want to say you did?"

Betty was silent for a beat before answering, "I guess I want to look back and know I was loved and gave love. I want a family, a house. Maybe a white picket fence." A wave lapped over our shoulders. "I want to go places, eat good food, and drink fine wines. I want to look back and not have any regrets."

Betty flipped over in the water, breaking her back-float in preference of treading water beside me. "How about you?"

I kept floating on my back, staring up into the blue sky. "I don't know. I haven't really thought about it."

"I don't believe you," Betty responded with a sing-song voice. "You asked that question for a reason. Now, tell me what you're thinking."

"I think I've been so consumed by trying to figure out what is wrong with me that I haven't given much thought to the future."

"Or maybe you were afraid of the future? That's fair. Not knowing what was wrong with you was a slow form of torture. I understand that. But things are different now that you have a diagnosis. And you know what to do to control it."

"Yes, I do." I agreed.

"So, now's the time to move past that fear. You can't let your narcolepsy control your life anymore. It might be part of you, but it's not who you are."

With Betty's words had come a moment of pure clarity, as clear as the bright sky above me. She was right, of course. I could determine my future.

"You're right." I declared, giving up on my back float, so we were treading water, face to face.

"Of course I am." Betty flashed her smile at me. Her

crooked canine glinted in the sun. "So, what do you want?"

Now, almost sixty years later, staring at the Atlantic, a whole lifetime removed from that summer, I still remember how that question changed me. The realization that I could decide what happened in my life and was free to make my own path and set my own course was like being handed a gift.

And I responded with a passion I hadn't felt before that moment. "I want it all."

Betty, being a bit more practical, had laughed. "Well, if that's all you're asking for, you should have no problem then."

But I was already making plans. "No, you're right. I don't have to let my narcolepsy control my life. I can work around it. I can live the life I choose. I never thought about it like that. I want to experience love too. I want to laugh every day. I want to be an active participant in all life has to offer me."

Betty squinted her eyes at me and nodded. "If I know anyone in this whole world who can have it all, it's you." Then, to my surprise, she raised her hand and skimmed it over the water, sending a splash directly into my face. "Just promise me you won't mess it up. Once you have it all, that is." She shrieked and dived into the clear blue Aegean Sea as I tried to splash her back, leaving me to silently vow to her and the universe I wouldn't mess up after I got it all.

Chapter Thirty-Seven

Give it a Category
Cassy

The boats bob enthusiastically in the increasingly choppy waters outside my window as Parker and I cross the A1A bridge in Parker's newly acquired red Tesla roadster, but Parker has worked me up into such a state of giggles that I can hardly pay them any attention.

"No way, you did not do that." I manage to say through deep breaths.

"I did. I swear." Parker takes his right hand off the steering wheel and holds it up like he's pledging the Boy Scouts' honor.

"I'm trying to picture it, but I can't," I say, trying to regain control of my laughter. I turn in the buttery-soft white leather passenger seat. Squinting my eyes, I ask, "Is there a picture of it?"

Parker scoffs at me. "If there is, I can guarantee you'll never get your pretty little mitts on it."

"Oh, that's what you think. Now that I know it exists, my life's goal is to find it." I wonder if my face portrays just how much amusement I'm getting out of torturing Parker at this very moment.

Parker hangs a left, and we zip down North Flagler Drive, headed toward my apartment. The wind has picked up, and the roads have become deserted, but the change in traffic and weather barely registers because

Parker has just told me the story of his first on-air assignment as a weatherman. Complete with a green bodysuit to match the green screen behind him and a cut-out paper sun with a hole in it for his face.

Taking his eyes off the road for a fraction of a second, Parker shoots me the look of death before refocusing on his driving. "Nope, not gonna happen. Besides, you'd probably have more luck finding the video footage." Parker allows himself a laugh. "It's actually pretty hilarious. Picture this beautiful face, surrounded by paper sunbeams, floating over the great state of Florida." Parker adjusts his voice to his announcer persona. "Florida will be seeing scorching hot temperatures for the next five days. So make sure to stay inside, stay hydrated, and stay safe."

I fall into another fit of giggles at the thought of Parker's sunny face. My body shakes, which causes Bo, sitting on my lap in the front seat, to make another attempt to cover me with doggy kisses.

"Okay, okay, boy. That's enough." I gently push Bo's face away, watching as his tongue laps the air mere inches from my face, and adjust his position on my lap.

"That's right, Bo, you tell her to stop laughing at my painful memories."

"Hey, you're the one who volunteered the information, remember." I protest before saying, "You've always been a good sport. Do you remember the time in Mr. Strobel's science class senior year?"

Parker squints his eyes as though he's trying to remember the class.

"You, Bri, and I had to present on sunscreen and the effects of different chemicals on the layers of skin." I offer, hoping to help jog his memory.

Parker lets out a laugh so deep it practically vibrates the electric car.

"Oh man, I tried to block that one from my memory. Thanks for bringing it back to the forefront."

I smile as we both recall how Bri and I had sprayed and rubbed every inch of Parker with various sunscreens until he resembled a slicked-up Q-tip, white from head to toe with sunscreen.

"I'm totally blaming you for that one. You always could talk me into doing crazy things." Parker wags his finger at me.

I contemplate what Parker has said. "You're right. I remember convincing you to do a few crazy things for me." I pause to adapt my best Scarlett O'Hara voice, "However, shall I repay you?" I clasp my hand over my chest in a damsel in distress kind of way.

I bat my eyes at Parker and wait for his quick comeback, something sarcastic and flippant. But instead of shooting off a quick jab at my expense, his grip tightens on the wheel, and when he turns to face me, all the blood rushes from my head to the bottom of my toes.

Parker is looking at me the same way I look at him every morning while watching WESH 2. I blink and clear my throat, trying to convince myself that Parker couldn't possibly have the same feelings for me that I still harbor for him. That kiss was between teenagers eight years ago on the night of senior prom. I search my mind for a way to try and figure out if this is what Parker is thinking, but at the last second, I waiver and instead say, "I remember Bri playing a hand in convincing you to do those things too."

The fire leaves Parker's eyes as he returns his attention to driving, pulling the Tesla over to the side of the road in front of my apartment building.

I glance up through the passenger's side window, and disappointment rushes through me when I realize this is the last time I'll see Parker.

Parker puts the car in park and turns his whole body to face mine. "Cassy, you must know you were the person I did those things for." I playfully push his arm, but he grabs my wrist in his hand, forcing me to look him in the eye. "I'm sorry I left the way I did. I should have been there for you."

I avert my eyes from his. "You don't have to apologize for leaving, Parker. You went to college. It's what you were supposed to do. I would have been mad at you if you didn't go."

Parker doesn't move, and I get the feeling he's planning what he wants to say next. "You're right, I needed to go, but that doesn't change the fact I abandoned you."

Parker squeezes my wrist, making me look into his eyes again. "Jesus, Cassy. It was only a year after your parent's funeral, and I left," he says.

A memory of Parker standing shoulder to shoulder with me at the cemetery, our pinkie fingers interlocked under the blazing Florida sun as they lowered my parents' caskets into the grave, flashes through my mind.

"And then you wouldn't return my calls or texts. I let you shut me out instead of coming back to check on you. I took the easy way out, pretending like you were fine. How can I even call myself your friend? You deserved so much better. I should have tried harder..." Parker trails off, and I assume it's because he doesn't know how to fix what he believes he's broken.

I shift Bo on my lap again and try to adopt a cheerful

voice. "Parker, it's okay. Really. Everyone was leaving for university. It all happened so fast. No one knew what to do, especially Nick and me." I pause, conscious of the cheerfulness evaporating. "I mean, it was eight years ago. Things have changed, I've healed," I say, while simultaneously trying to ignore the image of Nick and me clinging to each other after graduation as we found out the bank was repossessing our family home.

But as soon as I erase that image, another replaces it—an image of Auntie Claudia sitting on the couch in our living room. Nick and I are sitting on either side of her. Our hands clasped firmly in each of hers as she kindly yet firmly walked us through her plans for our future.

"It was like Nick and I were the last two people standing on a deserted island," I say, speaking slowly as the memory unfolds. "Our parents were gone, you were gone, Bri was gone. We were all alone until Auntie Claudia stepped in." I pause, considering all that transpired last night and how my memories no longer provide the same sanctuary. "I was so naïve to think she was doing everything out of the kindness of her heart. When in actuality she was doing it to appease herself of her guilt."

Parker looks at me, his facial features wrinkling together. "No, Cas, you weren't naïve. I know she did all those things because she loves you."

"How can you say that?"

Parker reaches over and grabs my wrist forcing me to look at him. "Because I know her. I know how much of a force she can be when she is motivated, but I also know she wouldn't have bothered expending that kind of energy for someone she didn't love." Parker holds my gaze before saying, "You need to talk with her. Let her have a chance to explain."

"I'll think about it," I answer him, not wanting to make any promises just yet. I still need time to think about this new information before my opinion is influenced by someone else.

Parker gives me a disappointed look but must decide to let it rest because he says, "There's still one thing I don't understand. Why didn't you return any of my calls if you felt so alone?"

I appreciate Parker not pressing the issue of Auntie Claudia, and in return, I want to offer him the most honest answer I can. "I guess I was ashamed. We all have different ways of dealing with grief. Nick drowned his sorrow in easy women and late-night hookups." I shrug my shoulders. "I guess my way of dealing was to avoid the conversation entirely."

Bo whines with impatience, and I scratch him behind the ear. "It wasn't just your calls I didn't return. It was everyone. I couldn't stand the pity and the "I'm so sorry" calls that flooded my phone. The only person I would talk to was Bri, and that's because she came to find me. Every weekend she would drive back and sit with me for hours. Sometimes we would talk, and sometimes we would just sit in the living room, staring at the TV in complete silence. She was the only person who treated Nick and me like we were the people we were before everything changed."

It's not until Parker squeezes my wrist that I realize he is still holding onto me.

"Cassy, you have no reason to feel ashamed around me." He squeezes again, causing me to look him in the eye. "I know you, and I know who you were before. To me, you're still Cassy. You're still the girl I feel the most comfortable around. You're still the one who knows all my secrets…" He stops and looks off into the distance like he's trying to find one of his secrets to tell me now. "Like I used to hate tomato soup and grilled cheese sandwiches."

"Seriously, what was wrong with you?" I laugh at him, thankful for the ease in the conversation.

"I know. What was I thinking?" Parker smiles and winks at me. "But more than that, I know the real you. I know how kind you are, how thoughtful you are, how generous you are. Just look at the present you gave *Giagiá* and *Pappoús*. How many people can come up with such a thoughtful gift?" he asks rhetorically. "I know you've been through hell. But do me a favor. Next time I call, pick up the phone."

I bite my lower lip between my teeth and nod my head slowly up and down. "Okay," I agree, "next time, I'll pick up the phone and talk to my friend when he calls."

I expect Parker to smile, happy I've agreed with him, but he narrows his eyes at me instead.

"Cassy, I care for you a great deal."

I give a quick nod. "So, you've said. Don't worry. I'll take your calls. I will."

Parker stares at me without responding until I feel him pulling gently on my arm, guiding me toward him in the car. It's not until his lips are on mine that my brain can comprehend that my body never stopped drifting into his.

I can't move. I'm a statue leaning into Parker as he kisses me. His lips are soft and warm against my own. The smell of soap and citrus invades my nostrils as I breathe him in. We stay this way for only a second longer before Parker pulls away, still staring into my eyes.

I try to read his features as my mind switches from paralyzed to stunned. "Wait, where did that come from?"

Parker blushes, and I get the feeling he doesn't quite know himself. "God, I'm sorry, Cassy. I don't know. I just…" He pauses, shakes his head so slightly I almost miss it, before saying, "I care for you."

"You mean, you care for me, care for me?" I blurt out before I can stop myself.

My oh-so-eloquent outburst elicits a deep laugh from Parker. The kind of laughter that turns my insides into hot lava.

Once the last breath has left his lips, Parker says, "Cassy, I've always cared for you, cared for you. We just never got the chance to finish what we started." He looks at me, and I no longer wonder if he still remembers our kiss on the dance floor. He is making it perfectly clear he does. He pauses and then says, "But you know something? I'm glad we didn't."

I can feel the heat touch my cheeks as the embarrassment of his statement permeates. But, of course, Parker is glad we didn't get together. He is a famous television personality who has spent years working to achieve his status. How could I possibly think he would want to be with me? A girl who has stayed in the same town for the past ten years and works at a café. "Right, yeah," I say as I look down at the center console between our seats.

Parker lets go of my wrists and reaches up to my chin, tilting it up with the pressure of one finger. "You didn't let me finish." He looks me in the eyes, and I'm lost in the deep blue as he says, "I'm glad we didn't get the chance because I wouldn't have been ready for something serious back then."

My breath catches in my chest as I whisper, "And now?"

"Now, I couldn't be more serious."

My stomach plummets as though I've just been thrown over the crest of a rollercoaster, and I instinctively hug Bo to my body. I've dreamt of this moment more times than I care to admit, but now that it's happening, I don't know what to say.

I open my mouth, but all that comes out is a garble of words. "I…But…" I close my mouth and try to gather my thoughts before speaking again, but the ringtone on Parker's phone cuts me off before I get the chance to string together a comprehensible sentence.

Parker grunts out of irritation and grabs the phone, pushing the silence button, not bothering to answer it. Instead, he shows me the screen flashing "studio" across the top.

He sighs and sticks his phone back in his pocket. "I'm sorry. I have to go. I should have been at the studio a long time ago."

"Right, of course. You need to go." I stupidly repeat after him. I pull on the handle of the passenger side door while grabbing Bo's leash with the other hand, but Parker grabs hold of my arm, halting me in my attempt to leave.

"Hold on." Parker opens his side door and jumps out, coming around the front and opening my door for me. He offers his hand to me, and Bo and I climb out of the car.

The wind whips my hair across my face as I stand facing Parker. He reaches up and tucks the strawberry strand behind my ear. Letting his hand linger on the side of my face. "Can we revisit this conversation later?"

I lean into his hand, savoring his warmth against my cheek. I nod my head yes.

Parker's eyes light up. "If Bri can help Nick conquer his demon, maybe I can be the one to help conquer yours."

I lift my head away from Parker's hand. "Bri did what? What do you mean?"

"You said Nick was drowning his sorrow in women and late-night hookups. That's obviously stopped now that he's dating Bri. I have to say, it came as a shock to me at first, but the more I think about it, the more it makes sense."

"Um, no. No, that does not make sense. I think you might be mistaken. Nick and Bri aren't dating." I adjust my posture, standing ramrod straight and wrapping Bo's leash around my hand. "What would make you think they were?"

"*Giagiá,* she mentioned something about them being together this morning." Parker's forehead crinkles. "Wait, they aren't together? *Giagiá* seems to think they are. She sounded fairly confident of it this morning at breakfast. She said it was obvious to anyone who saw them together that they were a couple." Parker glances over my shoulder and then returns his eyes to look into mine. "I get the impression she likes the idea of them together.

"Well, that's absurd. Auntie Claudia is obviously mistaken. They aren't together. If they were, I'm sure I would know about it."

"Hmm. Well, it's possible she's wrong. But look, I have to go. I'm going to be busy reporting on the storm and the aftermath, but I'm going to call you as soon as I can, and this time you'll pick up."

Even though he says it as a statement, I have the need to answer him. "Yeah, okay, I'll pick up."

He grabs my hand and gives it a final squeeze. "I hope so." A shiver travels down my spine as he lets go of my hand, gets back into the Tesla, and drives away.

Chapter Thirty-Eight

Storm Surge
Abigail

"No! I don't want to go back there." Riley, clearly playing hardball, stands with her arms crossed over her chest and her feet planted firmly on the sidewalk.

Riley and I have been standing in a face-off, across the street from the Flamingo Café, for the last twenty minutes. We didn't make it very far after leaving the café this morning. In fact, we didn't go anywhere at all because the second I turned on the ignition for the Mercedes, the gas light pinged, letting me know only a few gallons of gas remained in the tank. Not wanting to repeat my mistake of driving aimlessly and wasting what precious fuel we had, Riley and I had crawled into the G-wagon and hid behind the tinted glass. It was mere minutes after scrabbling into the SUV that Cassy and her crew had showed up and started working to board up the windows. Riley and I watched Cassy, and a guy who looked just like the weatherman on the television, as they worked in tandem to secure the Flamingo Café as though we were watching a movie in the cinema.

There was a rhythm between the two of them I found fascinating to watch as they brushed against and supported each other in their task. The only problem was they had worked for so long my limbs had started to go numb from keeping still. So, of course, I figured Riley would be as excited as me to return to the café the second they were gone. It never even crossed my mind she wouldn't be willing to go back inside. But apparently, I still have a lot to learn about seven-year-old's because Riley has just explained to me that her "conscious"—seriously, where does she learn these things?—won't let her go back in when she knows we aren't supposed to be there.

"Riley, *Mijá*, I've told you. This is our only option right now. Look around." I flail my arms to the side, so Riley will notice the deserted town surrounding us. Bright orange barricades are lined up across Royal Palm Way, blocking traffic from coming or going from the island.

Riley doesn't bother to look around her. Instead, she stares right at me. "No."

"Come on, *Mijá*, we have to."

"I don't have to do anything you say. You lie." She jerks her head in the direction of the road.

"I don't lie Riley. It's just that as an adult there are some things I keep to myself."

Riley doesn't buy it for a second. "Okay, then why did you tell me your friend wanted you to check on the café?" She narrows her eyes at me in a challenge, and I feel as though I'm not worthy of my opponent. She is constantly two steps ahead of me.

I grunt in frustration and say, "Okay. Fine, you win. I lied. But I'm still telling you we can't stay out here. We need to go back in."

"No."

Oh my God. This child is going to be the end of me. I've got to get her into that café, and from the look of the skies, I need to do it quickly. But how? If Julian were here, I'd just have him pick Riley up and throw her over his shoulder, kicking and screaming she would be no match for him, considering he throws down against two-hundred-fifty-pound linebackers daily. But he's not here, and he's the one responsible for this situation. I grind my teeth together at the thought. I've got to keep it together.

I could try bribery. I stare at Riley, still standing with her arms crossed, and search for anything I can bribe her with. Unfortunately, we've had enough pastries in the last few hours to last us for weeks, so I can't use the Key lime pie roll. "Ugh," I throw my hands up as I realize I have nothing in my possession to offer as a bribe.

I could go back to begging, but technically I've been doing just that for the last twenty minutes, and so far, it's only progressed into *esto está en candela*. But I'm desperate, so against my better judgment, I try one more time. "Come on, Riley, please. We need to get out of the rain. It's going to show up any minute, and when that happens, we won't have much time before the hurricane hits us for real."

Riley hesitates, breaking eye contact with me for the first time and looking up at the sky. "No." she looks back to me, pushing her glasses up her nose. "We should go back home."

Damn it, when is she going to understand? "We can't. I've already told you that."

"Why should I believe you?"

"Because I'm telling you the truth."

"But you haven't been telling the truth. So why should I believe you now? Why do I have to do what you tell me to now?"

I let out a sigh of exasperation and flap my arms at

my side. "Because I said so."

Riley looks at me disgusted and, sounding more like a teenager than a seven-year-old, says, "Oh, real original *Mamá*."

And it's at that moment that I can't keep it together any longer. "*Coñó*. Look, this is the first time I'm a mom. And believe it or not, this also happens to be the first time I've had to seek shelter when a hurricane is less than minutes away. Your *Papá*—he locked us out of the house. And, no, we are not allowed back in. I'm doing the best I can—*entiendo?* I don't have all the answers. I think I've proven that to you already. But I do know that I love you, and I will do anything in my power to protect you, and the way I'm going to protect you right now is to get us shelter. And the Flamingo Café is the best shelter option we have right now. I have a key, and I'm going to use it."

In a huff, I bend down, grab the duffle bag by my feet, and walk right past Riley, leaving my bewildered child on the street alone as I march over to the side door of the café and start to remove the sandbags piled in front of the door. It takes me a few extra minutes as I struggle with the weight of all seven bags, but channeling my frustration into the job, I eventually clear my path, use the key to unlock the door, and let myself in. I don't bother being quiet like the last time I entered. I know Cassy is gone for good, and the streets are deserted, so there is no reason to be cautious. I walk straight into the kitchen and flip on the television. Then I close my eyes and start counting.

At ten, I wonder if I've done the right thing. Should I go back out and check to make sure Riley hasn't decided to run off? I decide to wait her out, figuring she is probably playing the same game, and keep counting. I'm on fifteen when I hear the side door squeak open, and I finally let out the breath I didn't realize I was holding.

I open my eyes as Riley sheepishly enters the kitchen, pushing up her glasses and biting her lower lip between her little teeth. "*Mamá?*"

I open my arms, and she walks straight into them, burying her head in my stomach. I hug her tight as I do my best to soothe her. "We'll get through this. We will. We just have to stick together."

Chapter Thirty-Nine

Too Late to Get Out
Bri

I did it.

I peed on the stick. It's such an infantile thing to be proud of, but after over half an hour in the bathroom, it was literally turning into "pee or get off the pot." After all the time spent staring at a toilet, I shouldn't have been surprised when the first tinges of having to go had rapidly morphed into an all-out necessity to urinate. With no options of procrastination left, I gritted my teeth and preformed the first step of the scientific analysis that will determine the rest of my life. Now all I have to do, according to the directions, is wait for the next ten most suspenseful minutes of my life before I can discover my fate. A tingling starts at the back of my eyes as I stare at the little window engraved into the white plastic stick, trying to determine if I can make out the faintest blue lines parallel to the control line. Then, just as I bring the test in for closer inspection, a knock sounds on my bathroom door. I'm so startled by the sudden interruption that I drop the stick, cringing as it clatters to the ground.

"Hey, Bri?" Cassy's voice cuts through my thoughts. "You in there?"

I quickly pick up the stick. "Hey," I call, wincing at the high pitch of my voice. I clear my throat and start again. "I didn't hear you come in." Even though there is a closed door separating Cassy and me, I tuck the evidence behind my back, "I'll be out in a few minutes."

"Sure, no rush. I just thought I'd let you know I was back. Parker dropped me off," Cassy says, and I think I can hear something in her voice when she says Parker's name, but I don't have time to linger over it because she continues, "He was saying the craziest thing. He said something was going on between you and my brother."

I freeze, turning into a stone-cold statue. If ever I had a chance to experience x-ray vision superpowers, now would be the time. I would give anything to see Cassy's face right now. How could Parker know about Nick and me?

"Uh, what do you mean?" I say, trying to sound preoccupied, like I don't understand what she means.

"Of course, I told him he was being ridiculous." Cassy says without answering my question.

I close my eyes and give a silent prayer of thanks that Cassy has retracted the statement, saving me from a direct lie. Omitting the truth is a skill I have practiced to the point of perfection. Straight-out lying is a level of deceit I have not yet accomplished.

"Anyways, he's headed to the station now."

"Oh, okay," I say, doing my best to match her casual manner.

But after a long pause, another knock sounds on the door, causing me to jump for the second time within minutes.

"Are you feeling any better?"

For a second, I panic, thinking she is talking about my stress of hovering over the toilet only moments earlier or her bringing up Nick and me as a couple. But, before I can say anything to give myself away, I remember my nausea from this morning.

"Um, yeah, a little. I think I might have a bug or something."

"Oh no. Is there anything I can get you to help you feel better?"

"No, no. I'll be fine." The guilt of lying to Cassy for the umpteenth time slams into my chest, and I have to sit on the side of the tub. "Let me just finish up in here, and I'll be out in a few," I call to Cassy through the door as I scan the bathroom, desperate for a reason to delay facing her. I'm about to use the lame excuse of brushing my teeth when I spy the WaterBob sitting in the bathtub. "I'm filling up the WaterBob," I call through the door.

"The what?"

"The WaterBob," I repeat. "You know, in case the water main breaks or the storm surge contaminates the water supply." I grab the BPA-free plastic liner stretched across the tub basin, attach the fill sock to the faucet, and turn on the water. A loud hissing of water courses through the pipes, and the bladder changes shape.

"Oh, right. Of course, the WaterBob." Cassy laughs, obviously amused with my disaster preparations.

I can't help but bristle at Cassy's laissez-faire attitude toward the storm, but then I consider my goal of achieving a few more minutes of bathroom solitude and say, "You have one in your bathroom too. Why don't you go fill it up, you know, just in case we need it?"

"You always think of everything. Okay, I'm on it."

"It'll probably take twenty minutes to fill up," I add, so she doesn't feel the need to come back and check on me. "I'll meet you in the kitchen when it's finished."

"You got it. Do you want to watch the news with me when we're done? Parker won't be on the air for another

292

hour, but we can catch the latest storm updates together until the power goes out."

"Yeah, sure."

"Okay, I'll go fill up the WaterBob now. See you in a few."

There is a rustle of fabric as Cassy shuffles away from the door. I let out a deep breath as she calls out, further from the door, "what would I do without you?"

I figure it's a rhetorical question, so I don't bother answering her and instead gather myself together so I can stand from the side of the tub without my knees buckling. Once I feel steady, I step toward the counter, where I left the pregnancy test next to the sink.

My heart is beating at a rate sure to induce a cardiovascular episode. The idea that Parker could have told Cassy about Nick and me—I take that back. He *was* the one to tell Cassy about us—makes me want to vomit all over again. I have to tell her. It has to come from me, and I have to do it now. Thinking about it, I realize this could be the prime opportunity to tell Cassy the truth. While we are alone together in the apartment, waiting out the storm. I'm already manufacturing the perfect scenario in my head. We will settle down to watch Parker report on Odette, and I'll bring it up by saying, "You know that thing Parker mentioned? Well, what if it wasn't such a crazy idea?" and I'll tell her everything. I mentally prepare for her reaction, likely anger, hurt, and possibly even sadness, as her synapses fire and process the new information. But with enough time passing, I know I can get her to forgive me. The only problem is I need to know what to tell her. Do I tell her Nick loves me? Do I tell her I love him? Do I tell her how scared I am that Nick's lifestyle will make having a family together almost impossible? And I guess the most important question I need to answer is: Am I about to have a family with Nick? And if I am, how is Nick going to react? Will his love for me be as solid as he claims, or will this be the true test of his devotion?

My head is swimming with questions, and I know there is only one way to answer them. I pick up the white plastic stick with shaky hands and slowly turn it over to reveal my fate.

Chapter Forty

Flood Planes
Claudia

A big fat raindrop lands on the window I've been staring out of, breaking into my memory of Betty and the Greek Islands and making me realize I've done the exact opposite of what I said I would do.

I've broken my original vow.

I've messed it all up.

The desire to make amends with Benedict sends a spike of adrenaline straight to my nervous system, erasing any tiredness I was feeling before. The determination to come to a resolution with Benedict moves me at a surprisingly brisk pace as I rise out of my chair and cross the work studio.

"Benedict?" I call, realizing I can't remember whether Benedict returned from his meeting this morning. A chill runs down my body in the form of goosebumps as silence meets my address to the house.

Pamela took her leave directly following breakfast, and the absence of her companionship coupled with Benedict's scarcity makes me feel disoriented, as though I'm unsure which direction to turn. When I reach the foyer, I pause, straining my ears, but the only sound is the wind whipping the house beyond the sturdy walls. So, I concentrate again, deciphering if Benedict could be hiding amongst the seventeen thousand square feet of our estate. But when I don't hear anything, I accept that I am indeed alone and, at the very least, I should go upstairs and secure the shutters in the bedroom.

I progress through my well-secured home, satisfied as I pass the French doors and catch a glimpse of the pool, that all things not nailed down have been cleared off the patio and secured in one of the storage sheds at the estate's back.

My gaze continues to reach across the property, landing on the neighbor's beach cabana. Chairs and various other beach supplies are still out on the deck. And I can only assume the staff left before the outdoor furniture could be taken in and secured. I shudder at the thought of where these trinkets, so thoughtlessly left behind, might eventually end up after Hurricane Odette has left her mark on Palm Beach.

The single rain drop that touched the window in the study has, in no time at all, morphed into a certified downpour. I've reached the bedroom and am standing next to the bed, just slipping the lock closed on the windows, when Benedict enters the door with water dripping off his hair and onto his shoulders, causing the top of his dress shirt to become almost see-through.

"*Agápi mou*, you are drenched!" I say, startled. I quickly grab a towel from the linen closet and cross the bedroom to pat Benedict dry.

He takes the towel from my hands, his paper-thin skin brushing against mine, and rubs it through his hair. "I thought I'd make it back in time, but I must have caught one of the rain bands. The rain came before I could get home." Once he is done drying off, he sets the towel down on the seating bench at the bed's end and unbuttons his shirt.

"Well, I'm glad you are back now. You've been gone so long," I say, watching Benedict reveal a white tuff of hair on his chest.

"I needed to get some papers signed. The fellas at the office thought it would be best to meet today and get it out of the way—not being sure when we'd see each other again, with what's going on with the weather and all."

Benedict sets a black leather portfolio containing a batch of papers on the nightstand and finishes removing his shirt. I eye it curiously but am distracted when Benedict throws the shirt haphazardly on top of the discarded towel, no doubt forgetting our house is no longer full of staff to clean up after him. He disappears into his separate gentleman's closet and re-emerges a few seconds later with a pale blue polo shirt, pulling it over his head as he re-enters the bedroom.

"So…" Benedict says, coming to a stand-still in the middle of the room.

"I'm sorry," I blurt out, not bothering with a more elegant apology.

Benedict looks up and makes eye contact but doesn't respond.

I take a few steps, closing the distance between us until I'm right before him. "I'm sorry for how I reacted last night," I repeat. "You were right. I don't want to wake up years from now and feel like we missed our time together."

Benedict nods, encouraging me before saying, "I don't want that either."

"I know we only get to live life once, and I don't want to have any regrets." My voice is shaky with emotion.

Benedict closes the space separating us and takes me in his arms. I melt into him, leaning my head against his shoulder. Once a shoulder of brawn, skintight muscles developed from years of handling his sailboat's sails. Now, bony with loose skin, soft to the touch. When did we both become so timeworn and weathered?

"We've had a lot of good years between us. But we still have a lot of years left." Benedict says, repeating his sentiments from last night.

I nod, my head rubbing against his cotton shirt. "I'm worried about the children."

"Oh, they'll be all right. They've been through a storm or two. They know what to do."

"I know. But I miss the children," I say.

Benedict pulls back to look at me. "They've been out of the house for almost a decade." He peers at me closer. "What happened while I was away? What can I account for this change in demeanor? And why are you so nostalgic for the past all of a sudden?"

I stare over his shoulder, out the window now streaked with trails of water. "I had a chance to remember some things, some promises I made that I haven't kept."

Benedict looks at me closer, waiting for me to expand on my thoughts. But I don't want this moment to be about Betty. I want to keep it about Benedict and me, so I say, "Don't you miss the sounds of young people?"

"I suppose it depends on how young we're talking about," Benedict says straight-faced.

I let my memories wander back to the baby and toddler years and smile fondly at the images I conjure up. Benedict chasing Andrew around the yard at Christmas and Easter Sunday. Then again, at the memories of

Andrew expanding his own family years later, blessing Benedict and me with a grandchild.

But as the children grew, so did the silence in the house. Only to be broken up occasionally with holiday get-togethers or celebrations. Over the years, the obligations and responsibilities that go along with having a young family simply dried up, and our days became filled with mundane tasks and a vow to assuage my tragic mistakes.

I sigh and lean my head against Benedict's shoulder.

"I suppose we could always get a dog." Benedict proposes.

I let out a laugh. "Oh, dear God, what would I do with a dog?"

"Same as what Cassandra does with one. Feed it, walk it, talk to it like a baby."

I let out a hoot of laughter, a mixture of amusement and disbelief. "No, that is definitely not the answer."

"You could take Parker's advice," Benedict whispers next to my ear, and I can feel his hesitation to reiterate the subject. "We could travel the world. We could go back to Greece. Travel—Africa, Asia, Australia." Benedict's voice rises as he continues. "We could go on one of those World Cruises."

I scoff at his suggestion. "You? On a cruise ship?"

"Okay, scratch the cruise. We will stick to the private jet. Come on, *Agápi mou*, what do you say?" He holds me at arm's length, really taking me in. "Have an adventure with me? I know you are scared to leave this house. But I'll be with you the whole way. We can start small. Just one trip and see how it goes. We're still young enough to enjoy life. Let's soak up every last drop of it."

And this time, when he suggests it, I don't

automatically start to panic at the thought. Instead, I let myself envision what life would be like if I prioritized my marriage instead of appeasing a guilty conscious. And to my surprise, a sense of excitement fills me. Similar to the excitement I felt on the beaches of Santorini.

I slink my arms around Benedict's neck, pulling him to me for a kiss. When we break away, the surprise is evident in his eyes. "Yes, let's have an adventure."

Chapter Forty-One

Power Punch
Cassy

"Oh my gosh, Bri, are you done yet?" I call toward the bathroom, where Bri has been hibernating for the last twenty minutes. "Bri? My WaterBob is all filled up." I call again.

"I'll be right out," She answers, muffled by the door.

"Okay, because you've got to come and check this out." I turn my attention back to the sliding glass door of our apartment where I've been standing, watching the ocean transform into a menacing frenzy of waves and froth right before my eyes. When we moved in two years ago, Bri had picked the apartment complex's eighth-floor, corner, east-facing unit. She had declared it good for my psyche to look beyond the four walls surrounding me. And begrudgingly, I had agreed. But every time I stare at our direct view of the Atlantic Ocean, I can't help but concur with her choice of adding the extra fee to our monthly rent. Watching the orange and yellow sunrises transition into bright blue skies reflected in the turquoise waters reminds me that I'm part of something much bigger than myself and that while I can't control what happens, I can still search for beauty in the world. But now, as I press my nose against the glass, the scene before me sends chills up and down my arms. A literal wall of rain clouds is traveling toward us over the chopping sea at a surprisingly rapid pace—our condo and the rest of Palm Beach lie in its direct path.

Goose bumps rise on my arms and legs as I process the reality of the hurricane approaching. I dig my phone out of my back pocket and snap a picture to text Bri. I am just finished hitting the send button when a knock sounds at the apartment's front door.

"Coming," I call as I leave my post, glancing over my shoulder one last time as I cross through the living room—with Bo tight at my heels—and peer into the peephole.

"Nick? What are you doing here?" I say, as I open the door. "You shouldn't be out. The storm is literally right there." I point to where I was standing by the glass door.

Nick breezes past me like his being here is no big deal—like it's the same as any other day or last-minute visit. "I got my hands on some walkie-talkies at the hardware store." He wanders into the kitchen completely nonplussed, sets the walkie-talkies on the counter, and opens the fridge. He takes a soda, pops the top, and takes a long drink, belching as he brings the can away from his mouth. "Thought I'd bring them over. But now that I'm here looks like I should stay."

"Looks like it," I repeat and give Nick the stink eye, which he either ignores or doesn't even notice as he plops himself on the couch and kicks his feet up onto the coffee table. Bo, who has been bouncing around Nick since he arrived, is now up on the sofa, trying to snuggle under Nick's arm.

I let out a heavy sigh and throw up my arms. Nick knows, as well as I do, I'm not about to send him back out the door now that I've seen what is headed our way.

So, I simply ignore his self-invitation and point at his blue suede loafers resting on the coffee table. "Shoes?"

"Oh sure, right." He hooks his toe onto the heel of one shoe and flips it to the floor, repeating the process with the other shoe until his bare feet return to resting on the table.

I wrinkle my nose in disgust.

Nick, satisfied with himself, affectionately rubs Bo's head and glances around the apartment, "Is Bri here?"

"She's been in her room for a while."

Nick makes a non-committal humph and continues rubbing Bo, who has curled up beside his side, oblivious to any unannounced interruption.

"Hey, Bri. Nick's her—" But I'm cut off mid-sentence as Bri opens the door to her room and emerges before I can get the whole sentence out. Looking disoriented and wearing her black t-shirt with a cartoon of a world wearing sunglasses and the words "make the earth cool again," Bri glances up and down the hall before entering the kitchen.

I glance at Nick, wondering if he is as alert to Bri's odd behavior as I am. But Nick just picks up the television remote and starts flipping through the channels, checking the news before we officially lose power.

"You okay?" I ask Bri, coming into the kitchen behind her.

She takes a glass from the cabinet and fills it with water from the tap, drinking the whole thing in one long gulp.

"Hmm? Yeah, fine. I'm fine. What—?" she stops short when her attention is drawn to Nick sitting on the couch.

"Hi." She breathes as though she is seeing him for the first time.

"Hey," he grunts in return.

Bri turns back to me, ignoring Nick, and solidifying my opinion that Parker was misinformed about Bri and Nick.

"What was it you wanted me to see?" Bri asks, still staring across the room unseeingly.

"Come look at this." I point to the glass doors as the wall of darkness continues to close in on us.

"Wow, that is one solid rain band," Bri says.

"I know."

"Can you believe our man Parker is in that gnarly weather right now?" Nick comments over his shoulder, his eyes still glued to the television. "I can't believe he's going to brave that beast."

My heart starts beating double time at the mention of Parker's name. "What do you mean brave that beast? He's not outside," I say, pointing out the window. "He said he was going to the studio, as in indoors."

"Nope. Not true. Didn't he tell you?" Nick raises one shoulder in a whatever gesture. "He's going to try to get footage of the storm, like those storm chasers all over the internet. He has his sights set on some news award or something. Like the Emmys, but for anchors. Crazy shit, if you ask me."

Without thinking, I snatch my phone from my back pocket and dial Parker's number.

"Cassy, hey. You called me. Look at that. We are already making progress." Parker says jovially into the phone after picking up on the third ring.

"Are you really out there? As in, you're not at the studio right now, under a roof with four walls?" I say, ignoring his lighthearted comment as my voice rises, making me sound half accusatory, half-hysterical.

"Well, it's great to hear from you too." Parker chuckles into the phone, which only makes me more agitated.

"Um, hello. Were you, or were you not the one who was preaching evacuations, boarding up, and staying safe? You told everyone to gather supplies and make sure we stayed above flood level, and now what? You figure just because you look like a Greek god, you can battle the storm and win?" I pause for only a second to catch my breath before continuing. "Parker, what is wrong with you?"

Out of the corner of my eye, I catch Nick mimicking animated faces as I talk, as Bri stares out the window. But I don't pay him any attention and instead wait for Parker to offer a response that will help me make sense of his poor decision-making skills.

Instead of offering a logical explanation, he says, "Look, Cas. I'll be fine. I'm going to take some shots as the storm rolls in—just easy stuff like wind and rain. Once we have what we need, Larry, my camera guy, and I will move to the van. We'll shoot the rest of the storm from the inside, parked under a shelter."

I roll my eyes even though he can't see me. "Under a shelter somewhere? Gee, I feel so much better now. Knowing the copious amount of thought you've put into this plan."

"Good, I'm glad you feel better."

"Nooo." I draw the word out. "Not better. Parker, are you kidding me? You're going to get killed. Do you not remember talking about flying debris, gale-force winds, flooding tides, finding shelter?" I rub my hand down my face, trying to gain an understanding that won't come. "Do you just say all that stuff for fun, or do you actually believe it?"

"Ah, so you have been listening to what I've been telling you?" I can practically hear his smile down the line, and I want to reach through the phone and grab him by his neck.

"Parker?" I say in a low voice, all the fight evaporating from me as I realize that no matter what I say, Parker will do what he wants.

"Yes?"

"You have to. You have to promise me you won't be stupid. I can't lose anyone else."

There is a pause before he responds, and I think I've finally gotten through to him. "I promise to be careful, okay?"

"If that's all you're willing to give me, then I guess that's what I'll have to take." I turn to the sliding glass doors as the first few drops of rain slap against the glass, and I know I've lost this argument.

"Look, the storm will probably knock out all the power and cell services. I'll be shooting around Via Bethesda, right next to the Breakers. We can always take shelter in the hotel lobby if we need to. I'll be at one location until this thing passes. I'll be fine." Parker pauses, and his voice is softer when he continues. "You stay put, and I'll call you as soon as I can. If I can't get through, I'll come to you, okay?"

"Fine, but, Parker?"

"Yeah?"

"Stay safe."

Parker hesitates again before responding, "Of course. Okay, it's action time. I gotta go."

"Bye," I hang up the phone, and without glancing toward Bri and Nick, I head into the nearest bathroom.

I sit on the closed toilet lid and try to collect myself. I hate that I'm so worked up over Parker and that he is out in the storm. No, I take that back. I don't hate that I'm worked up about it. I hate that Parker doesn't seem to care that I'm worked up about it. If Parker cared about me like he said he did, wouldn't he understand I can't lose any more people I care about? How can he expect me to open my heart to him if he insists on playing Russian roulette with his life?

"Rrr," I let out my frustration in a low growl, wiping my nose with the back of my hand. I'm surprised to find teardrops along my skin as I pull my hand away.

I touch my cheeks and feel the trail of wetness running from the corners of my eyes. Seriously? Am I seriously crying over this? When did I start caring about Parker so profoundly that I would cry over him?

But I know the answer to that too. I've always cared about Parker and opened my heart to him long ago. A sob escapes my lips as the realization of just how much I care for Parker comes crashing down on me. I clasp a hand over my mouth and focus on taking long, even breaths, telling myself Parker will be okay. He promised me he would.

Frustrated, I stretch for the toilet paper to wipe my eyes, but as I'm gathering the tissue, wadding it up in my hand, something in the trash bin catches my eye. Abandoning the paper, I reach into the trash. It takes my brain a few seconds to register what I'm holding. A little white plastic wand with a stick that looks like a tongue depressor poking out the end of it rests in my hand. I flip the white rod over. The other side has a little rectangle box cut into the center. I peer closer at the window box, where two visible blue lines stare back at me.

"What the…?'

Chapter Forty-Two

Surfing the Surge
Bri

The rain, pelting the sliding glass door, has the same rhythmic pounding as the heart beating in my chest. I tap my fingers against my legs, doing my best to calm my rapid breathing, and try to decipher if the impending sense of doom I'm experiencing is from the torrential downpour happening on the other side of the glass or from the start of a panic attack.

"Hey?" Nick says from his position on the couch. Bo is still snuggled up by his side.

I glance over my shoulder, turning away from the sliding glass door. It's the first thing Nick has said since I noticed him after coming out of my room, but he's still staring at the television, not looking at me, so it's impossible to judge if he can tell something is different.

"Hey," I say.

"Everything okay?" He asks.

"Yeah, why?"

"You seem a little off." Nick shifts his eyes to my bedroom door, where Cassy disappeared a few minutes ago, and pats the spot next to him on the couch. "Com'on, take a load off."

The television flickers and then comes back to life as I round the arm of the couch and take a seat next to Bo. I can feel how stiff my actions are and scold myself for being so obvious when Nick glances at me and gives me a crooked smile.

"Seriously, what's up with you?"

"I think I might know," Cassy says, shocking me with her re-appearance at my bedroom door.

Also surprised by Cassy's sudden reappearance, Nick swings his head in her direction. "Huh?"

My gaze drifts from the back of Nick's head to Cassy's face, and I know the second we lock eyes. Cassy knows. Cassy remains silent but breaks eye contact to glance at Nick before meeting my gaze again.

"Cassy," I say in a hushed voice as I rise off the couch.

"I wasn't going through your trash, I promise," she says in a whisper, "I saw it when I was in there."

I nod, moving toward her in slow motion as she holds up the white plastic stick. As I get closer, I can see she has tears in her eyes.

"This is yours, right?" She says it in the form of a question, but it sounds more like an accusation.

I nod again as I reach out and take the test from her hand. "Yes."

She lets me take the test from her and drops her hand to her side. "Oh my god, Bri. You're pregnant?" She doesn't bother to hide the hurt laced in her words. I've been keeping secrets from her, and now she knows it. "But how?" she asks.

The room starts to sway around me as adrenaline floods my bloodstream. Fighting shallow breaths, I focus on Cassy's face, desperate to communicate my remorse to her but unable to find the words.

At the mention of pregnancy, Nick shoots off the couch, causing Bo's head to bounce off the cushions under him. Cassy and I swivel our attention to Nick as Bo snorts in disgust and moves to the end of the couch. Bo turns in a circle twice before curling into a ball against the armrest, tucking his snout under one paw.

"What are you guys talking about?" Nick asks, breathless, looking directly at me. A prickle passes through my body as dopamine and adrenaline accumulate within me. At the same time, Nick's gaze drifts to the object in my hand. "It's yours?"

I stare at Nick wordlessly as the hair on my arm stands up. I shift my eyes from Nick to my best friend and back again.

"Is it mine?" Nick asks.

I see Cassy take an involuntary step backward out of the corner of my eye, but I can't bring myself to break the eye contact I've just established with Nick. Now slapping against the window, the rain is the only sound in the room as I hold Nick's gaze.

Desperate for a second to collect myself and utterly conscious of the audience of one watching Nick and me, I close my eyes, take a deep breath, and raise my chin. A horrified gasp erupts from Cassy as I squeeze my eyes tighter, blocking any light from reaching my retina, bringing my chin down, and bobbing it twice in a nod of affirmation.

And now Nick knows. It's all happening too fast. This wasn't the way I wanted to tell him. And this isn't the way I wanted Cassy to find out.

With my eyes closed, I'm floating, lost in a sea of emotion. Guilt for lying to Cassy for so long. Relief that I don't have to keep this from her anymore. Fear that I've just ruined two of the most important relationships in my life and sorrow for the life the three of us will no longer be able to return to. Because no matter how this all turns out, this baby is coming, and change is inevitable.

All the air leaves my lungs at the cumulation of each overwhelming sensation. It's too much. And suddenly, I'm freefalling. It feels like my feet have left the ground, and I'm floating. But then I realize with a start that I am literally in the air. My eyes shoot open, and I see Nick's hands grasping my waist as he lifts and swings me in circles.

"I'm going to be a dad!" Nick's words start to permeate my muted senses as he sets me down and kisses me roughly on the mouth. "I'm going to be a dad, and we're going to be a family." He repeats as he breaks away from kissing me and presses his forehead to mine.

I'm rooted to my spot, unable to move a muscle or comprehend what is happening as Nick straightens up and then drops to one knee, taking my left hand and sandwiching it between both of his.

Over Nick's shoulder, Cassy's hand flies up to cover her mouth as she lets out a shriek of disbelief.

"Bri, I've loved you for as long as I can remember. You are my everything. And now you're going to have my baby. Bri, make me the happiest man alive. Will you marry me?"

"No!" The word flies out of Cassy's lips before I can process and respond to what Nick is saying. I swivel my head and step toward Cassy, but I'm yanked back when Nick doesn't let go of me.

"Cassy, I didn't mean to—" I say as Nick tugs on my hand, trying to bring me closer to him as every cell in my body screams in protest, demanding to get closer to Cassy.

I struggle against Nick, determined for him to let me

go, but Cassy holds up her hand, indicating I'm not to come any closer. "How could you?" she says in disbelief and anguish. "Stay away from me."

"Oh, come on, Cas. Don't be so dramatic." Nick says, finally letting go of my hand and standing up. "You should be happy for us. Hell, you should be happy for yourself. Your best friend is going to be your sister-in-law." He turns back to me as he says that last part. "That is if she'll have me."

"Happy for you?" Cassy says, "Happy for me? Nick, I still don't even know what's happening."

"I mean, it's pretty obvious, isn't it?" Nick says. "Just give it some time to settle in. You'll get over this. It's going to be fine."

"No, Nick, it's not going to be fine. How can it be fine when I'm just now finding out my best friend and brother, the two people I trusted most in this world, have been keeping something so deceitful from me for…" Cassy trails off as the sound of the rain pelting the glass increases even more rapidly, and the television channel cuts in and out. "…how long? Months?"

"Something like that," Nick says.

"Something like that? Longer? A year?" Cassy asks.

Nick shrugs sheepishly in answer.

"Oh my God," Cassy whispers and then looks at me. "I trusted you. You said you would always be there for me, that I could count on you, but you didn't mean it. Did you?"

"I did mean it. Cassy, this doesn't change anything."

"No, this changes everything. I can't believe how stupid I was to trust you."

"You weren't stupid, Cassy. I was. I was the one who was stupid to keep this from you." I say, waving the pregnancy stick in the air, trying and failing to explain that my decision to keep this all a secret from her stemmed from my own stupid inability to see Cassy as the mature and capable person she is. That this whole mess is my fault. "This is all such a big mistake. I've made the biggest mistake."

"Now, hold on just a minute?" Nick asks. "Are you saying I'm a mistake?"

My head swivels back to Nick, who looks at me like I've just slapped him across the face. "No!" I take a step toward Nick. "You're not a mistake."

"Right," Cassy scoffs at me. "Obviously, the only mistake here is my choosing you as my friend. I can't even stand to look at you anymore."

"Oh, Cassy, you can't be serious." Nick rounds on his sister, and suddenly they are yelling at each other in the way siblings do, not bothering to listen to the other's point of view. The arguing is so loud I can't decipher what is being said, and suddenly the room starts to spin around me. The sound of Cassy and Nick's voices blur into one. A ringing begins in my ears as I stand rooted to my spot, acting as a bystander in this war between siblings. But as I stand there amongst the commotion, the only thing clear in my head is Cassy's words playing repeatedly. "I can't even stand to look at you anymore."

With blind determination, I leave my spot on the carpet and briskly walk into the kitchen, grab my keys off the counter and leave through the front door. It's not until the elevator doors are closing that the ringing in my ears stops, and I can hear Nick say, "What the fuck? Where's Bri?"

Chapter Forty-Three

Land Fall
Abigail

The day I found out I was pregnant with Riley is as clear in my mind as if it was only yesterday. The combination of pride and panic coursed through my gut as I sat in our little apartment, holding the positive test strip—the knowledge of finally succeeding in my quest to snare Julian settling into my consciousness. I had figured out a way to effectively flip the middle finger for stringing me along all these years. In my mind, my cunning genius would have the two of us heading straight for the altar. Julian would, at long last, be forced to reconcile his fate as my husband and the father of our child.

Getting pregnant out of wedlock was a risk, Sure. But I was *me resbala*, because it wasn't being pregnant that excited me. It was the idea that I had found a power I could suddenly yield over Julian and anyone else who doubted our relationship, like my parents. With the Catholic religion strong in their Cuban veins, my parents had shot daggers with their eyes at Julian and me when we had shared the news. But I was so confident in my plan that I had boldly stared right back, daring them to question us.

I suppose I should give them credit for not being too arrogant when the day my water broke came, and I still wasn't married to Julian. However, my own shock when Riley was born, and I was still waiting for Julian to settle down and fully commit to the two of us, was like a slap in the face.

I thought for sure the second he saw his daughter's ten little fingers and ten tiny toes, Julian would know we were meant to be a family.

How very naïve I was.

It only took one week after coming home from the hospital before Julian returned to his old ways, leaving Riley and me alone at the apartment in favor of a guy's weekend in Miami. That little instance should have served as the real moment of truth. I should have wised up and seen what was right in front of my face.

But I didn't. I held on until it was too late.

I smooth my hand over Riley's cheek as she sleeps on the pink velvet couch, her head propped in my lap, and realize it has always been her and me. Just because Julian was physically present doesn't mean he was there for us. Riley was mine from the start. I figured out how to care for her on my own back then and can do it again now.

I stare at the palm frond wallpaper across the café and contemplate what life will be like for Riley and me. The wind whistles against the side of the building as the storm intensifies. I strain my ears past the low murmur of the television, listening for any hint of what I might be missing outside.

There is a low rumble as the wind passes through the buildings, cut only by the rhythmic pelting of the rain against the boards blocking the windows on the outside. Something slaps against the wall every so often, like someone is playing basketball against the side of the building. This is why I don't notice the back door bumping against the kitchen wall until the addition of nails scratching against the wooden floor refocuses my attention on the inside.

My hand halts in its motion on Riley's cheek as a rush of adrenaline courses through my body. I keep still, holding my breath as I listen, trying to decipher what has entered the café.

I don't have to wonder for too long because a burst of conversation travels from the kitchen into the café.

"Damn it, Cassy, how many times do I have to tell you before you get it through your stubborn head? No body was trying to lie to you."

"How can you even say that when that's obviously what you and Bri have been doing?"

There is a pause in the conversation, and I bring my feet up and tuck them under me on the couch, trying to make Riley and me as small as possible in our dark nook under the bookcase.

The voices grow louder as they get closer to the swinging door separating the two rooms.

"The only reason we didn't tell you is because Bri wanted to protect you."

"What is it with everyone thinking I need protecting? First Auntie Claudia, and now you and Bri? What am I? Some frail damsel in distress? How do I get that label and you don't? Huh? We went through the same thing, and just because I'm the girl, I have to be protected, whereas you're expected just to handle it? Take it all in stride?"

"No. That's not it."

"I know that's not it! And you know why? Because I at least try to process my emotions. All you do is push them away and pretend everything is all honkey dory all the time. Your denial is just as detrimental as my panic attacks."

"That's what I've been trying to tell you. Bri helps me deal with my emotions. In a way no one else can. She's important to me."

"Well, she's important to me too! And you just took her."

"Good grief Cassy, can't you just let it go? We have more important things to worry about."

"Like what?"

"Like *finding* Bri. You said she might be here, right? Let's find her and get home. We can try to work it out there."

"Ugh!" Cassy lets out a growl of what I can only interpret as frustration as they burst into the café, smacking the swinging door against the wall.

The sudden commotion as Cassy and Nick explode into the café wakes Riley. I keep my hand pressed to the side of her head as she blinks, trying to figure out her surroundings.

"Who—" Riley starts to ask, but I cut her off with a finger to my lips, making a shushing motion with my head.

Riley eyes me warily but, thankfully, decides to follow my lead and remain quiet.

"Bri?" Nick calls into the room.

As barking closes in on Riley and me, I brace myself for what's about to come next. Riley stiffens against my arms as Bo barrels around the corner, stopping to show his teeth when he sees us.

"Bri?" Cassy calls, following right behind Bo.

"Bri, thank god you're here. What were you

thinking storming out in the middle of a hur—" Cassy stops short as she rounds the corner and comes face to face with Riley and me, frozen on her pink velvet couch. "What the—?"

My cheeks burn under Cassy's reproachful gaze as she takes in the scene before her. A tray full of pastries on the table, a glass of milk, the small portable television on the table, set to a low hum. Our duffel bag of clothes is open on the couch next to us, with Bo, now nose-deep in the bag, helping himself to our belongings.

"Cassy, did you find—"

Cassy snaps out of her trance as Nick joins our haphazard group, stopping behind Cassy's shoulders.

"Okay... Not Bri..." Nick breathes the word out, clearly searching for clarification.

"No, definitely not Bri, and definitely not okay," Cassy says.

I glance down at Riley, who stares at the shocked pair, and I do my best to send them the subliminal message that Riley is innocent. "Riley and I needed a place to stay for a while." I start to explain, but Cassy cuts me off.

"And you thought my café was the best solution?" Cassy jaunts her head forward like she can't believe what she's seeing.

"I think this is all a big misunderstanding," I say as I rise from the couch, placing myself as a barrier between Cassy and Riley.

"No. There is no misunderstanding here. It's completely clear to me. You're just another selfish person with no regard for anyone else." Cassy shakes her head like she's experiencing a whole other side conversation inside her head. "I can't for the life of me figure out why everyone thinks they can lie to me and get away with it. It's people like you who feel like they can walk all over people like me."

"People like me. What's that supposed to mean?" I ask, even though I'm reasonably sure I already have an idea of what she's talking about.

People like me account for people who haven't worked a day in their lives but still act like they own not just the road but the entire town. The kind of people she probably deals with every day, walking around her café as though they own it. Making demands of the staff, declaring the food not up to their standards, flaunting their black credit cards and wads of hundred-dollar bills. The type of people who put their desires above the needs of others. Clearly, this is the kind of person Cassy thinks I am.

"It means what I said it means. You think you can do no wrong; that you can lie to me and get away with it. Well, I'll tell you what. I'm tired of people playing me as the fool. If you think you get to break into my café and I'm not going to do anything about it, you're wrong."

A chill runs down my back as I realize she's serious. She is going to have me put in jail for trespassing. I need to correct this situation. "I think you have the wrong idea about me."

"Why don't you enlighten me then?" Cassy places her hands on her hips and stares me down, waiting for my explanation.

A loud bang rattles through the café as the wind blows the side door open and it smacks against the wall. I jump at the sudden disturbance, but Cassy doesn't even flinch. She just keeps her gaze locked on mine as she waits for my explanation.

I swallow and clear my throat. "Fine. Look, you're right."

Cassy raises her eyebrows.

"I used to be like that, but recently I've been given a chance to gain a little introspection about the kind of person I was—and who I want to be in the future."

The door continues to knock against the sidewall, the wind whistling as it passes the open door. I stare after it, resisting my instinct to go and shut it as I form a mental picture of rain pouring into the café from the storm swirling around outside.

"He kicked us out. Julian did." I force myself to say the words aloud for the first time. "Locked us out is more like it. I left to pick Riley up from camp, and when I got back home, the gates were locked, and that—" I point to the duffle bag next to the couch. "Was all he left us. I-I didn't want to break into the café, but the storm was coming." I gesture to the rain and wind still howling past the open side door. "I couldn't stay in the car with Riley."

"And how, exactly, do your domestic disturbances become my problem? Last time I checked, this wasn't a hotel, my cash register wasn't an ATM, and I wasn't a therapist."

I open my mouth to respond, but Nick interrupts our conversation before I can comment. "Come on, Cas. We can deal with her later." Nick rolls his eyes in my direction as though I'm no longer worthy of his full attention. "Right now, we need to focus on finding Bri." He points to the side door, rain now blowing into the café in sheets, soaking the floor directly in front of the opening. "We don't have time for this. Obviously, you can't kick them out now. She has her kid with her. Let them stay, and we'll come back to deal with it after we've found Bri."

Cassy looks at me, and I think she's about to concede to Nick's suggestion of letting Riley and I stay here, but as she takes me in, she changes her demeanor like she is seeing me for the first time.

"No," Cassy says, shaking her head. "No. I'm done with everyone. I'm not helping her."

"Come on, Cas. You can't be serious." Nick reaches out to take Cassy's hand, but she shakes him off.

"No, Nick, I'm serious. I'm tired of being lied to. I'm not going to let anyone manipulate me anymore."

"But where do you suggest we go?" I turn to indicate Riley, hoping Cassy will see how senseless she is being, but when I look at the couch, Riley is gone.

"Where's Riley?" I ask.

Cassy and Nick glance behind me and then at each other like they expect the other one to reply with the answer.

Nick recovers first, calling, "Riley?" over his shoulder toward the coffee counter.

I turn toward the kitchen and call out, "Rye? *Mijá?*" mimicking Nick.

I listen for a reply, but when there is no response, I walk swiftly in the direction of the coffee bar. Not seeing her, I push through the door into the kitchen.

"Riley?" I call again.

The only response is the muffled sounds of Nick and Cassy calling her name in various corners of the cafe.

I rush back out to the seating area where Nick and Cassy meet me. Unfortunately, all of us are empty-handed.

We stare at each other briefly before Cassy surveys the area one more time and, clasping a hand over her mouth, gasps, "Bo?"

Silence.

Cassy removes her hand and calls out, "Bo? Here, Bo." Louder this time.

But the only reply is the wind howling and the door knocking on the wall again, making it crystal clear Bo and Riley are gone.

"Jesus, Cassy, look what you've done now," Nick says.

"What?! And how is this my fault?" Cassy asks.

"When you keep telling people to leave, what do you think is going to happen!?" Nick storms past Cassy in the direction of the open side door. "Jesus." He mutters again as he grabs a walkie-talkie off the counter and exits the café.

"What are you doing?"

"I'm going to find them."

"Well, there is no way I'm going to stay here with her." Cassy points her thumb in my direction, and I can't help but cringe.

"I don't care what you do. Just try not to kick anyone else out into a hurricane. I have as much as I can handle as it is." And with his last words, he disappears out the door and into the storm.

Cassy and I look at each other, bewildered, until I remember it's my child he has just gone after. "No way in hell I'm staying here while my daughter is out in that." And before I even know what I'm doing, I grab Cassy's wrist with one hand and the last walkie-talkie with the other and drag Cassy out of the café, following behind Nick. "And you're coming with me."

Chapter Forty-Four

State of Emergency
Cassy

"Oh, my God! What have I done?" Abigail wails from the driver's seat next to me. She slaps the steering wheel with the palm of her hand, and I jump in my seat. "We have to find her."

Of course, we have to find Riley, but we also need to find Bri and Bo. But I don't get the chance to voice my concerns because Abigail lets fly a string of Spanish I don't understand. The only thing I catch that I can interpret is *arroz con mango*, which I think translates to "a big mess."

I fidget in my seat, my soaking wet clothes making our drive along North Country Road impossibly uncomfortable. I search for something to distract me from the feel of cotton sticking to my skin and pick up the walkie-talkie from the middle console. I switch the knob, and a crackling sound cuts through the air, adding to the noise of the wind howling around us.

Setting the walkie-talkie back down, I strain my eyes past the sheets of water cascading down the window in front of me as we crisscross the streets heading toward the Palm Beach Country Club.

"What have I done?" Abigail asks again. She has been repeating the same question over and over since we left the café. And, while I know I should probably make some kind of attempt to soothe her, I'm still too numb from earlier to feel particularly inclined to do so.

I glance at her from the corner of my eye, taking in her disheveled appearance and animalistic stare. She catches me looking at her. "I can only imagine what you must think of me," she says, keeping her eyes trained on the road.

I don't respond, just shrug my shoulders and keep staring out the window, looking for signs of life on the deserted street.

"It's disgusting how my personal life is plastered across the news." Abigail looks at me again. "I'm sure you've seen it, and you've already formed your opinion about what kind of person I am."

I can't handle her self-preservation for another second. I straighten up in my seat and let the words I've kept locked down inside me fly. "I don't care what is said about you on the news. What I do care about is how people treat one another. People can't just lie or keep secrets or act like animals and get away with it." I pause as the memory of Bri coming into the café earlier flashes through my mind. "You almost ran over my best friend on the street and drove away. Who does that?"

"I—" Abigail attempts to cut into what I'm saying, but I hold my hand up, halting her.

"And you're right. I do care about your lack of concern breaking into my place of business. The Flamingo Café is not your hotel; you can't just check in when you feel like it."

"So, you said." Abigail says, "And I'm sorry about Bri." She pauses as I scoff at her apology, not buying for a minute that she means it. "Seriously, that whole thing was an accident. It's not like I go around purposely trying to run people over. You're right. I should have stopped to check on her, but I wasn't thinking straight." Abigail pauses again as she gathers her thoughts. "Please, let me explain."

I struggle with my conflicted emotions regarding Bri but choose to remain silent and let Abigail continue uninterrupted.

"That night, when Julian got kicked out of THE NEST, he didn't come home. I learned when everyone else did that he had been running all over town and getting into trouble. It wasn't the first time it happened, but it was the first time it was a top news story. I wasn't thinking about anything besides how I was going to clean up the mess he made." Abigail shakes her head at the memory. "But apparently, damage control wasn't what Julian had in mind."

"How so?" I can't help but ask.

"When he got home the next morning, he kicked me out of our house. He said he was calling off the engagement and that I needed to pack my things and get out. I had no money, nowhere to go. I was desperate, so when I was at the cafe, and I saw the keys sitting on the counter by the register, and the opportunity presented itself, I didn't hesitate. You need to understand, it was out of desperation. I was desperate for a place for Riley and me to stay. To be safe…" Abigail's eyes start to tear up. "I never meant any harm. I was just trying to keep my daughter safe." Her voice catches on the last word. "God, I was so naïve."

I turn to look out the side window of the Mercedes as we pass another property, straining to look past the gates. And even though I hate to admit it, I hear Abigail loud and clear. Of course, our circumstances are completely different, and our lifestyles are a world apart, but I understand what it feels like to realize you've been ignorant of what is happening around you.

"How could I have let Julian do this to us? I trusted him," Abigail says so softly I almost don't hear her over the pounding of the wind and rain, and it's as though her words have sparked a fire within me. Abigail and I have both been naïve, trusting people only to have it backfire.

"I trusted someone once," I say slowly, not entirely sure why I'm offering this information to Abigail, of all people. Maybe it's because I feel like she is the one person on this island who can finally relate.

Abigail glances at me out of the corner of her eye. "I'm guessing it turned out about as good as it did for me?" The rain continues to pelt the windshield, the wipers working double-time to push the water out of the way.

"Worse."

"I don't know how getting kicked out of your own house with no money, a child, and in the middle of a hurricane could get any worse." Abigail scoffs at me.

"You have a point." I acknowledge. "Ever heard of the Mastiff scandal?"

"Um yeah, you'd have to be living under a rock not to have heard about it."

I raise my hand like a child offering the answer in a classroom. "That was our family. My dad invested everything we had with him. Our whole life savings, Nick's and my college educations. Everything."

Abigail makes an ugh sound but keeps driving, knuckles white from gripping the steering wheel.

"My parents lost it all. Every penny was gone. My dad became incensed with guilt. It would eat at him every day until he was driving with my mom one afternoon, and I think he saw a way out of how he was feeling. He wrapped his car around the telephone pole a few blocks from our house. He must have been traveling at a speed much higher than the limit because the impact was so intense it killed them both instantly." I fight the bile rising in my throat, recalling the scene. "It happened when I was getting dropped off from school at the bus stop. I saw the whole thing."

"I'm so sorry." Abigail has enough grace to say.

I nod, squeezing my hands between my thighs. "Anyways, my grandmother's best friend took in Nick and me. She looked after us for years. I thought she was doing it because she loved us, but I just found out she was doing it because she felt guilty for being the one to get my family to invest with Ernie."

Abigail glances at me out of the corner of her eye. "Are you sure about that? Only doing it because she was guilty, I mean?"

"She said as much when we had dinner last night."

"Hmm…" Abigail hums like she doesn't quite believe me.

"What do you mean 'Hmm'?"

"It's just that it seems like a lot of effort to go to if she's only doing it because she's guilty. Raising children isn't for the faint of heart, you know. I mean, look at me! I'm doing the best I can, but I've lost my child in a hurricane!" The wildness returns to Abigail's eyes at the mention of Riley.

"We'll find her. What about your parents or a friend? Would she try to go there?"

"My parents are already gone, evacuated. And the friends I thought I had, well, I guess they weren't my friends after all." Abigail trails off, and I know full well what she is implying about the people who call you their friend in Palm Beach.

"I don't know what's worse, friends that abandon you or friends that lie to you." I ponder out loud.

"How about friends that lie *and* abandon you?" Abigail counters.

I shake my head in disgust and say, "Right." Before lapsing into silence.

"What did your friends lie to you about?" Abigail asks as the tires split the water in the road, spraying droplets covering my window.

"My best friend lied about sleeping with my brother; now she's pregnant with his baby."

"Ouch."

"Yep."

"Why didn't she tell you? About being with your brother?"

"She claims it was to protect me." I sigh. "I'm so tired of people lying to me under the pretense of protecting me."

"Maybe," Abigail says, looking thoughtful while keeping her eyes laser-focused on the road before her, scanning the streets for any sign of Riley. "But you can look at it from their point of view. I don't know them, and I don't know you, but I'm willing to bet the people you are talking about are only keeping things from you because they love you and don't want to see you get hurt again. It's their way of taking care of you. I mean, I did the same thing with Riley. When Julian kicked us out, you better believe I didn't just offer up that information to my daughter—because I was trying to protect her."

"That's messed up."

"Maybe, but it's the best I knew at the time, just like these people are doing the best they can at the time. But Riley showed me she needed to know the truth, and you have to do the same with your people. You are the only one who can teach them how to treat you. Show them you're strong enough to handle the truth. What you do with the information now will determine how they treat you in the future. Show them you're ready, strong, and can handle anything." Abigail stops abruptly in her conversation, and I look out the window to see waves of grey water washing over the roadway, cutting the street in front of us in half.

"Damn it," Abigail says under her breath, throwing the SUV in reverse. "Even the G-wagon can't pass through that kind of flooding. *Cõnó*, now what do we do?"

"Let's think about where Riley would go. If she wouldn't go to your parents or a friend's house, is there someplace else she feels safe? Someplace she would try and get to?"

"She would try to go home."

Chapter Forty-Five

In the Dark
Bri

An involuntary shriek leaves my lips as a palm leaf sails through the air and smacks against the Jeep, slapping as it plasters itself across the driver's side windshield, completely obscuring my vision. In an attempt to dislodge the unwanted foliage, I bat at the windshield wipers, but it's useless. The wipers only push the palm further into the Jeep's crevasse, firmly attaching itself to the vehicle. Cursing, I glance out the side window and take the first turn I see, swerving into the Flagler Steakhouse parking lot and shutting off the engine.

Now that the Jeep has stopped and I'm no longer fighting the steering wheel for control against the wind, my thoughts automatically shift back to Cassy and Nick. I hold my breath as images careen around my head like the debris in the parking lot.

Nick, down on one knee in the middle of our apartment, declaring his love and proposing marriage. Over his shoulder, Cassy looks at me as if I've just punched her in the gut.

How could I have done this to my best friend? The one person I was supposed to stand by and protect from other people's deviance. How would she ever be able to trust me again? And how could I possibly think we could all be one happy family after the destruction I've caused?

I shake my head as an ambiguous object wheels past my line of vision, pulling me out of my reverie. Yanked back into the present, I glance around and notice for the first time that the light in the sky has diminished since embarking on my foolhearted departure from the apartment. The atmosphere has new electric energy despite the almost complete darkness surrounding me. I can just make out the blackened shadows of the palm trees lining the road. And judging by how they are shaking their leaves—as if they're overzealous cheerleaders—it is time I stop my daydreaming and find protection from the storm.

I place my hand on the handle, intending to open the door so I can remove the palm frond, but the steady force of the wind on the other side prevents me from accomplishing the easiest of tasks. It's not until I push with my shoulder, increasing the counterbalance of force, that I am able to achieve a sliver of an opening that I sneak my body through before letting the door slam shut behind me. The rain saturates my clothes in less than a second while the gale thrashes my hair around my face, obscuring my vision. Already feeling a chill as a deluge of water penetrates my skin, I reach up and struggle to gather my hair into a ponytail. Frustratingly, I can only contain half of my amber locks. I'm forced to secure a rubber band around the wad of hair while the rest tangles wildly in the wind. With my hair no longer in my face, I reach out to release the palm leaf—watching as the wind rips it from my hand, leaving me with a cut on my fingertip. It's not the tiniest of cuts, and as I peer closer at the two halves of skin now separated by a deep valley, bright red blood starts to bubble to the surface. I stick my finger in my mouth to abate the bleeding as I watch the leaf whip away.

A howl assaults my body and ears, drowning out any other audible sounds as if the ocean has manifested its way straight into my eardrums. The waves are crashing in regular succession, making it impossible to hear anything besides the storm.

I release my finger from my mouth and rest both hands on the Jeep hood, bracing myself against the gust. I need to get inside. I glance at the steakhouse and am not surprised to see it boarded to within an inch of its life.

Squinting my eyes, and peering into the distance, I scan the yellow building again, desperate to discover any opening I can get into. It takes effort to focus past the rain and debris as I grasp the details of the boarded-up windows and locked front doors. But just as my gaze passes the porte-cochere, I see something.

Crouched down and huddled against the yellow wooden planks of the building are a child and a dog. Squinting harder, I can just make out white fur with black dots through the rain. It doesn't take me more than an instant to recognize Bo. I trace his guarded stance to the child behind him, sandwiched between his body and the wall, and let out a gasp.

Folded into a ball, Riley sits with one hand extended from her body, grasping Bo at the collar. Her face is tucked into her chest, shielded from the wind and rain.

"Riley!" I call out, the wind ripping the words away before they even leave my mouth.

I try to step toward the tangled pair but almost topple over from the force of the wind pushing back against me. Without the buffer of the vehicle, I'm no match against the increasing storm.

Unable to push my way forward, I retreat to the Jeep. Pulling at the handle again, I sneak back into the interior sanctuary, start the engine, and cautiously make a U-turn in the parking lot. Fighting the steering wheel, I pull up under the porte-cochere and press into the side of the door, pushing against the gust and ciphering my body through the opening one more time.

"Riley!" I call out, but it is of no use. Again, the words don't make it past my mouth, the wind tossing them to the uproar surrounding us. With the storm picking up force, it is impossible to get my message to the balled-up mass of child and dog just outside my grasp.

Riley's knuckles are white from holding onto Bo, who is now biting at an unseeable threat. Making snapping motions as he tries to catch the pelting rain between his teeth.

"Riley!" I try again, waving my arms above my head to get her attention.

As I move closer, Bo dips his head and gives a low warning, "Grrr."

Riley lifts her head at Bo's guarded stance, and I can see that tears are streaking her cheeks under her glasses. Whether from crying or the wind and rain stinging her face, I can't tell.

She is on her feet the instant she sees me, trying to get to me. But as soon as she puts pressure on her foot to walk, she winces and falls into Bo, who instinctively stands steady and offers her the support she needs.

With one final push, I reach Bo and Riley. "Are you hurt?" I ask, bending down to eye level with Riley while patting her leg with my hand, looking for obvious injury.

Riley nods. "I hurt it when I was trying to catch Bo."

A dozen questions fly through my mind. Like, where is Riley's mother? Why was Riley trying to catch Bo? How did Riley and Bo come to be together? And what in the world are the two of them doing alone, out in a hurricane? But instead of berating Riley with questions that don't matter, I nod in understanding and turn so my back is to her. "Do you think you can climb onto my back?"

"Like a piggyback?"

"Yeah, like a piggyback. You think you can do that?"

Riley places her hands on my shoulder. "I can try." She hops on one foot as she clambers onto my back and wraps her arms around my neck. Once I feel Riley is secure, I push off the ground and struggle to stand, grabbing Bo by the collar. The additional weight of Riley's frame and the dense punishing wind and rain force me to stay hunched over as I drag our trio back to the Jeep.

Once at the Jeep, I open the passenger side door and rotate backward so Riley can scoot into the seat. I ensure she is settled before gathering Bo in my arms, heaving him into the carriage at her feet, and shutting the door. Then, keeping my hand on the hood for support, I push to the driver's side and get in.

"Miss Bri?" Riley whispers once I'm seated next to her.

"Yes, Riley?" I turn to her and watch as her chin trembles.

"I want my *Mamá*."

I nod again and suppress the desire to ask a million questions. "I know."

I pull her across the middle console and wrap my

arms around her. She heaves a sob into my chest, and I hug her tighter. "I promise, as soon as we can, I'll make sure you get to see your *Mamá*. Okay?"

"But, what if we die!?" she wails.

I pull back in surprise. The thought of death being imminent never even occurred to me. But now that Riley's put it out there, I can see the real danger we've placed ourselves in. But, of course, these are not the thoughts that will comfort a scared child. So instead, I grasp Riley by the shoulders, look her in the eye, and say, "no, no, we aren't going to die." As I'm trying to comfort Riley, the canvas roof of the Jeep rattles over our heads, and I can't help but break eye contact with Riley to look up. The sense of escape was why I bought this Jeep in the first place. Visions of driving along the coastline with the top down had beckoned to me to the point that I had easily forked over the money for the down payment, but now, as the zipper pulls and rattles in the wind, my decision of vehicles feels more like a death trap than an adventure.

I release Riley and turn to start the engine. "Why don't you put on your seat belt? We need to get out of here."

"*Mamá* says I can't sit in the front seat while driving. I'm not old enough yet."

"And your *Mamá* is absolutely right, but just this one time, I think we need to break the rules. I'll drive real slow." Riley looks uncertain but puts her seat belt on anyways.

I put the Jeep in drive and take a left out of the parking lot, not confident as to where I'm heading but making sure to drive slowly as promised. As we inch our way down South Country Road, I take the opportunity to

336

finally ask, "What happened? Why are you out here all alone with Bo?"

Riley tucks her chin to her chest, speaking to the floor. "*Mamá* and I were at the Flamingo Café when that lady, Miss Cassy, and a tall guy with red hair—"

"Nick?" I ask, not able to stop myself from interrupting her.

Riley lifts her head and looks at me quizzically. "Yeah, Nick."

I nod as a pang of longing rips through my heart, "Okay, so you were at the café when Cassy and Nick came in." I pause, trying to put the pieces of the puzzle together. I don't bother asking why Riley and her *Mamá* were at the café in the first place because I am certain I can piece together a hypothesis from all the information I have, to know that Abigail needed to find shelter from the storm just like we do right now. So instead, I say, "Is that where you left them?"

Riley looks sheepish and nods in affirmation.

"We should go back. I'm sure they're frantic by now and looking for you."

"And you."

"What do you mean?"

"Cassy and Nick, they said they needed to find you." Riley pushes her glasses back up her nose, pausing to wipe a tear from her eye before looking at me. Did you run away too?" She asks.

I pinch my lips together and shrug my shoulders, focusing on the road before me. I had run away from Cassy and Nick. At the time, it had seemed like the only solution. But now, sitting here across from Riley, I realize it was the childish one. Here I had been worried the whole time that Nick wouldn't be able to handle the responsibility of becoming a dad when, in actuality, he had been the stronger half of us, standing up to the task. He had proposed marriage, and I had done what I expected of him. I ran away. And all because I wasn't able to deal with Cassy's response. What was I expecting her to do? Give me flowers and tell me she couldn't wait to be an aunt? I should have been more prepared. I should have been more patient with her. I need to get back to the café. There has to be a way we can work through all of this. Haven't I always said I love Cassy like a sister? Sisters fight and make up all the time. I just need to devise a way to show Cassy I am her sister, her best friend, and I'm not going anywhere.

But before I can formulate a plan, sparks shoot across the sky a few feet in front of us.

Riley shrieks as the power line next to her side of the car breaks free, snapping in the wind before the whole pole bursts into a blinding white light. Horror grips me as the pole starts to tip over, falling in what seems like slow motion right across our path.

Before I can fully process what is happening, instincts take over, and I slam my foot onto the brake, causing Riley to lurch forward in her seat and Bo to hit the glove box, letting out a yelp.

The first pole hits the ground with a loud crash, shaking the road beneath us and pulling the next pole down behind it.

I adjust the gears on the Jeep and throw my arm over the passenger side seat, turning to look out the back window as I steer the Jeep backward, away from the chain of poles toppling like dominoes, chasing us down the road.

"Hold on," I yell at Riley, who is eerily silent,

clutching her seat belt.

My stomach lurches as another pole topples to the ground a few feet from the Jeep's hood. I press my foot down harder on the gas pedal and redirect my attention backward.

In all the commotion, Bo has clambered onto Riley's lap and is now clawing at the window, trying to dig his way to safety.

"Bo. Sit!" I shout in an unusually authoritative baritone. The command does the trick, and Bo sits his butt firmly on Riley's lap, who wraps her arms around Bo's neck.

"We're going to be okay." I hear myself say as if I'm detached from my own body. "We're almost there." After offering this small reassurance, I pinch my lips together, even though I want nothing more than to scream in holy terror. Opaque milky water is now gushing down the road, rippling as the wind and rain push against it, causing tiny waves of foam to race us as we continue our retreat.

I'm doing my best to control my adrenaline surge and not freak out when I catch sight of the familiar red bricks of Breakers Row on our right. I rotate the steering wheel in a hard turn and start to drive backward down the long driveway, watching as the golf course recedes from in front of us—the uniform line of palm trees whizzing past our line of vision as we continue down the drive. I don't pause as we pass the security check stand, the wind now tearing the canopy away from the Jeep's frame.

Riley shrieks as she stares with wide eyes at the opening, slowly morphing into a gaping hole, letting the rain pour through.

I slam on the brakes and squeal to a stop when we finally reach the circular drive, customarily used for valet services. The stately fountain is no longer spouting its water in a welcoming gesture but is now being hammered by the rain and flying debris.

I stop the engine and pop my seat belt free. "We need to get inside." I glance at the front doors and say a silent prayer that there is still a skeleton crew of workers inside the iconic hotel who can let us in.

I point to Riley's seat belt. "Come on. I'll carry you."

Wishing my hands were swift and confident, not fumbling and awkward, I reach into the back of the Jeep and grab a piece of rope from my work box. I tie one side around my waist, creating a makeshift running leash like I've seen Cassy do a thousand times with Bo. I secure the remaining free rope around my hand and use my legs to push the driver's side door open.

The rain is pouring down in sheets, pelting my skin with an unforgiving torrent from the sky. I feel like I'm pushing against a brick wall as I shove my way to Riley's door, wrench it open, and quickly tie the rope to Bo's collar.

With eyes wide and round, Riley climbs onto my back and grasps her legs around my waist. "You okay?" I call to her as I yank Bo out of the Jeep.

"I'm scared," Riley says, her breath warm against my ear.

"I'm going to get you back to your *Mamá*. I promise. But first, we need to stay here."

Riley buries her head into my neck as water cascades off her forehead. I tilt my head to the side in a vain attempt to block the wind from her face. But no matter which way I turn, it is of no use. So, I start the short trek to the front of the hotel. My breath is ripped out of me before I can even finish exhaling. I take in gulps of air, trying to keep my lungs from burning.

We need to get into the hotel.

I glance toward the Breaker's front doors, my line of sight passing straight through the foyer to the Atlantic on the other side of the building. The waves are building in intensity and crashing past the concrete barricade in rapid succession, flooding the footpath just feet from the doors.

It will be a matter of minutes before the grounds are entirely submerged.

Using the herringbone pattern of the red bricks as a focal point, I lean into the wind, placing one foot in front of the other as I slosh through the water, and pull on the rope attached to my waist, dragging a reluctant Bo along with me. Riley adjusts her grip on my neck as we continue to push forward. Only a few feet separate us from the front doors when I see a figure pass by one of the windows.

Relief courses through me as I lift my hand to wave, trying to get the attention of whoever is inside. I know it's of no use trying to call out. There is no way I can compete with the sound of the storm raging around us.

But as I release my grip on Riley's leg, a loud snap makes me look up. There is enough time for my brain to register the large palm frond sailing through the air before it slams into me. I topple backward, releasing Riley, who falls to the ground at my side. I hit the ground hard, first with my back and then with my head. Pain shoots up my spine, blurring my vision until nothing is left to see.

Chapter Forty-Six

Eye Wall
Abigail

Water sprays from the tires as we cut through the flooding over the roadway. "We'll find them. I know we will." Cassy says as the rain relentlessly slams against the hood of the Mercedes. A sharp gust pushes against the tires, and I have to tighten my grip to avoid swerving off the road entirely. I clamp my lips closed, not answering Cassy, and focus on making it home.

Home. Of course, that's where Riley would go. Shame rips through me as I wonder why it took so long to come to that conclusion. Could it be possible that I no longer view Julian's *casita* as *mi casita*? I shiver as I consider what it might mean that I can so easily detach from a whole life in such a short time. But I don't have the chance to think about it for too long because we round the corner and pull up to the closed front gate.

A memory of the last time I was here flashes through my head, and I have to convince myself I have nothing to be embarrassed about before I turn to Cassy and say, "It was locked the last time I was here. Julian changed the code." I throw the ignition in park and turn off the engine. Cassy and I stare at the gate in front of us.

"Do we try to climb over it?" Cassy asks, sizing up the wooden planks currently being battered by hurricane-force winds and rain.

"I think that would be going about it wrong. If we can't do it, there's no way Riley could."

Cassy nods, "or Bo."

I stare at Cassy, momentarily forgetting I'm not the only person missing a loved one. I close my eyes, desperately trying to calm the screaming *Vieja Loca,* who has been dictating my every move since Riley went missing. If I were a seven-year-old, how would I do it? How would I get to the place I was sure would offer me security? With my eyes still closed, I mentally scan the perimeter of Julian's property, trying to remember Riley's actions as she played in the yard in the late afternoons. And then it hits me.

"Come on, follow me."

Cassy removes her seat belt, following my lead. We are drenched the second we step outside the Mercedes. My body naturally leans into the wind as I hold my arm up to shield my eyes from the rain. Keeping one hand on the hood of the SUV, I push my way to the gate, only pausing as I transfer my hold to the posts running the length of the property. Wordlessly, I crouch down and peek through the break. I remember Riley playing in between the uniform hedges surrounding the property. This is how Riley would do it. I can feel it in my gut. I just need to push through, and I'll have *mi bebé* back in my arms. Then, as if tethered to Riley on the other side of the shrubs, I spring forward, catapulting my whole body through the hole, leaving Cassy on the other side.

The saltwater from the storm stings my eyes and blurs my vision. The branches from the hedges dig into my exposed skin as I continue to shuffle on my hands and knees through the hole—mud, and leaves sticking to my body. Keeping my head ducked as I emerge from the shrubs, the rain again batters me as I struggle to stand. Not bothering to dust myself off, I reach behind for Cassy's hand, instinctively knowing she'll be right behind me.

I drag her to standing and immediately notice blood dripping from a fresh gash on her forearm. Cassy sees me looking at her and shifts her gaze to where I'm staring at the blood as it mixes with the rain, flowing down her arm in red-pink rivers toward the ground.

I don't hear as much as I see Cassy mutter the word "shit" and grasp her arm with her opposite hand, applying pressure to the wound. Without thinking, I grab the hem of my soaking shirt and bring it to my teeth, ripping it at the seam. Then, pulling the shirt away, I tear a small strip and rush over to wrap it around Cassy's arm. The stream of blood visibly slows after I've secured the fabric, and I can see relief flash through Cassy's eyes. But it doesn't last long as she brings her gaze back to mine and then continues to look over my shoulder. I follow her and turn to look at the yard behind me. It takes me a while to even process what I'm looking at. These are not the same grounds I had been luxuriating on just a few days ago. The patio, stripped of any outdoor furniture, is now littered with palm leaves and other debris skating across the tile with every new gust of wind. The windows and French doors are boarded up, leaving no opportunity to enter the casita.

Cassy squeezes my hand before I turn back to look at her. She jerks her head toward the backyard, and I nod. I'm not leaving here until I search every corner for Riley. Still holding onto each other, we inch through the courtyard, slowly turning our heads left and right, scanning every inch of the property. I don't lock eyes with Cassy again until we've done a complete circle of the property and are back where we started. I can feel the tears sting my eyes as they mix with the saltwater already streaming down my cheeks. Cassy bites down on her upper lip and shakes her head. "No."

They aren't here.

Cassy motions to the opening in the hedges, indicating it's time for us to head back the way we came. But I can't move. It's as though the absence of Riley has caused all my senses to stop functioning. If she isn't here, then where is she? How do I find her?

I hardly notice Cassy pulling on my arm, tugging me behind her as she makes her way back through the shrubs to the street. She guides me back to the G-Wagon, but I grab her arm when she opens the driver's side door. "I thought she'd be here." my voice and hands are trembling. "I can't leave her."

Cassy pauses under my touch. "We aren't leaving her. She's not here. And we can't stay here. We'll find them."

"But what if we don't? There's no way Riley can survive in this storm."

Cassy doesn't answer me but again tries to open the driver's side door, but I refuse to move. I can't drive away from my baby.

Cassy shivers as the wind howls around the SUV. "Where else? Can you think of anywhere else she could be?"

I remove my hands from Cassy's and bury my face in them. "I don't know," I cry in a muffled wail. "I don't know." I can feel my body shutting down. My shoulders slump, and my knees feel like they are about to buckle. I'm sure I'm about to hit the ground when I feel Cassy's hands under my arms, firmly guiding me to the passenger's side of the Mercedes. She opens the door and shoves me inside the SUV with more force than I thought she was capable of.

I watch numbly as she rounds the vehicle's hood, pulls open the driver's side door, and gets in. Once safely back inside the G-Wagon, Cassy reaches into the back seat, grabbing a shirt from my duffle bag to dry off.

She passes me the makeshift towel, and I grab hold of her hand again.

"We'll find them," she repeats.

I close my eyes and try to picture where else Riley might go, but my concentration is interrupted when Cassy says, "I don't know how to drive. But we can't stay here. It's too dangerous." She turns to look at me, searching my face for comprehension. "You have to teach me. Now." She places both hands on the wheel, reaches down to start the ignition, and then turns to look at me again. "Tell me what to do."

The authority in her voice and the surprise of Cassy not knowing how to drive, snaps me back to the present. Cassy needs me to perform a task. If Cassy is willing to drive for the first time with a gash running down her forearm, I can do this. All I have to do is focus on the here and now and walk her through the motions. "Put your foot on the brake and shift into drive." I wait for Cassy to do as I say. I watch as her knuckles turn from red to white as she grips the wheel. "Now, slowly take your foot off the brake and press on the gas pedal." Again, Cassy follows my lead, and we are suddenly moving down the road. As I continue to give Cassy directions, I become conscious that she doesn't have to fight the vehicle like I did while driving earlier. I lean my head against the window and notice the wind has died down considerably. There is no longer a howling and pounding on the other side of the Mercedes. Seconds later, the rain stops pouring down the side of the window.

"What's happening?" I ask.

"We are in the eye of the storm," Cassy says as she quickly turns into a driveway and pulls under a porte cochere. "But it doesn't last long. The strongest winds in a hurricane are on the right side of the eyewall. If we thought it was bad just a few minutes ago, it's about to get a lot worse. We have twenty minutes—half an hour tops—before it starts up again. "

"I have to find Riley," I say, feeling the panic rising again.

"Which is why we're here." Cassy shuts off the engine and opens her driver's side door.

Not understanding where "here" is, but trusting Cassy, I copy her actions and step out into the hot, humid air that is as still as a summer's night. On the other side of the SUV, I watch Cassy. We lock eyes for a second before she raises hers to the sky.

Above us are a million tiny stars.

Chapter Forty-Seven

Inside the Eye
Claudia

"Benedict?" I roll over onto my side, adjusting the pillow so it still cradles my head, and reach out to grasp Benedict's upper arm. I give a slight shake. "Benedict."

I wait for Benedict's shallow breathing to change rhythm. "Benedict?"

With his eyes still closed, he rolls toward me in bed. "What is it, *Agápi mou*? Can't sleep again?"

"No. Well, yes, but that's not why I'm waking you."

"What is it?" Benedict mumbles, still in a half-sleep.

"The storm, it's stopped."

Benedict shifts, rousing from his grogginess. His eyes flutter open, and he takes in his surroundings.

"So, it has." Benedict reaches his arm out and winds it around my waist, pulling me to him. "Let's wait until the morning to assess the damage."

He is speaking loudly next to my ear, which makes me assume he has removed his hearing aids and placed them in the dish on the nightstand next to his water carafe and the stack of papers he brought home from his meeting earlier this afternoon.

I place my finger on his lips to shush him but giggle like a schoolgirl as he drags my body against his, spooning as we used to years ago. The warmth of his body wraps around mine, making the decision to stay right where we are easy.

"Not much we can do in the dark anyway." I concede, snuggling further into the covers. Not caring whether or not I'll be able to achieve sleep, but just enjoying the feeling of my husband close to me.

Benedict kisses my neck, and a longing that has been dormant inside of me starts to unfold. I rotate to face Benedict, our heads even on the pillow, as I kiss my husband.

I can tell I've caught him off guard with my new-found passion, but he quickly catches on, tightening his grip around my body.

I'm about to fully express my intent when we are interrupted by a loud banging, followed quickly by the chimes of the front door.

Startled, I pull away from Benedict, who looks just as perplexed, and I realize he can't hear the banging without his hearing aid.

"Someone's at the door," I explain.

"What?" Benedict says, and I think it's because he didn't hear me, but he quickly follows up with, "Who would be at the door in the middle of the night after a hurricane?"

"I don't know. Could it be emergency personnel?" I wager a guess.

Benedict doesn't answer me but untangles his body from mine and tosses off the covers. I follow his lead and rise out of bed on my side, placing one hand on my nightstand as I wait for my body to adjust to supporting its own weight. Benedict switches on a flashlight, illuminating the dark room in a blueish glow. With the help of the dim light, I locate my night coat and throw it over my shoulders. Benedict threads his arms through his bathrobe and exits our room, moving down the hall.

We carefully descend the staircase together, the small stream of light leading the way, and pause at the front door. Benedict glances at the security camera screen tucked into the side wall next to the front door. It only takes a glance at the screen before Benedict throws the front door open.

I gasp and hurry forward.

"Cassandra! *Agápi mou*, what in the world?"

Cassandra and another girl I don't recognize are standing on the doorstep. Their clothes are soaked through and clinging to their bodies. Their hair is plastered to their heads as though they are wearing helmets, and on closer inspection, it appears as though Cassandra is bleeding, but from where I can't be sure.

"Come in, come in." Benedict wastes no time ushering the girls inside.

Before he shuts the door behind them, I am able to catch a glimmer of the destruction caused by the storm. The south side of the lawn is completely flooded, and there are fragments of furniture floating in the murky water. Trees are toppled, and debris is scattered everywhere. How the girls got to our house is beyond my comprehension.

Benedict closes the door on my view to the outside world, and I focus back on the girls. I approach Cassandra, who is shivering uncontrollably, and take her by the arm and lead her farther into the foyer.

"Darling! You poor thing, you're soaked to the bone. And is that blood?" I continue to usher the pair toward the stairs. "What happened?"

Cassandra, wide-eyed, turns to her friend. "Auntie Claudia, Uncle Benedict, this is Abigail. Abigail, this is my aunt and uncle." She is still shivering uncontrollably, and I notice she didn't directly answer my question.

I know I won't get any information from her until the shock of what these two have gone through wears off. So, even though it is ridiculous, I follow Cassandra's lead and nod politely at our new guest. "Abigail, having you in our house is a pleasure."

Abigail, who has the same wide-eyed expression as Cassandra, nods and mumbles something indiscernible but might have been, "I need to find her."

I take her mumbling as her best effort at a gracious welcome and move on. "Now, that's enough small talk. Let's get you two out of those drenched clothes. Come along, girls."

Benedict leads the way, casting the flashlight along the hallway until we reach the bed chamber.

He stops at the doorway and clears his throat. "I'll give you some privacy while the girls are changing. Why don't I go down to the kitchen and try to wrestle us up some tea and biscuits?"

My heart swells at Benedict's thoughtfulness. I smile and nod my head. "Good idea, *Agápi mou*. I'm sure that would be much appreciated." I give him a peck on the cheek before heading into the bedroom to help the girls, leaving him to navigate the hallway back to the kitchen alone.

As I pass through the bedroom into the en-suite bathroom, I catch sight of Cassandra and Abigail waiting for me. They are standing in the darkened room, heads down and limbs limp, as though they've just been forced through an industrial washing machine and are lucky to be coming out the other end.

Any energy they once had is completely evaporated,

leaving them with zombie-like stares. A hot shower would do them wonders, but I remember hearing warnings somewhere that using a shower during and after a hurricane is a bad idea. I can't recall why it is dangerous, but I heed the warnings and focus on getting them out of the wet clothes and into something warm.

Propelled with a sense of maternal concern for these young women, I do quick work instructing them to remove their soaked garments, tossing them into a pile in the bathtub. I grab each a towel and dry their dripping hair. Noticing the cuts and scrapes on the girl's hips, knees, and hands, I remove the first aid kit from the cupboard, place it on the counter, and do my best to attend to their wounds.

As I assess my patchwork on the girls, Abigail repeats what I thought she said earlier. Only this time, her words are clear and determined. "I need to find her."

"Find who, darling?" I ask as I usher our group into the dressing room from the bathroom. The room is dark, so I grab a flashlight from the counter and turn it on, cutting the room in half with the beam. Moving around quickly, I flick on several battery-operated candles until the room is bathed in a soft orange glow. Opening a set of drawers, I pull out two cashmere jumpsuits from my past collection and hand them over.

Cassandra quickly changes into dry clothes, but Abigail continues to stare blankly at her surroundings. "Riley." Abigail glances at Cassandra. "We can't stay here. We need to go back out there and find Riley."

Cassandra places a hand on Abigail's arm, clearly trying to calm her down.

I'm about to ask who Riley is when there is a soft knock at the dressing room door before Benedict pokes his head around the frame. "Everyone decent?"

"Yes, you may come in, *Agápi mou*."

Benedict enters, holding a tray of tea and biscuits. Crossing the closet, he sets the tray on the tufted ottoman beside the chaise. Then, settling on the lounge, he pours four cups of tea.

Patting the cushion next to him, Benedict hands Cassandra a saucer as she leaves Abigail's side and sits down.

I pick up the remaining two teacups and hand one to Abigail, directing her to sit on the second ottoman. But instead of sitting, Abigail takes the teacup and starts pacing around the room.

I glance at Benedict, and he tilts his head at me in response, clearly seeing Abigail's level of agitation. Then, in a purposefully calm voice, Benedict sips his tea and asks, "Well, now, you girls have obviously been through the wringer. Why don't you tell us why you were out in the storm?"

And it's as though Benedict has opened the floodgates because both girls start talking at once. I can only catch parts of each conversation because the girls are talking over each other, not caring that making sense of what they are saying is impossible. Nevertheless, I am able to pick up something about Bri being pregnant with Nicolas's baby, Abigail getting kicked out of her house and staying at the Flamingo Café, and the disappearance of Bri, Abigail's daughter—Riley, and Bo. My head is spinning with revelation after revelation to the point I can't keep up.

"Okay, girls, that's enough." I hold up my hands for them to stop. And it's when the conversation dies down, I'm surprised to hear the wind howling against the side of the house. "I thought the storm was over."

Abigail and Cassandra glance at each other, and I catch what can only be described as terror etched in their eyes.

"That calm was only the eye of the storm," Cassandra says in almost a whisper.

"What's that?" Benedict cuts in, having not heard her.

"She said it was only the eye of the storm," I repeat for him at a louder volume, then turn back to Cassandra. "You mean we've only survived half of the storm?"

She nods her head. "From what Parker has told me, the worst is still to come."

As if on cue, a crack of thunder reverberates throughout the house as a flash of light cuts through the sky just above our heads. Illuminating the stained-glass skylight, and walk-in closet, so they resemble the daytime for a fraction of a second.

"Oh, God! Riley!" Abigail wails.

I wait for the rumbling to stop before turning to Cassandra. "You said you came here after checking for Riley at Abigail's house?"

"What used to be my house," Abigail says.

I can tell there is a story hidden in her comment, but I do not want to uncover it right now. Right now, we need a plan to find her daughter.

I turn to Cassandra. "You mentioned Nicholas went to look for Bri on his own. Do you have a way to communicate with him?"

Cassandra's eyes light up at my suggestion. "Yeah, we have a walkie-talkie. I think it's still in my pocket." Cassandra says, pointing to the pile of clothes in the bathtub just outside the closet door.

I am starting to piece together the information the girls spewed out earlier, and it is clear we need to devise a plan. As the rain pelts against the domed skylight, I turn to Abigail and say, "I understand your fear for Riley. I don't know what I would do if something happened to Cassandra or Nicholas. We will find your daughter."

"Auntie Claudia?" Cassandra rises from her seat next to Benedict, coming over to stand in front of me.

And I don't need her to say anything more. I can tell from the look in her eyes that she forgives me. That she understands everything I've done for her and Nicolas was purely out of love and no other reason. She understands that if something were to happen to them, I would feel an ache in my heart so deep that nothing could fix it just as Abigail is feeling. I stretch my arms out for Cassandra, and she walks right into them. I enclose her in a hug and whisper in her ear. "I know. It's okay. We are okay."

Cassandra pulls away and wipes a tear from her eye, and I smile at her. "Okay, now let us get started." I'm about to morph into CEO mode in order to find Riley when I stop dead in my tracks.

What I see in front of me makes me think I am experiencing one of my hallucinations again. The stairs leading to the balcony above us are literally expanding and contracting right before my eyes. I gasp and shift my gaze to Benedict. At the same time, a wheezing sound starts to emit from the stairs.

Benedict, sensing my tension, glances over his shoulder to see what I am looking at. I can tell from his expression that what I see is not a hallucination but actually happening.

Horrified by the scene before me, I move toward

Benedict and open my mouth to tell everyone to move. But as I start to speak, my words are eclipsed by a blinding white light and thunder so loud I am momentarily rendered deaf.

Instinctively, I reach my arm in front of my face to shield it from the light. But immediately pull it away again when I hear a loud crack overhead. I look up at the stained-glass dome, which is now split down the center by a jagged crack, progressively spreading its way down the entire length of the glass to where it meets the roof line.

Next to me, I hear Cassandra gasp as the domed roof gives away and the antique chandelier attached to it drops from the sky, closing in on the three of us in a tangle of white glass, wire, and light until there is only blackness.

Chapter Forty-Eight

Catastrophic
Abigail
What the hell was that?

My face feels singed, like my eye sockets are burned out of my head. I blink repeatedly, but black blobs still scatter and dance across my vision—the lasting effects of the blinding flash of light.

My sudden blindness, combined with the wind and rain invading the dressing room from the gaping hole in the ceiling, has rendered me completely disoriented. I reach my arm out before me as I try to regain my bearings. The last thing I remember seeing before being rendered practically blind was the glass chandelier whizzing past me in a blur of white as it fell to the floor.

I've been groping around the circular room, trying to find Cassy, but with my blurred vision and unbalanced equilibrium, I have yet to find her. The closet doors, pulled open by the change in pressure and the howling wind, are slapping open and closed, making it damn near impossible to navigate the room's perimeter without getting slapped in the face or back.

My hair is drenched, and I have to keep wiping the water off my face so I can see where I'm going. But, as I leave the sanctuary of the walls and round the island separating me from the rest of the closet, my vision clears enough for me to take in the scene before me. A cry gets caught in my throat as I stare at the mass of tangled limbs and body parts intermixed among a pile of sharp wire and crushed glass. There is no way for me to decipher what body part belongs to whom, let alone if the person attached to it is injured. Or dead.

I drop to my knees and start crawling toward the mass just a few feet away. The black splotches in my vision have reduced to a small scattering of dots, making it slightly less challenging to navigate the floor.

When I reach a leg, toned and tight-skinned, I automatically know it belongs to Cassy. I pull on it gently and wait for a response. A soft moan escapes from under the wires and glass. It's the only encouragement I need before I dig through the rubble, pushing away the shards of glass with my bare hands. With one final effort, I manage to uncover her lower body and torso. Upon first glance, everything appears intact, and I can't help but whimper in relief. It's not until I try to remove a mass of tangled wire from atop Cassy's head that I hear her scream, "Stop!"

The sudden presence of a voice breaking through the storm causes me to immediately release my hands from the wires. I pause and then bend down, placing my face at ground level. "Cassy? Cassy? What is it? Are you hurt?" I yell into the pile above her head, hating how I cannot control the shaking in my voice. I can't bear to imagine what might be below the mass of wires. The thought of Cassy's angelic face crushed underneath the rubble makes me want to retch. Instead, I lift my head and take a deep breath to steady my nerves before returning my face to the floor again as drops of water pour off my nose and onto the ground below me.

"Cassy, can you hear me?"

"I hear you."

I almost fall flat to the floor with relief when I hear her choked voice.

"Cassy, where are you hurt? Can you tell me?"

"I'm okay. I'm not hurt."

"You are? You're not? Oh my God. *Gracias a Dios*." I sit back on my legs and reach for the broken chandelier. "I'm going to get this off you," I call to her.

"No. Wait."

I pause, my hands suspended in the air above her.

"My hair. It's tangled."

It takes me a second to understand what she means. But when I look closer at the mass of wires and glass, I can see Cassy's strawberry red hair, crossing and weaving through the debris, like its sole responsibility is to hold it all together.

"*Mierda*. How am I going to get it untangled?" I ask, more to myself than to Cassy.

"You're not," Cassy calls back. "You're going to have to cut it off."

I think of Cassy's long red locks and flinch at the vision of chopping them away like weeds I'm removing with a machete. "I don't think I can do that."

"Yes, you can, and you will. It's only hair. It will grow back." Cassy counters me.

Her directions are unpredictably commanding, considering she is trapped beneath a pile of broken glass. "Auntie Claudia keeps fabric scissors in one of the drawers of her dressing table. Find them and come back."

I don't question Cassy any further and do as I'm told, shuffling on my hands and knees as I stay close to the ground. I brace against the storm streaming in through the roof, swirling around the room like a tornado. After a few wrong drawers, I finally find the one that houses the scissors. Clutching them in my hand so they don't slip out, I crawl back to Cassy's side. "I got them."

I take a quick breath, trying to suck more air into my lungs than the wind will allow, and start to clip away pieces of red hair. It doesn't take long before the cables come loose, the sharp edges of the scissors easily slice the tangled strands away, and I can lift the mass of filament and wreckage off Cassy's upper torso, revealing her face to me.

Cuts lace her forehead and cheeks, and she winces as I gently pull her up to sit. Without thinking, I drag her to me, embracing her. We are still clinging to each other, when one of Claudia's designer shoes, displayed on a nearby rack, lifts in the wind and whizzes past our heads. We stare at each other in disbelief before releasing our arms and struggling to a standing position. "We need to get out of here," I call loud enough to pierce the surrounding noise. Cassy nods but doesn't move, pausing as though searching for a distant memory before twisting and surveying the rubble behind her. "I can't leave. I have to find Auntie Claudia and Uncle Benedict."

Cassy crouches back onto her hands and knees and starts pawing through the glass, just as I had done when I was trying to reach her.

I follow her lead and search the opposite direction, squinting through the darkness. Another shoe flies past and I turn my head but not before it clips me on the shoulder, causing me to draw back in pain. Just as I bring my head back around, I catch sight of an arm resting on the ground, palm side up, fingers stretched open.

"Over here," I call to Cassy, who immediately

swivels and crawls over to where I'm pointing. Once she is by my side, we work in tandem to unearth what I can only assume is the body of Cassy's Aunt Claudia. Once we have fully uncovered her body, Cassy and I hover over her, trying to assess any injuries. Cuts crisscross her bare shoulder, where the chandelier made impact and her arm is bent at a weird angle, but more disturbing is her lower jaw, hanging ajar as though detached from her mouth. Her eyes are open, staring unseeingly at the gaping hole above us. I'm certain she is dead. And I can tell by the look on Cassy's face she thinks the same thing.

But as we move closer to check if she's breathing, she blinks. Next to me, Cassy lets out a tiny cry before reaching out and grabbing Claudia's hand while trying to shield her body from the flying debris. "Auntie Claudia? I'm here. I'm right here."

Claudia's gaze drifts lazily from the ceiling, passing through the room and finally settling on Cassy. Her eyes are still glazed over, but her jaw moves and snaps back into place as she croaks out, "Betty? Betty, why did you cut your hair?"

I think I might be sick as I snap my attention to Cassy, who stares at me with a look of confusion. "She thinks I'm my grandmother," she stage-whispers over the hiss of the wind and the pounding of the slamming doors.

I motion with my hand, indicating I think she was hit in the head, but Cassy shakes hers in the negative. "No, she's hallucinating. She does that when she's coming out of an episode. I've seen it before."

I nod in understanding, even though I have no idea what Cassy is talking about. "What do we do now?"

Cassy glances around us, like the answer is buried beneath the rubble, and then back up to meet my eyes.

"We need to get her out of here, but it will take both of us to move her."

I nod again and crawl closer to Cassy and Claudia, positioning myself next to Claudia's body, on the opposite side of Cassy. Following Cassy's lead, I gingerly lift one of Claudia's arms around my shoulder and prop my own shoulder in the crook of her armpit. Claudia lets out a groan of pain but doesn't stop us. Claudia turns out to be surprisingly light as Cassy and I push to stand, sharing her weight between us. The carpet squishes under my feet as Cassy and I stand and carry Claudia out of the closet, past the bathroom, and into the bedroom, where we gently deposit her on the bed.

"We need to get her out of these clothes and under the covers," I yell as if I know what I'm talking about. Only after I've spoken do I realize I'm still shouting, and, in the relative quiet of the bedroom, my voice comes out loud and overbearing.

Not fazed by my shouting, Cassy glances one more time at Claudia before heading back into the bathroom. "No, leave her for now. She'll be okay until we get back. Uncle Benedict is still in there somewhere."

I'm not entirely comfortable leaving Claudia alone in the bedroom without first attending to her needs. But Cassy is correct. There is still one more person we must find. So I grab a throw blanket off a nearby chair and drape it over Claudia, whispering, "We'll be back, I promise." before following Cassy back into the dressing room.

I'm halfway through the bathroom, trying not to slip on the wet marble floor, when a scream so loud and piercing it drowns out the hurricane pounding throughout the house reverberates up my spine.

Forgetting about not slipping, I run to the closet door, where Cassy stands completely still, staring at the floor. The island is blocking my view, and my hair has started whipping around my face again, making it hard to see, but I keep moving until I am shoulder-to-shoulder with Cassy. And when I look down, following Cassy's stare, I know what has made her cry out. Under the iron base of the chandelier, Benedict is lying in a pool of blood.

"No. No. No. No." Cassy is now repeating over and over.

I wait for Cassy to jump into action, but when she continues to stand there, not moving a muscle, I leave her and crawl on my hands and knees to Benedict's side, pushing the heavy iron mold off his body and shoving it to the side. My hands shake as I reach out and touch Benedict on the neck. His skin is paper-thin and cold against my fingers as I search for a pulse.

The doors to the built-in closets are still slamming open and shut around me, and the wind is still swirling inside the dressing room. Benedict's skin is slick against my fingers, and Cassy still chants above us. All of it combined makes it damn near impossible for me to tell if Benedict has a pulse. I slide my fingers up his neck and press them harder under his jawbone, desperate to feel any rhythm in his veins.

When a faint thump presses against my fingers, I let out a little cry of joy and call out to Cassy, "He has a pulse."

I expect Cassy to jump into action, but she continues to stand there as though she is looking at a ghost. Feeling as though I'm losing my patience with a child I glance at Benedict and then stand up and walk back to Cassy, grab both her shoulders and give her a good shake. "Snap out of it! Look, I need you to help me here. We aren't able to save anyone standing around like statues."

Cassy blinks once and then again and then nods slowly.

I give her arms a little squeeze to make sure she is with me before releasing her. "We need to figure out where he's bleeding from and stop it."

Cassy nods again, and this time when we both sink to the blood and rain-soaked carpet, relief washes through me at not having to do this alone. Together we inspect Benedict's body, but it doesn't take long for us to find the large gash on the side of his head where blood is still oozing out.

No longer registering the blood and immune to its presence, I bend closer to the cut, inspecting the skin. "It looks like it's just a surface wound," I shout above the noise surrounding us. I glance around the room, looking for something to stop the bleeding, and grab a t-shirt and a shawl off a stack of clothes. Gently I press the t-shirt to the side of Benedict's head before wrapping the shawl tight around the t-shirt, securing it all in place.

Applying as much pressure as I dare without causing further damage, I press my hand to the makeshift bandage and look up at Cassy. "What do we do now? He's too heavy to move."

Cassy looks down at Benedict and seems to sway backward. I think I'm losing her again when she squeezes her eyes shut, takes a deep breath, and whispers, "If only Nick were here."

I'm about to shake her again, but I don't have to because her words seem to wake her up. Without looking our way again, she opens her eyes, stands up, and strides out of the closet. Leaving me stranded on the ground, still applying pressure to Benedict's head.

"What the hell?" I say to myself before calling out louder, "Cassy? Cassy, come back."

Seconds later, Cassy reappears at the door and rushes over to my side, holding out the walkie-talkie as though it's the answer to her prayers. She pushes the TALK button and calls into the mouthpiece, "Nick. Nick, are you there?" She releases the button and waits. Static crackles through the speaker. Cassy pushes the button again, this time speaking louder. "Nick. I need you. Nick, please answer me."

Again, she releases the button, and we wait.

This time the static is interrupted with a quick beep, and then we hear, "Cassy? Cassy, is that you? It's me, Bri."

Chapter Forty-Nine

Down Grade
Cassy

My heart blooms at Bri's voice crackling through the walkie-talkie, only to wither within seconds of remembering I'm supposed to be mad at her for keeping secrets and being deceitful. But with one glance at the ground where Uncle Benedict is still lying in a pool of his own blood, I realize all thoughts of retribution need to be put on hold. I do my best to shove any choler back down into the recesses of my existence and focus on the task at hand. But when I fumble the walkie-talkie, I discover regulating myself is more challenging than I anticipated. My emotions are swinging like a pendulum, and if I thought my hands were shaking earlier, they are damn near vibrating like a tuning fork now. I grip the walkie-talkie with both hands, and this time, concentrate while pressing the TALK button. "Bri!? Is that you? It's me, Cassy!" I release the button before the sob I'm holding in can escape my lips and travel down the line.

Abigail and I stare at each other as an unbearable amount of time passes before Bri's voice returns to the line, again breaking through the hissing and sputtering storm surrounding us.

"Cassy, Nick's not here. He went with Parker and the cameraman to shoot some footage inside the hotel. What's going on? Are you okay?"

I realize I should ask her the same thing, but the lack of matching hysteria in her voice leads me to believe Bri is not in the same kind of life-threatening predicament as I am at this moment, so I ignore all the questions starting to build in my head, such as—where is she? What hotel is she talking about? And how did she end up with Parker and Nick?—and dive in.

"Bri, I don't know what to do. Uncle Benedict, he's hurt, and I don't know what to do. We have to get out of this room." Right as I say the words, a "crack" sounds from above our heads. Abigail and I look up simultaneously to watch as one of the remaining pieces of glass splinters and spins out from the center, like a windshield hit by a flying rock.

"Holy, Shit," Abigail whispers next to me.

With new urgency, I grasp the walkie-talkie "We have to get out of here," I repeat, "but we can't lift him on our own." I realize my words are all mixed together, and I wonder if my rambling makes it impossible for Bri to put the pieces of my explanation into any coherent picture.

But I don't have to wonder for too long because the second I release my finger from the TALK button, Bri's voice calls through the line. "Cassy, slow down. I need more information. How is Benedict hurt? Where are you? Why do you need to move him?"

"We are in Auntie Claudia's dressing room. The glass dome…there was a flash of light, and then it shattered. The whole thing just caved in. The chandelier…it landed on Uncle Benedict. He's cut on the head, he's bleeding, and he's unconscious. But we need to move him because the hurricane is pouring in from the hole in the ceiling above us, and the glass is still shattering. We're not safe here."

I pray that Bri can make out all the words I'm saying. It's impossible to tell if the thumping of the doors and the howling of the wind is breaking into our communication or if she can hear me above the commotion.

Luckily it seems as though she has caught the majority of my message because she replies, "Benedict's head injury. I need to know how bad it is. I need you to look at his head. Does it appear sunken in or depressed? Is it still bleeding? Are there any bruises around his ears or eyes?" Bri is asking a lot of questions at once and I can only assume it's because she doesn't want to risk getting cut off.

Abigail, who has been quiet until now, applying pressure to the side of Benedict's head, speaks up as I hold the walkie-talkie to her mouth and gesture for her to give Bri a report of what she knows.

"Bri, it's Abigail. I'm here too. There isn't any bruising. I checked his head and didn't see any depression, just a nasty cut. It's rather deep, but I think I've been able to stop the bleeding. I used a t-shirt, and I've been applying pressure with my hand." Abigail's voice is shaky as she relays the information. But she seems to visibly relax just the slightest bit when Bri replies, "Good, that's all good."

We wait for Bri to continue, to provide us with directions or more encouragement, but we are met with silence from Bri's end of the line, broken up by crackle and static. I glance at Abigail, who meets my gaze with wide eyes of her own. She wordlessly shakes her head and shrugs her shoulders, all without removing her hand from the side of Benedict's head.

As time passes, a rising sensation of panic overtakes me as I can only assume we have lost the connection with Bri. "Bri?" I call into the walkie-talkie as I stand up and begin to move toward the bathroom door like the walkie-talkie is a cell phone and Bri's disappearance has something to do with the device in my hand being dependent on reception. I'm about to call Bri again when her voice burst through the silence.

"Cassy, your aunt and uncle have a first aid kit, right?"

And it's like Bri's words lift a veil that has been covering my eyes for the last hour, and I can see everything clearly once again. In a burst of adrenaline, I call, "Yes! It's in the safe room! They have everything in the safe room!" Without a backward glance, I drop the walkie-talkie into Abigail's free hand and sprint through the bathroom and bedroom, only slightly registering Auntie Claudia sitting up in the bed, leaning against the headboard with her arm propped in her lap as I race past and hurry down the hall, only stopping once I've reached the very last room in the wing. I yank on the steal door and step into Auntie Claudia and Uncle Benedict's safe room. A room Uncle Benedict had insisted on adding to the house. A room that resembles nothing of the concrete bunker Jodi Foster had to hunker down in in the movie *Panic Room* but rather an elaborately decorated hotel room explicitly designed to protect the family from disasters ranging from hurricanes to mass shootings to poison gasses.

I streak past the sitting area, complete with a leather sofa and flat-screen TV, only to be halted in my tracks as I catch sight of a display of framed photographs sitting atop an armoire. It's not the display that has stopped me

but the pictures being displayed. They are a combination
of family memories. Andrew and Joanna on the beach
with a baby Parker, Claudia and Benedict dressed up
while attending one of Claudia's shows at Paris Fashion
Week, the whole family on the whitewashed slopes of
Aspen, skis propped on their shoulders as they smile at
the camera. But mixed in among these are photographs
of Nick and me. Us baking in Auntie Claudia's kitchen,
us at the beach, us at our separate graduations, us as
children, making tents out of sheets with Parker. The
sheer number of photographs is dizzying. Rooted to my
spot, dripping onto the clean dove-grey carpet, it hits me.
Even in this tucked-away corner of the house, Auntie
Claudia has placed trinkets and memories of Nick and
me. They are here, in this place where she would be if
disaster struck, and she needed comfort. These are items
she has intently chosen to offer her comfort and solace
in a time of stress. She has placed these memories here
not because she feels guilty or needs to repay some kind
of fabricated debt but because she has always seen us as
her family. Because she has always loved and cared
deeply for Nick and me. And that has nothing to do with
guilt. There is no longer any question of Auntie
Claudia's love for me. For only a second, I let myself
marinate in the memories each picture evokes as I gaze
at the images scattered before me. But when my eyes
land on a photo of Benedict, Claudia, and me at the grand
opening of the Flamingo Café, I snap back to reality. If I
want to ensure a future of more photographs with the
three of us, Uncle Benedict needs my help.

Leaving the photos, I bend down and wrench the
cabinet door open, riffling through the stockpiled
supplies until I find the first aid kit. Breathlessly, I tuck

the red and white package under my arm and race back to the closet.

"Auntie Claudia!" In my absence, Auntie Claudia has fully regained consciousness, moved off the bed, and is now standing in the middle of the closet. Tears stream down her face as she cradles her arm, taking in the scene before her. She looks up when she hears me call her name, and the look of anguish in her face crushes my heart. I take a step closer and place my hand on her shoulder.

"Please," she says. And I can only nod in response. I can't make her any promises, but I know I have to calm her, so I motion for her to follow my lead and bend down as I kneel next to Abigail. Abigail flips me the walkie-talkie and I grab it hungrily, pressing the TALK button and calling, "Bri, I found the first aid kit."

Bri's response is crackly but immediate, "Okay, that's great. If you can remove the t-shirt without starting the bleeding again, go ahead and replace it with the sterile gauze." There is a beep and white noise as the conversation cuts out and I nod at Abigail to go ahead and remove the t-shirt. Gingerly she pulls back a corner of the fabric revealing two pieces of skin that are now pressed together and are no longer bleeding. Abigail and I glance at each other, and I know we share the same relieved expression. Quickly I remove the gauze pad from its sterile wrapper and apply it to Uncle Benedict's head in place of the blood-soaked t-shirt that Abigail wads up and discards in a corner.

As though we are passing a baton Abigail takes the walkie-talkie from me as I keep my hand pressed to the side of Benedicts head. Auntie Claudia has crawled closer and is now stroking Benedict's arm repeating,

"I'm here *Agápi mou*, stay with me, stay with me."

As I listen to Auntie Claudia plead with Uncle Benedict I can't help but make my own bargain with the universe that if we all get out of here alive, I'll promise to hear Bri and Nick out, to give them another chance like I decided to do with Auntie Claudia. Because the thought of having to live even one day without these people who are a part of me is simply unbearable. Whatever hurt feelings exist between us are nothing compared to the idea of losing any more members of my family. And that is what these people are, my family.

Bri's voice cuts through my thoughts with more instruction and I'm snapped back once again. "Now wrap a bandage around his head. Sweatband-style. Circle the head at least three times while you keep the gauze underneath in place," Bri says.

"Okay, hold on." Abigail calls into the walkie-talkie before setting it down and helping me remove a strip of bandage from the first aid kit. We work in tandem passing the fabric back and forth as we circle Uncle Benedict's head as Bri instructed. I'm on the third pass when Benedict's eyes start to flutter open.

"He's waking up," Abigail cries.

Upon hearing Abigail, Auntie Claudia lifts her head and regards Uncle Benedict, watching as he opens his eyes and squints up at us through the torrent of rain still pouring in from above.

"Ouch." Benedict says, drawing out the word and reaching up to touch his head.

But before he can disrupt the bandage Abigail is now securing with a clip, I grab his hand and bring it to my chest. "Uncle Benedict, it's me Cassandra."

"Well of course it is. You didn't think I'd mistake

you for Nicolas, did you?"

A gasp of laughter escapes my lips at Uncle Benedicts question as a cold wave of relief washes through me from head to toe. "No, I guess not." I answer as Auntie Claudia pushes her way past me so she can grasp Uncle Benedicts face between her hands.

"*Agápi mou.* Oh, I thought I lost you." She bends her head down and places a gentle kiss on his lips, careful to not move his head.

"Now, now dear, that would have been too easy. I'm not going anywhere until you make good on your promise to travel with me." Uncle Benedict smiles at Auntie Claudia and they both chuckle at their little inside joke.

"Anywhere, *Agápi mou.* I'll go anywhere with you." Auntie Claudia releases Uncle Benedict's face to hold onto his hand.

I'm so caught up in the tender moment between Auntie Claudia and Uncle Benedict that I'm startled when Bri's voice calls out from the ground beside me.

"Cassy? Cassy, what's going on?"

I grab the walkie-talkie and press TALK "Bri! Uncle Benedict woke up!" I call, unable to keep the enthusiasm out of my voice.

"That's great news! But Cassy, don't move him yet." Bri calls back down the line. "I need you to check to see if his pupils are dilated. Then, see if you can have him trace your finger as you move it slowly across his vision. If he can do that, then ask him an easy question and see if he can answer it."

As Bri has been calling out her directions, Abigail has been leaning over Uncle Benedict, peering into his eyes, and then waving a finger across his vision, watching as his eyes track it back and forth.

But as I report everything back to Bri, Uncle Benedict presses his hand into the carpet and pushes himself into a sitting position. "Okay, that's enough hovering. I'm fine." He waves Abigail and me away as he uses Auntie Claudia's hand and struggles to a standing position.

We all stare at him in amazement, as though we are watching Jesus himself rise from the grave. Then, unbothered as if he had just come home from a day at the office, and not dripping in blood with a bandage around his head, he wraps an arm around Auntie Claudia's good shoulder and starts to steer her toward the bathroom. "Come my dear, this is no place for you to be."

Abigail and I trail behind them as Abigail reports back to Bri. "Bri, it's Abigail again. Benedict is standing and walking. We are headed to the safe room now."

There is static as we pass the bathroom and bedroom and move into the hallway, destined for the saferoom. We are only feet away from the steel door when Bri's voice cuts the hallway's silence. "Abigail? Cassy, are you still there?"

"Yeah, we're here," I say when Abigail presses the TALK button.

"Great. Now that you're out of danger, I should let you know—I have Bo and Riley."

The walkie-talkie clatters to the hardwood floor, as next to me, Abigail sinks to her knees with a sob. "*Mi Bebé!*"

Chapter Fifty

Clean Up
Bri

"Bri? Do you have Riley? It's me, Abigail. Is she okay? Can I talk to her?" Abigail's shaky voice cuts through the walkie-talkie, echoing off the beige-white walls of the Ponce de Leon Ballroom.

"Yes, Abigail, she's here and she's fine, I promise, but she's asleep now. She's been through a lot today." I say, trying to explain to Abigail why she can't speak to her daughter while I scan the massive space before me. I couldn't be more thankful for the solid structure surrounding us. The power is out, and Hurricane Odette continues its frenzy on the other side of the walls, but a string of lanterns runs along the ballroom's perimeter. A white glow encompasses the blue swirl carpet, giving the room an eerie-calm feeling. A handful of Breaker's staff mill around the ballroom, and a couple of them shoot curious glances our way when static sputters from the walkie-talkie in my hand. I turn the volume down to a lower decibel to appease the onlookers. I can only assume they wonder what I'm doing here, laying on a cot sandwiched between a sleeping child and a curled-up Dalmatian. I offer them a polite smile as they drift past and let my gaze stray from them to the thin crowd, searching for Nick.

Nick left Riley, Bo, and me on a makeshift cot in the

middle of the ballroom after Parker had suggested they try to get a few more shots of the storm. Reluctant to leave my side for even a second, Nick initially waved Parker off. But I had encouraged him to go, promising I was fine and needed to rest, which was the truth. I was still groggy after being slammed by the palm frond and ending up flat on my back. But Cassy's frantic call had interrupted any rest I might have gotten, and the boys were gone the whole time I was walking Cassy through her crash course in first aid. And now I'm starting to wonder where they've gotten off to. Before they left, I made Nick and Parker promise to stay inside the hotel and keep a safe distance from the windows. Of course, they both assured me they would, but now that I'm no longer distracted with Cassy, I'm starting to worry about why they are taking so long.

"Bri? Abigail cuts into my thoughts, bringing me back to the conversation. Even though I've already explained myself, I'm half expecting Abigail to insist I wake Riley up so she can talk to her daughter, but instead, she surprises me by saying, "I can only imagine what she's been through. You're right. Let her sleep."

"Okay," I start to reply, but Abigail keeps talking on her end, having not released the TALK button yet. It takes me a second to catch up to the conversation Abigail is still having, but when I do, I'm startled to realize she is in the middle of an apology.

"I'm so sorry. I know you know it was me driving the Mercedes. It was an accident, I promise you, but I don't want to use excuses anymore. I should never have left you standing there. I was scared. Scared of losing everything." Abigail pauses but doesn't end her control of the walkie-talkie. "I realize now everything I thought

I was losing wasn't what matters. People matter, and how you treat those people is what matters. I never meant to hurt you. I was so awful, and here you are, saving *mi bebé*. I hope one day you can forgive me. I promise you; I'm going to be a better person. I'm gonna be a better mom…You deserve so much more respect than what I gave you."

Just as Abigail apologizes, Nick shows up at the back of the cot, approaching us from behind and immediately alleviating my stress. He bends down next to me, patting Bo on the head, where the dog rests, curled into a tight ball of spotted white fur. Then, having caught the last line of Abigail's speech, Nick gives the walkie-talkie a quizzical look and mutters, "You're damn right." Even though I'm sure he has no idea what Abigail is talking about.

With Nick's fresh attention, Bo whines and shifts on the cot, causing a sleeping Riley to murmur and stir under the sheet. I gently touch her head to comfort her, and at the same time, I try to figure out the best way to reply to Abigail. She's right, what she did was awful, but I like to believe I can hear the conviction of change in her voice, so I decide to try my hand at a balanced perspective and envision myself in her position. What would it be like to find myself broke, alone, and responsible for my child? My hand drifts to my stomach, and I suddenly understand what Abigail means when she says she was scared. I stare at Riley sleeping peacefully beside me and can feel the fear of caring for a child when what seems like every door is slammed in your face. And while our situations aren't even close to being the same, I can finally empathize with her fear. Trepidation can make you do irrational things without thinking of the consequences. Abigail ran away from a scary situation—just like I had.

I turn to Nick, who looks me in the eye and then laces his fingers through mine. Holding his gaze, I lift the walkie-talkie and press TALK. "Abigail, I understand. You were scared. I appreciate your apology, and I accept it." I pause, my thumb still on the TALK button, debating only a fraction of a second before adding, "But I want you to know, you don't have to be scared anymore. I know we don't know each other very well, but if you need help, I'm here." I look at Nick, who nods his agreement. "We're all here."

I release the TALK button, and a low crackle fills the silence as Nick sits on the ground next to the cot, and we wait for Abigail's response.

A beep sounds, and then, "Thank you." Abigail's voice is tense, like she is struggling to speak through her crying, and I want to reach through the little yellow box and hug her. But Cassy's voice takes over before I can figure out how to comfort Abigail.

"She has us, too," Cassy says, piggybacking on my earlier sentiment.

Hearing Cassy's voice, Nick sits up straighter and holds his hand out to me. I hand over the walkie-talkie, and he immediately brings the receiver to his mouth. "Cassy, it's Nick. Are you there?"

"Nick! Oh my God, Nick, it's so good to hear your voice. You won't believe what we've been through."

Nick starts to respond but quickly remembers it's a one-way radio, and Cassy controls the conversation. "Auntie Claudia woke up, and when she came into the closet, she was holding her broken arm, and she almost had a heart attack—seeing Uncle Benedict surrounded by a puddle of blood. You should have seen it. It was unbelievable. He woke up and started talking like nothing had happened. We're all headed to the saferoom now. Auntie Claudia insisted we shelter here for the rest of the storm. And now that we know you have Riley and Bo, we have no reason to leave. Have you ever been in here?" Cassy asks, not bothering to wait for a response before continuing, "It's like being inside a bank vault with every amenity you need. Uncle Benedict is propped up in a recliner, and we've been checking on him every few minutes, but he seems to be doing fine right now."

Nick's eyes have grown in size the whole time Cassy talks, trying to take in everything she tells him. He turns to me now, eyes still as big as saucers. "A pool of blood surrounded Benedict? Auntie Claudia has a broken arm? What the hell happened while I was gone?"

I squeeze Nick's hand in mine and say, "A lot. But I'll tell you about all of it later. Right now, you just need to know Cassy did great. Everyone's going to be okay."

"You mean you did great. I have a feeling you played a starring role in the reason Cassy was able to handle everything." Nick says, and I'm shocked when a tear escapes from the corner of Nick's eye. I release my hand from his and reach up to wipe the tear away. Nick grasps my hand again before I can pull it back. He brings my knuckles to his lips, kissing the wetness.

"God, I love you so much," Nick whispers as he slowly releases my hand from his.

I can still feel the warmth from his lips on my fingertips. And right there, in the middle of the Breakers' ballroom, on a cot, in the middle of a hurricane, surrounded by a child and a dog and waiting for Nick to process the danger his family was in…I know.

I love this man sitting before me more than I've loved anything. I know when Nick says he loves me, he means it. And I know what the right thing to do is. So, with the most confidence I've felt in a long time, I whisper back, "I love you too."

Nick hesitates only a fraction of a second before leaning over the top of Riley, careful not to wake her, and kisses me on the mouth. I can taste the salt from his tears as he claims me as his own. I could stay here forever, kissing Nick and sealing our love for each other, but another crackle on the walkie-talkie interrupts our moment.

There is a pause and a beep, and I realize Cassy has released the TALK button on her end of the connection. I wiggle my thumb at Nick, indicating his turn to talk. Nick smiles sheepishly at me and then snaps back into action, speaking into the walkie-talkie. "Oh shit, Cassy. Thank God you're all okay. I'm so glad everyone is okay."

I make a face at Nick and glance down at Riley, who is sleeping, and back up again. Nick makes a face as though to say, "Hello, she's asleep," before Cassy's response comes.

"Me too! But wait? What about you guys? Where are you?"

"We're at the Breakers," Nick replies. "It was Parker who found Bri and Riley. I got here after the fact. Parker and his team were inside when they saw Bri through the window. She carried Riley on her back and had Bo tied around her waist. Parker watched the whole thing happen. A palm frond broke off from one of the palm trees and sailed through the wind at Bri. Took her straight out and knocked her unconscious. But only for a few minutes." Nick squeezes my hand as he relays my experience, second hand to Cassy. "The guys were able to get to her quickly. They got Bri, Riley, and Bo into the hotel and out of the storm. They're a little banged up. Bri caught the worst of it. She hit the ground hard when that palm frond took her out. And Riley twisted her ankle chasing after Bo. But they're going to be fine. They'll be okay."

"Oh my gosh. You guys. That's so scary. The idea of Bri hurt...She never said anything while she was talking to me. Nick, I don't know what I would have done without her. She helped me save Uncle Benedict."

"I just walked her through a little first aid," I whisper as if Cassy can hear me. Nick raises his eyebrows and gives me an "I don't believe it for a minute" look.

"The three of us still need to work on our communication," Cassy laughs, continuing, and it's like a song vibrating through the walkie-talkie. "But I want you to know I'm happy for you. It might take a little while to get used to you as a couple but tell Bri we're going to be okay. We're going to be a family. I understand why you didn't tell me. Just don't do it again." Again, her laughter crackles down the line before it changes to static, and we know it's our turn to talk.

"You just told her yourself. She's right here next to me." Nick smiles at me as he talks to his sister, and I can see the release of tension on his face as he speaks.

"Well, in that case, I should probably add. If you hurt her, you're a dead man."

I can't help but let out a burst of laughter as the pent-up tension of the last twenty-four hours tumbles out of my mouth. Nick shushes me and makes an exaggerated glance at Riley. I quickly regain control and settle back into the cot.

"Cassy, I can promise you; I'll never hurt Bri. I love her, and I know you love her too." Nick's eyes bore into mine as he speaks. "Now that we know everyone is safe and accounted for, we should all get some much-needed rest. We'll talk more soon. Stay safe."

"Okay, soon." Cassy calls through the line before signing off with, "You stay safe too."

****

Light streams through the open double doors on the far side of the ballroom, making it hard to open my eyes.

I blink a few times and try to reorient myself to my surroundings. Nick is on the cot he pulled up next to mine last night as we fell asleep listening to the dying wind and rain. He is lying on his side and staring at me with a dreamy look.

"The hurricane is over," he whispers.

I glance out the doors one of the employees must have opened in the early morning hours and catch sight of the blue skies peeking through the window across the hallway from the ballroom. "So it is."

"Still love me?" Nick asks, still whispering, conscious of Riley and Bo sleeping soundly between us.

I pretend to look surprised but quickly crumble when I see his face turn sour. "I do." I laugh at his expression.

"Say it."

"I love you."

"Say it again."

I raise my eyebrow at him, but I do as he asks. "Nicholas Green, I love you!"

Nick pretends to think about what I've said for a minute and then breaks into a goofy grin. "Does that mean you'll marry me and have our love child?"

I can't help but let out a bumbling laugh, which makes Riley stir at my side.

I'm thankful for the distraction from Nick's question as Riley turns to me, blinking in the bright light. "Is the storm over?" she asks in a groggy voice.

"Yes, it is," I say, pointing to the doors.

Riley sits up with such unexpected energy that she almost knocks me off the cot's backside.

"Then we can go see *Mamá*?"

I glance at Nick as I struggle to a sitting position.

"Absolutely," he says, also sitting up. Once upright, Nick glances around the room and waves when he spies Parker on the other side of the ballroom.

Parker, impeccably dressed, and already awake and in conversation with his cameraman, catches sight of the three of us waving at him and excuses himself to come and join us.

"Well, good morning, sleepyheads." Parker greets us as he gets closer. "Can you believe Hurricane Odette is finally gone?"

"It's certainly been an adventure," I say.

Nick choke-laughs and says, 'That's one way to put it."

I playfully punch Nick in the arm, but I can feel Riley getting impatient next to me. So, I redirect my attention to Parker and Nick and ask, "Up for one more adventure? This little lady would like to go see her *Mamá*."

Nick and Parker smile at each other before turning to Riley.

Parker says, "They just let me off the hook. The coverage is switching to aerial views of the aftermath

Jackie Kang

from the chopper." Parker smiles at Riley and snaps his fingers like he's just remembered something. "You know what? I just happen to know a guy with a really big car that can get us there."

Riley hops off the cot, seemingly unbothered by yesterday's ankle injury, grabs my hand, and pulls me up. Then, still holding my hand, she starts toward the Ballroom's entrance, calling over her shoulder, "Bo. Come."

Bo rises from the end of the cot and stretches forward and back, yawns, and then launches himself next to Riley in one swift motion. With her trusty companion once again at her side, Riley pauses, looks over her shoulder at Nick and Parker, and says, "Well? What are you waiting for?"

****

Nick's Hummer proves to be the ideal vehicle in our quest to traverse from The Breakers to the Castello property, quickly cutting through the twelve-plus inches of flooding over the roadway and smashing over the palm fronds and other debris littering the roads.

I've been staring out the backseat window while holding Riley's hand, who is also staring out the window, trying to absorb the destruction surrounding us.

"Oh wow," Riley says as we round the last bend in the once immaculate Castello drive, emerging from the broken and loose tree branches blocking our view onto the massive estate property.

I shift my gaze from my own window to look out Riley's, curious as to the reason for her exclamation. "Oh my gosh," I say as my vision lands on the scene before us. I know what we are looking at is real, but the sheer amount of destruction is almost impossible to

384

comprehend.

Broken furniture—from God knows where—entire boards of CDX plywood and a plethora of tree branches and palm fronds litter the grounds. The bougainvillea vines that once climbed outside the mansion have been ripped off and now hang at broken and wild angles. Shutters are hanging by the hinges, and some of the windows even have cracks in them. Shingles are missing from the roof, but the most shocking is the massive hole where the glass dome skylight used to stand. Now instead of brilliant colors of tinted glass reflecting the sun, shards of jagged glass jut into the sky like a pitchfork.

"Holy crap," Parker says from the front seat, repeating our sentiments of disbelief, as Nick slows the Hummer to a stop a few feet from the porte-cochere, now half ripped from where it attaches to the house and dangling dangerously close to the ground.

I squeeze Riley's hand as she looks from the house to me and back to the house again. Her eyes are wide, and her mouth is open to an *O*. The four of us stare at the Castello residence, shock preventing us from making any immediate movement. Until a glint of reflected light catches my eye, I shift my gaze to watch as the double front doors are pulled open, and Cassy, Claudia, Benedict, and Abigail all emerge.

As they file out, the sight of them is just as shocking as looking at the house. Cassy's hair is loose around her face but cut in wildly alternating lengths and angles, making her look like a lion's mane surrounds her. Next to her, Benedict stands, supported by Abigail and Cassy, a bandage wrapped around his head. Claudia follows nearby. Her arm is cradled in a nylon sling as she steps onto the patio and shades her eyes from the sun.

The second Riley lays eyes on her *Mamá* she drops my hand and claws at the door handle until it pops open, and she leaps from the Hummer.

"*Mamá! Mamá!*" Unable to contain her excitement a moment longer, Riley hurls herself out of the massive SUV and straight into Abigail's outstretched arms with the force of a hurricane. Slamming into her *Mamá* with an "oaff" and wrapping her little body so tightly around Abigail, she can't help but grunt from the impact.

I watch as Abigail brings Riley in for a long embrace, tears streaming down her face, before holding Riley at arm's length to inspect her daughter. "Oh, *Mijá.* I love you so much. I don't know what I would have done if something happened to you." Then, satisfied she is void of injuries, Abigail pulls Riley back for another hug, encapsulating Riley's tiny body with her own.

Sensing activity, Bo bounds out of the SUV behind Riley before I can grab his collar. Then, yelping excitedly, he sniffs the air and makes a beeline for Cassy, who bends down with arms outstretched.

Finally shaken back to the present, Nick, Parker, and I follow suit and exit the vehicle. Nick and Parker both head straight to Claudia and Benedict, hugging and patting them down as though they are inspecting each body for more damage than what is present to the naked eye.

Feeling unusually tentative in Cassy's presence, I hesitate as I reach the rear of the patio, stepping off to the side.

Sensing my nearness, Cassy hugs Bo one last time and stands up to face me.

"Your hair," I say before I can stop myself, realizing

after the fact that this is probably not what I should lead with.

"It was tangled," Cassy says, fingering her strawberry locks. "Abigail had to cut it to get the chandelier off me."

And I don't know if it's the mental image of Cassy caught under the wreckage of glass and wires or if I'm over-exhausted, but years of sisterhood take over, and I launch myself at Cassy, hugging her to within an inch of her life, just like Riley had done with her *Mamá*. "Oh my God, Cassy. I'm so glad you're okay."

Cassy starts to sputter laugh as she hugs me back and slowly extracts herself to say, "Okay, okay. I'm okay. Just need a haircut, is all."

I hold her at arm's length and regard her as we smile at each other before I hear, "Well, I think you look great no matter what your hair looks like."

I glance over my shoulder as Parker leaves Benedict's side and stands beside me, staring directly into Cassy's eyes.

Cassy visibly colors and says, "Thanks."

And then, without warning, Parker takes a step forward, tenderly takes Cassy's face between his hands, and says, "Anytime." Before he kisses her right on the lips, in front of all of us to see.

I'm sure the surprise is evident on my face as Parker pulls away and another voice over my shoulder calls out, "Oh, thank goodness. It's about time the two of you figured it out."

Parker chuckles good-naturedly and grabs Cassy's hand as they turn to face Claudia. "Okay, *Giagiá*. Don't go getting ahead of yourself. You might have known all along but we're just starting to figure it out over here."

"Well, don't take too long." Claudia nods in my direction and says, "If you want the cousins to be close in age, you're going to have to get a move on."

"Now that's what I'm talking about," Nick says, laughing as he moves to embrace me from behind, letting his hands settle on my stomach—right where our child is growing inside me.

Like parting the sea, Claudia leaves her spot next to Benedict and glides through our little crowd, stopping when she is in front of me. "I hear congratulations are in order. Now I must say, I was a bit surprised when I heard this news." She turns over her shoulder to smile at Cassy. "But maybe not as surprised as others." She turns back to me after seeing Cassy smile sheepishly. "Bri, I want to officially welcome you into the family."

Nick's arms tighten around my waist before he lets go and steps around me to hug his aunt. "Thank you," he says.

"Oh, *Agápi mou*, I couldn't be more thrilled for you," Claudia says, regarding Nick and me. "You're going to be wonderful parents."

"They will," Abigail agrees from the perimeter of our little circle as she steps forward with Riley. "Thank you for taking care of Riley. If you love your child even half as much as you showed Riley love, I know you'll be an amazing mom."

"Thank you. And you're welcome." I say. "But we took care of each other, didn't we?" I ask Riley, who leaves her mom's side, to hug me, which prompts Bo to start yelping in excitement as he circles our group.

Laughing, Riley lets go of me and bends down to grab Bo around the neck with her little arms, hugging him to her body. "You too, buddy!"

We all laugh as Riley gets Bo to calm down and then looks up at us from her crouched position.

"What do we do now, *Mamá?*" she asks, holding Bo in her arms.

Abigail looks down at Riley and offers her a small smile before saying, "We move forward, *Mija*."

Claudia nods and places her hand on Abigail's shoulder. "But we do it together."

Cassy, clearly touched by the moment, wipes a tear from her eye and says, "By forgiving each other."

"And relying on each other," Parker calls out, looking directly at Cassy.

"And trusting each other again," I add as I regard Cassy and Parker.

Benedict, quiet until now, clears his throat and looks around, making eye-contact with each of us before declaring, "That's right. We pick ourselves up and rebuild this destruction together."

Epilogue
Two Months Later
Abigail

My phone, propped in the Mercedes' middleconsole, pings with yet another incoming text, interrupting my conversation with Claudia and Benedict. "Sorry," I say and reach down to silence the ringer until we reach our destination.

"Are you sure you don't want to get that?" Claudia asks from beside me. "Is it possible it could it be Riley?"

"No, it's okay. My parents have Riley today. If it were an emergency, they would have just called. I'll check my phone once we're at the Flamingo Café."

"Well, if you insist," Claudia says, shifting slightly to address Benedict, sitting in the back with all the luggage. "Where was I?"

I glance in the rearview mirror and catch Benedict's eye. He winks at me before addressing Claudia, "I believe you were telling this young lady how invaluable she has been to us these last few weeks."

I return Benedict's smile and adjust my gaze back to the road as the memory of how, after the storm was over, everyone had easily paired off, heading to their apartments and homes to assess their damage runs through my mind. I had stood awkwardly on the steps of the Castello residence, Riley's hand in mine, only to proclaim the pair of us still had nowhere to go.

Claudia didn't hesitate even a second before she shepherded Riley and me into her house, declaring we would stay with them in the guest suite until further notice, no arguing. Of course, I was eternally grateful for a place to stay, but I was serious about my earlier declaration. I didn't want my words erased simply due to the storm being over. I meant what I said when talking to Bri. I am going to be a better person and *Mamá*. And part of that means I need to stop expecting something for nothing.

So Riley and I lived in the guest wing during the week my parents stayed with *Tia* Benita and I did my best to help sweep up the broken glass and wires, remove the debris from the yard and return the Castello home to its original state. Each day, after exhausting ourselves working to bring the property back to it's original glory, I would make the four of us meals and we would sit around the table reliving old memories and getting to know each other better. It was during one of these meals that I revealed my history with Julian and how I came to live in their house. At which point, Benedict insisted on taking on my child support case pro bono. Eternally grateful, I accepted his offer, promising I would pay him back once I was back on my feet.

In return for my honesty, Claudia did her best to explain to Benedict and me how she had slowly become averse to leaving the house. How it hadn't been a sudden ailment but rather something that had grown over the years as she continued to blame herself for each family tragedy as it happened until she was sure if she left the house, something awful would happen.

This is why today is such a momentous day for Claudia and Benedict. We are on our way to the Flamingo Café so they can give their farewells to Cassy and Nick before I drive them to the airport.

Next to me, Claudia snaps her fingers and says,

"That's right. Now, I realize how wonderful to us you have been. But you know Pamela will return to work once we are back from Ireland. And you, my dear, are meant for much better things other than taking care of Benedict and me."

I can feel a sense of panic start to rise at the thought of no longer being needed. I have grown accustomed to helping Claudia with her schedule these last few weeks and I'm scared that I will succumb to my old ways without a purpose.

Claudia, perhaps sensing my uncertainty says, "But you know I'm not ready to give you up just yet." I can feel not so much as see Claudia look me up and down from across the seat. "You look very nice today."

My cheeks *se vuelve rosa* as I keep my eyes trained on the road and recall what I am wearing today—one of Claudia's Caftans but with a few alterations. I've removed the long sleeves and at least five inches in length from the hem line, cinching the look with a fashionable belt at my waistline. The whole effect is new and unexpected from Claudia's typical designs but also fresh and modern.

I quickly glance at Claudia and say, "I hope you don't find it offensive that I've changed your original design."

Claudia breaks into a wide grin. "My child, I'm not offended in the least. On the contrary—I love what you've done with it. You have taken a classic and given it vivacity. Something I have not been able to do with years of trying. Just like you and Cassy were able to provide Benedict and me a new chance at life together, you are breathing new energy into my clothing line."

I smile and say, "That might be a little dramatic. We

just did what needed to be done at the time. Anyone would have done the same."

But Claudia isn't having any of it. She narrows her eyes and fixes me with a stare. "Maybe so, but I still have a debt to settle with you. As you might have noticed, I keep a penance for repaying my debts. You helped save my life in that hurricane, and you brought the love of my life back to me. I don't know what I would have done if I had lost him." Claudia glances at Benedict and smiles bashfully. "So, now, I owe you in return."

I start to protest, but Claudia holds up her hand, silencing me.

"I would like to offer you an internship with Claudia's Caftans. A paid internship. Of course, it won't be close to the amount you were used to living off of, but if you work hard and prove yourself in the industry, I believe there is no limit to how far you will go."

I am momentarily stunned into silence. Working with the team at Claudia's Caftans would be a dream come true. A start on the path I always wanted but never thought possible. I will show Riley how to be an independent woman who can provide for herself and not have to rely on a man.

I pull the G-Wagon over to the side of the road next to the Flamingo Café, noticing Cassy, Parker, Nick, and Bri are all standing on the sidewalk waiting for us. Before we leave the SUV and join them, I turn to Claudia, "I would be honored to work with you. You don't know what this means to me."

Claudia winks at me and places her hand on the door handle before saying, "Oh, I think I might have a clue."

****

Claudia

Benedict, Abigail, and I exit the SUV and walk down the sidewalk toward Nicolas, Parker, Cassandra, and Bri. The four of them are admiring Cassandra's new addition to the café, a pink and white striped canvas awning with green palm script boasting Flamingo Café over the front door.

"*Agápi mou*, this looks ravishing," I say as we approach the children.

"Thanks, I just had it put in yesterday. I think it brightens the place up a bit," Cassandra says, shielding her eyes from the sun as she basks in my praise.

"It does. It looks great," Abigail chimes in. "And so does your hair."

Cassandra reaches up and fingers her newly styled pageboy haircut as Parker looks on adoringly. "Thank you," she says.

"It suits you very nicely indeed." Benedict agrees as he stands next to me, holding his black portfolio at his side. He smiles and turns his attention to the entire group of young ones. "Thank you for meeting us before we head out."

"Of course! We wouldn't miss seeing the two of you off." Nicolas says.

Parker chimes in after Nicolas. "You're going to have a great time. I've made sure of it." He winks at Benedict and me, and I can't help but feel my heart swell at my *Engonós* persistence. It turns out he knew what was best for me all along.

Nicolas shoves Parker playfully on the shoulder and adds, "Make sure to send us lots of pictures."

Benedict chuckles and places a hand on my arm. I know he is anxious to tell the children his excellent news—the news he shared with me only a few days prior. And after seeing how Abigail reacted to my offer of an internship, I am just as anxious to see Cassandra and Nicolas response as Benedict is. I gently nudge him and whisper, "Now or never."

Benedict nods briskly and turns his attention back to Nicolas. "I'll do that, but before we go, your auntie and I have some news for the two of you." He nods at Nicolas and Cassandra.

"What's that?" Cassandra asks.

"Well, you probably didn't realize, but your auntie here has had me working on a case for a while now." He holds up the portfolio in his hand. "We've been trying, for almost a decade now, to recover some of the money your parents invested."

Benedict turns his gaze to me, and there is only affection in his eyes as he says, "Your auntie wouldn't rest until she knew you and Nicholas were taken care of. And, as it turns out, she knew what she was doing. Because these papers are from the office of Levi Pascal, stating that as of two months ago, they have recovered eighty percent of your family's losses."

Cassandra and Nicolas stare at Benedict until Cassandra finally asks in a hushed voice, "What does that mean exactly?"

I squeeze Benedict's arm, too excited to let him take the lead, and tell Cassandra, "It means Benedict was able to recover all the money. The two of you are going to be okay. No, you're going to be better than okay. You're going to be millionaires."

"Oh my gosh! You guys!" Bri exclaims from beside Nicolas, obviously happy for both of her friends.

I watch as Parker places a hand on Cassandra's arm and says, "Oh wow."

I reach to hug Cassandra, who hasn't moved, and I assume it's from the shock of the news. "Oh, *Agápi mou.* I couldn't be happier for you. This is going to change everything."

"I know we can't take back what happened to your parents," Benedict says, hugging Nicolas. "And I wish with all my heart that we could have done something to prevent that tragedy. But we couldn't. So, even though you will be set financially, we need you to know that you both will always be part of our family. We will never stop loving you and looking after you."

I drop my arms from around Cassandra, holding her at arm's length as she wipes a tear from her eye and finally says, "Auntie Claudia, I'm going to pay you back the loan. But I'm keeping the café."

To which I laugh and say, "Well, of course, you are, *Agápi mou.*"

****

Cassy

So many questions are buzzing around my head. Nick and I have our inheritance back? How is that possible? What do we do now? But I don't get to ask about any details because, over Auntie Claudia's shoulder, I am startled to see Officer Jackson walking up the sidewalk, heading toward us.

He stops just short of our gathering and tips his chin in greeting.

"Officer Jackson," I say as I instinctively reach my hand out for Parker's. I'm a bit confused as to why Officer Jackson is here and I'm still reeling from Auntie Claudia and Uncle Benedict's news but the strength I pull from the squeeze of Parkers hand in mine helps me to continue. "It's nice to see you again."

"Cassy. It's nice to see you as well. How's that dog of yours?"

"Bo—he's doing great. He's spending some time with a new friend today," I smile at Abigail who gives me a knowing smile back.

"Good to hear it. I hate to interrupt, but I have some information regarding the break-in you reported some time ago. I was hoping to review it with you if you have the time."

"Of course, yes. What kind of information?"

Officer Jackson glances around at our audience, and I nod, letting him know he can speak freely in front of my friends and family.

"Okay then," he coughs into his fist and starts talking, "We've been reviewing some footage from video surveillance cameras in the area for recording the timeline of Hurricane Odette and the damage caused when we came across the video from your neighbor's security camera."

I look down the sidewalk at the Italian restaurant, and sure enough, they have a security camera pointing straight at the Flamingo Café.

"I can't believe I never noticed that."

Officer Jackson nods in understanding. "Yes, sometimes we get so used to our surroundings that we pass by things and don't even notice them. Anyway, while we were reviewing the video, we accidentally went too far back and came across the footage from the night of your break-in."

I can feel my eyes getting wider as Officer Jackson continues. "The perpetrator who broke in wasn't wearing a disguise, so with facial recognition and some big sports fans on the force, it was fairly easy for us to identify him as Julian Mendez."

"What?" Abigail springs forward, and I'm grateful for Uncle Benedict when he places a hand on her shoulder, holding her in place.

"He was on quite the bender that night. After being kicked out of THE NEST for disorderly conduct, he headed straight to your café. In the video, he displays the actions of someone intoxicated and not within his right mind." Officer Jackson says, letting me process everything before continuing, "So, I guess the question now becomes, would you like to press charges?"

I turn to face Abigail, not knowing what the correct answer is. I don't want to hurt Abigail after all she has been through. "What do you want me to do?"

But instead of answering me, Abigail turns to Uncle Benedict, addressing him with her questions. "Would pressing charges change anything regarding custody and child support?"

A glint of ruthlessness reflects in Uncle Benedict's eye as he answers Abigail. "I would see to it that you receive full custody of Riley. And as for child support, it won't change a thing."

With Uncle Benedict's final words, I no longer have to guess what Abigail wants me to do. With my free hand I reach out and grab Abigail's, letting her know she no longer has to be alone. In unison, we turn to Officer Jackson and say, "Press charges."

****

Bri

After briefly discussing the details, Officer Jackson says his goodbyes and retreats to his patrol car, leaving us on the sidewalk.

"Well, that's Karma for you," Nick says, coming

from behind me to place his hands on my now minuscule baby pouch as we watch Officer Jackson's figure retreat down the sidewalk. I set my own hands on top of his, looking down at the thin braided gold band encircling my ring finger.

"Oh, now dear," Claudia shifts her gaze from Abigail to Nick and me. "That's letting Julian off too easy. Life is not simply Karma coming back to get you. A dear friend of mine taught me a long time ago. Life is an accumulation of your choices." Claudia reaches out and takes Benedict's hand in hers. "How you decide to carry out those choices determines your fate. Of course, we all make mistakes and make the wrong choices occasionally, but if we're lucky, we get to learn from those mistakes and make better choices in the future."

Claudia locks eyes with Benedict. "You're never too old to learn from your mistakes."

Benedict reaches up and taps Claudia on the nose before winking at the rest of us and saying, "Well, I, for one, am ready to go experience one of those better choices."

Abigail glances at her watch and says, "Oh no, we have to get you two to the airport before you miss your flight!"

Benedict chuckles at Abigail's sudden animation. "It's okay, dear. I think they'll wait for us. They tend to do that when you own the plane. But you're right. We should get a move on."

Benedict walks around Claudia and hugs each of us before stepping back as Claudia repeats the process. Once they have finished their goodbyes and are being ushered down the sidewalk by Abigail, I can't help but realize I was wrong all along. Nick does have the perfect role models for what a family looks like. Claudia and Benedict have taken our mismatched group and created a team out of us. And I know, as I take in our little family circle, that whatever challenges we might face in the future we will face them together, because that's what you do when you love someone.

~*~

In memory of
Jewel Fay Monroe
March 13, 1948 – October 11, 2021
I love you every day.